"Wife," he said cuttingly, "you call me a barbaric animal, yet you continually feel safe to taunt me. I suppose I must prove to you that I am a civil man wishing nothing other than your most pleasurable existence. You do not care to scrub my back, therefore I will humble myself and scrub yours."

Erin could not free herself from him and one glance into the blue fire of his eyes started her shivering with dismay. There was little time for her to do more than issue the single protest "No!" before finding herself dropped into the tub.

"How remiss of me," he muttered. "I can't scrub your back when there is cloth upon it, can I?"

"Damn you, Viking! I don't want my back scrubbed!" Erin cried desperately as he held her with one hand while he eased the soaking linen up and over her head. She struggled with him, attempting to stand. But that only brought her nude and wet body colliding with his, and she shuddered as if touched by fire.

"Relax, Princess," he murmured, massaging her. "I would not think of demanding any service of you I wouldn't gladly give in return." His hands moved lower and she gasped. "Perhaps my thorn can be gentled to a rose. . . ."

GOLDEN SURRENDER

Heather Graham

A DELL BOOK

GOLDEN SURRENDER
A Dell Book

PUBLISHING HISTORY
Dell mass market edition published 1985
Dell mass market reissue / February 2009

Published by Bantam Dell
A Division of Random House, Inc.
New York, New York

This is a work of fiction. Names, characters, places, and incidents
either are the product of the author's imagination or are used
fictitiously. Any resemblance to actual persons, living or dead, events,
or locales is entirely coincidental.

Dell is a registered trademark of Random House, Inc., and the
colophon is a trademark of Random House, Inc.

ISBN 978-0-440-24548-3

Printed in the United States of America

www.bantamdell.com

OPM 10 9 8 7 6 5 4 3 2 1

*For my mother, Violet J. Graham; she was born in Dublin,
and gave me the fascination. For my cousins Katie DeVuono and Peggy Lassila;
they helped give me the past. For Granny and Aunt Amy;
they are gone now, but they let me believe in banshees
and leprechauns.
They gave me both truth—and magic.*

For Cindy Kay with deep gratitude; she always cared.

*And for Lydia E. Paglio, my editor, guide, mentor, and friend.
Without her, this book could have never been.
My deepest thanks.*

PROLOGUE

IRELAND, A.D. 848

From the cold and hostile mists of the north he came, his sleek black longboats, his "dragon ships," resembling a rush of awesome sea serpents as they appeared on the horizon, gliding over the waves with their broad red and white sails, seeking out the emerald coast of Eire.

His men were fearless, ferocious, terrible. They were like huge beasts, howling fiercely as they leaped from their ships to the shore, waving their swords, axes, and spears. They honored not the Christian God nor were they servants to morals or scruples. Yet the man who led them, Olaf the White, a prince of Norway, known far and wide as the Lord of the Wolves, was different.

He was a man above men, magnificently golden, towering above even his own countrymen with a lean and muscled strength that demanded respect and loyal, admiring obedience. His mind, so bred to bar-

barism, stretched beyond it. He did not come to ravage this land but to forge himself a kingdom upon it.

From the moment his dragon ship first brought him to the shore of Ireland, his steel-blue gaze lit upon the rugged terrain with its wild beauty, and he knew he had come to stay.

The tales that had come to his father's house in Norway when he was a lad had taught him much. Even as his chilling and indomitable gaze swept the rugged landscape, he knew that he must take and nurture this land as he might a child. He would not desecrate the abbeys and monasteries, but would force the monks and friars to do his bidding as teachers, to make him understand ever more fully the complex literature of the Irish, the history so carefully preserved by their exquisite artistry. He would understand the people, the culture of these indomitable Irish people who could be invaded time and again, subdued but never conquered.

Aye, he would come to understand them and, in so doing, he would conquer where others had failed.

He thought of all these things as he studied the coastline, his hands upon his hips, his legs planted squarely on the ground.

Ireland, She was to be his—or he hers. He felt it within his blood, within his bones, and the feeling was like a potent mead. I will make my mark upon this land, he decided, cocking back his head with its rich mane of sun-gold hair and laughing joyously as the sparkle of the morning sky touched the teal blue of his riveting eyes. Ireland, aye, this was where destiny awaited him. He craved the land; its possession was a fever within him, drawing him with fascination as surely as a sultry and seductive maid.

He spun about and the planes of his face were both ruggedly handsome and chilling as he faced his men with a broad grin. "Inland!" he called above the whipping wind as he raised his sword high to the sky.

"We go a-Viking inland, and on horses. And upon her, this rich green isle, we will dig deep roots! A kingdom awaits us!"

The cries of the men rose high with the wind.

And indeed, the Lord of the Wolves had come to Ireland.

CHAPTER

1

From a window in the Grianan, the women's sun house, Erin mac Aed stared out upon the graceful wooden buildings and rolling slopes of Tara, the ancient and traditional home of the Ard-Righ, or High King of the Irish. Not long ago the meeting in the great banqueting hall had ended, and her mother had been called from the Grianan by her father. Since then Erin had kept her vigil by the window, for she desperately wanted to seek out her father.

She chewed upon her lower lip as she waited impatiently to see her parents return from their walk. It was a beautiful scene she stared upon. The verdant green grass dazzled beneath the sun until it appeared as a field of glistening emeralds, and in the distance the little brook that rounded the southernmost dun took on the hue of sapphires. Geese ambled about the brook, and cows and horses grazed lazily upon the hills.

Yet today Erin could not focus on the beauty and peace spread before her. She stared upon the grass and sky feeling as if the world spun. She could not help being haunted by memories. Visions of the past took precedence over reality, and although she swallowed furiously and blinked, the memories remained of fire, of blood, and the trample of horses' hooves that was like a thunderous beat. . . .

Mist seemed to settle over the sunblaze of the golden afternoon, and she saw herself too clearly, two years past, as she sat with her aunt, Bridget of Clonntairth, in the garden. Bridget, sweet, beautiful Bridget, had been laughing so gaily. But then the alarm had come and Bridget had forced Erin to flee. Erin had turned back in time to see Bridget burying her small pearl-handled dagger deep into her own heart in terror of the Norsemen coming. Then high-pitched screams had risen and risen to vie with the terrible drum-beat of the Norsemen's horses as they bore down upon her uncle's kingdom of Clonntairth.

Even now Erin could hear the bloodcurdling war cries of the Norsemen, the shrill wailing of the unprepared Irish. Even now she could smell the fire, hear the earth itself tremble with thunder. . . .

Erin blinked and forced herself to dispel the image. She drew in a deep breath and exhaled shakily, her excitement suddenly growing as she saw that her parents were at long last returning from the copse by the brook. She had sat with her eyes unwaveringly fixed on those trees since Maeve had been summoned, her fingers pulling knots in the threads of the robe she mended. In the two years since Clonntairth, she had tried to settle into living again. She had tried to enjoy being a princess of Tara, and she had tried very hard to convince her father and gentle mother that she had been able to put Clonntairth in the past. but she had never fogotten, and she never, never would.

She knew that today the kings and princes of Eire met to discuss their stand in the coming battle between the Danes and the Norwegians. And though she hated the Danes, she despised the Norwegians—and one in particular: Olaf the White.

Just thinking his name made her palms grow damp, her body flush and tremble with fury and loathing.

Erin desperately wanted to know if the Irish chiefs who had debated all morning in the great banqueting hall would take a side; if they did, she prayed that they would not decide the Norwegians were the lesser of two evils.

"If you paid attention to your work, sister," Gwynn said sourly, interrupting her vigil, "your stitches would be small and neat. You should bring your head in from the window anyway. It hardly befits a princess to stare out with the ill-concealed nosiness of a farm wife!"

Erin started and drew her gaze from the window to glance at her older sister with a sigh of resignation. Gwynn had been picking at her all day, but Erin could feel no rancor in return. She knew that Gwynn was terribly unhappy.

Her marriage had been a dynastical one, to be sure, but Gwynn had been smitten by the young king of Antrim long before her royal wedding. Belatedly she had discovered that her prince's gallantry was the type to last only to the altar. Heith was handsome, suave, and charming, and now, with his wife five months pregnant and in her father's house, he was apparently practicing that charm on other women. But Gwynn dared not complain to her father; Aed would either chastise her for being a jealous wife or, worse still, vent the terrible rage he was generally known to control on her husband.

"You're right, sister," Erin said softly. "When I sew, I will try not to allow my mind to wander." She smiled at her sister, sensing the depth of misery that had taken Gwynn from a cheerful girl to a morose woman. "But you know, Gwynn, you always were the most talented of us! Mother used to despair of all our stitches, while applauding yours."

Gwynn slowly smiled in return, aware that she didn't particularly deserve the charity of one whom she had spent the day harassing. "I'm sorry, Erin, for truly I've been a miserable lot for you to draw today."

Erin dropped her stance at the window to go to her

sister. She knelt beside her and placed her head briefly upon Gwynn's knees before meeting her eyes. "You are truly forgiven, Gwynn. I know that the babe makes you most uncomfortable!"

"Sweet Erin," Gwynn murmured, her eyes, so like her sister's, growing misty. Despite the bulk of her pregnancy, Gwynn was still a beautiful young woman. Her face lacked the ultimate perfection of her youngest sister's, but she had been sought by many a prince across the countryside. That fact made her life all the more bitter now. She laughed suddenly, for Erin had always been her favorite and guilt because of her harassment of her sister plagued her. "Off your knees, Erin! I'm behaving like an old witch, and you are humoring me. We all know it is not the babe who plagues me and makes me old before my time, but that worthless husband of mine."

"Gwynn!" Bride, the oldest sister, a matron now of three and a half decades and mother of grown sons, spoke sharply. "You should not speak so of your husband. He is your lord and you must give him homage."

Gwynn sniffed. "Homage! If I had any sense I would consult a Brehon and demand a separation. The laws declare that I would keep what's mine, which would hurt my noble husband. He would lose half his gambling assets!"

"Gwynn." The address came this time in a soft, quiet voice. It was Bede who spoke, and even the simple intonation of Gwynn's name was musical.

Bede had never possessed the beauty that even Bride still retained; her hair was a plain mouse brown, her face was thin. Her only true asset was the deep emerald eyes that she shared with her siblings.

She had always been the happiest of the brood, always able to find pleasure in the smallest things. That she had been promised to the church since birth had brought her complete happiness. She had joined her order at twelve and came home only for special feasts. She was here today because her father had requested that all his family be present, and as Ard-Righ his word was law.

"I do not believe you would be happy to set your husband aside," Bede said wisely, "for you love him still. Perhaps when the babe is born, things will improve. Remember your pride, sister, but remember too that time can be your friend. When trysts of the night have long since passed, you will still be wife and mother of his heirs."

Still at Gwynn's knees, Erin glanced at Bede's sweet face. Her sister's intuition was often startling. A nun Bede might be, but she was far from innocent or sheltered. She met the world with commendable good sense.

Gwynn sighed. "You are right, sister. I would not set the man aside for I am fool enough to love him. I crave him; I accept the crumbs of his affection and weep and scream when I discover his wenching! But . . . still I love him, and so I believe, as Bede suggests, that I will dazzle his heart again. When the babe is born. . . ." Her lashes lowered as she sighed and gazed once more upon Erin. "Do forgive me, sister. I thought to inflict misery upon you because I have become such a bitter wretch! You are wise, Erin, and in my jealousy I resent your wisdom in not marrying. *Never* marry! And never, never be foolish enough to love! Give your heart to God as Bede has done, if you would, but never, never let it be trampled by mortal man!"

"What rubbish you feed her!" Bride interrupted with derision. "She is past the age she should have married already, and you would have her go merrily on playing swordsman with our brothers until all hear of her lack of maidenliness and despair of her! She is the daughter of Aed Finnlaith! It is her duty to wed, as we have, sister, to better our alliances and hold safe our father's and brother's crowns!"

Bede, still and dark in her long black habit, suddenly moved impatiently. "Bride, leave the girl be—"

"I will not!" Bride snorted. "Father fears for her

feelings like a foolish, besotted old man! Well, Clonntairth was a fact of life and Erin must get over it.''

Mention of Clonntairth suddenly reminded Erin how faithfully she had watched for her parents to return. If she didn't hurry now, she would miss her father before he sent his servants for his bath, and then she would not be able to speak to him till late in the night.

She hopped to her feet, aware that her unseemly hurry would send Bride to Maeve with warning tales of woe, but Bride would not be at Tara much longer. When the meeting split and the tribes broke, Bride would return to her own province with her husband and sons. "Excuse me, sisters," Erin muttered. Then she fled them and the Grianan, smiling and acknowledging the other ladies who sat about sewing and conversing.

As she reached the open air, Erin overheard her father speaking with her mother about the meal that would be served that evening. Erin did not want to see her mother. Maeve was not half so critical as Bride, but she would look at Erin with such weary sadness that the young woman would feel riddled with guilt. Erin didn't believe she would ever capture any of Maeve's qualities of kindness and sweetness.

She allowed herself a brief, wry smile. She was justly proud of both her parents. Aed Finnlaith was the High King of Eire, ruling over a number of lesser, constantly squabbling Irish kings. A magnificent warrior, he had banded the Irish together with a force greater than any king before him. And still he had always been a tender, loving father and husband. When his heart and soul were clouded by worries such as today, he would seek out his Maeve, and she would always lighten his heart with gentle laughter and wit and amusing tales from the rivalry within the Grianan.

To avoid a confrontation with both parents, Erin slipped around to the rear of the Grianan and paused by the gnarled trunk of a great tree. Her father would have to pass her to reach the handsomely adorned building that was their residence.

As she waited, she bit her lip. She would have to watch each of her words carefully. She didn't want her father to know that vengeance was the ruling factor in her heart.

A crackle in the velvet-green grass warned her of her father's approach. Erin looked up, smiling to meet him.

"Father!"

Aed raised his graying red head and smiled warmly in return. "Daughter! How sweet of you to come and ease the strains of a tired old man. You are a breath of spring to see, my Erin."

Erin went to his side and accepted his hug.

"What do you here, daughter?"

Erin shrugged. "I've come to walk with you a spell, Father."

Aed stopped in his tracks and stared down into her face, raising his brow doubtfully. "Come to walk with me, have you, minx? Or to ply me with questions?"

Erin grimaced. "Well, I would like to hear the decision of the council."

Aed looked at her long and hard. She was an uncommon beauty, this last of his ten children. In her eyes was all the green beauty of the land; in her shapely and straight form, its strength. Beneath the sun her ebony hair gleamed gloriously, framing a face that was both fair and sharply intelligent, and in no need of powders or paints. His daughter's skin was like a rose petal, soft and fair and naturally blushed. He took a terrible pride in her. She understood every nuance of politics, she read with a comprehension superior to any of her brothers', and she wrote with a beautiful hand. Her voice, like Bede's, was like a melody, and she could play the harp, surpassing her sisters in talent.

And she had a wicked sword arm. Though his sons complained, Aed would not refuse his daughter's tutelage by their masters. He was secretly pleased when she would best her brothers, and he silenced his boys' grumblings with the reminder that they must work even harder. If their sister could bring them to their knees, what would a Norseman do?

But now Aed frowned with her query. He had watched her carefully since the day she had stumbled home cross country after the Viking raid at Clonntairth with only her half-crazed cousin Gregory beside her.

Clonntairth had been destroyed. Its buildings razed, its people taken in slavery by the Norwegians. Yet by crawling through wreckage and ancient tunnels, Erin and Gregory had escaped. Aed had had to send Gregory to the monks at Armagh. But Erin had been strong and recuperated at home, living on hate.

Aed was a wise man who knew hate could lead to desperate gestures. It was not a feeling one could forget, but neither was it one that should be fostered. Acting with passion but without wit was foolhardy. It could too easily lead to destruction.

He had tried to teach his daughter these things, yet despite her pleasantry, her apparent ease with the womanly arts, Aed knew that Erin still harbored her terrible hate. That it seemed to be a personal hate surprised and bewildered Aed. Bridget had died by her own hand; Brian, her husband, in battle. The attack had come from the troops of Olaf the White, a strangely merciful man for one of his heritage. He allowed no slaughter of children or of women; nor, for that matter, would he allow the senseless murder of warriors. That those conquered became slaves was but the way of the world, and slaves did not always live in misery. It was said that the vassals of the Norwegian Wolf ate better than many a prince and were clothed in wool in the winters.

Aed stared at her a moment longer and then shrugged. "They have chosen to support the Danish princes, for the Danes have sworn to pray to Saint Patrick and offer up great riches to his honor should he help them in battle. And"—Aed paused a moment, but he could hold few secrets from Erin's sharp mind—"and I am glad we support the Danes, for I believe they will take the coming battle. They are stronger now; they are united.''

Erin lowered her lashes and smiled, but not before her father saw the glitter of pleasure in her eyes. ''Don't take this to mean much, daughter,'' he warned sharply. ''I believe the decision we make means less than the time it took to come to. We do not raise arms for the Danes. They too are murdering barbarians, no matter what cloak they wear. Oh, a few Irish tribes will fight. But I warrant, despite the decision reached here today, that a few Irish tribes will also fight on the side of the Norsemen. I tell you this, daughter: I will be glad to see the Norwegians fall, but we pass merely from one set of hawks to the next. The Viking is here to stay, and I care not his nationality. In the years to come, we must look to men carefully, and weigh our enemies.''

Erin nodded, although she wasn't particularly interested in her father's wisdom at the moment. She kept her eyes carefully downcast, for she dreaded her father reading her thoughts. Just as she could too clearly remember the carnage at Clonntairth, she could too clearly remember the Wolf. . . .

The battle had ended, and she and Gregory had escaped to a dun overlooking the town. She had held back her screams by biting her wrist, for what she had turned back to see was Lady Moira, the wife of one of her uncle's warriors, being raped. Again and again Moira had been ravaged. Then *he* had ridden up, like a sun-god upon a midnight charger. Taller than his own men, he stopped them with a single shout, rebuking them for their treatment of the woman. What good, he had demanded, were half-dead slaves? Dear God, how she had hated him!

Erin understood her father's reasons and his thoughts. No, the Norwegian Wolf had not murdered her aunt, nor had he raped poor Moira. But Clonntairth had been taken by his command and the residents as slaves. *Slaves!* The Irish were not meant to be slaves to the barbaric pagans who invaded from the north.

On that day at Clonntairth, Erin had solemnly sworn to avenge her aunt and her uncle—and Moira. And so now she could not help but be pleased with the belief that death might come to the Norwegian Wolf and slavery to his she-wolf, the woman as blond as he who had ridden with him that day, a warrior like him. Though she had been beautiful, her sword had carried the sheen of blood. When the Wolf had seen her, he had smiled, and his granite features and ice-blue eyes had almost appeared human. Human! The Wolf of Norway! Erin wanted to spit. Olaf the White, Prince of Norway, was a barbarian, an animal!

But now it was decided. The Irish and the Danes would fight against the Norse, and likely, very likely, he would die.

She tried to control the excitement in her voice. "Fennen mac Cormac told me that the armies were mustering at Carlingford Lough. He says that you plan to ride out and observe the battle. I would go with you, Father."

"Oh? And why is that, daughter? Such bloodthirstiness is unattractive to God and man, Erin. I should send you to Bede so that she could work on the cleansing of your soul."

"Father!" Erin protested. "You hate these heathens! I have seen the fire in your eyes, I have heard you swear against them, and—" She bit her lip but then continued. "And I have often wondered why you have not let that hate raise you to swift and sure ven—"

"Enough, daughter!" Aed commanded. "I am the Ard-Righ, Erin, I cannot run about like a maddened schoolboy. Yes, I have hated. In my dreams I have slain many a man. But I am a king of many kings, Erin. My hold upon my throne is tenuous, at best. I cannot lead men to senseless slaughter because of my personal hatreds or losses. Your uncle's death is most recent in my heart, Erin, so aye, I will be pleased to see the Norwegians down upon the field of battle. But that is patience and wisdom, daughter. The Danes will do what *I* cannot." He paused for a moment, glancing at her sadly. "Even for you, daughter, I can never forget that I am Ard-Righ. The decisions I make will always be for the land."

Erin lowered her head. She respected her father, she even understood his wisdom; and besides being her father, he was her king. Without his blessing she could do nothing, and so she kept her head lowered so that he might not see the sparkle of cajolery that had come to her eyes.

"I understand what you say, Father," she told him solemnly. "But I would ride with you for another reason."

"Oh?" Aed lifted his shaggy brows. "And what might that reason be?"

Erin hated lying to her father, but she could never explain the horror of her vision at Clonntairth. According to Saint Patrick, vengeance is mine, saith the Lord, but Erin's heart cried out for vengeance. To her father many things were lamentable, but they were also the business of politics. She could not see how the taking of Clonntairth had been an admirable military move, nor could she see the temperance of Olaf the White. She could see only her aunt, beautiful Bridget of Clonntairth, lying in a pool of blood. She could see Moira dragged and mauled and screaming. She could close her eyes and remember the stench of the fires. . . .

She looked up and smiled into her father's face. "It is not vengeance I seek, Father, it's . . ." She paused, blushing prettily. "It's Fennen mac Cormac. I think he woos me, Father, and as yet, I know not what I think. If I could be near him for a while . . ."

Aed lifted his bushy brows with interest. "Fennen mac Cormac, eh? Well, well. He seems a likable man. He fights well, but still thinks with his mind rather than his fists. I'm pleased, daughter."

"Then you will let me ride with you?"

"I don't know, Erin. They are heathens. It might be dangerous. We must have a deputation to know who takes the victory, but whereas a truce holds men safe—"

"Father," Erin interrupted. Her excitement was showing, but she could allow that now since Aed Finnlaith seemed to be pleased with her interest in the young king Fennen. "The old Druid Mergwin has a cottage near the lough, remember. I would be safe there while you met with the Danes. And yet I could still be with the party."

Aed shrugged. He was a Christian king, but he bore no rancor to the scattered Druids who still practiced their old beliefs. He was quite fond of the ancient Mergwin; in fact, he had entrusted Erin to Mergwin's care many times. And Erin was right. No harm could come to her in the cottage deep in the woods. But he didn't mean to give in to his daughter immediately. He wanted her to think deeply on duty and obedience and charity, the qualities necessary in a princess and a wife.

"I will make my decision with your mother and speak with you in the morning, daughter," he said firmly. "And for tonight, well, you may sup beside this young king who holds your fancy, and then you will spend the hours with your sister Bede and study her serenity."

Erin dutifully lowered her head and humbly said, "Yes, Father."

She accepted his pleased kiss upon her forehead and waited until his footsteps took him away toward their dwelling.

Then she raised her head with a very real and very mischievous smile on her face. She knew her father well; she knew she had won. Tomorrow she *would* ride with the envoy.

CHAPTER

2

The Druid, Mergwin, was a vision to behold in his long robes of white and his fiery, burning eyes. His hair was long and wild, and it blended with the thick gray beard that fell below his knees.

It was rumored that he was the son of a Druid priestess and a Viking rune master who had come with the first tide of scavengers to raid the Irish island at the turn of the century. Mergwin never spoke of his background, but it was believed that the man was indeed a rare sorcerer, blessed by dual gods thanks to his distant and hazy paternity. But whatever the secrets of his past or the usage of his craft, Mergwin *knew* things; it was a fact no one denied.

Within the walls of his cottage his earth-banked fire burned with a blue glow, and in a pot above it, he was known to mix a number of concoctions for any number of causes. A maiden might well celebrate the Sabbath on her knees in chapel, then run to the home of Mergwin to plead that he give her a potion to win the favor of a certain warrior.

There were those who crossed themselves and muttered to the Virgin Mary as they passed his home in the woods, thinking him insane. There were others who railed against him, saying that the days of sorcery were over, that Mergwin was naught more than a witch who should be dealt with harshly. But those who would cry out against him would be compelled by a wise look from those eyes as deep as time, and they would fall silent. So Mergwin remained in his cottage, welcoming and harboring those who would come to him.

Mergwin loved the child of Aed Finnlaith, as he loved and respected Aed. The Ard-Righ of Tara was to Mergwin's mind a just and unusual man who preferred negotiation among his continually bickering chieftains to the mass battles that too often answered minor disputes. Aed was capable of justice even when his own sons were concerned. He would listen, he would close his eyes, and when they opened, they would be opaque, hiding all personal feeling.

Yet the emotions and wisdom of the man ran deep. Since his daughter had been but a child, Aed brought her to the woods to stay with Mergwin. The priests and monks might teach her of the life of the Christ, but Mergwin would teach her about her own soul and about the earth that surrounded her.

To Mergwin's mind, the princess Erin would have made a fine priestess for the Druid cult. But as Mergwin and Aed had a silent understanding, Mergwin cherished the child as student and ward, nothing more. He taught her to respect the trees, to love and honor the earth. He taught her to foretell the signs of the sky so that she might know of sun and thunder. He taught her which herbs could heal, which could ease pain. And he watched her with the creatures of the forest, loving her more each time she tenderly mended the wing of a tiny robin or brought the wild hares of the deep burrows to her feet to pet and fondle and feed.

She rode to him today with the young king of Connaught, Fennen mac Cormac. Something troubled Mergwin as he left his doorway to meet her. It was as if a shadow fell over the sun. He frowned as he watched the princess being helped from her horse by the young king. It appeared that the shadow fell by the person of the mac Cormac.

Mergwin shook himself slightly. Erin's eyes were alight with laughter and pleasure; she enjoyed her fair escort. Foolish old man, Mergwin reproached himself silently. Fennen mac Cormac was a respected and carefully watched king. He was said to be strong in wisdom and charity. For the daughter of Aed Finnlaith, Ard-Righ of Tara, he would be a most appropriate match. I must reread the signs, Mergwin warned himself.

"Erin mac Aed!" Mergwin called to her. Stepping forward, he bowed low first to her and then to the young king at her side. "And Fennen mac Cormac. I welcome you. What brings you here this day?"

He knew, of course. All the land knew that the Viking forces gathered to meet near Carlingford Lough. Mergwin had felt the coming tremor of the earth; the breeze had whispered of the blood that would feed the land.

"A slaughter," answered the young mac Cormac, with barely a glance at Mergwin. His eyes, Mergwin noted, already coveted the princess. Fennen finally looked at the Druid. "It is justice, old man, don't you think? I ride with the Ard-Righ as an envoy. We will view the carnage and we will collect the tithe of gold and silver due Saint Patrick by the Danish victors."

Mergwin nodded to the powerful young lord while considering him a fool. Dane and Norseman alike had ravaged the land; both would do so again. The Irish envoy would be lucky to escape alive.

"Aed Finnlaith, Maelsechlainn, and myself will secure the treasure, then we shall return for my lady Erin. Keep her well, old man."

Mergwin stiffened. He didn't need to be told a thing about the lady Erin. He would serve her well of his own design and for her father, not for an upstart lord who knew not his place.

"The daughter of Aed Finnlaith always abides well

with me, King of Connaught,'' Mergwin at last said
severely.

Fennen seemed not to notice the old man's tone.
His eyes were upon Erin. Last night in the banqueting
hall, he hadn't a moment alone with her. And he had
suffered the agonies of the damned as he had watched
her brilliant-eyed gaiety as she had performed the role
of perfect princess, perfect hostess for her father,
dancing with all the kings, charming the oldest and
youngest of the princes.

"Druid,'' Fennen said gruffly, "I would have a
moment alone with the lady, and then she will be left
in your care.''

Mergwin set his jaw and barely stepped away from
the young couple.

Fennen held out his hand to Erin, ignoring the
Druid's stern, paternal expression. "Erin, let's walk a
bit into the woods.''

Erin grinned, raising a brow at Mergwin. At the
cunning twinkle in the princess's emerald-green eyes,
Mergwin almost laughed. He knew her so well. She
liked Fennen—and why not? The young king of Connaught was handsome, athletic, and powerful—any
girl's vision of a fine man. But Erin was, as always,
assured of herself. She could walk in the woods with
the man who sought to woo her; she could charm and
bedazzle him. But Mergwin would be more than ready
to wager that she gave him nothing and promised not
a thing. The Druid's frown became a smile as he
watched the pair walk away.

It was Fennen who kept his smile as he escorted
Erin through a path in the trees to a sheltered copse,
for he was secretly damning the Ard-Righ. Erin was
twenty, and Fennen had been enamored of her for
many years. Her sisters had been wed at the age of
sixteen. Aed had never discouraged Fennen's suit, but
he had shied away from any conversation of commitment, telling all that he would not give his youngest
daughter in marriage until he knew the bent of her
heart.

But she had bewitched Fennen. The king of Connaught, to whom most women flocked, wanted only her, she who would not fall prey instantly to his charms.

She was a spirited girl, and as a wife she was going to need a lot of taming—especially after having been her father's favorite for so long. But Fennen would love to tame her—gently and lovingly, of course. And as her husband, he would at last be able to put his foot down.

Erin was also thinking along the lines of marriage as they walked. Her own smile was a bit strained, especially when she would catch Fennen's handsome dark eyes upon her. She did like him so well! But since Clonntairth, she had desperately valued her freedom.

She sighed softly. Some day she would have to marry but for now, she had to come to terms with her fevered desire to see the Norwegians laid waste.

"Oh, Erin! Why do you take such pleasure in torturing me so!"

Startled, Erin gazed into his eyes. She saw the love that he bore her, and she felt terribly guilty. "Fennen . . . I-I don't seek to hurt you," she answered truthfully.

"Then promise yourself to me. We will speak with your father—"

"Fennen! Please, know how much I care for you, and don't press me! In time . . ." Erin hesitated carefully, knowing that her future hung in the balance. Her father would, she knew, eventually tell her she must marry, and she would choose Fennen. So she wanted only to prolong her freedom as far as she might—without losing the suitor who would keep her father from deciding her future for her.

"Fennen, allow me the time to know you fully, to—to love you. Time and the subtle searchings of souls together make for the most applaudable unions, don't you agree?"

Fennen's jaw tightened, for he knew exactly what she was saying. She would have him but in her own good time. And while he waited, watching her supple form and imagining all the beauty beneath her royal tunics and mantles, he would suffer heartily. He would dream of her at night, of the fullness of her breasts, the slimness of her waist. . . . He would wait, but he wouldn't be denied everything. He pulled her suddenly into his arms. "A kiss, my beauty. Grant me a kiss, and I will wait into eternity."

"A kiss," she agreed, fascinated and flattered by his need.

He touched his lips to her reverently, massaging the small of her back with one hand, cradling her nape with the other. His heartbeat was strong against hers, and the feel of his strong arms was pleasant. It was not the grand sense of excitement she had anticipated, but it was pleasant.

The tip of his tongue moved over her closed mouth, prying gently so that her lips might open to his. Curious, Erin allowed the contact. His tongue moved into her mouth, delving deeper and deeper. Again, the sensation was pleasant. But it did not give her any indication of great rewards to come from such play. She moved her fingers from his shoulders to his chest, attempting to draw away. He held her tight, and suddenly panic descended upon her. Visions of rape, of the lady Moira in the hands of the Norsemen, flashed through her mind. She heard the screams in the air. . . .

Her protest rumbled deep within her throat and she brought her hand furiously against her suitor's cheek. "You said a kiss, my lord of Connaught! Yet you abuse my consent when you are entrusted by my own father with my welfare!"

Anger was Fennen's first reaction as he rubbed his cheek, but then he realized that he had pushed too far. It had been so easy to do when he held her in his arms. "I apologize, my lady," he said with a humility he was far from feeling. One day he would not have to release her. He would calm her fears, and he would teach her all the beauty that there was to loving. In her kiss he could feel a smoldering sensuality, one she didn't yet recognize herself. He could console himself with the knowledge that patience would award him his prize. One day he would have her forever, laughing, touching, bedazzling him, him alone, and he would love her.

"Oh, Fennen! I'm sorry too!" Erin murmured, again feeling the pangs of guilt. She had accepted him, she had wanted his touch, until . . . until she had thought of the Norwegians. But he was smiling at her again, and she returned his look mischievously, enjoying the power she had over this handsome and coveted Irish warrior and king.

"You must take me back to Mergwin, Fennen," she said sweetly, "for then you must return to the envoy and see what fate the Vikings have met in battle. Oh, Fennen, Father believes that the Norwegians will be the losers—and a multitude of them will be slaughtered upon the field!"

Fennen nodded, holding her arm respectfully as he led her back to the cottage. "The Danes are strong in numbers and unity, and they promised us great riches!" He laughed.

Mergwin still stood before the cottage. "The day wanes quickly, King of Connaught," he said pointedly.

Fennen ignored the scowling Druid. He turned to Erin. "Take care, my princess. I will see you soon."

"Fare thee well, my lord Fennen," Erin said prettily, dipping a low curtsy. Mergwin saw that she twisted her face demurely when he kissed her; he also saw the spark in her eyes beneath the lowered lashes.

Mergwin was hard put not to laugh. Think not that you hold the treasure of the young princess yet, my lord, he thought silently. I do believe the princess will have much to say in the matter.

Fennen mac Cormac dropped a finely embroidered scarf into the Druid's hand—a present from the lady Maeve and Aed—and made a fine show of remounting his charger.

Erin waved as he disappeared through the path in the trees, then turned to Mergwin, her laughter coming to her lips. "What think you, Druid?" she demanded, the sparkle in her emerald eyes deep. "Is my lord Fennen not a bit like a puffer fish? As are all men?"

Mergwin lifted his brows and pursed his lips against his own laughter. "What is this, Erin? You mock the king of Connaught? I had thought at long last you brought me a betrothed."

Erin shrugged, averting her eyes as she slipped past the Druid to enter the cottage. She sighed as he followed her. "No, Mergwin, I do not seek to mock Fennen. He is a good man, a good king of his province. I-I just don't know, Mergwin. I believe it is me. I frustrate my father and my fair lady mother, I annoy my sisters. But I have no desire to marry."

"Perhaps," Mergwin suggested shrewdly, "you would enter a religious order as your sister Bede."

"Oh, no!" Erin laughed, spinning around to smile at her old friend and mentor. "Bede is suited to her convent. I fear I am not so charitable as Bede, nor can I so blindly love her God—"

"Or purge the hatred in your heart," Mergwin suggested in quiet interruption.

Erin shrugged and turned away once again, and strode to the earth-banked fire to warm her hands. "I saw a town razed, Mergwin. My cousin was torn and shattered, and sent to the monks to be tended. My aunt and uncle were food for buzzards, and they were not avenged. Do you wonder that a hatred remains to sustain me?"

Mergwin sat at his table and began to grind a mixture of roots before him. "Your father could not avenge Clonntairth, Erin. The kings of Ireland were scattered and fighting among themselves. The Norsemen were very powerful then, as they will be again. Aed's first loyalty must be the protection of Tara and the Brehon laws. He could not leave the high seat of government unprotected and open to attack. And think on this, girl: Aed could easily spend his life in the pursuit of vengeance. His brother was lost to an attack by Danes; his father was murdered by a fellow Irish king. Tell me, Erin, where should your father start, with the total collapse of what little centralized order there is?"

Erin was an intelligent girl; he knew she fully understood his arguments. Yet Mergwin was well aware that all the reasoning in the world could not ease the pain that haunted her spirit.

"So what do I do, Mergwin?" she demanded. "Marry Fennen mac Cormac and become a docile wife and keep turning my head as my country is ravaged?"

You will not marry the son of Cormac, Mergwin thought with certainty, but he didn't say so. He returned his attention to his roots. "You could do worse."

"Ahh . . . you think I could do better!"

He should warn her; he should tell her there was an aura of darkness around the king who would have her. The darkness meant tragedy or pain—but for whom? The young king, or the princess he coveted?

Mergwin didn't answer and Erin exploded. "I cannot marry and bear children and watch daily as my men go about their business until the longboats or the horses come and my province too is destroyed!"

Mergwin looked up, staring hard into the vehement emerald eyes that met his. "The longboats will come no matter what you do. They will come in your children's time and in their children's time—"

"And we just sit like sacrificial lambs!" Erin exclaimed furiously. "And the great provincial kings like my lord Fennen will cry Irish while siding with the slaughterers—"

"It will not be all slaughter," Mergwin intoned emotionlessly. "Nor, in the end, shall the invader triumph."

Erin drew in her breath sharply. On the table sat a fine doeskin bag. Within it were Mergwin's runes—exceptionally fine pieces, stones with beautifully carved glyphs. She grasped the bag and rattled it beneath Mergwin's nose. "Tell me my fortune, give me an oracle. Cast the runes for me, Mergwin," she pleaded.

"No!" Mergwin protested sharply.

Erin knelt at his feet, but the gesture was far from humble. She lifted her chin proudly and met his eyes with her implacable green stare. "Then I shall tell you, Mergwin. Last night at the banquet my father's new poet told the story of Maelsechlainn's daughter—how she and fifteen other maidens tricked the Norwegian Turgeis. She slew him, Mergwin—a woman rid the Irish of the pagan Turgeis! And when the Vikings took Clonntairth, I saw a woman warrior. She fought alongside her men. That, my dear Druid, is exactly what I intend to do. Perhaps the invaders will ravage our countryside for the decades to come, but I will do something about it, Mergwin. I may die, but the invader will die alongside me! *That* is a fortune I can live with, Druid!"

"Fool girl!" Mergwin rose to his feet, his eyes blazing, his robes shaking with his fervor. "Enough will die! Would you break the heart of your father? Leave your mother wallowing in tears?"

"Men die in battle. And I am more proven than most! My brothers grow more and more irate because I can best them—"

"Stop!" Mergwin raised his hands, his sleeves floating behind him. He glared at her a moment longer as the silence stretched between them. Then he whirled like a gigantic bird to stare at the fire, then again to stare at her. "I will read the runes for you, girl, and you will see that such dreams are but foolish imagination."

She laughed softly. He saw the affection and manipulation in her eyes. "Oh, thank you, Mergwin!" she exclaimed. She lifted her hands and grinned. Though she was hard, bright, and determined, Mergwin smiled in return for she was also very much a lady. She spoke against marriage, but there was a brilliance to her eyes and an understated sensuality to her well-formed body that spoke of great underlying passion. When she loved, Mergwin thought, she will do so with all the fervor she now fed to her dreams of vengeance.

"I hope," he muttered, "that the runes show you respectably married, mother of a score of children, dutifully following the will of father and husband."

Moments later they sat across from one another at the table. Darkness had come fast to the copse within the trees, the only light coming from the fire and the one precious candle. Mergwin laid a linen cloth over the table, then cast the stones upon it, glyphs downward. "You will touch three," he ordered Erin.

She did so decisively. Mergwin turned over the first stone. Thurisaz. The Gateway stone. Erin should be standing still, viewing the world about her carefully, not impetuously rushing about.

Without a word he turned the second stone. Hegalez. The stone of great disaster and upheaval, a stone of the gods. Something coming of destiny, something man could not control, like a massive wave of the ocean . . . like the endless tide of the invaders.

Still silent, Mergwin turned the third stone. The rune was blank.

Erin, watching the old Druid's eyes becoming narrow and clouded, felt a nervousness creeping through her and edgily prompted him. "Mergwin! Tell me! Tell me what it is that you see!"

He did not wish to speak of what he saw. The blank rune was the unknowable. To the Vikings, it was Odin's rune. It could be death; it could be a beginning, a rebirth. Following Hegalez, the stone marked vast and dangerous obstacles looming before her. She must accept the change that was coming. If she did so, her life could be long and, in time, he believed she would find happiness. But the pathway before that happiness seemed laden with danger.

He closed his eyes in deep concentration, his fingers caressing the coolness of the stones and absorbing their symbols. He saw her clothed in mail as she had threatened and sensed the agony of the punishment that would come to her because of her armor. The punishment was caused by a man, but the man was not Fennen mac Cormac. He was a golden man. Light shone around him. He was powerful; he was dangerous. Yet his aura was not of evil, but of determined strength. The runes seemed to whisper that he was of the land and that the pathways of his life were irrevocably interwoven with those of Erin mac Aed.

Within his mind, Mergwin heard the howling of a wolf. A standard bearing the animal was raised high . . . a Viking standard. Mergwin began to shake. It was not the usual reading of the runes; he had touched upon a destiny that was of the earth, eternally consequential to the land of Eire.

"Mergwin!" Erin demanded.

His eyes snapped open. "Hush, Erin of Aed!" he snapped with wide, fever-eyed irritation. "I see exactly what should be seen for the daughter of Aed. You will grow old, you will bear many children. Your sons will people the land."

"You lie to me, Druid!" Erin accused reproachfully.

Mergwin rose from the table, his robes flowing about him. He left the runes as they were with feigned disinterest. "I do not lie, daughter of Aed. And I am a tired and hungry old man who would have my supper and my bed." Irritably he returned to the table and dropped the stones back into their doeskin bag.

Erin hesitated a moment and then smiled. Mergwin did sound like a crotchety old man, but she loved him dearly. She stood and straightened her robe and followed him to the fire. She reached on tiptoe to massage his shoulders as she often did for her father. "Tired old man, eh?" she demanded with a light tinkle of laughter. "You will not be old, Mergwin, when you have outlived all the trees of the forest! But come, this stew you have simmered all day smells delicious! We shall eat and I will tell you all the gossip that floats about Tara and then you shall tell me more legends of the old days and we shall sleep!"

Erin lifted the cover from the pot and carefully ladled out two portions. "Oh, there is fine wine from the province of Alsace in my saddlebags! I bought it myself when the peddler brought silks to Mother. We shall get a little tipsy as we talk, Mergwin!"

Mergwin brought his wooden bowl of stew to the table and glanced wearily at his beautiful charge. "I will not be so tipsy, Erin, as for you to manage to bring to my lips words I do not intend to say."

Her eyes went very dark for a moment. She was still and straight and proud as she lifted her chin to him. "I have no plan to connive you, Druid," she said, her tone steady and dignified.

She set her food upon the table across from him and moved to the door so that she might go to the horse shed and retrieve the wine. She hesitated, then turned back to him, her words soft but vehement. "You see, Druid, I care not what your stones say. I shall forge my own destiny."

CHAPTER

3

With his hands upon his hips, he stood beside the gnarled ash, and in the twilight of the day he created a stunning silhouette. His mantle of red, emblazoned with the wolf's head, blew about his magnificent body, his tendrils of sun-blond hair swept back across his forehead.

His eyes held a cast of indigo as he beheld Carlingford Lough below him. The Danish camps could be seen across the banks. Thousands were gathered there that night for the battle that would begin at dawn.

Olaf shook a chill from his body. The Danish raiders were talented and clever men. The very chain mail that he and some of the Irish chieftains wore was the result of the Danes' ingenuity, and that cunning would be what he would be fighting come morning. There was so much more there than most men, Norse or Dane, realized. He, a prince of Norway, sought more than battle and plunder. Even as a child, sitting through the frigid nights at the feet of the storytellers, he had dreamed of Eire. As a younger son, he would not inherit his father's kingship. His destiny was his own to make. He thought of his uncle Turgeis, who had once held most of this emerald isle beneath his thumb. From the banks of the Liffey, to Dubhlain, Turgeis had stretched out his conquering hand. Olaf felt he even knew his uncle's weakness. Turgeis had been determined to create a pagan empire—but the Irish were a people not willing to give up their own god.

I would conquer and then learn to coexist, Olaf thought. He cared not which god he worshipped. In his mind he saw a great new race, created of the raw strength and architectural talents of the Viking—and of the great social laws and learning of the Irish, which held them together against all force.

He sighed. Foolish thoughts for a warrior with a feeling of doom. He was conqueror of nothing at the moment. He was but a warrior-prince, as many other generals who would lead the Norse into battle come the dawn. Yes, tonight his thoughts were foolish. He had taken many towns; he had given riches to himself and to his men. But Eire was still a battlefield, and he shrewdly felt that no terror by the sea would ever fully quell the Irish. Coexistence . . .

The Norseman who becomes Irish is the man who will survive, he thought with a strange poignancy. He shrugged, impatient with his own thoughts. He was the son of a king—minus a kingdom, and he craved to be a king.

There was a touch upon his shoulder. He did not spring about or reach for his sword. He knew the touch. He placed his hand over the hand that lay on his mantle, slowly drawing her around until she faced him. His sweet Grenilde. So tall a woman, she could almost meet his eyes. So courageous that she blazoned into battle like a man. So uniquely beautiful that she held his heart and soul.

Now she raised a golden brow at him and taunted, "Would you not come to bed, my Wolf? I would hate to see you falling off your horse due to lack of sleep come the morn."

He laughed and drew her tight as he teased, "Do

you ask that I sleep, my lady barbarian? Or have you other thoughts in mind?''

Her laughter in return was like a bubbling brook. It amazed him still how many things she could be. He had found her leading another group of Vikings in a raid that coincided with one of his own. When the village was taken they had faced one another. Squared off, they had stared into one another's eyes, and their swords had fallen to their sides with their laughter. Ever since, they had ridden together, lovers and adventurers alike. She had known other men, she was not of royal blood, yet while others married princesses and kept them in spoils at home, he had made her his hearth-wife, finding that other women paled in comparison to her beauty and spirit.

She had taken away his desire to rape the innocents he discovered in his plunder. A screaming woman held no lure for him, not when this creature of the gods came to him to please him, to cry her pleasure at his touch. He could not keep his men from demanding the women who were a part of their spoils, but in his raids he had demanded certain rules—and because of them, they now had warm, living bodies to do their bidding. Several of his warriors had held dear to their Irish maidens, making of them wives rather than slaves.

He touched his lips tenderly to Grenilde's. Her mouth opened sweetly to him, then as their tongues began a silken duel, the desire in him rose. He broke from her, seeing that he had pressed the soft flesh of her partially exposed breasts so hard against his mail that he had left marks. "Come," he murmured, "to bed.''

In the seclusion of their tent she set to removing his mantle, mail, girdle, then tunic and rough leather leggings. Her pleasure with her task was evident and stirred his blood even further. The throbbing within him rose unbearably.

When he stood naked before her she stepped back as she had countless times before, her eyes caressing his warrior's body. Her tongue touched her lower lip and her breathing became raspy. She stepped forward, her lips touching upon a battle scar that cut across his bronzed and golden-haired chest. She ran her tongue over his nipples, which stood upon wire-taut muscle. Then she was roughly grabbed, her makeshift tunic torn asunder. Olaf held her for a moment against the beating of his heart, then he dragged her down, unable to bear a moment's more hesitation. He glared down at her a moment, his eyes hungrily appreciating the blue veins that lay beneath the milk white of her breasts, her hardened nipples that rose with their own desire to be cherished and touched. He met her eyes again, then stared at her mouth, fascinated. Her lips were parted, her tongue wetting them against the rapid force of her breath. Their mouths met thirstily again, and the fever that ensued sent them both seeking the other's body with hands and lips and teeth. In his ardor he devoured her flesh from head to toe, the whirling that pounded in his head becoming more and more thunderous as he found her woman's places and elicited strangled cries from her lips, pleas that he make her whole.

In her cries muffled against his flesh was the promise that she would give, she would torture as he. Her golden hair tangled about him as they rolled together, her mouth found him and his fingers wound into that golden beauty of the hair that enwebbed him. She was strong, his Viking love, yet all woman. Undaunted and uninhibited, she met his passions with her own, and then she gave to his superior strength, falling willingly to his demand as he rolled over her. He placed his hand upon her and parted her thighs, whispering his joy and pleasure as she arched toward his fingers, at the warmth that welcomed him. Her long legs wrapped high around him and then he rose to give himself to her as she cried out for him, taking her so that they blended together in a need both sweet and savage.

He lay beside her and stroked her glistening body when they were spent. How he loved her. She was so perfect, bronzed as he, both sinewed and slim, firm of breast and thigh. She was the only mate for him, insatiable lover, fearless fighter, recipient of his dreams. Still tangled within her golden hair, he slept.

But in the darkness of sleep he could see serpents coming for him. They raised their heads high above him and came in wave after wave, fangs dripping. With his sword he tried to slay them, but there were more and more. Their vicious fangs could not penetrate him, but they were getting past him and there were screams, terrible screams coming from behind. . . .

He awoke covered with sweat, and for a moment he froze, alert to danger. He was shaking, his teeth were chattering. But there was nothing in his tent of furs and leathers, nothing but the woman who lay beside him, meshing her heartbeat with his.

He closed his eyes, clenching them tightly. When he opened them once more, she was raised above him.

"What is it, my love?" she demanded, frowning, then trying to make light of his situation. "The Wolf who never flinches in battle shakes over a dream? Tell me of it, love, and I will chase the darkness away."

He stared into her sapphire eyes, so beautiful in the pale moonlight, and the fever of fear clenched him once more. "I don't want you to join the battle tomorrow."

She stiffened, her golden hair trailing proudly over her breasts. "I am more a warrior than most of your men," she spat contemptuously. "And I am my own mistress. I will fight my enemies as I choose."

"You are not your own mistress!" he declared heatedly. "I am your prince—you are near my equal, but you are my mate. You will do as I say."

Grenilde hesitated a moment, wondering at the anger that glistened so irrationally deep within his eyes. She would have argued, she would have reminded him that even as a woman she had earned the respect and loyalty of her own troops, but she loved him. He was her lord, and so she would humor him and demurely promise obedience, and then do as she wished.

Grenilde curled once more to his side. "As you

choose, my lord Wolf," she murmured with a yawn. "As you choose." She stretched her arm around him, pretending to settle back to sleep.

But it was she who lay awake when exhaustion reclaimed him. She held him long against the spirits of the night, and she prayed to the god Thor to keep him safe on the morn.

The battle of Carlingford Lough was the bloodiest ever to take place upon the emerald-green field. And by midafternoon, Olaf knew that it was a battle lost. All around him lay bodies. The human carnage was so great that a man could not take a step without sliding on blood.

He himself was covered with blood, which mingled with the sweat on his face to drip into his eyes. He could scarcely see. At one point he was saved from certain death only by the hideous cry of his attacker.

His arms, so accustomed to the heavy weight of his sword, were weary, and his mind, so accustomed to carnage, was rebelling. The smell of death around him was terrible, and the battle was lost. Viking kings and princes lay dead all over the field. He didn't yet realize that he was one of the few royalty and generals still standing. He knew only that if any Norse lives were to be saved, it was time to retreat. The retreat would not be an orderly one. Those who had survived would have to flee into the countryside and find shelter until they could meet and rally once more. Raising his arms high over his head, he sent the signal for retreat to those Vikings who could see him. As he tiredly lowered his arms, he knew that the Danes now held Dubhlain. But he and his men would arise again from outside its earthworks and they would seek their revenge. He would have vengeance for this day.

His resolve strengthened, Olaf sidestepped a Danish battle-axe, and the heavy weapon was imbedded in the earth. Olaf took that chance to bring his sword down upon the Dane, swiftly slaying his enemy. Then he looked about and saw his remaining forces disappearing into the trees of Eire. Now he could make good his own retreat. He stepped cautiously through the field and looked to a cove of thick bark and leaves.

But then he saw Grenilde. She was still in the thick of battle, her grace and poise allowing her to dance about her would-be assassins. At first he was furious; she had disobeyed his direct order. Then fear riddled him once more. He had seen it in his dream; the Danes had been the serpents.

He called to her; he shouted. Her sapphire eyes met his across the field. And then she was coming to him, running, stopping to cover her rear, running once more, pausing to slay a sword-wielding hulk. And then she was running again, toward the cove.

But there were more Danes coming with battle-axes, with spears, with chains and swords. Olaf ran out to meet them, screaming for Grenilde to get behind him. They were two now against ten, but the bodies fell around them. "Go!" he screamed to her. Olaf met the last of his contenders, vaguely aware of the blood dripping down his mail from a wound beneath his arm and the weakness in his leg from a deep, gaping wound on his thigh, but he couldn't give in to his fatigue and pain. He had to keep fighting like a demon, forgetting all else but the need to survive.

The battle continued across the field, until the last man before him fell. Olaf tore from the field, into the trees shouting Grenilde's name until she answered him. Following the sound of her voice, he found her, lying on leaves and moss. As he saw her there, she was more beautiful than she had ever been. He didn't see the sweat, the dirt, the blood. Beneath the grime that covered her skin he saw only her eyes, beautiful eyes, sapphire eyes. They beheld his with love, and then they began to glaze.

Then she screamed a cry of agony, a cry of death.

He knelt down beside her. "No!" he cried, twisting her body to find her wound. But even as he slipped his arms around her, he was drenched with her blood. The wound was in her back, and even as he cast his great, sun-capped head back to howl against it, her life began to slip from her body. Her arms that reached piteously for him were cold, too limp to hold him.

"My love," she whispered.

Smoothing her torn and matted hair from her brow, he bent over her, touching his lips to hers, unaware of the fetid scent of death upon them. "For eternity I will love you," he swore, his breath mingling with hers. "You must not leave me."

Somehow she smiled, but then her chest heaved with a great rattle and she broke into a spasm of coughing. Blood trickled from her lips, and heedlessly he kissed them again.

"Don't die," he pleaded, "please, don't die. . . ."

Through her parched, cracked lips, she whispered, "Hold me, love . . . Your warmth belies the cold of death. Oh, hold me . . . my lord . . . hold me . . . I am cold . . . so cold . . . cold as our native icestorms." Then her broken whispers ceased.

He held her, shook her, sat clasping her dead body to his chest. And there he rocked her, whispering to her as if she were a sleeping child.

The sun had set when he finally laid her on the ground. He stood trembling, the rage and pain wracking his already weak and tired body. Casting his massive golden head back, he screamed his grief and despair to the heavens. He ranted of his torment, his anguish, his loss, and his cries rattled the land. Wherever they were heard, even the Danes, the staunchest barbarians, quivered and prayed to their gods. It was the mighty howl of the Wolf, and it brought chills of terror and doom.

From his vantage point atop a high hill overlooking the lough, Aed Finnlaith viewed the bloody field. Those standing amid the carnage were Danes. Whether it had been their superior numbers or organization, or if Saint Patrick had heard their heathen prayers, he would never know, but the victory was theirs. Dubhlain, city of the Norwegians for years, now belonged to the conquering Danes.

Bent on one knee as he looked over the scene, Aed suddenly closed his eyes in silent prayer. The bodies that covered the field were those of his enemies, but he could take little pleasure in the hideous toll of death. Let it end, God, he prayed silently. Let the Danes hold their city of Dubhlain and build their walls. Let them cease their countless scourges throughout the country. Let us live in peace. . . .

He felt nothing from his prayer; he knew deep within him that it would be ignored, and he had the strange intuition that what he witnessed that day would be just the beginning for him. "Thy will be done," he murmured with a surge of pain.

"Father."

There was a tap on his shoulder. Aed twisted his head to his son Niall of Ulster standing behind him. Niall was a powerful man of thirty years, a handsome young giant with the wisdom learned from his father reflected in his somber green eyes.

"Fennen and Maelsechlainn await us, Father. We must ride down and receive the tribute for the shrine from the Danes."

Aed nodded and rose to his feet, wincing a bit as his bones cracked. With Niall, he didn't care if his bones cracked. His son had no desire to attempt to seize his crown during his lifetime; in fact, Aed sometimes doubted if Niall would ever covet the position of Ard-Righ. It was not a title that was necessarily hereditary; it passed between several of the powerful royal tribes. Niall was burdened down with his own affairs in Ulster and with the constant Viking harassment that occurred in the north.

Yet there were always men ready to topple an unwary king, and a man in Aed's position could afford to show no weakness. He gathered his horse's reins and mounted with an agility that belied his aching bones.

"We ride to the Danes," he called to his son.

The Ard-Righ's trumpets sounded and the Irish began their approach.

Dusk fell as they rode. By the time they picked their way through the fallen to the tent of Friggid the Bowlegs, the Danish chief, fires were flaming within the hastily erected campsite. Danes stopped in their camp preparations and looting to watch the Irish. They wore the grins of victors, sly looks that chilled the heart, looks that warned that truces were promises waiting to be broken.

Yet Aed was not afraid as he faced Friggid, despite the foul temper of the wild, red-haired Dane. In fact, Friggid took pleasure in the fury that tautened his features as he raged to his men. "Find him! The Wolf must die!" Friggid controlled his temper as he faced Aed. "A slaughter, Ard-Righ."

Aed found that he could grimly smile. The murdering Dane was afraid, afraid that one Norwegian lived . . . the Wolf.

Olaf held Grenilde through the night. In the morning he was quiet, a changed man, a man even more determined. His leg wound was festering, but he thought nothing of it. He lifted her high in his arms and began to walk, seeking water. The sun beat down upon him, but he kept his pace even, one step after the next. At midday he came to a stream, and then he bathed her tenderly. He touched her with reverence, cherishing the silk of her hair, the satin bronze of her flesh.

He spent the rest of the day building her bier. When the platform was complete, he laid her on it and placed her sword in her hands. He piled the plentiful kindling high as he wished her journey to Valhalla to be easy. She would travel with the wind to sit beside the war god Wodon, for surely there she would lead the life of the princess she had not been on earth.

When all was complete, he kissed her cold mouth. Determinedly searching, he found a piece of flint and sparked a fire. With a torch, he set it to his love. The bier burned ferociously. As he stood by the banks of the stream he watched it, burning still as the sun set once more. His eyes were distant and yet hard. He no longer howled out his grief. It had become a part of him, a part of his heart.

In the morning, he discovered it was difficult to stand. His wounds had weakened him. He bent to the stream and drank hungrily, then staggered in to soak his wounds. The pain in his thigh was a burning that equalled the fires of Grenilde's bier.

He attempted to cleanse the leg wound, but fatigue overwhelmed him. He fell on the bank of the stream, half in, half out of the water, his face lodged in mud, his golden head dirty and matted. But his nose and mouth were still above the water. The Wolf was felled, but still he breathed.

CHAPTER

4

❧

Tiptoeing about the cabin, Erin dressed quietly, donning a short wool tunic, heavy leather leggings, and a girdle of engraved gold. The need might arise for her to ride hard and she didn't want to be impeded by proper maidenly dress. Dragging her forest-green mantle from the hook by the door, she cast it about herself and secured the brooch. Just as she touched the heavy wooden latch, Mergwin's snoring ceased.

"Where do you think you're going, Erin?"

"To the stream, Mergwin, where else?" she inquired innocently.

"You should not go riding, Erin. The woods will be full of danger today."

"I shall take my sword, friend Druid," Erin said, adding with a mischievous smile, "after all, Mergwin, what can happen to me? It was you who said I would grow old with children at my feet!"

She closed the door quickly behind her, laughing as she heard the Druid's soft curses follow her. He would not be really worried, Erin was sure. Mergwin knew that she was one with these woods; she would be wary of stragglers from the battle. She would be careful; she would listen to the sounds of the wind and the earth as he had taught her. But she wanted to find the battlefield. She had to see . . .

What drove her she herself really didn't know. That she should hate the Norsemen was, logically, ludicrous, for she knew the Danes to be, if anything, even more barbaric. But her father could weigh logic and politics; he was the king. She could only take the torture of her own soul personally, and that torture had been inflicted by the Norwegians—Norwegians led by the Wolf, Olaf the White.

She paused many times as she led her horse through the overgrown paths and sloping fields that led to the duns above the lough, heeding Mergwin's warning to keep her eyes and ears sharp. She intended no stupidity. Her goal was to see the land run red with the blood of the Vikings—not her own. But it was difficult to sense the danger on the air. The sky was a sapphire-blue that morning, touched by only dreamlike puffs of white clouds. The long green grass seemed to reflect the morning dew like a million glittering emeralds. Rich clumps of heather spotted the fields, adding a touch of amethyst to the beauty of the day.

She rode nearly an hour before she dismounted from her horse and began to scurry carefully through the high dun above Carlingford Lough. Briars and branches pulled at her hair and mantle as she made her way through the dense foliage, but she didn't feel them, so intent was she to reach her destination.

Yet when she reached a spot near enough the cliff to survey the immense field below, she closed her eyes. A dizziness came over her; she had to grab a branch and hold on tightly to keep herself from falling. Her stomach began to writhe and heave. Despite her best efforts, she had to bend low over the grass as she was violently sick.

The world spun black for a minute, then she steadied herself. You came to see, she admonished sharply, to see Norwegian carcasses.

But nothing in her life, not even Clonntairth, had

prepared her for the horror of the scene below her.
Birds of prey were already among the torn and muti-
lated bodies. How many men lay dead and rotting?
she wondered. Thousands. Literally thousands. She
choked back a surge of hysterical laughter that would
surely do nothing more than make her retch hideously
again. In one day, one bloody day, the Vikings had
decimated more men with more vengeance than the
Irish had inflicted in years.

Oh, God, Erin thought, over and over. She closed
her eyes tightly, trying to close out the nightmare of
the field. Oh, God . . . Just as she had been so
determined to come, now she had to get away. Suddenly it seemed that the air was permeated with the
smell of death and decay.

She didn't realize that she sobbed her horror as she
backed her way rashly out of the thicket to her mare.
Her flesh was roughly torn and ripped, and a bramble
tore across her cheek. She touched her face and
vaguely realized that her tears were mingling with the
thin line of blood. She took a deep breath, and then
another, and as she swung her leg high and remounted
her horse, she realized that she had been too horrified
to try to discern if the bodies were Norse or Danish.
She didn't really know who had taken the victory.

With all those dead, it had to be the Danish. She
swallowed sharply, still tasting the bile in her mouth.
It would have been too great an irony for the Wolf to
escape. If there indeed was justice, and all those men
had been left for the scavengers, then Olaf the White
had to be among them.

Make that so, God, she prayed, so I can forget the
past. Let him just be dead and I will try to learn
wisdom like my father, forgiveness like my sister Bede
. . . for truly, God, what I have witnessed is horrible.
I cannot love this carnage. I cannot, I cannot. . . .

She couldn't stop her shaking, nor control the horrible taste of sickness that kept rising to her mouth.
She smelled death all around her; it had permeated her
mouth and nose. She wanted nothing more than to find

water and wash and wash until she could wash the horror from her mind.

But she rode a distance before she dismounted and once more battled through a heavy tangle of trees to the brook that raced through the forest. Even then she was alert and careful. Before she tethered her mare, she stood silent, listening, looking. But the forest was quiet and peaceful; she was alone. Still, she pulled her heavy steel sword into her hand when she left the mare to venture to the water.

Seeing the crystal stream sparkling beneath the sunlight, Erin forgot caution and ran to it. Flinging herself on her knees, she dropped her face into the water and then flattened to allow the rush of cold wet cleanness to cover her, clothing and all, so that it might purge the terror. She pulled her head up and began to breathe more easily, then lowered her face again to drink and clean her mouth. She breathed in the air deeply, her eyes closed as she brushed wet tendrils of hair from them. She began to blink the water from her lashes, then froze as her eyes lit upon a body in the water not fifty feet away.

She knelt there stiffly as seconds ticked by, not blinking, holding her breath. She raised herself lithely to the balls of her feet, her eyes never leaving the body as she fumbled around until her fingers closed over the steel of her sword. Then she stood, sword raised high, her eyes glued to the body.

That he had come from the battle was evident. Half immersed in the water, his massive body was clad in bloodied and dirty mail. He wore no helmet, but it was impossible to discern the color of his hair because it was covered with mud, and she could not see his features as his head was turned from her.

Warily, her sword poised to strike, she began to move toward him. A fish jumped in the water and she leaped back at the sound. But the body hadn't moved, and she forced herself to move forward again. When she stood beside him, she first thought him dead, but then she saw the rise and fall of his heavy shoulders.

She stood, poised to strike, but the awful carnage she had just seen made her loath to take a human life, and she didn't think she was capable of murdering a scarcely breathing man.

She noticed that blood was caked to his temple and matted with his hair. Beneath the water's edge she could see the flesh of a bent thigh. A terrible gash had rent away leggings and flesh.

He groaned suddenly, and once again she almost jumped back to the trees. But after that one emission of pain, he was silent again. A pity she didn't want to feel welled within her. The man was sorely wounded.

Erin was truly at a loss. She couldn't slaughter him as he lay there, yet she would be a fool to let him go. He would probably die anyway, just another dead Viking. And didn't she want all Vikings dead? It was one thing to think so in the luxury of her father's home, but it was quite another when she had just stared upon a profusion of broken bones, crushed skulls, and mangled bodies. And she had heard his heart-wrenching groan . . . Dear God, could she be this weak?

It occurred to her then that he might be a Viking of note—a worthy prisoner to bring to her father. Actually, her situation was a brilliant one. She could save this man and, in so doing, prove to her father that she could be as worthy as any of her brothers.

But how to capture him? She would have to render him helpless before attempting to revive him and forcing him to move to the threat of her sword. She was good with the weapon, but it would be only intelligent not to rely upon her prowess alone. The man at her feet was incredibly long and massive.

Erin thought only a moment, then hurried back to her mare and rummaged through her saddlebags. She had nothing. Then it occurred to her that the leather thongs that held the bag together were sturdy and supple enough for her to bind the man's wrists quickly. She would wet them, and they would dry and become so tight and strong that he would never free himself.

Excited with purpose, but wary still, Erin returned to the fallen Viking. She knelt beside him and placed her sword at her fingertips as she reached gingerly first for one wrist and then the other. The dead weight of the man's arms was such that she almost staggered beneath them, and she reflected that she was very lucky he was barely alive. If this man was conscious, it was doubtful that, for all her skill, she could deal with him with any hope of victory.

She couldn't quell the pity that arose within her again as she glanced at the broad hands and long fingers that feel limply from the wrists she bound. Tiny tufts of gold hair dotted his fingers and backs of his hands. Absently Erin dusted away the dry mud that clung to that hair. Strange, how that gesture made the man seem so human. I am crazy, she thought. His hands and fingers are strong because they wield weapons against the Irish.

He groaned once more, and she clenched her teeth together. Her mind fought a silent battle, one side saying he was a barbaric animal and should die, a deeper side unable to bear his suffering.

Finally she shrugged. He was bound; he was her captive, and should he dispute it, she would kiss his throat with the ready tip of her sword.

She had to move him, at least roll him over, if she was going to be able to bathe his face, ascertain the extent of his wounds, and make him walk. Once she returned him to Mergwin's cottage, she would have the Druid give him a sleeping potion. If he lived, this was one Viking giant who would be dangerous awake.

Erin first attempted to roll him over by his mail-clad chest, but she quickly realized the effort was futile and ludicrous. All she had to do was lever the elbow of his arm, and—if there was life in him at all—he would naturally roll to the balance. She put all her weight into her pull, and, as she had reasoned, his weight followed behind hers. The movement was accompanied by a deep, low, anguished groan. She took the large, sodden head into her lap and began to smooth the hair from the man's brow. Without thinking, she began to speak soothingly. "Shh . . . you are all right. I will cleanse your wounds."

She broke off as the man's eyes opened, instantly sharp and alert and as cold and blue as a frosted morning. She stared into those eyes and her own narrowed dangerously. Now there was no mistaking the roughly hewn and rugged features of the man. Not even blood and mud and the filthy beard could hide the raw, hard planes of the sharply arrogant and indomitable countenance.

Her tone changed radically, her voice rising high and shrill. "You!" she gasped. For his was far too familiar a face. It was one she had long envisioned in nightmares. "You!"

Her exclamations had become snarls. Instant warning and the reflexes of the warrior came to Olaf. His head was ringing, his body ached with pain, he knew not where he was nor his circumstances. He knew only that the face above his was filled with shock and hate.

"You! Wolf bastard of the North—"

He attempted to move, to grab the screaming harpy who tormented him, only to discover that he had no power over his arms because his wrists were securely bound. And then it all came back to him. The battle . . . Grenilde. . . . His eyes closed again.

When they reopened to his tormentor, they were curiously empty, devoid of fear, anger, anything. He watched Erin as if he were the captor rather than she, just staring at her almost absently, as if she were totally inconsequential.

She pulled her body back sharply, allowing his head to fall back to the earth with a sharp crack. He winced, and his eyes narrowed sharply as they looked up at her with irritation. Erin sprang for her sword and quickly held it to his neck. "Up, Olaf the White! Dog of Norway."

He ignored her command. Erin tightened her lips and pressed her sword more firmly against his jugular.

She received great satisfaction from the surprise that filtered through his eyes.

Still he didn't make a move. Erin smiled. She would have been surprised to see the intensity of cruelty in her own eyes.

She brought her sword in a casual line down his torso, scraping the mail. Her sword hovered below his hips. "Up, now, dog. You raping, plundering, murdering bastard. I wish to prolong your suffering. Oh, Viking, what I would do to you! But you will be my father's hostage. So we will go to him. But I warn you now, bastard dog of the North, one wrong move and I will sever your manhood and roast it before your eyes!"

She had hit a core of anger. His eyes flashed blue fire as his jaw tightened, but he began a painful attempt to rise. When he wavered on his feet before her, Erin inadvertently took a step backward. She was fairly tall for a woman, but this man towered over her. The giant muscles in his arms and thighs bulged with his strain to stay afoot. She saw his teeth clench more tightly together beneath the mud-matted growth of his beard as he was forced to place weight upon his wounded thigh.

"Turn slowly, Viking," she hissed. "I assure you the caress of my sword can be a long one. I would not kill you swiftly, Viking. The Danes would show greater mercy." He turned. Erin pressed the point of her sword in his back. "Walk, Viking, and don't, *don't,* make the mistake of turning."

He began to walk, wavering badly. He stumbled and fell. A flash of compassion tugged strongly at Erin, but she closed her eyes and remembered, Clonntairth, the smell of the fires, the screams of the women. . . . Her sword dug into his downed back. "You have five seconds to get up, Viking."

He stumbled back to his feet. Once more they moved for the trees and Erin's tethered horse. She didn't take her eyes off him as she gathered her mount's reins. But he was half dead, weary, encrusted with blood and dirst. His mail armor must weigh down on him terribly, Erin thought. She bit into her lip as she watched him waver, thinking she wasn't going to be able to take him far in his condition. But once again, bitter memory rose above her compassion. He would walk until he dropped.

Carefully, with one eye upon her barely conscious prisoner, she cut through the left rein on her mare's bridle to use as a rope. The rein was not particularly strong, but then, at this point, neither was the Wolf. "Put your hands out," she commanded him sharply.

He refused to oblige until she raised the point of her sword to his neck once more and pressed threateningly against his flesh. He blinked, but not even then did the empty, arctic ice leave his eyes. He raised his hands.

It was difficult to keep her sword raised with one hand and loop the rein securely around the bounds that held his hands, but despite his condition, she couldn't trust him, couldn't let down her guard for an instant. It was even more difficult to mount her horse while holding both prisoner and sword but she didn't dare release either. Thankfully the mare was a docile creature, and although she was occasionally skittish, she remained as meek as a lamb while Erin struggled into the saddle. She dug her knees against the mare's flanks and began a crisp trot.

From her vantage point Erin stared down at the captive. Another flash of unwanted compassion swept through her and a trace of grudging admiration. He was as pale as clouds, his face was strained with pain, and yet he ran. Clonntairth! she reminded herself, and she closed her eyes quickly, forcing the images of terror to her mind. To feel compassion for this dangerous beast was to betray the memory of those she had loved.

She opened her eyes to find the ice-blue ones staring up into hers. They were so strange, so devoid of life and yet they seemed to mock her from a ruggedly structured face that was handsome and supremely arrogant even now. He stared at her as he struggled to run and a cold wind seemed to send shivers up her spine. There was something terribly frightening about him. He seemed to be more than mere man. Wounded, ragged, muddied, tethered and dragged, he still managed to walk, still managed to stare at her with contempt and arrogance the only distant emotions in his cold, cold . . . empty eyes. She shivered, staring again. He was a giant of a man, muscled and yet trim, with his golden head at a level with her waist even as she sat on her horse. If he had his customary strength, I would not still be riding, she thought. He would have attacked her, dragged her from the horse, broken his bonds. . . . She leveled her sword carefully at his eyes. "I warn you, Viking, one move and you will suffer hideously."

His eyes were still on her when he fell, sinking to his knees, then careening flat on his face.

She leaped from the mare, wary at first that his action had only been a ploy. But when she carefully skirted around him and pressed the point of her sword into his spine, he didn't move. She stood, perplexed, berating herself for not thinking more fully about the extent of his wounds. She might have already killed him. She shrugged. Didn't she want this particular Viking dead?

"Oh, God . . ." she whispered aloud. She wanted him to suffer, as the Irish had suffered. But there was a thin, fragile line between life and death, and though she did not understand her feelings completely, Erin knew she didn't want the responsibility of murder, of snapping the fragile line of life, on her hands and heart. Such responsibility belonged to her father, to her brothers, to the warriors who met their enemies on the field.

Erin sighed, bending to touch his broad back. He still breathed. She stood again, looking into the trees. She hadn't come far, and she had followed the trail that wound around beside the stream. Somehow she had to get him back to the water. Sighing once more, she knelt down and maneuvered him onto his back. A bitterness gnawed at her stomach as she again studied his face. It was no wonder that he was known throughout the Viking and Irish worlds alike, thought to be touched and guarded by the ancient Scandinavian gods. Even down, unconscious, a prisoner, he seemed to radiate an aura of golden power as if he were one of those blond and blue-eyed gods. Hah! He was no god. He was her prisoner. And he would never possess the power of any god again because she would see that, if he wasn't executed, he would be incarcerated by the very Irish he had arrogantly assumed he could conquer and subdue.

"I am the conqueror, Viking!" she whispered. "You are the captive . . . the conquered . . . my prisoner!"

Gritting her teeth, she stood and firmly gripped his bound wrists. She groaned aloud as she attempted to drag him, his weight tremendous against her more delicate strength. It was terribly slow going, and she grunted and panted most of the way, but eventually she moved him the twenty feet through the foliage back to the bank.

Drawing upon her remaining strength, she dragged his torso up against the trunk of an oak and secured his bound wrists to it with a piece of the rein. Once she had assured herself that he was secure, she tethered her mare and hurried to the stream to drink thirstily. Then she looked back to her prisoner. He too needed water.

Erin returned to her mare and procured the little silver drinking cup she always carried, filled it with water, and returned to the Viking. The full lips beneath the golden curls of his matted beard were parched. His eyes were still closed, but she gingerly brought the cup to his lips, allowing water to trickle over them and into his beard. His eyes began to flicker and his lips to move. She pressed the cup against them again and he instinctively began to drink. "Slow!" she warned him sharply as he began to gulp and the penetrating blue ray of his ice eyes looked at her.

Apparently heeding the wisdom of her command,

he paused, taking a deep breath and closing his eyes before drinking again. He attempted to move, then realized that as well as being bound at the wrists, he was tied to the tree.

One of his arched brows cocked slightly and he smiled dryly, his lips twisted into a snarl. "Thank you," he muttered in Norse.

She moved away from him. When he was conscious, he frightened her, no matter how he was tied. She was too keenly aware of the breadth of his chest, of the steel-hard strength in his sinewed arms.

"Don't thank me, Viking," she snapped. "I keep you alive so that you may suffer more fully. Quick death would be too good for you, dog of Norway.

Hoping to prove her point, Erin stepped over his sprawled legs disdainfully and hurried back to her mare. From her saddlebags she brought out a piece of bread. She was about to hold it for him when she halted. He was a Viking, and Vikings were known for terrible atrocities. He might just very well attempt to bite her fingers.

Smiling grimly, Erin stuck the piece of bread on the end of her sword and leveled it beneath his nose. "Your meal, Viking," she mocked haughtily. "All that you eat in my land comes to you through the use of a sword. Today should be no different. Except take heed, Viking, you would not want to swallow the point, or find that I allow it to slip.

She was glad Aed had made her learn the language of the invaders when she was young. She knew the Wolf understood her every word clearly. The emptiness left his eyes and was replaced with pure hatred and vengeance. But looking at the bread, he carefully began to eat. Erin controlled a little shiver as she watched him bite into the bread and she remembered the day he had laughed so handsomely, so captivatingly with his blond she-wolf at Clonntairth.

Erin jerked her sword away with the bread still on it, forcing him to twist his head quickly to avoid slitting half his mouth. Her eyes were emerald daggers in the twilight now descending. She yawned elaborately. "Excuse me, Lord Dog of Norway. I'm too exhausted to further satisfy your appetite." She took a position ten feet away from him and curled up on the bank, her sword beneath her, the hilt beside her hand. "Sleep well, Viking," she hissed. "Tomorrow you will run alongside my horse and you will meet my father's wrath—the justice of the Irish!"

CHAPTER

5

❦

Erin awoke, damp, cramped, and miserable, with a start. Blinking fog from her eyes, she noticed first that it was barely dawn. She recalled instantly where she was but wondered why she had awakened. And then she knew. The Wolf was glaring at her again. And despite his icy gaze, she felt heat, as if he could penetrate her mind with those extraordinary cold blue eyes.

She stood and walked to the stream to wash her face and to drink, then returned to her captive. "Today you walk, Viking, or you die," she told him sharply. She lifted her sword over him, smiling as she assumed he must be certain she meant to bring it down upon him. But then she carefully slit the length of leather that held him to the tree. His arms fell in front of him and he sat for several seconds, allowing life to seep back into him. Erin placed her sword against his neck. "Up," she told him. "Walk to the stream. You may wash your face and drink water—but no tricks. As I have warned you, I am talented with a sword. Give me the slightest cause and you will begin to lose your extremities one by one."

He staggered as he attempted to rise, but Erin could immediately see that the night had given him greater strength. Forewarned, she kept the point of her sword firmly against his spine as she followed him to the stream. She allowed him to drink only a mouthful of water, then dug her sword up against his ribs. "Enough. Up."

He rose, teetering still.

"Head straight toward my horse, and don't turn a hair. Remember, Wolf, you are my prisoner. Now move!"

Having him obey her commands made the joy of victory race through her blood. But as they approached the tethered animal, Erin was still very aware that she couldn't let down her guard for an instant.

When she reached her mare, Erin untied the tethering rein from a branch, and a startled morning bird suddenly flew from the tree, squawking like a demon of hell. The mare bolted, rearing and neighing in skittish panic, and Erin was forced to drop her sword and turn her strength to the reins to calm and hold the mare.

It was her complete undoing. The second her back was turned, the rock-muscled arms of her captive came around her, his bound wrists about her waist, squeezing tightly.

"Your prisoner?" the Wolf snarled. "I think not, Irish bitch."

She was barely breathing, half paralyzed with terror, but fully aware that somehow she had to fight him. For a moment she held perfectly still, aware of the fierce male body pressed to hers, aware of the scent, the heavy breathing, the suffocating strength.

His beard brushed her cheek as he lowered his head and whispered a spine-chilling command against her ear. "Now you will move."

Erin twisted her head to sink her teeth into his shoulder as she kicked backward furiously, hoping to hit his injured leg. His agonized groan was a sign of her success, but she was still imprisoned by his bound arms, and as he staggered with pain, she staggered along with him until together they fell to the earth.

She was beneath him, panting desperately for breath. For several seconds they both merely lay there, trying just to breathe and gather their resources. Then he twisted, ignoring the slight pain under his arm, to bring himself around so that he could stare into her eyes. Shocking blue met deepest emerald. And more than anything else, both pairs of eyes registered an incredulous surprise that the owners should be in such positions.

Olaf was weak and torn. Erin was staggered and helpless from his weight. Like opponents in a ring they watched one another, still drawing desperately for breath.

Erin attempted the first move, as Olaf, whose eyes were still bleary, continually shook his head to clear his vision. When his lids fell, she dove desperately to escape from his arms.

She'd almost succeeded but he let out a biting growl and dug his fingers into her hair, the wound under his arm no longer paining him. Erin screamed at the wrenching pain and fell back beneath him, then brought her nails raking across his face. He swore furiously and pressed an elbow deep into her ribs. Erin gritted her teeth together from the pain and desperately struck at him, fists pummeling furiously and feet flying. He jerked his arms up from around her while swearing again, then brought his folded fingers down and backhanded her hard across the face.

The blow was stunning. Her head reeled with the sharp agony and she lay still, her eyes closed as she fought the tears and waited—waited to feel his death blow, or the barbaric revenge that he would exact.

Nothing came. Slowly she opened her eyes. He lay a foot away from her, staring at her tiredly as he panted for breath. For countless moments their eyes locked.

She fought a scream of terror as he rolled toward

her again. Dazed and paralyzed by her terror, her body refused to function. He brought his bound arms around her again. She began to struggle against him, certain that he meant to crush her within his grasp. But he didn't. He laid his weight atop hers and went still again, breathing deeply. Panic again filled her in new waves as she felt him against her, the steel strength of his chest, the muscled heat of his legs, the iron clamp of his arms. Even the easy brush of his beard against her throat and cheek was terrifying and threatening. He was not hurting her, yet he frightened her far more than if he were. The golden aura she had sensed about him was unleashed and she was held by a power both mercilessly strong and mercilessly male. Never before had she been more aware of a man. Never before had she been so powerless, or more acutely aware of the weakness of her sex. And the power of his.

She gasped for breath as shivers seized her. All manner of horror swept through her mind. Surely he would kill her. Perhaps rape her first. Torture her. She fought a scream as she waited. . . .

Finally he pulled his arms up over her head again and rolled away from her. She realized blankly that he had just been holding her still and immobile while gathering his strength. She swallowed sickly. Now he would tear her to pieces.

But though his eyes remained upon her, irritated and watchful, he made no move toward her. He struggled to his feet and returned to the bubbling cool water where he lay again to drink deeply and then cleanse the mud from his face and hair, his task made difficult by his bound hands.

Erin attempted to rise, but the blackness that rushed to meet her sent her sprawling again, struggling for consciousness. By the time she cleared her head of the debilitating mists, he stood over her, water dripping from his beard upon her face.

"Have you more food?" he demanded.

She continued to stare at him, but he nudged her

ribs with his foot and she winced at the pain. It surprised her that he spoke in her tongue, especially since she had been ridiculing him in his own, but she didn't dwell upon it. She closed her eyes, and then rose slowly to her feet.

"In my saddlebags," she told him tonelessly.

He looped his fingers through her hair and aimed her toward the now docilely grazing mare. When they neared the animal he shoved her. Without turning around Erin dug into the leather satchels with trembling fingers.

When she turned to offer him the bread and dried meat she carried, her eyes widened with amazement and she dropped her forced offerings. His eyes were closed, his features drawn and tense with strain as he held his hands before him, the muscles of his arms bulging, the veins blue from his strength as he clenched his fingers tightly and pulled. The leather thongs that bound him snapped and fell to the earth.

He opened his eyes, glanced at Erin and then at the food on the ground. "Pick it up," he told her tonelessly, still in her own language.

Quaking in uncontrollable shudders, Erin stooped to obey. He stared at her as he wolfed the food down where he stood, first the bread, then the meat. Erin returned his stare but didn't move a muscle.

But then his freed hand shot out to clamp around her wrist and in panic she brought a knee up hard, brushing his wound and striking his groin. He grunted loud in pain, and his eyes narrowed while his teeth ground down so hard that she could hear their grating. But he didn't release her. He gave her arm a savage wrench and dragged her along with him back to the water's edge. He sat, and she was pulled beside him to watch as he ripped the fabric from his wounded thigh.

It was a long, deep gash. Erin saw a pulse tick hard within his cheek below the threads of his beard. He was in great pain, and she attempted to avert her eyes from both his face and the wound.

He placed a hand around her chin and jerked her face back to his. "You will clean it," he commanded, his voice still toneless but rasping and harsh.

"No," she murmured, feeling ill and queasy again.

His fingers tightened around her chin, hard and biting. "Do it."

Erin swallowed and ripped away the hem of her tunic. She wet it in the cold water, then paused.

His eyes were like glittering hard diamonds, his jaw was again clenched. "Do it," he repeated.

Her eyes lowered from his and she gingerly touched his ravaged flesh. Then she too gritted her teeth and began to scrub the wound.

Nothing more than a groan, quickly choked off, escaped him. His face turned white, but he let no more evidence of the agony the thorough cleansing caused him come to his lips.

Erin was biting her own lips and trembling as she finished the task. Touching him, she felt his warm flesh. She was aware of the golden hair that flourished on the leg, of the hard strength of the sinewed limb, of the panted breathing of the man who braced himself against his pain. She swayed a second herself, clamped her teeth hard, and glanced at his face. For a second his eyes remained closed, then they opened, the startling, sapphire blue denoting no emotion.

"It should be burned and closed." Why she opened her mouth to speak, she didn't know. The words had simply come out.

He nodded and closed his eyes once more. She thought he intended to ignore her, but he rose and began to search the ground.

Erin again thought of flight. But his eyes riveted to her just as she bunched her muscles to spring into a desperate run, causing her to hesitate—just a second too long. He limped to her side with the agony of his haste clearly apparent in his eyes. And then, instead of running, she was sent sprawling into the water.

She was ignored once more as he discovered the flint he sought. Moving painfully, he gathered kindling.

With deliberate care he created a fire upon the bank, then moved across it once more to retrieve Erin's sword from the brush where it had fallen.

Only then did he turn back to Erin, limping determinedly to draw her from the water. He gripped her wrist as he heated her sword in the flames, then forced the sword into her hands as he dragged them both down. "Now!" he hissed to her.

Her hand was shaking. His grip around her wrist tightened. "Now—and let your hand be sure," he warned.

She brought the heated metal against his thigh, feeling faint as she smelled the burning flesh. This time he did scream out. He released his hold on her and fell backward in his agony, fists clenching the earth.

Erin was immobilized for an instant as her heart cried out for the pain he was enduring. But then alert reasoning flashed into her mind. He was the enemy, and she had been a fool not to kill him. She jumped back and skirted around his prone form to run. She could reach her horse.

He twisted his body and grabbed her leg, his face portraying the agony his effort caused him, but he was determined. He pulled her leg sharply, causing her to fall.

Pure panic raced through Erin's veins. With every ounce of her own estimable strength, she brought her elbow down hard into his wound. He rolled onto his back, but his hold did not ease, as she sprawled on the earth beside him.

His eyes, she saw, were closed against his pain. He was barely conscious. She jerked her leg furiously, but to no avail. He turned toward her and his eyes opened. He clasped her wrist so tightly that she cried out, certain that her bones would snap beneath his strength. But he knew when to stop, how to deliver pain without inflicting permanent damage. He stared at her and grated, "Irish bitch! I have much to repay you for. Don't nurture the vengeance that might fall upon you. You are my prisoner. In my power."

How could he endure his pain to remain conscious and speak? Erin wondered bitterly. She had so injured and angered him now that she was more certain than ever that he would kill her or torture her slowly. She was cornered, but being cornered gave her an absurd bravado.

"Never, Viking. I will never be in your power," she hissed. "The Irish will find you . . . my father will find us . . . and you will become food for the rats—" She broke off with a scream as he wrenched her wrist.

"Shut up!" he commanded, rolling his weight on top of her with a sudden fury and gasping at the renewed pain of his thigh wound with the effort. His face was a strained and chilling mask as he placed his hands on either side of her face, and she fought tears as she realized he could crush her skull, the delicate bones of her cheeks, if he so desired. She winced and held still, staring into the hypnotizing blue of his eyes. "Shut up," he repeated in a growl. "Bitch, you do sorely push the benevolence of the gods!"

In mounting terror, Erin held her peace. She met his sharp stare as long as she could, and then, despite her will to show him no fear, she closed her eyes against the power of his, wincing at his painful hold.

Slowly it eased. For several moments Erin kept her eyes tightly clenched, too frozen with her fear even to shiver. But she felt nothing, no blow to body, no touch of cruelty or revenge. There was only the shift of his weight upon hers, one that even more securely pinioned her.

Moments passed, and unable to bear further suspense, Erin tentatively opened her eyes—and realized the cause of her safety. The Wolf was not inhuman. Pain on top of injury had finally taken its rightful toll. He had passed out atop her.

For several seconds she barely breathed, but his head on her shoulder didn't move. His arms were on either side of her, his torso over the length of her, his legs sprawled over hers, so that his limbs created a steel band of imprisonment. She had to move him to move herself.

Hating each second that his heat pressed her to the ground, Erin forced herself to wait. The sun-blond hair tickled her chin, the breadth of his chest crushed against her breasts, and his thighs were hard against hers, absurdly intimate. Had he raped her, he would not have fallen any differently.

That thought made her panic, and she decided she had waited long enough. She gingerly attempted to edge from beneath him, watching his right arm as she tried to gently lift it. The muscled bicep began to move at her careful touch and she held her breath, even more carefully sliding her leg from beneath his. By rolling slowly to her stomach she discovered that she could more easily escape from his weight.

Erin had her body half freed from its prison of flesh and muscle when she chanced to notice a shift against herself. She quickly turned her face and shifted her eyes toward the head of the captor, only to scream aloud when she saw that his face was now twisted to hers, his eyes open and staring sharply as his hand clamped around her waist and the small of her back. Her scream became a choked yelp of pain and indignity as his hand moved from her only to descend swiftly and fiercely upon the rounded padding of her buttocks. Tears she could not prevent glazed her eyes. She would have rather endured another blow to the jaw than this humiliation, which reduced her to the status of nothing more than a troublesome child.

But even as her mind reeled against the assault, it ceased, and she found herself swept beneath him again, staring into his eyes, with her own threatening to spill over and her lips trembling despite her best efforts. He spoke tiredly as he held her.

"Girl, I haven't yet the strength to move. You do so again, and I will break your leg. Your bones would snap easily—and such a feat is also one I can also accomplish with one hand and little energy."

He stared at her long before he resumed his position and rested his head upon her shoulder and breast.

As tears fell silently down her cheeks, she noted dismally that the dawn had not as yet fully broken. She lay in rigid, silent misery until the need for rest which the Wolf so craved overwhelmed her too and she dozed into the escape and oblivion of a restless sleep.

Olaf saw a glorious building. It was the great hall of Valhalla, shrouded in mist as the hall of the gods should be. It was resplendent, as only such a place should be. The glimmering chalices were inlaid with precious glass, the warriors and their ladies were gowned in silks, they laughed and they feasted and the men raised great drinking horns to their lips. But Olaf didn't stop to drink with his comrades. He hurried along the hall, seeking out the doors that rose in mist as he floated along. Grenilde . . . she would be waiting. And she was, with her eyes of the sky that offered heaven, dazzling in her welcome, her arms outstretched wrapping him in them.

He held her, feeling part of the love she had given him, a knowledge of that gentle time. It was not the wild beauty of body craving body, rather the peace and tenderness of souls that reached out. Just holding . . . touching. . . .

In the misted dusk between sleep and wakefulness, it was a spell of tranquility. He smiled as he held her, and he shifted slightly, feeling the caress of her hair against his cheek, the supple warmth of her curved woman's body. He trailed his knuckles down her cheek, stroked the soft column of her throat with his thumb, savored the firm and heavy feel of her breast within his palm. She stirred, sighing in a soft whimper, moving closer against him.

His eyes opened and pain riddled through him from the glare of the sun overhead. But a deeper agony ripped through his soul at the loss of his dream. He gazed with his jaw tightening at the woman he held.

The hair that teased his bearded chin was not the gold of the sun, but the ebony of the night. The long, lithe limbs that entwined with his were not Grenilde's, nor was the delicate face that appeared deceptively sweet and innocent in sleep. He cozened to his side the Irish bitch who was so eager to see him castrated and torn asunder.

She sighed softly again, as if comfortable and content, and twisted more closely to him, her breast filling the palm he held upon it. She nuzzled against his shoulder with the tender instincts of a kitten, and he realized with both dry humor and bitter pain that she cherished dreams of her own.

Erin was not dreaming as Olaf had been. She was coming from pleasant dusk, slowly awakening. It was instinct she responded to. She nestled against a warmth and unyielding strength that was yet secure and comforting. It gave more warmth to her stiff and chilled body than even the rays of the sun, and all that she felt was light and pleasant and stirring, until her eyes flashed open with sudden alarm and she stared into those blue-ice eyes of the Wolf.

Olaf's eyes narrowed sardonically as he saw a flush of horror rise in her creamy complexion. She gazed at him, and upon her own position, her tunic hiked, her slender legs entangled with his, her body curled suggestively . . . his hand . . .

Erin's cry died in her throat as she met his contemptuous gaze again. She had done this. She had come against him like a lover might. She had responded with pleasure to his touch, and even now her breast tingled against the touch of his palm.

He laughed suddenly, but it was the sound of dry leaves rustling, hollow. Empty. Distant, so distant. . . .

Still it was laughter, and her humiliation and loathing came to her full force. Forgetting the threat he had given her about snapping her limbs—a threat she hadn't doubted for a moment—she lashed out with arms and legs, catching him unaware and causing new pain to his injury.

The laughter left his face to be replaced by the fury she was coming to know so well. He straddled her quickly, catching her wrists and securing them high over her head. He had found his strength again, she thought bitterly, her rash anger cooling as regret for her impulsive and foolish action turned quickly to a rebirth of terror.

"Irish, you are a bitch to be taught a few lessons," he snapped irritably. "Thank your God that my mind is full, and my body wounded—and in need of your gentle touch," he added sarcastically.

He let go of her wrists, his brows rising in questioning mockery as he dared her to move against him again. He placed his fingers lightly over her cheeks, smiling grimly at her battle for the control to remain still before him. His light touch held her as his eyes became clouded by shadow. "Be glad that I need you, girl," he said, his anger almost absent, "and that a Dane did pierce my leg, for I do not forget when I am aggravated sorely. And, Irish bitch, again and again you have given me grievance."

He released her face and pushed himself painstakingly to his feet. Then he reached down for her, dragging her to her feet. "You will help me to the water," he commanded.

At the water's edge he pushed her down before staggering down beside her. He swallowed and leaned back upon his arms. "Clean it again!" he demanded. "And rinse it well, Irish, for still I feel the burn. Ease the pain."

With trembling hands Erin began to cool the damaged flesh with the fresh water. She glanced nervously at him and saw that his head was tilted back and his eyes were closed. But they parted in gleaming slits of warning and she turned her eyes back to her task.

He is distant now, she thought, preoccupied. But he had stored in his mind everything she had done to him. What would happen to her when the disinterested distance that held him at bay was no longer with him?

"The mud in this bank is a special clay," she said

falteringly. "When your wound is rinsed, it will be best to pack it with the clay and these river weeds. The burn will be eased and—"

"I will eventually rot with the poison?" he queried her sharply.

"No," Erin murmured. "I am telling you the truth."

"Then you will pack it—carefully."

Still shivering, Erin ripped away the fabric near the wound and tore more of her own clothing to create a bandage.

And all the while she was aware of him. She felt the whisper of his breath against her neck as she bent over his thigh, the brushing of his sinewed arm against her when she moved. Even when she wasn't looking at him she could feel his eyes, envision the full handsome lips, nestled in the trimmed beard, that could twist with both mockery and amusement.

Any brush against his body, any thought of him, made her shiver. She had to get away, but if she hurt him again, she would have to make her escape good.

As if sensing her thoughts, he spoke. "They say, Irish, that the taste of revenge is the sweetest in the world. . . ."

"Yes," Erin bit back. "Revenge is sweet, Viking." She touched the binding over his wound, as if checking her work, and then stood, carefully pretending to stretch her muscles cramped by her efforts in his behalf. As she had hoped, he dipped his golden head over his wound to survey her ministrations.

He is weak, Erin told herself. He had barely eaten, and although he had rested, he was still wounded; still exhausted. Despite the great strength of his body, he was weary. He had to be enduring a draining pain. He wasn't holding her, and he couldn't possibly run, and if she didn't escape him, he would seek a revenge that he had warned her would be very, very sweet.

She stooped carefully to grasp a dead branch from the stream's edge, praying he wouldn't hear her. He did, but he glanced up a second too late. The blue eyes met hers just before she brought the branch careening against his skull. And just before his eyes closed she saw a message within them. He would never be distant or disinterested in her again. If he were ever to hold her in his power again, his revenge would be sweet and enduring.

He fell against the bank, but Erin was certain her blow had not been lethal. She doubted she had even rendered him unconscious. But she didn't wait to find out. She ran, forgetting her horse—and the absurd idea she could ever have taken him prisoner.

Half-hysterical, she dove through brambles and thorns, foliage and trees, thinking of nothing but putting distance between herself and the man, the creature of incredible power, the Wolf.

CHAPTER

6

A.D. 853

Erin leaned heavily against the broad trunk of an ash, closing her eyes and breathing deeply.

Spring was coming to the land and, with it, heavy rains. The ground was damp beneath her feet, and the forest smelled heavily of earth and greenery. The air itself was heavy and humid. Soon rain would fall again and the earth would turn to mud and slush.

She adjusted her stance, wincing slightly and clutching her shoulder. Her hand came in contact with something sticky and she looked at her fingers with surprise. Blood oozed from her flesh. Strange, she had felt no pain.

She reached upward to remove the gold-gilded helmet that shielded her head and hid her features, and then slid to sit at the foot of the tree. Somewhere, not far behind her, her raiders would be making an end of the Danish camp by the sea. She did not hear the cries of men—she had taught herself not to listen, just as she had taught herself not to think of the carnage.

A twig snapped and her eyes flew open as she reached for her heavy sword, trying to still the panic that rose within her. She was amazed to see Mergwin standing before her. But as her panic subsided, so did her amazement. The old Druid had a habit of managing to be places when he should have been miles and miles away.

Erin met his relentless stare silently, waiting for him to speak.

"Women," he said quietly, "are exempt from carrying arms, my lady Erin, as well you know, since 697 when the mother of Saint Adamnan saw two fair ladies in battle. Those docile creatures, before Ronait's vision, tore into one another with iron sickles in a manner so savage and barbaric that Saint Adamnan issued at Tara that year the law we refer to now as Cain Adamnan. Know you not that law, Erin?"

She wanted to outstare the Druid, but her eyes fell. She exhaled a tired sigh. "I do not enter the battles, Mergwin."

"No, you lead the men, you position them to fight from the forests, to attack when you have lured the Vikings to their traps."

Color rushed into her face, and she felt miserable. "What are you doing here, Mergwin?" she asked resentfully. Her arm was beginning to pain her and the gold-gilded mail she wore upon her chest seemed incredibly heavy. She felt gritty and tired and far more unclean than simply dirty. Why did Mergwin have this effect on her? She had been victorious that day, as she had been many times since she began her raids. But her victory felt hollow. She wanted to be home at Tara, to be with her mother, dressing her hair carefully, choosing silks for new gowns. . . .

"Oh." Mergwin shrugged in answer to the question she had almost forgotten she had asked. "I thought I might find you here, daughter of Aed." He sat down beside her and parted the chain on her arm, muttering beneath his breath at the sight of her wound. "I will tie and bind it for you with a poultice," he said. "Then you must take care to keep it clean or the career of the Golden Warrioress will end with no honor or great deed but with a rotting disease. Do you understand?"

Erin nodded silently.

"I assume," Mergwin continued, his tone a firm scold, "that neither Aed nor my lord Fennen of Connaught knows that they harbor against their bosoms the lady who drives the Vikings to such great distraction with her devious tactics?"

Erin shook her head, still not meeting Mergwin's eyes. "No," she murmured with a bit of a nervous gulp. It was strange how she could now meet a horde of oncoming warriors with little more than a tremor, yet Mergwin could make her feel like a naughty child. But she was not the "Golden Warrioress" to Mergwin and she knew it well. She was a young woman, terrified both of capture and discovery by her own, often wondering how she had even set upon her path.

She finally turned her eyes to her old tutor. "Mergwin, Father must not know that it is I who lead these raids. He will stop me, Mergwin, and he will marry me off to Fennen."

"I should tell your father," Mergwin muttered darkly, making her gasp as he pulled tight a band of his own robe around the slash in her arm. "You should be married to Fennen and locked well in his royal residence, away from this bloodshed and foolishness."

Erin started shivering, feeling a fear worse than that of her first raid. Most of the time she didn't allow herself to think. After the day in the forest when she had encountered the Norwegian Wolf and found herself inept, she had lost all dreams of battle. She had learned she was fragile and she had discovered she had no wish to die, nor to be injured.

But it had been at that same time that her cousin Gregory had come home well and hearty again, and Gregory's dreams of vengeance rekindled her own. Only she and Gregory had been at Clonntairth; only they could remember the horror. And so they had created fantasies together, daydreams in which they were the victors, in which the Vikings who had destroyed Clonntairth were butchered one by one. Erin had told Gregory of both Maelsechlainn's daughter who had brought about the death of Turgeis the Norseman and about the Viking woman warrior who had impressed her. Gregory had seized upon her words. And Erin had discovered that her cousin had gained not only new strength and health from the monks, but a cunning that far surpassed his years.

But even as she allowed herself to spin tales with Gregory, Erin had remembered the horror of the field at Carlingford Lough and she had remembered the feel of the cold eyes of the Norwegian Wolf on her.

Peace had supposedly reigned after the Danes took the battle of Carlingford Lough. But the fact of peace hadn't lasted a day. Not even the Danes were a totally organized foe. Bands of them had been scavenging tiny coastal villages even as the Irish kings had met with Friggid the Bowlegs, and the defeated Norwegians had returned like weeds. Their raids became more and more fierce, and in their vengeance they preyed more cruelly upon the Danes than ever before.

Gregory cared little whether the raiders were Norwegians or Danes. He had a fever about him to destroy all the foreigners. Even more than the foreigners, he wanted to destroy the outlaw Irish who turned their backs on their land to join with groups of Vikings to prey upon their own.

During his recovery at Armagh, Gregory had studied the tactics of warfare. He combined all he had assimilated with Erin's tales of the brave, conquering females, and the Golden Warrioress had been born.

To her cousin, Erin had finally admitted she was a coward. She told Gregory she had met with a Viking in the woods after the great battle, and that victory had quickly become defeat in her panicked hands. Gregory had been fascinated, assuring Erin she had behaved commendably and that she had obviously been saved by the powers of the forest because she did have a heroic destiny.

Erin wasn't terribly sure she was destined for heroism, but Gregory had designed the beautiful gilded helmet and tunic of mail, and before she had quite known she had agreed to his audacious plans, she had become the Golden Warrioress now admired by kings, revered by poets—and respectfully feared by the Vikings.

At first it had been only she and Gregory and a handful of young men. They had been nothing more than a small group of youths, crying out at their first sight of blood. But conviction had held them to their purpose, and after nights when they had sobbed out their terror, screamed with agony from their wounds, and watched friend and brother die, they had toughened into a formidable force. And with the success of their swift and cunning raids, more and more Irish princes and warriors had joined the secret ranks.

They met infrequently, only when Gregory and Erin could escape the work and formalities of home, thinking up excuse after excuse to ride from Tara. They had had more time lately; Aed was busy worrying about the resurgence of Norwegian power that seemed to grow like wildfire. He traveled the land trying to rally the kings together, for an organized defense was vital if they were to survive. Maeve had never had much control over her youngest daughter, and it was doubtful if she ever considered Erin might be lying about the "pilgrimages" she set on with her cousin.

Erin met her troops in the golden outfit, her helmet carefully in place. She had been terrified for months that her voice would give her away, but the delicately molded visor created an echo within the frame of the strange structure and her voice was well camouflaged. Her troops were loyal, placing her upon a pedestal and respecting her wish to remain anonymous. Any man who chose to allow his curiosity to outweigh his honor would quickly find swords held to his throat.

"Mergwin," Erin said softly, "please, you mustn't tell my father, or Fennen, or anyone. Not now. I could not be any man's wife, Mergwin, I am needed. We have been striking the only decent blows against the Vikings. We have saved countless Irish villages, countless Irish lives." She touched the old Druid's bearded cheeks and whispered, "Please, Mergwin. I swear to you, I carry my sword only so that I may defend myself if—"

"If the Golden Warrioress can't disappear quickly enough after seducing men to their deaths?"

Erin lost her temper. She was tired and worn and her arm was paining her, and Mergwin was behaving as if the Vikings were the injured party. "Mergwin," she said coldly, "these men whom I 'seduce' to their deaths are rapists, murderers, and thieves. Butchers plundering a land that isn't theirs! I don't take off across the seas to bring them harm. They've come here, Mergwin, to *my* land. They need only to leave to keep their bloodthirsty hides safe! We attack their camps when we know they are about to decimate *our* villages."

She had stood as she spoke, squaring her shoulders, straightening her spine. Mergwin could see how she had rallied a group of ragtag boys into inestimable valor. Her eyes glittered with righteous dignity. Within their emerald depths, one saw the land in all its beauty. He couldn't even argue with her logic. Nor in fairness should he fight against her since her secret exploits had ironically done much to assist her father in rallying the kings of Eire together.

He was simply frightened for her, scared in his bones. But just as he knew a great danger lay before her in the hands of the blond giant, he also knew that he was powerless to steer her course.

He stood beside her and was glad for a moment that he was a tall man. With this willful daughter of Aed, one needed every advantage to appear as a figure of authority. "Go and disband your troops," he told her shortly. "I have come to escort you back to Tara. Your father is calling council, and this is one time he will surely note your absence."

Erin stared at the irascible Druid for a moment, hearing the pounding of her heart. He was not going to betray her to her father; he had come only to find her. "All right, Mergwin," she said quietly. He handed her the golden helmet and she righted it upon her head, adjusting the visor.

Erin mac Aed, sweet-spirited beauty of Tara, was gone. The visor stole away the gentle girl he had known who healed robins' wings and shed gentle tears for the least of the forest's injured creatures. She wore her gold with a frightening amount of authority.

Erin made her way quickly and quietly through the forest, returning to circle the clearing where the Vikings had been ambushed. She steeled her eyes to the sight of the dead. As many brave men before her, she had simply learned not to look upon death. As she had from the beginning, she began to pray fervently that Gregory was not among the fallen.

The forest was silent, and she forced herself to pause for a minute as Mergwin had long ago taught her. At first she heard only the slight stirring of the leaves in the breeze, but then the breeze also brought a murmur that was the distant sound of men. She followed the sound, realizing her band of twenty-odd had gone on to raze the Viking camp.

She trod softly to come upon a second, larger clearing filled with the tents and cold campfires of the Vikings.

She swallowed her revulsion at the sight of the damage done by her Irish raiders and fought back a ridiculous rush of tears. These were Danes, she told herself, but sometimes, seeing destruction and loss hurt just the same. An old man lay slaughtered near a cooking fire, a woman—a camp follower—lay dead before her tent, an Irish pick through her heart.

A quivering horror ripped through Erin and she almost doubled over. I am losing control, she thought sickly. *They* are the butchers, the barbarians. We are the educated, the literate . . . the Christian.

She stepped into the clearing and her voice rang across the camp. Men began to emerge from tents, booty in their hands, but as she railed against their heathen ways, their faces became sheepish. A man broke from the crowd and lowered himself to a knee before her.

"Our pardon, lady. The woman was killed in the frenzy of our attack. She appeared and our spears and picks flew without our careful scrutiny."

The man looked up, and chills of shock swept through Erin. The warrior on his knees before her was none other than Fennen mac Cormac. Dear God! He will know who I am, she thought with panic. No, she assured herself. He could not recognize her. Only her eyes were visible through her visor. Stop shaking, and think! she warned herself. Take great care with your words, or you will lose your brave fighters. Forget that this is Fennen.

"Rise, please," she said aloud. "I pray merely that we not rid the land of pagans to become pagan again ourselves."

The majority of the men now stood near by, their war trophies in hand. Erin didn't mind that they plundered the camps. What the Vikings had had generally belonged to the Irish first.

She lifted her gold-skeined gloved hands. "My friends, we disband. Word will come when and where we will meet again."

The troops silently melted into the forest. Erin hastily scanned faces. She came upon her cousin's and inwardly whispered a little prayer of gratitude.

Gregory's eyes met hers across the camp. He twisted his lips in a quick smile that indicated he was fine, then inclined his head slightly. He knew that she was in panic over Fennen.

Erin spun about, carefully taking an opposite direction into the forest from the one Fennen had taken. She met with Gregory in a prearranged spot, throwing herself into his arms, finally allowing herself to shake with the aftereffect of the confrontation.

"Fennen!" Erin whispered, "Gregory, he might have recognized me. Why didn't I know that he was with us? You should have warned me!"

"I couldn't, Erin, he rode in too late. All I could do

was accept him graciously, as we accept all Irish who wish to band together. I couldn't distract you before the battle.'' He fell silent, holding her close, then spoke again. ''Why have we disbanded, Erin?''

''Oh, Gregory, my father has called a council at Tara, and we must return home! And now we are in for trouble, for Fennen knows you are among the raiders who so successfully plague the Vikings! And Mother believes we humble ourselves and ride to the chapels together. . . .''

Gregory shook his head. ''Fennen will not mention this raid, I'll warrant. Your father cannot condone the exploits of the Golden Warrioress and her band because we are basically outlaws—doing what we please. Fennen is the king of Connaught. He is supposed to be following the policies of the kings, which right now suggest that all lie low until some organization can be established. He will not admit his complicity any more than I would.''

Erin shrugged. ''I hope you're right, Gregory,'' she murmured. ''You'd best get the horses, and we need to strip ourselves of this mail.''

Gregory frowned. ''How do you know your father is calling a council?''

''Mergwin appeared in the forest.''

''Mergwin!''

Erin nodded and smiled wryly. ''That old Druid does have his talents.''

Muttering beneath his breath, Gregory slipped away to find their horses. Erin continued to muse about Fennen. He had greatly endeared himself to her by his actions that day.

By the time Gregory reappeared, she had stripped off her helmet and visor and was struggling with the gold-tinged mail. He helped her silently, then likewise received her assistance.

''Erin?'' Gregory queried, strangely hesitant.

''Yes, Gregory?''

Gregory's back was to her as he carefully bundled their war gear together to be stowed in saddlebags and

hidden before they reached Tara. "How did Mergwin
find us? How could he have known?"

She shrugged. "Mergwin . . . well, sometimes he
does just know things. Come on, Gregory, we have to
find him again and then get going. It is lucky he did
find us. My father will believe we have been with him
a spell."

They didn't have to search for Mergwin. He trotted
up to them on his bay gelding, his cape and beard
flowing in the breeze. "Well?" he demanded irritably.
"May we go?"

Erin and Gregory silently mounted their horses and
followed behind him. They had ridden a fair distance
before Erin thought to query him. She dug her heels
against her horse's side and came abreast of him on
the trail. "Mergwin, why does my father call a council? Has something happened?"

His brooding eyes looked at her strangely, as if he
saw something in her face. But then the look was gone
and he shrugged his shoulders.

"You might say that something has happened, my
lady Erin. Olaf the White has routed the Danes from
the Liffey—and taken Dubhlain. The lord of the
wolves has returned."

A shaft of icy fear like none Erin had ever known
ravaged her. He was back. Dear God, he was back.

Mergwin's eyes lit on her again, dark and fathomless
as he spoke with a disturbingly emotionless tone. "It
is said that he will not be content with Dubhlain. That
the Wolf will ride across Ireland. That he marches
toward Tara."

CHAPTER

7

"You will not leave Tara, daughter, while I am gone. I have tolerated all this nonsense about you and Gregory praying at the different shrines, but you will not leave while we fight. Do you understand me, girl?"

Erin felt a terrible lump in her throat. Tears shimmered in her eyes. Her father, her brothers, and Gregory were all leaving to face the Wolf who, it was said, traveled with thousands of warriors. The valleys of Tara were in chaos as the Irish kings banded together at last beneath the Ard-Righ to fight the common foe. "Yes, Father," she said meekly.

He touched her chin lightly with a finger. "Ah, Erin, I have such a soft spot for you in this old heart. . . ." His voice roughened again. "But mind me, girl, for I mean it. We will truly have a reckoning if you disobey me when I have this Wolf to contend with."

Erin nodded again. Her father mounted his horse and she hurried after her mother to kiss her brothers, pausing to adjust Niall's mantle brooch. "Take care, Niall," she whispered, trying to smile in return to her brother's gentle grimace.

"Chin up, little sister. We will soon meet each other again."

For him, she smiled a dazzling smile. He moved forward to say his final good-byes to his wife and Erin next came to Gregory.

"It seems the Golden Warrioress must disappear for a time," he whispered. "I'm glad, Erin. You'll be safe for a while."

"Gregory, this is worse. I'm so frightened for you and my father."

"I will come back, Erin. So will your father and brothers."

"I believe so, Gregory. In my heart, I believe so."

A tap on her shoulder distracted her from Gregory. Fennen stood behind her. He pulled her around and kissed her lightly but tenderly on the lips. "I will return, Erin, and when I do, we will wait no longer. We will speak to your father and be married at once."

She opened her mouth to protest, then closed it. Perhaps when they returned, the Wolf would be dead and the Viking threat would be over. "Take care, Fennen mac Cormac," she said softly.

He kissed her again, gently. "We will not be away long, I promise, emerald beauty," he murmured, then made a great display of mounting his horse and galloping off to whip the men of Connaught into their ranks.

Erin turned to search for Gregory, but he had already ridden on. She saw her mother staring after her father, but Aed too was riding, cantering to reach the front of the mass procession.

Maeve slipped an arm around Erin. Together they watched as the last horse disappeared into the glare of the midday sun.

The days passed slowly at Tara. Chores became more and more tedious and mundane. To Erin had fallen the task of tending the sheep, and instead of letting her mind fill with graphic visions of bloodshed, she would lie in the grass while the sheep grazed and dream that the Irish returned victorious. The Norwegian Wolf had been slain, and she was freed from haunting memories. . . . Fennen gallantly threw himself at Aed's feet, begging for his daughter in marriage, and, proud of Fennen's courage and victories, Aed had agreed, as long as his daughter might be won. . . .

Just dreaming sent little thrills down Erin's spine, and she began to wonder with a poignant and bittersweet pain what it would truly be like to know and love a man with her every breath.

She was musing so on the afternoon that marked the fifth week of the army's departure from Tara when she was suddenly startled back to reality by the thunder of horses' hooves. As the sound permeated her consciousness, she sprang to a crouch, the gallop of her heart matching that of the coming sound. How far had she wandered with the flock? It could not be danger. Surely the guards would have seen an intruder.

The pounding of her heart slowed as she saw with pleasure that the rider now slowing to a canter so as not to disturb the sheep was Gregory. She stood in her worn linen robe and shouted his name joyfully, racing down the hill to throw her arms around him as he finally dismounted from his horse.

"Gregory! You're here! Are you all right? Father—how is he? Gregory, is he all right? Niall, my—"

"Shh . . ." Gregory murmured, moving away slightly to smile lovingly into her anxious eyes. "Your father and brothers were fine just two days ago when I left them." He saw the relief flash into her eyes, and he took a moment just to stare at her, never more aware of her stunning beauty. Even in old and drab work clothing, she shone, her eyes so brilliantly, flashingly green against the smooth ivory of her elegantly chiseled features, her midnight hair contrasting with the rose-flushed ivory of her skin, her fine arched brows high with inquiry.

He hugged her again, whispering, "Oh, Erin, you look so wonderful. So very wonderful after all I have seen."

She pulled away from him anxiously. "Gregory, does it go badly? Why are you here?"

"No," he said quickly, "things are going well. Your father wanted a messenger to return to Tara with news." He paused, wondering whether to get to the real point of his return, or to simply allow her the pleasure first of seeing a kinsman alive and well. He opted for the latter. "It's strange, Erin, that Wolf is a cunning fighter. We have entered into only a few battles. Those that we have joined have been ferocious and ter—" He paused; he didn't need to describe battle to her. "Olaf strikes a village—but he kills only those who take arms against them. He steals what little he can find in the farmlands, resupplies his troops, but burns nothing and then withdraws." Gregory frowned. "Do you know, Erin, I don't believe that Olaf intends to march on Tara. I don't believe he ever did. I think he is counting on our believing that he will behave as all Vikings before him and we are falling right into his trap and doing just that."

Erin slipped her hand into her cousin's and led him up the tiny dun where she had just recently been dreaming of days of peace. She had forgotten all such foolishness now. A frown furrowed her brow as she mulled his words and made him sit so that she could feed him from her packed meal of cheese and fresh bread.

"I don't understand, Gregory," she said as he began to eat voraciously. "Why would that sly Norseman want to take on all of the Irish? If he had never threatened Tara, he might have been left alone. Dubhlain has belonged to Vikings for decades. As long as they stay there, we skirt them."

Gregory shook his head and accepted the gourd of fresh brook water she handed him. He drank a long time, the water spilling over his chin, then he wiped his chin with his sleeve, sighed, and shook his head again.

"I don't know, Erin, but that's exactly what worries me. No one can understand exactly what he's up to.

We harry him backward daily; soon we will hound him back to Dubhlain, and yet I don't believe that we harry him at all. I just don't know. . . ."

"I do!" Erin said with venomous enthusiasm. "My father has bested that wolf, that dog of Norway. We will be victorious!"

Gregory sensed something behind her words, something not quite natural. A personal hate so intense . . . Clonntairth, of course. But it was his family that had been lost to the troops of Olaf the White, and he no longer focused his hate in any particular direction. He fought Vikings any way he could; it was he who had created the spectacular troops of the Golden Warrioress. It was Erin's faultless courage and dignity that had made the venture a success, but the dream of vengeance had been his. But he had experienced logic and tactics and politics with his uncle, and he had seen Aed's controlled wisdom save many a situation in which rash behavior would have been suicide.

He fought the Wolf of Norway now, and that he did was sweet. But warfare could not be personal, and Gregory realized now, a bit amazed, that he did not personally blame Olaf for the loss of his parents. He had, in fact, left a battlefield upon which he stood a chance of meeting the Norwegian face to face. Perhaps it was best that he had for he had seen the golden giant engaged in combat. No man seemed quite so powerful. He was like the wind when he came, flattening all in his path.

He glanced back to Erin, wondering why she was brooding. Then he shrugged inwardly. She had been stronger than he at Clonntairth, but Clonntairth had been three years ago. Despite the valor that only he could appreciate, she was a woman, more emotional than a man. It never occurred to him that the "Viking" she had stumbled across near Carlingsford Lough might have been the Wolf of Norway.

"Tell me, Gregory," Erin murmured, staring ahead at the sheep, "have you seen Olaf the White?"

"I have."

"He lives, then? You have not seen him injured?"

"Not even scratched. Many men believe he is protected by Norse gods." He didn't like the look in her eyes, and so he decided it was time to talk. "Erin, I petitioned to your father especially to be the messenger to bring news of the battle home. And I selected all who rode with me."

She didn't reply, but continued staring at the sheep. He was about to speak again when she finally murmured, "I'm glad you could come home, Gregory. I value your life as dearly as those of my brothers."

He squeezed her hand. "We shall always be sister and brother," he said. There was a silence between them for a moment, and then Gregory cleared his throat and spoke again. "I am glad to be home, but a visit is not why I petitioned the duty."

She finally turned to him, her expression puzzled. "I don't understand what you're talking about."

"I need you, Erin."

She frowned. "I understand even less now, cousin."

He drew in a breath and held it for a moment. "The Golden Warrioress must ride again."

"What? Gregory, you must be crazy! If my father were to catch us, I would rather face a score of Danes singlehanded—"

Gregory shook his head. "We are going nowhere near your father. Athrip has been riding scout throughout the countryside. The Wolf does not threaten Tara but a group of outlaw Irish and Danes do. Althrip discovered a camp not a day's ride from here. He believes that they will attack because Tara is presently stripped of manpower. The wives of the nobles are here, prime picking for use or sale."

Erin thought for a moment, then spoke. "Gregory, I don't know how I will be able to manage it. My father made me promise I would not leave, and my mother spends an hour each morning charting out the chores I must attend to about Tara."

"Erin, there won't be a Tara if we don't act."

"I cannot believe that my father would not send troops."

"We are the troops. There is no one else. Each day the fighting becomes more critical as Dubhlain is reached. I have all who can be spared! Your father trusts me to win, Erin, and I trust myself. But we must have that element of surprise."

"Gregory, the guards—"

"Are not enough. You must think of something, you must act."

He saw the pain flash through her face. He wasn't quite sure which hurt her the most—donning the costume again and facing the barbarians, or going against the direct orders of her father.

She winced only momentarily, then her beautiful features became devoid of emotion. "I know what excuse to use," she said, clearly, concisely. "You must tell my mother that Mergwin is ailing. That you will escort me to him. The men will be told the same story, and then it will not seem peculiar to them that their golden lady is to meet them in the same area."

"Well thought, cousin," Gregory murmured.

Erin stood and dusted dirt and grass from her robe. She gazed at the beautiful buildings in the distance. Tara seemed to glitter beneath the sun. She thought about that long-ago day in Mergwin's cottage when she had dreamed of being a heroine. Now she was one. Ironically, she wanted to be anything but.

"Come," she said, reaching a hand to her cousin. "Let us go and allow my lady mother to feast upon the sight of you and hear the good tidings about my father and brothers. Gwynn will plague you mercilessly. And then . . . then you will have to speak to the wives who will not see their husbands and sons again."

Gregory slipped an arm around her shoulder. They walked down to his horse and Gregory looped the reins over his arm to lead the animal. Erin whistled loudly to the dogs and the sheep were harassed into movement.

The silent, sad little party made its way home.

Olaf the White played an incredible game of cat and mouse. For days he had struck small villages, disappearing again like lightning, always a step ahead of the Irish, always retreating toward Dubhlain.

But today he had made a stand to fight before the earthworks of Dubhlain. Employing the very forest tactics that—unknown to Aed—his daughter also incorporated, the Viking had enticed the Irish into an ambush. The battle had raged all morning and all afternoon, and continued even now, as dusk began to fall.

Caught in the midst of the bloodshed, Aed bemoaned his age even as he fought. It had seemed that the Irish had long held the field before the hilltop forest. Now he realized that it had all been illusion. One moment he had been fighting among his men, then it seemed that he had no more than blinked to find that he was surrounded by Norsemen on all sides.

I am old, he thought, I have lived a lifetime.

But no man could follow that argument when faced with certain death. He thought of Maeve, of his children, and of the Ireland he had fought to preserve and despite the odds, raised his sword, swinging, slashing.

As suddenly as he had found himself amid the enemy, he found himself standing alone. All had stepped away from him. His head seemed to ring, his eyes to blur. He closed them and opened them again, and saw before him Olaf the White.

It was true that an aura seemed to radiate from the man. Even for a Viking he was tall, and beneath his emblazoned mail he seemed to be a mass of sinewed power. As he walked forward, tension seemed to spark from him.

I do not want to die! A shudder rippled through Aed as he gazed into the frigid blue eyes of the Norseman, but no sign of that shudder appeared in his countenance. Good Lord, I am an old man who fears death, he thought as be began to pray. Yea though I walk

through the valley of the shadow . . . Aed raised his
heavy battle sword high as the prayer drifted from his
mind. And it was he who struck first. Blow parried
blow. It appeared to be more a dance of agility than a
dance of death as the two men faced each other. Each
strike of steel upon steel seemed to screech.

Aed's arms shuddered from the force of each strike
he parried. He noted vaguely that they were left entirely alone. At least he had the advantage of not
worrying about an axe to his back. But he was a man
past his prime meeting a superb warrior who never
failed to best even the most ferocius and talented of
his peers. That Aed held his own as long as he did was
a consolation, enough of one at least to slowly bring
him to the acceptance of a proud death, a warrior's
death, a king's death.

A blow from the Viking's sword sent him faltering
to his knees. He tried to stand again, but he slipped in
the blood-slick mud, unable to wield the heavy war
sword effectively. He closed his eyes and thought of
green grass, of the smell of the earth after the rain, of
Maeve's smile and blue skies. And he tried to brace
himself for death, tried not to tremble as he felt the
point of the Viking's sword touch his wrinkled throat.

The swordpoint was removed and Aed opened his
eyes, wondering why the Viking king would not grant
him death in battle. He could not believe that this
extraordinary man known for a strange type of mercy
would grant none to the Ard-Righ of Ireland, a man
who had fought him bravely.

To Aed's amazement, a hand partially clad in leather
to the knuckles reached out for his. There was a trace
of thawing amusement in the arctic eyes.

"Rise, High King of Tara," a deep and surprisingly
pleasant voice bid him in his own tongue. Rather
blankly, Aed accepted the hand. "Would that I have
your strength and courage when I reach your years,"
the blond giant continued quietly.

Aed stood, praying he wouldn't wobble. "If you
would kill me, Wolf of Norway," Aed replied, using in

his turn the Norse tongue, "grant a king his due and end it here."

The Viking laughed. Aed did not know that he saw the first trace of warmth in eyes that had long been cold. "By your Christian God, Aed Finnlaith, Ard-Righ of Tara, I would not take your life. Only that God of yours knows who might follow in your footsteps, and I am partial to men of reason. Go back to your troops, High King. You will not be molested. You are a man of honor and courage."

Scarce believing his ears, Aed watched as an ocean of the burly giants parted to allow him through. He stared at the hard handsome face of his enemy, then turned and forced himself to lift his chin without faltering as he began to walk.

Any second an axe will fall into my back, he thought as he slowly made his way. But as he had been promised, he was not molested. He walked past the Vikings and through the now-quiet battlefield. The fighting was over for the day. A strident trumpet sounded; and the Norse seemed to melt into the trees.

As Aed finished his silent but fervent thanks to God for the extraordinary quirk within the Wolf of Norway that had granted him his life, he began to study the results of the day. And for the life of him, he did not know who had taken the victory.

Forty miles inland, Aed's daughter was leaving the scene of her own particular battle. Tara had been saved by Gregory and the troops of the Golden Warrioress, but Erin was not jubilant as they rode through the forest. Gregory had been wounded and she was anxious that they reach Mergwin's quickly so that he could be treated. Even Gregory, who had once voiced a certain fear of the Druid, longed for his magic touch.

Erin caught her cousin's eyes on her as they rode in silence. He smiled, but she could see the pain in his eyes.

"Mergwin will know we are coming," Erin assured him. "Your pain will soon be soothed."

Gregory shrugged. "I worry about you, Erin, not me."

Erin made no attempt to reply. She had almost been caught that day. She had become embroiled in the battle, forced into hand-to-hand combat with a bulky Dane. She had managed to elude his lethal axe but she had not been forced to deliver a death blow. Gregory had come to her rescue. Yet she had been forced to realize that she could kill but only to survive. She hadn't the heart for warfare. She knew that Gregory worried she might be caught again, and that she would be too hesitant to strike.

"Gregory," she said finally, "please don't ever worry. If the need ever comes and I am alone, I will do what is necessary for my life."

Gregory half smiled, but his smile was miserable. "I pray, cousin, that you never have to don your suit of gold again."

They fell into a silence as they continued onward through the forest.

As Erin had sensed, Mergwin expected them. He cared for Gregory's wounds, he fed them, and he made them rest. He didn't scold, he delivered no lectures. He stroked his long beard continually, his eyes mirrors of distraction.

They spent the night in the cottage in the woods. Erin slept well, a deep sleep, like that of a very young child. She almost felt gay in the morning, as if she were a child again, staying with Mergwin merely to learn to listen to the breeze and delight in the sight of a rainbow. Mergwin's cottage was warmth; it was safety. She flirted outrageously with the old man while they prepared a breakfast of smoked fish. But not even her coddling could bring him out of his distracted mood.

She and Gregory left after the meal. Erin turned back to wave, which she did with a smile. But when she turned away again, her brow was knit in a furrow. She almost asked Gregory to turn around and look at the Druid, but her cousin was semislumped over his horse and his expression was tired and irritable.

She shivered suddenly, unable to shake that final vision of Mergwin's eyes. They had stared upon her so sadly. She had never seen anyone glance upon her before with such agonized . . . pity.

They were able to slip back to Tara with no incident. Gregory remained another day, then rode off to return to the battlefield. Erin quietly resumed her tasks. She spent her evening hours with her sisters and since even Bride was jubilant with the news that the Irish were pushing the Norse back to Dubhlain, Erin quickly found herself allowing her near-fatal deceit to fall into misted memory. Once more she allowed her dreams to surround her as she tended the geese or sheep.

Mercifully she was unaware that her dreams, the substance of her existence, were about to be shattered. In the most incredible way.

CHAPTER

8

❧

Aed Finnlaith stood, a weary man, against a tall tree as he stared at the earthworks of Dubhlain, already being replaced by a stone and mortar wall. His generals were boasting of the day. He knew the murmurs of the voices he heard from the central campfire were those of glory. Aed could not see the day as a victory. The green mounds of Ireland were well fed with the blood of her sons. Men he had supped with the night before were butchered beyond recognition. Indeed, even the night sky highlighted the display of grizzly death by changing with a shocking array of crimsons and mocking blood reds.

He closed his eyes, feeling sick. He tried to shut out the wanton waste of life, of both Irish and Norwegian men. The majority of the dead were young men, beautiful young men, strong, healthy . . . the pride of their fathers, the love and youth of their mothers.

God rot us all! he thought angrily. And his anger turned on his own generals as he thought of the work it had taken to draw them together. They had been born and bred to the Viking threat, born and bred to battle. Today they had faced the Norse, but though they called themselves civilized Christians, they were still murdering butchers. Aed began to wonder how long it would take the kings to go to war against one another again if the threat of the Viking diminished.

"Perhaps we deserve one another," he whispered aloud. And perhaps the Viking threat would never be over, he thought, discouraged. Olaf played cat and mouse so well.

Olaf the White. Aed had seen him again today, leading his troops, his heavy sword high as he charged the field on his immense black stallion. He had screamed a heathen war cry as piercing as any ever heard, he had ridden across the land as fiercely as ever a Viking lord before him.

But he was different. That had been proven yesterday. Aed had his life as testimony. Yes, Olaf was different—young, strong, and as steady as an old oak tree—and as tall and powerful. His golden-blond head, appearing over the hill like the wrath of God, had been enough to instill terror into the hearts of many a brave man. Yet he was still a man who battled only men. He preyed upon neither women nor children. He was a warrior, ferocious in battle, but not an executioner.

The sky slowly lost it shade of crimson mockery, but it did not bring relief from the gruesome pictures of the day. Instead, campfires flared with the breeze of night, seeming to flame a golden warning.

Impatiently Aed cast his helmet aside and strove to free himself from the heavy shackle of his mail. Many of the Irish troops still fought with nothing more than leather tunics and fell to the superiority of steel.

He sat on the ridge by the tree, suddenly a very old man, old beyond life. Perhaps his graying hair and beard were an outward sign of the weakness creeping into his bones and into his mind.

They wanted him to attack the city. Perhaps that was exactly what he should do. Why didn't he do it? Because he couldn't win. He knew that Olaf anticipated an attack and that he awaited Aed's next move with curiosity. And because if there was hope at all for their lives and for peace, the hope rested with the Wolf. He *was* different. A wild barbarian from the North, yes. But somehow civilized. Unlike the Dane Friggid the Bowlegs, Olaf was fastidious. It was rumored that he had taken on many Irish customs, including daily bathing. He was a builder and a dreamer. Already a stone castle stood within the growing walls, and Aed had also heard that in Dubhlain there was now water running directly to the houses through hollowed-out logs.

A cry of agony from a mortally wounded man pierced through Aed's eardrums like a hard-flung spear. He gritted his teeth and pulled his red-gray hair over his ears with clenched fists to relieve the haunting shrieks of the dying man. Then suddenly Aed Finnlaith, High King of Tara, the man who had drawn together the fighting nobles of the land to beat the common foe, cried. Tears, which had not touched his weathered face in forty years, swept down his bronzed and bushy cheeks. And for a moment he gave into the sickness of his heart. He cried for the beautiful sons of the land who lay in mangled heaps.

Slowly Aed staggered back to his feet. He did not touch his coat of mail, nor his sword with its crust of blood. He strode on his aged but still powerful legs to the campfire where generals and kings awaited his council, expecting that he would give the word that they would attack Dubhlain come morning.

The men looked curiously at Aed as he walked among them, their eyes bright with the lustful gleam of power and victory. Fools, Aed thought. You have watched him draw us ever closer, and yet you believe that this day has really been ours? Aed grimaced as he saw the eyes of his men. They were Christians, yet they appeared as animals, carnivorous and bloodthirsty. Dear God, Aed asked silently, are we, the men of your faith, no better than the beast that comes from the North?

His answer lay before him. The kings at the fire, those who had withstood the weeks of battle and today's horror with little or no injury, continued to boast of their feats. Aed warmed his gnarled fingers over the fire wordlessly as he waited for the conversation to die around him. Then he looked up with fierce eyes, nonetheless compelling for the smoky hue that had encroached upon a once-brilliant blue. "It is over," he said simply. "Come the morning, we will send a delegation to Olaf to offer negotiation."

The fire snapped and crackled, the only reply to Aed's surprising words. The expresssions on the faces of the men who ringed the fire differed; some were of scarce-concealed relief, some were of anger. It was Fennen mac Cormac who finally spoke, breaking the terse silence of the macabre scene.

"Look here, Aed," he protested, drawing his muscled body to full height. "You called us together. You demanded the ultimate defeat of the Vikings. Now you propose to withdraw when we are but a day from final victory."

Aed eyed Fennen with patience and then spoke quietly. "It is true that I called you together. Olaf threatened all of Ireland. But we will never be truly rid of the Viking. He strikes at will, he isn't a common enemy. The Viking is a Dane, a Norwegian, a Swede. He preys upon himself as we have seen. And as we have also seen, Olaf is not our customary foe. So think on this, my lords. We seemed to have won the day. The Norse took refuge behind their walls. But can we trust this victory? There stands the possibility that we have been drawn here in one group. We could attack tomorrow morning and we could discover that Olaf has thousands of warriors awaiting us.

"Or we could negotiate. He is stronger than any Viking before him. Men obey his word blindly. An alliance with him could grant us aid against the outlaw raids that chew upon the coastlines, slowly devouring the Irish. He has proven himself a better man than any Dane. We have seen him fight; we have also seen his generosity. He allows us to take away our wounded. He has left no trail of death in the villages behind him.

"This, my lords, is my belief. Mull on it as you will and at dawn we make our decision. But I believe that Olaf has cunningly brought us here. That he wants no more than Dubhlain, but he wants the recognition that the city is his. I say that we should let him have it; the city has always been Norse. Our option might be a final slaughter of the kings of Ireland. One last thing to think on. We have regained land today. We have not beaten Olaf. Should we not beat him, he has the power to raise his strength again and again, and perhaps eventually annihilate our kingdoms."

There was silence again around the fire. Aed surveyed the eyes of the kings, but then he waited for no more words or discussion. Let their minds brew awhile, he thought as he walked away. He was tired. He longed to be at home, hearing Maeve's gentle laughter, feeling her soothing touch upon his brow. I might be old, he thought, and the passions and fires of youth might have grown subdued, but still my wife is my lover and my friend.

He had not reached his tent before he was stopped by his son Niall.

"Father?"

Aed's lifted brow indicated his exhaustion.

Niall spoke quickly. "I believe the kings will side with you. Few still rave about victory." Niall shifted from foot to foot uncomfortably. "Many of the kings believe that Olaf does have the gods on his side, that he cannot be destroyed. They worry about only one thing—how to cement a peace, how to ensure that Olaf will not ride against us again."

Aed smiled and placed his hands upon his son's shoulders. "Thank you for telling me this, Niall." He knew that Niall had the confidence and respect of the younger kings. "I will rest now, and I will dwell upon solving that problem." He paused a moment. "Niall, what is your opinion?"

Niall hesitated, then cleared this throat. "I believe as you do, Father, that the Wolf is cunning. I believe that he allowed you to live because he respects you and that he hopes you will sue for peace rather than force him to senseless slaughter." Niall paused again. Then he spoke hoarsely, his voice thin. "Look at those walls, Father. God alone knows what horrors he has in preparation behind them."

Aed nodded and turned from his son. He ducked into his tent to find a young girl, a camp follower, a whore. He smiled dryly, thinking the lass would find herself disappointed. He was a faithful man, and if he weren't, he would still be too old to play warrior and lover in one day. "Go, girl," he told her softly, "for I have no use of your talents this night."

She was very young and very pretty, too young and pretty to be following this life. Her face flamed at his words, and he realized she believed he thought her not worthy. He relented.

"If you would provide me with water to wash the stench of blood from my hands, I would find pleasure in a little cleanliness."

The girl nodded with a gentle smile. "I will fetch water, m'lord," she murmured shyly. "And I can rub your shoulders to ease the tension."

"That will be fine," Aed said softly. Then as he watched the girl procure the water and bathe his hands, he realized that she reminded him a bit of Erin. She hadn't Erin's stunning coloring, nor the lithe perfection of form, but she was the same age as his daughter.

The girl began to massage his neck and shoulders. Aed smiled and closed his eyes, his thoughts still on Erin. It would be good to go home.

He had to stop thinking about home. He had to think about Olaf the White and a peace treaty that could be binding, but he was so tired. Thinking was a painful process but he had to think about the Wolf, aye, he had to think about the Viking. The girl was good at soothing him; she had a touch almost as gentle as Erin's.

He had begun to relax; then his entire body suddenly stiffened. Thoughts of the Norwegian Wolf and his daughter had merged together. As a father, he cringed with pain. As Ard-Righ, he had known instantly what he had to do, offer a truce, an alliance that couldn't be broken.

Aed spent a miserable night, but with the dawn messengers were sent to the walls of Dubhlain. The Wolf agreed to meet with Aed, and an unhappy Niall was sent to Tara to bring his sister Erin to his father. The Ard-Righ had struck his alliance.

Erin tried every feminine trick she knew as she traveled with her brother, from cajoling and wheedling to pouting and begging. When all else failed, she tried tears, but not even that effort could draw an explanation from Niall.

She had been ordered to travel as befit a princess, and the party that set out for Dubhlain was impressive. The finest silks and fur-trimmed satins adorned the men as well as the ladies. Even the horses were clad in silk trappings with silver and gold ornamentation. Erin's splendid mantle of deepest indigo flared from her shoulders to trail in soft folds over her horse's haunches. It was trimmed with snow-white winter fox, and against the fur her hair fell in cascades that gleamed like a raven's wing. She was terrified, and because of her fear, she kept her chin high.

Seeing her cheeks flushed with fresh air and her eyes shimmering with dignified caution, Niall of Ulster believed that Erin had never appeared more beautiful. He felt his sense of betrayal clearly, but because he not only gave his unfaltering loyalty to his father, but saw clearly himself the perfect sense of Aed's commitment, he forced himself to hold his secret. He didn't doubt for a minute that Erin would attempt to escape across the land if she had the slightest inkling of her fate.

"Niall?" Her voice broke into his thoughts and he braced himself. The sound was soft and seductive, and he knew he was in for another session of questioning.

"Yes, Erin?"

"Please, Niall, if I'm in some type of trouble with Father, I'll fare much better if I'm aware of what I've done! Oh, Niall—"

"Erin," Niall lied, "I'm only Father's messenger. I don't really know why he has summoned you. I'm sorry, Erin."

More sorry than you'll ever know, little sister, he thought sadly. If only we were children and you were to be chastised about the geese. . . .

They were on the road for several days, but despite the size of their party, which included a hundred men-at-arms because of the obvious wealth and importance of the group, they found Irish hospitality fires and the Brehon hospitality laws practiced in the villages where they rested. Erin was always given the finest room in the inn or in the house of the town's chief. They were well fed and entertained with enthusiasm in the poorest of the communities.

As they neared the Irish encampment before Dubhlain, Erin felt the tremors she had learned to live with over the past few days increasing to uncontrollable shudders. She tried to reason with herself, assuring herself that she was her father's pet. If he knew of her clandestine life, he might yell for hours, but what could he actually do? She was absurd to be afraid; what she had done had not been terrible, but righteous, and she would tell Aed so with dignity—after demurely begging with tears for his forgiveness and understanding. He would threaten her with confinement within a nunnery, or with marriage to some powerful but repulsive king, but he would never carry out such a threat. After all, it was the Golden Warrioress who had assisted in the protection of Tara when her father's troops had been needed to face the Vikings.

She blanched with the thought that all her reasoning had not changed the fact that Aed must have been furious indeed to summon her when he still maintained a position before the walls of Dubhlain. But she felt a rebellious fury herself; Niall had mumbled something about a truce being declared before the very walls that housed the Norwegian dog.

She was startled from all thought as they crested a hill and stared at the city. In the field before the walls, the tents of the Irish seemed to stretch forever. But it was the sight beyond the walls that stunned her. Dubhlain was huge, far greater than even the endless fields of tents. From her vantage point Erin could see magnificent buildings within the boundaries, buildings that combined beautifully carved wood and stone.

"Father will want to see you right away," Niall said curtly, nudging his horse onward. Erin's mount automatically followed. They passed the tents of the nobles and their servers, and Erin bowed in return to the men who stood to stare respectfully, occasionally shouting cheers for Niall of Ulster and the daughter of Aed. Erin tried to smile, but she suddenly wanted nothing more than to turn her horse, thread her way through her own party until she found her sister Bede, confess all to the family nun, and beg that Bede call upon God to spirit them both away.

Her father's tent was set somewhat apart from the others. She realized as they reached the slit opening that she and Niall rode alone. He drew his horse to a halt and dismounted to help her from her horse.

Erin met her brother's eyes, and the pity she read in them sent her into a panic again. Father knows, he must know, what else can it be? she thought, her mind racing. She had defied a direct order. . . .

It occurred to her then that she was within touching distance of the greatest enemy she had ever known. I am the one who has been betrayed, she thought. My father's army stands in force on the heels of the Wolf and they do nothing to annihilate him and his forces from the land.

She closed her eyes and momentarily envisioned the day by the stream. If only she had thrust her sword through his throat. . . . Another wave of panic engulfed her as she wondered if she would see the Wolf himself again. Would he remember her? It was possible. She

had heaped threats and humiliation on him at a time
when he was in pain, and she had quite adequately
added to that pain when she had escaped him.

She swallowed hard and straightened her elegant
mantle. No, she would not have to face the Wolf.
Whatever truces were being made. Aed would surely
not break bread with an animal. And no matter what
his anger, Aed would not expect her to be hostess to
the barbarians.

"Go in," Niall said softly.

"Aren't you coming with me, Niall?" she asked him
sharply.

"Father wishes to see you alone."

With that parting comment, Niall remounted his
horse. Erin drew in a deep breath, desperately making
last-minute plans. Should she be immediately humble,
or should she appear angered herself that her father
had drawn her from home and her mother to stand
before a Viking wall?

She opened the flap and ducked inside the tent, then
paused again. For perhaps the first time, she saw her
father as others saw him. He sat upon a chair before a
makeshift desk, studying parchments. His deep-violet
mantle draped over the chair and brushed the ground.
His face, in study, appeared fierce. The hand he rested
upon his knee was large and strong. He glanced up at
her, and she thought belatedly that she had never
known her father's eyes could be so sharp.

"Erin," he said simply.

He has never looked at me like this, she thought,
and felt as if her heart had ceased to beat. Something
was wrong, terribly, terribly wrong. Aed was her
father. He would not think of the good done by the
Golden Warrioress, he would think only that she had
directly disobeyed him and the law of the land, the
Adamnan Cain.

If only she weren't shaking, if only they were at
Tara and not before the walls of the Viking stronghold,
she would fly across the room to him, hug and kiss
him, and attempt to flirt her way out of the situation.

No, even at Tara she couldn't have done it, not with this terrible tension about him! She lowered her lashes and felt her heart pound again, too loud, too fast. She offered her deepest, most humble and graceful bow, keeping her head respectfully inclined. "I humbly beg your pardon, my lord father."

"For what?" The eyes which had so frozen her flashed with a moment of confusion.

He doesn't know, Erin thought, fearing she would faint with relief. Then nothing she could have done could be so terrible for him to summon her.

She kept her lashes lowered. "For however I have offended you, Father," she said demurely.

He adjusted his frame uncomfortably and averted his eyes from her to stare unseeingly at his parchment. "You have not offended me," Aed said flatly. "I have summoned you because I have contracted your marriage."

Erin frowned. If she was not in trouble, then she had every right to be indignant. "But, Father—"

"No 'buts,' mistress," Aed suddenly roared. "I have been generous and lenient with you, daughter, for far too long."

She could still argue him out of it, unless, of course, the noble should prove to be of her liking. Fennen? Of course! Her mind whirred as she stood before Aed, and she almost smiled as she thought of her dreams upon the hill. Perhaps it was finally a time for peace, a time to explore her feelings for Fennen. Yes, she decided, she would marry, but only if the man was Fennen. She was suddenly riddled with chills again, certain Aed had another man in mind. Why drag her out to a battlefield to wed her to a man she had known for years? She lifted her eyes and faced Aed with spirit. "I understand the duties of a princess, Father, and, as is your command, I will marry. But I must tell you, Father, that I can only marry a man of my own choosing. If you have decided that I shall marry Fennen—"

Aed waved his arm impatiently and interrupted her

speech. "It is not Fennen mac Cormac. I have contracted you to Olaf the White and you will speak your vows with him tomorrow before dusk."

"What?"

The blood drained from her face, and she felt as if a great wave of northern water had cascaded over her.

"You heard me!" Aed Finnlaith was roaring because he couldn't bear the shocked betrayal on her pale face. "Tomorrow you wed Olaf. The contracts are set, all is agreed."

"Father! No! You couldn't! You know how I despise the Vikings, how I loathe Olaf the White." Erin began trembling. She had tried to convince herself it was a trick of her hearing, that it couldn't be true, but it was, she could see it in her father's eyes. "I will not do it!" she said firmly, forcing her trembling to cease.

"You will." He was adamant.

Motion came to her legs and she threw herself at his feet, groping for his hands, and kneeled below him at his desk. "Father, please, I can't. He is a barbarian! You cannot give your own flesh and blood to a northern scavenger. Wolf of Norway! Dog of Norway! You can't, Father! I will marry Fennen, I will marry anyone, I will enter a religious order, but I cannot marry the Norwegian who butchered our family! Father, we are Irish. Brehon laws—our just laws—protect women—"

"And they also state that daughters should honor their fathers." He would not even look at her. He stayed perfectly still, and his eyes remained glued to his parchment.

"Father!" she screeched the word, "Don't you understand? I cannot do this, I would rather die! I will not say the words I must reply!" Still he didn't look at her. She burst into tears. "Oh, please, Father, *Please!*"

She collapsed upon his knees, her sobs hysterical. He had never been able to deny my tears before, she thought bitterly, but now that they were real, he was as cold as steel. "You don't understand," she murmured in gasps, new horror dawning upon her at the thought of facing Olaf the White. He would probably kill her, or find a way to make her life an eternal torture.

She realized suddenly that the tent flap had opened and two burly warriors she did not know stood inside. Her father lifted a hand slightly and they approached.

"See that she is confined," Aed said softly.

The warriors reached for her and Erin jerked away furiously, standing on her own power and lifting her chin. It was no hoax, no dream. The father she had adored all her life was throwing her coldly to the enemy. She had never thought Aed would offer the lowliest Irish whore to a Viking, but he was offering his own daughter. And she could not reach him. He had set up a shield that was unbreachable.

"Don't touch me," she told her bodyguards, sweeping the train of her mantle over an arm. "I am quite capable of walking on my own." She preceded the men with head tilted, then paused at the flap of the tent. "You have told me, Father, and so I will tell you. I will not marry the Viking. Attempt to force me to do so and there will be a scene such as will make the strongest warrior blanch."

Aed still did not look at her. "I am the Ard-Righ," he said quietly, staring straight ahead. "I am your father, and in all that I could, I spoiled you. To cause you pain is agony within me but what I do now I must. For Ireland. For the land. She is more important than you or I, Erin. And for the land, and for the centuries and people to come, you will be the wife of the Wolf of Norway."

Erin spun around, trying not to shake or cry again before the men. She walked regally between them as they led her past her father's tent to a copse in which a second tent stood.

There were more guards around the tent. She shook off the hand of the stoic man who would have assisted her beneath the flaps, and slapped them shut behind her. Only then did she begin to shake.

"Erin?"

Bede awaited her in the tent, her eyes full of care and sympathy. Erin burst into tears once more and fell into her sister's arms. "Oh, Bede," she sobbed piteously, "Father . . . he . . . Olaf . . ."

"I know," Bede soothed her, smoothing back her sister's luxurious hair. "Shh, now, Erin. . . ."

Erin kept sobbing and the great convulsions tore at Bede's heart. But it was when her sister stopped crying that she felt tremors herself.

Deadly calm with her beautiful and immense eyes feverishly dazzled to a shade beyond a gemstone, Erin whispered venomously, "I will not do it, Bede. I will not marry him, and no one can force me. They can place a knife to my throat and I will not do it." Erin stood and began to pace the tent with agitation. "I will hire a Brehon to speak my case."

Bede knew Erin was serious, and she trembled within. The look upon her sister's face went beyond chilling. "Erin," she interrupted softly, "you will never find a Brehon to take your case against the Ard-Righ. And I hear that the Wolf is a fierce fighter, but a gentle man. Niall tells me that his residence is the finest he has ever seen. Olaf has sworn to father that you will receive every respect due a princess of Tara. Truly, Erin, it will not be so bad. I will stay with you for a while, and you will have your ladies. And many Irish families will be beyond the walls. Our architects wish to study the Norse method of building. And he is a fine man, they say. His teeth are fine, no pockmarks mar his face. He will be gentle, Erin—"

Erin started to laugh and the laughing terrified Bede. Gentle! With her! The man would never, never, in a thousand years be gentle to her. Not that it would matter, for she would hate him past the grave.

I should have killed him when I had the chance, she thought furiously.

Then another thought took over. Maybe if she told her father about the meeting in the woods, Aed would realize that he was handing her over to an animal.

No, she could tell him, but that would only make Aed more determined that she be wed as planned. His mind had hardened against her and all he thought about was his precious land.

"You must lie down and rest, Erin," Bede murmured, interrupting Erin's internal battling.

Erin looked at her sister. "I am not going to marry him, Bede. I am going to escape tonight. I have given the people and the land enough," she said bitterly, and Bede frowned.

"Erin, how will you escape? The tent is guarded—"

"There are those who would help me," Erin said. "When it is night, I will escape. I have my sword with my things, and I know how to use it."

Bede was shocked, but more than that she was worried, both about Erin's state of mind and the consequences that could come from it.

"Well, sister," she said aloud, "if you would escape, you must eat. I'm going to fetch a full and nourishing dinner."

Erin glanced up, her eyes suddenly sparkling. "You're right, Bede, I'm going to need all my strength! See too if you can't find extra bread and dried meat. I don't know how long I will have to ride."

Bede felt a terrible twinge of guilt, but she nodded and smiled. "I'll be right back."

She left Erin and headed for her father's tent. He was in council with Niall and a group of the lesser Ulster kings, but as soon as he saw the worried frown upon her face, he asked that the room be cleared.

"Father," Bede said anxiously, "I am worried about Erin, very worried. She means it when she says she will not wed the Viking; she intends to attempt to escape tonight. Of course she will fail, Father, but that scares me even worse. I believe she'd allow herself to be killed—even at the altar—to escape this."

The agony that flashed through Aed's eyes made Bede catch her breath. She set an arm around his shoulders, knowing his pain. "She will one day forgive you, Father."

"Will she?" Aed patted her hand absently, then shook his head. "If only she would see reason. . . ." He lifted a brow in a hopeless gesture. "Do you know what is strange, Bede? I trust him far more than I do most of my own generals. He is an honorable man."

Bede said nothing but silently stood by.

Aed sighed wearily. "Whatever her heart or passions, she must marry Olaf." He paused in thought for a moment. "Stay here. Mergwin is somewhere in the trees. I will be back."

"I told Erin I would bring her something to eat and food to pack for an escape," Bede said nervously.

Aed nodded, called a guard, and sent him for an ample supply of food. He disappeared out the tent flap himself and Bede fidgeted about her father's large tent. She hated deception and wounding Erin. But like her father, Bede had the ability to forget the individual for the good of the many. The intercourse between the Vikings and Irish at Dubhlain was a miracle. Perhaps it was a miracle that wouldn't last. There were still many outlaw bands of Danes as well as Norwegian and Swedish raiders who would die rather than change their ways. But for the time, countless people were going to live because the strengths of her father and Olaf were combined.

Aed returned quietly. He handed Bede a tiny vial of powder. "Half, and she will sleep through the night. She will awake docile. You must see that she gets a quarter more in the morning, then the final dose before the evening. Do you understand?"

Bede winced, but nodded to her father.

I'm awake, Erin thought. But she wasn't really awake, she had to be dreaming. There was light streaking through the tent, and in reality, it had to be dark. And she had to be asleep dreaming, because Bede would have woken her long ago if it had been day.

Yes, it was a dream, because everything around her was a little hazy. She tried to sit, and she could, but the haze didn't go away. Bede was in her dream. She was standing before her. "I have brought you some breakfast, Erin. You must eat." Erin obeyed. It was a dream, and whatever was said, she responded to. It was really a nice dream. She didn't feel weak, but like air. "Drink the mead, Erin, you must drink the mead," Bede said, and she drank the mead.

Then there were other women around her besides Bede. She smiled, because they were all so nice. One woman began to comb her hair and the touch was very gentle and nice. She really didn't have to do much of anything except enjoy the delicious, cloudy feeling. They helped her wash, they covered her in silk that felt wonderful as it caressed her skin.

Her father walked into the tent and for a minute she frowned. She was angry with her father. He shouldn't be in her beautiful dream. Then her frown dissipated. She loved her father, so she couldn't be really angry with him, and he was looking at her so anxiously. . . .

She smiled and extended a hand to him. He took it and they walked together. "Can she ride?" Aed seemed to whisper.

"Yes, we'll stay right next to her."

Strange that they should doubt her ability to ride, Erin thought as she heard her father and sister exchange the hushed whispers. "Of course I can ride," she assured them with a smile. How funny her voice sounded, and she could barely feel her horse beneath her. This sensation was even more like floating.

Then she discovered that her dream became even more and more intriguing. She was in a beautiful hall of stone with the most beautiful of carvings, and there were people, so many people. They kept smiling at her, and she smiled back. It was a party, a wonderful, wonderful party. Everyone was so very happy.

She walked as they led her to the head of the hall. Her father's hand slipped away but that didn't disturb her because another hand, firm and guiding, reached out for hers. And Bebe was still with her. A funny little man who looked like a monk was saying things, and Bede was whispering that she must repeat them.

Erin had to try very hard not to laugh because it seemed so funny that Bede of all people should be playing jokes on a priest.

But Erin must have said the right words, because all of a sudden, the people were cheering. She smiled happily, having pleased them all. She glanced at the hand that held hers and thought with detachment what a beautiful hand it was, so strong and yet neat, the fingers long with clean clipped nails, and soft with little tufts of hair that looked like golden threads. She looked up, and her smile faded.

Olaf the White was in her dream. Tall and golden and awesome and beautifully bedecked, his mantle of deepest royal purple was held across his broad shoulders by a golden brooch. He stared at her with the greatest surprise, and then with a dark anger that sizzled his eyes to dangerous gemstones. Suddenly he laughed, and he wore a hard grin, and his eyes were very much like a blue fire. Fire? They were ice, an ice fire. He appeared as a wolf who had downed a rival in combat and now waited, savoring the capture.

Erin froze in terror, but then she laughed. It was so funny. The wolf thought he would have revenge. He did not know that it was only a dream. . . .

He lowered his head and his lips touched hers. They brushed them merely, but the touch was warm and firm and it made her feel even more as if she were deliriously floating on clouds. Then the feasting began. There was delicious food and there were jugglers and dancers and fine imported wines from the continent. . . .

Olaf had been stunned. Then he had itched to throttle the girl. But then the ironic justice of the situation had struck him and he had laughed with the greatest pleasure. It was incredible that he had been handed this of all Irish maidens. Maybe not. In the woods she had ranted on about turning him over to "her father." Who else would she have been but an Irish princess? And he was glad of the anger she invoked in him, glad of the interest. It drew him from the brooding thoughts that so often filled his mind even when he worked with his generals and builders. Seeing her seemed to make his blood heat and race through his veins as he remembered how she had doubled him over in pain with a well-aimed kick that day long ago. The little bitch had been placed directly into his hands. . . .

There would be a reckoning. By all the gods, yes, there would be a reckoning. But it would be quick; merely to clear the air. He wanted no more war with the Irish, not even with the bitch he had been given as wife who so despised him. It was a relief to feel again, to forget the pain of loss for a while, but the indifference that had become so much a part of him took hold again. He would do what was necessary to turn her into the hostess he required for his home, but no more. She would be left alone, granted all that he had promised her father. She was welcome to her hate if she learned it must be personal, kept to herself, as he made himself accept his grief. She would be his wife, but once he had made her realize that he hadn't forgotten all that she had put him through, she should be happy.

He had little interest in her. Yet her father, he thought analytically, had not lied. She surely had to be one of the most beautiful women he had ever seen. She was dark whereas the woman he had loved had been blond, but the dark sheen of her hair was an ebony so rich it hinted of blue. Her eyes with their fringe of equally lustrous lashes were bedazzling. Her face was finely, delicately molded as if carved to specific royal specifications. The pale violet of her silk robe molded to her young form like a glove, and he knew truly that Aed intended to keep peace when he had offered this perfectly lithe and sweetly curved beauty.

He felt a smile tingeing his mouth as he watched her beside him. He might be the Wolf of Norway, but surely Aed was the Fox of Ireland. The girl despised him—that Olaf knew well. At his first incredulous sight of her Olaf had wondered how the Irish king had forced her to marry him. It was unlikely that Aed Finnlaith knew that the Wolf had met his daughter; yet surely the girl must have vehemently refused to agree to the marriage. Apparently she had, and so she was drugged, and the potion had been well designed. She appeared normal. But a knowing look into those emerald eyes clearly told one of her circumstance. Except that the potion was beginning to wear off, which was good. He wanted her fully cognizant when they spoke.

He pushed back his chair with the emblazoned emblem of the wolf. In a far corner he saw her sister, the nun. A girl with wise, intelligent eyes. He made a motion, and she nodded. A second later she was coming for Erin.

Erin looked at her sister, then she looked at Olaf, and in that second, Olaf knew that she finally understood what had happened. She was still too far under the influence of the potion to fight, but she was aware.

She disentangled herself from her sister long enough to stare at him with pure loathing sizzling fire into the emerald of her eyes.

"Dog of Norway," she hissed, "I despise you. You are nothing but a barbaric, carnivorous animal. . . ."

Olaf clenched his jaw and his own eyes took on a look of pure frost. There would be a time of reckoning soon.

His bride was led away, lapsing back to docility. He stared after her, feeling the anger burn within him, then picked up his goblet and drank deeply. He wanted to break her, to repay her, to overpower the hatred in her eyes. He was the lord of Dubhlain, he had fought hard for the title, and he would be the master of his home.

But then his anger faded. The indifference that plagued him was back. Grenilde . . . her name was a cry in his heart.

He sighed, as the anger seeped through him again. His Irish wife was a spirited little bitch and had to be dealt with. She would learn that he was not a man to be abused by her sharp tongue. She had once made a damned fool out of him.

His anger grew, but like his eyes, it was a cold anger. A calculated and controlled anger. He looked about the hall. It was time, and the effects of the potion would have surely disappeared by now.

CHAPTER

9

For a bridal chamber, it had been strangely subdued. They had bathed her with rose water. They had washed her luxurious hair until it fell in curls about her like deepest ebony, and then they had adorned her in a gown of filmy silk and left her. Not even Bede had tried to speak. Not one of the Irish ladies allowed her had smiled during the somber proceedings—much less attempted a bawdy joke.

Erin had been quiet and acquiescent while she was being prepared; her eyes luminous, wide and barely blinking. But now the poppyseed that had brought about her soft-spoken "yes" during the ceremony was wearing off. Bede began to pray that the warrior-king would come to claim his bride before she again came to her full senses

Bede moved quickly to kiss her sister. "May Saint Bridget help you through this night," she murmured quickly, and then she stepped back, whirling to leave the chamber. The wide emerald eyes in the haunted pale face of her sister stabbed her deeply. For one painful moment Bede held tight to the gilded door jamb. The Viking was a splendid man, yes, but he was the very Viking Erin despised above all others. Bede winced, hating her part in the trickery. Poor Erin. . . .

She is going to want to skin Father and me alive! Bede shivered but then sighed. Her sister's fate was not an unusual one. It was the lot of a woman, and especially the lot of a princess. Without looking back again, Bede closed the chamber door.

The quiet click of the door brought Erin fully from her stupor. She suddenly became aware of herself for the first time in hours, and as she glanced down at the white gown, she whispered a ferocious "No!"

She covered her face with her hands and shuddered. *They had done it.* They had drugged her, they had tricked her into doing what she had sworn she would not. The Wolf, the animal, was now her husband. Soon he would come to her—no, not her, *his*—chamber, and she would be expected to receive him.

I will kill him first! she thought, and then she quailed, remembering that he too would be ready to extract vengeance for that day in the forest. "I should have told Father," she whispered to herself, the broken sound of her voice for once piteous. Erin closed her eyes, shaking, wondering what he would do to her for all she had wrought against him. He would surely debase her, torture her. . . .

"No!" she cried again, springing from her frozen stance to hurtle across the room and search through her trousseau until she found her pearl-handled scissors. It was fitting, she thought, that the instrument so resembled the dagger with which Bridget had taken her own life. Because now she, Erin, would end the conqueror's life. She was strong, she had spent long hours studying the art of murder with her brothers. He would be expecting a humble and drugged bride, one terrified of his entrance. She would have the advantage of surprise, and she would kill him or die trying because she would not be touched by his filthy wolf's paws.

She paled, thinking that all assembled, Viking and Irish, would shortly be whispering in the halls, giggling

over the activity of the marriage bed. They would be
thinking that the Viking would have her, that he would
be sweating and straining like the barbaric animal that
he was.

"Never!" she whispered.

She drew back the furs and sheets and got into the
bed, holding the scissors tight against her chest as she
drew the covers around herself. Her heart was thudding painfully, but she knew that her very anticipation
made her look like a terrified and innocent maiden.

The door began to open and the thudding in her
chest became so very painful she could barely breathe.
She stared at him as he opened the door, but as his
brooding indigo eyes met hers, she lowered her eyes.

"So, Irish," he murmured mockingly, "we meet
again." She didn't reply. Her eyes downcast, she felt
his eyes on her as he strode about the room, shedding
his wedding finery. He sat to remove his boots then
placed his girdle upon the wooden chest. He seemed
to be fastidiously neat, draping the embroidered mantle over a chair, folding his leggings and tunic and kilt.

Confusion mingled with her resentment. The Norse
were supposed to be pigs, filthy and slovenly. But even
as he moved about so meticulously, she noticed again
that scent of sandalwood melded with a male aroma
that was not at all unpleasant, but earthy and clean.
He is the enemy, she thought above her confusion, be
he clean or dirty.

He walked lightly for a man so large, and she was
startled into swallowing as she realized the he had
come, stripped at last, before her. The pounding of
her heart was so strong that she couldn't believe he
didn't hear it and suspect her. He stared at her still;
she knew it, yet she couldn't bring her eyes to meet
his. She could see enough of him through her lowered
lashes to know that his chest was massively broad,
that his waist tapered trimly to a remarkably narrow
but still muscled abdomen. His hips too were solid and
trim; the fine golden curls that riddled his chest ended

there to begin again lower, creating a fine nest for a sex that was relaxed, but shocking, strong, pulsating.

He will die, she thought. She would find his heart, his lifeblood, and then all his magnificent muscles and strength would mean nothing as the blood rose up to choke him.

If she hadn't the designs in her heart to slay him, she wouldn't have been able to endure the moment. Surely he intended revenge. He thought her in his power, and he would lord that power over her. He would beat her, mock her, make her pay the humiliating tribute for that time in the woods.

"Look at me!" he snapped.

She forced her eyes up. He stared at them for a moment with his countenance hard and unreadable. Then over his features a grim smile split that did not reach the ice in his relentless, brooding eyes.

It was that look that made her shiver. His eyes were so devoid of emotion. He felt nothing for her. If anything, he found her absently amusing; he seemed able to read her.

No, she thought, he thinks I cower with fear. He does not know that it is he who shall pay with a vengeance tonight.

Yet still she shivered because she knew she must wait, and she did not like that strange, contemptuous glitter in his eyes as he came nearer, his weight bearing over her as he crawled atop her, covers and all. She kept her eyes glued to his with defiant hate as he straddled his knees over her hips and placed a hand on either side of her head, holding himself as he stared down at her. Now, my lord Viking, she thought, two inches closer and you shall feel my shaft through your heart.

He held that twisted smile, his eyes hard, as he moved closer. Now, Erin hissed to herself, but the pounding in her chest was making her shake. She felt the weight of him, the warmth of him. She heard the beat of the heart she meant to strike. But she suddenly became aware of the sleek and bulging bicep that paralleled her head. She lost control. Her fingers cramped, nervous moisture making them slick. The scissors began to slip from her death grip.

The Wolf pounced. Sitting back on his haunches, he brought his right hand in a mightly blow across her covered hands. She gasped as the covers fell—and the scissors went flying harmlessly across the cold stone floor.

"If you hadn't lost your nerve when you did, Irish," he said coldly, "your marriage bed would have been stained with the blood of your jugular."

It wasn't courage that kept her silent at that moment, for she was too stunned to speak. Her eyes continued to glare into his, the hate shining through now without thought of deception.

She was spared the fear of what he might do to her as he acted swiftly, once more amazing her that such a powerful man could move so lithely. Stark naked as he pounced from the bed to rake the covers from it, he was even more awesome than when clad in armor. Each ripple of muscle could be clearly seen; the power that radiated from his toned bronze form was all the more chilling because it was purely physical. The naked form of any man would have given her pause; his made the breath catch in her throat, her body go as weak as water.

"Ahhh . . ." he murmured, his hands on his hips and his voice deathly quiet as he surveyed her in the bed. "The glitter in the eyes of the murderess turns to a plea of mercy! Sweet innocent—Irish bitch!" His long arm shot out and snaked around her wrist.

Dear Lord, no, she would plead no mercy, but as he wrenched her from the bed to her feet, she couldn't stop the cry of shock and pain that assailed her.

"I'll kill you yet, Viking bastard!" she hissed as she wavered against his hold.

If he had struck her, she could have borne it far better than his laughter. But before she could speak again, his other hand shot to her neckline and ripped the white gown from her with a single jerk.

He released her then and stepped back and executed a low, mocking bow. "By your leave, lady," he said sardonically, "I would see the goods your lord father has offered. I would not be cheated."

Erin shook with humiliation, but managed to stand before him, her head lifted, her eyes dry daggers. She bit into her lip as he took a slow, tauntingly slow assessment, his sapphire gaze resting first upon her breasts, then her waist, down to the spot between her thighs, and finally over the length of her legs. His eyes returned to hers. That terrible dry, mocking smile was still on his lips, his eyes cold.

For a maddening moment she was tempted to ask if he found her pleasing. Then as his mocking silence continued, and a thick arched honey brow lifted with further scorn, she felt impelled to speak. Her voice dripped with scorn. "I hope, lord sea pirate, that you find the bargain fair. The Irish pride themselves in their law and justice. My father would not break a vow."

He laughed again, then his laughter was gone, even his mocking smile was gone. She could have sworn a look of pain glazed through his eyes momentarily, but then even that was gone. He appeared hard and merciless and totally ruthless. His teeth locked, almost like the snarl of a wolf.

No matter what had happened, she had sworn she would show him no fear—nor would she cry out. But when he stepped toward her menacingly, she became aware of only his blatant and tremendous masculinity and panicked.

At that moment all resolve of courage and pride fled her. She thought only instinctively of survival, and she turned, crying out, to flee she knew not where.

She didn't hear him, hadn't even sensed his movement, but suddenly his fingers closed over her arm. She was spun into his arms, pressed against the length of him. Her body was spared none of the secrets of his steel-hard strength as he crushed her there and she struggled against him, horrified to find that her struggles only made her more aware of the sex that rubbed against her belly, of the crisp golden body hair that tickled and seared her breasts.

He grasped her shoulders then entwined his fingers into her soft curls, jerking her head back cruelly so that she was forced to meet his now blazing eyes. "So you do have some fear for your conqueror, Irish bitch," he hissed quietly, so quietly that her body, limp with terror, convulsively shuddered. "It is well that you have that fear, wife, for I promise you that all my shafts are strong and sure and merciless."

She was suddenly flung away from him, so hard that she sprawled, stunned, against the bed.

"But rape, dear lady wife," he spat, towering over her with his frame rigid and shaking itself with the depth of an emotion she didn't yet understand, "is one fear you needn't harbor tonight. Did you think I would be crazy with desire for your precious virgin flesh? No, wife, I find nothing desirable about a cold, murderous person. You offer me nothing!"

He turned from her suddenly. Stunned and reprieved, Erin could do nothing but stare at his broad back for several seconds, feeling her head reel, as if she had been struck. He stared at the fire for several seconds. Erin finally gathered herself together enough to crawl warily back into the far side of the bed, drawing the covers around her.

When he turned back to her, he stroked his beard, his lips traced with a partially grim, partially distant smile. "But then, my lady, you must hold more than the simple fear of rape. Surely you must wonder if I don't intend retaliation. What was it you threatened that day?"

He moved stealthily to her side, wrenching the covers from her so that she could not hide her shivering although she managed to sit still. His dry smile was so close to her lips that she could see the pulse beat of his throat.

She had to give her full concentration to the prayer that she did not scream out in terror as he touched her—lightly, and with just one finger, tracing a line that nevertheless burned from her throat, between the valley of her breasts, down over her belly. She clenched her teeth as that bronze finger wavered over the tender white flesh high on her thigh. "I believe you mentioned something about roasting my manhood in front of my eyes?"

His tone was almost politely inquisitive. That it was deadly did not escape Erin's mind. She had to fight hard to keep her eyes on his, to keep from clenching her knees to her chest in an effort to elude the burning brand of his finger upon her flesh. "Well, my wife," he said almost distractedly, "that is hardly something I could do to you—had I the inclination."

With one of his incredibly agile movements he stepped back from her, contemptuously throwing the covers back around her. He walked a few feet away and stood in silence as she watched him, still in shock and shivering madly, her mind in a dark whirl. But when he turned to her again, the emotion was gone. He appeared tired, barely aware of her presence.

"I harbor you no malice," he said wearily, pushing a handful of straying gold hair back over his temple with an offhand gesture. "I seek no revenge for your treatment by the stream. Offer me no trouble, wife, and you will find your life tolerable. But I tell you now, I am the lord of my castle—a Viking, if you will—and if you defy me, you will be dealt with harshly. I brook no petty opposition. Do you understand?"

She stared at him long and hard, then nodded slowly. It seemed the only course open to her at the moment. You will never be *my* lord, Viking, she thought, but it didn't bother her to momentarily pretend submission.

He turned from her again as if totally disinterested in—no, oblivious now to—her presence. He snuffed out the oil lamps, then came to the bed and crawled in, his back to her.

Amazed at the turn of events, Erin remained curled

in her corner away from him. He wasn't dead; he didn't intend to rape her. If she didn't hate him so, she would be insulted; then she realized that she *was* insulted, that he had compared her to his Viking mistress and found her lacking. Good! Thank God! *She* would not be the recipient of his barbaric desires. It was strange, though, that his words had the power to hurt and humiliate her. They festered inside of her along with her hate.

She remained sitting in the darkness that was barely alleviated by the low flames of the fire for what seemed like forever.

Then she heard the even breaths of his sleep. Her mind geared into bitter action once more as she thought of how he had wrenched her from the bed, stripped her mockingly, tossed her aside with punishing strength as if she were nothing.

She ground her teeth together to fight off the tears of mortification that were threatening to spill from her eyes. She couldn't bear this, she simply couldn't bear it. He expected her to fall asleep beside him, to do his bidding, to be his vassal like a groveling dog. How could her father have done this to her?

She glanced at the man beside her. He slept easily, while she endured torture. Biting then into her lip to keep the tears from flowing, she turned from him. Her eyes lit upon the pearl handle of her scissors, glinting in the pale glow of firelight.

Erin covered her face with her hands. She could not murder even the Viking in cold blood with a stab in the back. But she wanted the scissors near her. If he moved to touch her again, humiliate her with his greater strength, she would strike. She would not falter a second time.

She glanced back at the broad and bronzed shoulders of the despised man beside her. They rose and fell rhythmically. Very carefully she moved, easing her weight from the bed, tiptoeing across the cold stone floor until she could bend to retrieve the scissors.

His voice cracked like a deep whip over her shoulder and his fingers dug into her hair. "May all the gods be damned, woman but you are a fool."

Tears sprang to her eyes as she was wrenched to her feet by her hair. The pain was so excruciating that she longed to plead for mercy, but she could not. She gasped and swallowed, and struck out blindly for his face. He caught her arm and twisted it behind her back and the cry that she tried to suppress escaped her. Once more she felt herself pushed back to the bed, and she fell across it.

"One more thing, Irish bitch," he warned, the blue of his eyes glittering in the darkness, "and you will find yourself learning that Vikings are not averse to beating their wives—even on their wedding nights."

Rubbing her scalp where she was sure she had lost half her hair, Erin righted her sprawled position and backed in a crouch toward the headboard, watching him warily. She had tempted him sorely; he believed that she had meant to stab him in the back.

But for some reason, his insulting disdain of her resulted in a strange temperance. As she nervously became aware that they were still naked and tried to draw the furs about herself, she prayed that he would take her silence as submission and come back into bed.

She saw his silhouette as he moved about the room, then heard him as he rummaged through his chest. A moment later he returned to her side.

"Give me your wrists," he demanded.

She realized then that he was going to tie her up and she panicked.

"No!" She hadn't meant it to be a shout, but it was. With impatience he reached for her, and instinct rose over intelligence to make her fight. She kicked out at him, her arms flailing, her nails curved in hopes of gouging an eye.

He cursed her soundly, but subduing her came as little effort. He cast his weight over her torso and legs, then ably pinned her wrists with one hand. The effort

had, however, left them both panting. For a moment
he just lay there above her, his body pressing hers into
the down of the bed. Erin twisted her head, crunching
her teeth hard into her lips. His beard tickled her neck
and ear, she felt the moistness of his breath. To her
horror, she could feel her nipples hardening against
the crush of his hard but warm chest and the touch of
the crisply curled hair. His thighs were atop hers and
she was painfully aware of him resting against the soft
tender flesh of her upper thighs.

He shifted suddenly. "You should definitely stay
still and fight no more, Irish wife. I just might decide
that my physical needs outweigh my abhorrence for
cold virgins. I now know no woman I care for, but I
have been known to appreciate the talents of a good
field whore. I just might be tempted to consider you in
such a light. After all, there will be many waiting in
hopes that this match will create an heir to combine
the forces of the land."

Erin closed her eyes against the sight of him, but
she couldn't close her eyes against the surging feel of
his strength. She swallowed convulsively, shivering as
she realized the pulse against her thighs was growing
stronger. She could feel him so thoroughly that it was
shocking. She was aware of the vital feel of his every
inch of flesh against hers—

Her wrists, tensed against his hold, went limp. She
went perfectly still and was treated to another spurt of
his dry, humorless laughter.

He straddled her hips, still totally unselfconscious
of the nudity that distressed her as he pulled her wrists
to him and carefully bound them together with a belt.
Pulling her binding tight, he leaned above her as he
drew her arms high, then secured her to the headboard
of the feather and rope bed. His belly and hips rose
before her face as he tied her and she swallowed hard,
wanting to close her eyes, but discovering they stayed
open with the tumult of her mind. The soft golden hair
that was below his navel teased her nose as he worked
to secure her bonds, and she found that she quivered

with her fury and humiliation despite her best efforts not to. She felt faint with the heat that rose with her anger and the indignity of his forced intimacy.

He shifted once more, grunting as he secured the knot. The shaft of his maleness nudged between the hollow of her breasts and a rush of blood came to her face. She felt as if she had become raging, molten steel with the world whirling like a black tunnel around her. I'm going to faint, she thought desperately. She was burning so with anger, with humiliation, yet still fighting fear. Her head was reeling. She couldn't breathe. She had to keep trying to swallow.

He finished his task without a glance at her, then turned his back on her once more and lay to sleep.

She could no longer hold her tears as she shivered with her weak, miserable feelings and utter humiliation. They slipped silently down her cheeks. It didn't matter; he had disposed of her as an annoyance and now found his rest.

But he wasn't sleeping. She started at the surprisingly gentle tone of his voice.

"I'm sorry you forced me to do that to you. Perhaps it is a justice, but I didn't intend it to be so. I'm afraid I simply can't worry all night about your stabbing me in the back."

Erin thought about pleading, about telling him she hadn't intended to stab him in the back, only arm herself should he attack her.

But if she opened her mouth, he would hear the tears in her voice. After the heavy toll of subjugation he had already extracted from her, she could bear no more. Besides, she could plead herself hoarse and probably receive no mercy. He had warned her. . . .

There was an air of expectancy hanging over them as if he waited for a reply. But she gave him none.

She heard a barely perceptible grunt of impatience, then he resettled himself. In time she heard that rise and fall of breath that indicated he once more slept.

But she lay awake a long, long time, the silent tears still falling. She was the bride of the Wolf, most powerful of Viking kings, and absurdly she was still a virgin, shackled to her marriage bed. The strange encounter had left her knowing that her husband considered himself undisputed lord and master. She was a virgin still by his whim only, his vassal by his command. And she was vowed to him as wife.

Her most hated enemy.

CHAPTER

10

Erin awoke slowly and miserably, her arms cramped and sore. Unable to move, she had slept restlessly during the night, ready to cry out many times. Somehow she had made it through to morning.

She didn't need a second's thought to know exactly where she was, and under what circumstances. It was still difficult to comprehend that all that had happened was truth and reality, but she had been thrust into her position so swiftly that even comprehension bred confusion. What did she do now, where did she go from here?

She closed her eyes and then opened them, suddenly aware that she was uncomfortable for a reason beyond her bound arms.

Olaf the Wolf still slept disgustingly comfortably. The tip of his golden head edged her rib cage; his arm was haphazardly cast low over her abdomen.

She studied his pose, wondering if there weren't a way she could twist to escape his touch. She gazed at his long-fingered, broad hand, dangling over her hip bone. Perhaps she could shift . . .

Little tingles suddenly pricked her nape as she

shifted her gaze quickly to the golden-blond head. A flush of horror filled her face. He was no longer sleeping, but watching her, and his blue eyes denoted a clear knowledge of and amusement with her perplexity. She averted her eyes quickly from him as he chuckled, and stared upon the beautiful linen draperies that framed the carved wood cabinet bed.

"I'm sorry," he murmured with mockery lacing his apology. "Does my position distress you? Then surely I shall change it."

His hand instantly moved from her hip so that he could trail the calloused tips of his fingers lightly and slowly low upon her belly in circles. Erin sucked in her breath and held it, determined to show him none of the trembling that ran rampant within her at his touch. She stared at his hand, willing herself not to falter or flinch as his fingers continued their hypnotic encroachment to her navel, up her rib cage, and to her left breast. He cupped the mound within his hand, and grazed the nipple with the coarse texture of his thumb. Sensations unlike any she had ever experienced before suddenly made her warm, the trembling within her making her feel as if hot liquid poured from some invisible inner location deep in her belly to her limbs, rendering them weak and useless. To her horror she saw her nipple harden and peak beneath his thumb. She could no longer control the trembling, and the hot liquid feeling was becoming terrifying and overwhelming. It was making her head spin in a whirling vortex that threatened to rob her of conscious thought as well as strength of limb. Before she could stop herself, she closed her eyes and exhaled an anguished beseechment, all the more pathetic because it was a broken whisper.

"Please . . ."

To her vast surprise and relief, he ceased his torment immediately. She slowly opened her eyes to find him propped on an elbow, his lips still curled by a small twisted grin of dry amusement, but his eyes strangely probing.

"So, wife," he murmured, "you are capable of entreaty. That is good. Perhaps there is a chance we may live in peace."

Erin closed her eyes again, ignoring him. She felt that he continued to stare at her, and without opening her eyes she quietly asked, "Could you untie me now?"

He raised himself to release her and she still kept her eyes tightly closed. She didn't want to see his body, the lean belly with its down of gold, brushing her face. She held her breath against the clean and very male scent of him.

Her arms fell to her sides as he unbound her wrists. He moved away, and she finally opened her eyes. The Nordic blue of his seemed to impale her and she quickly looked at her wrists as she rubbed them.

"Why do you hate me so much?" he demanded sharply.

"You're a Viking," she said briefly, suddenly remembering her nudity and attempting to casually draw a fur over her. From his low chuckle she knew that her movement hadn't been at all casual, but he did nothing to stop her.

"There's more to it than that," he said flatly.

Erin shrugged, still refusing to look his way. "We met once, Lord of the Wolves, and it was not an amicable meeting. My feelings should make perfect sense to you."

"No," he said. "You were going to assist one of your hated Vikings at that stream until you discovered who I was. I repeat, why do you hate *me*?"

"Because you killed my aunt!" Erin exploded, facing him with rage.

She was startled by the surprise that filled his usually fathomless ice stare. "I have never killed a woman," he said flatly.

Erin knew that she was close to tears and she had no intention of letting him see her cry. "Clonntairth," she said, her tone harsh and bitter. "The king of Clonntairth was my uncle. Bridget was his queen."

He rose from the bed suddenly, cold again. "I did not kill your aunt. I have never killed a woman, nor have I allowed my men to do so."

"No," Erin countered in a biting voice, "your men don't slit their necks. They merely attack them in mass until they are so misused they wish to be dead."

"You really are a misinformed little bitch," he told her with little emotion.

"Misinformed!" In the turmoil of despair and rage that boiled within her, she forgot her circumstances and sprang up to stare at him across the expanse of the bed. "I saw what you did, Olaf the do—"

With shocking speed and agility he leaped across the bed and pinioned her wrists to drag her back down on the bed before she could finish her word. Held beneath his weight with the steel of his features and the ice of his eyes challenging her hotly, she could only stare back and pray to Bede's God that He not allow her to let her tears flow.

"Please," he ordered, "continue."

She closed her eyes and swallowed, wishing desperately that he would move his weight from hers, the hips that crushed her, the manhood that burned the softness of her inner thighs.

"I was there," she whispered. "I was at Clonntairth."

His voice seemed to soften a shade. "I didn't kill your aunt," he repeated.

Erin found that she had to swallow again. "She—she stabbed herself because you were coming . . . and, and I saw—"

"What?" His tone was still low, but forceful in a way she didn't dare deny.

"Moira . . . a woman I knew well. She . . . was attacked."

"What did you say her name was?"

"Moira."

He was silent for a moment, unrelenting in his hold upon her wrists and body. Then he spoke coolly. "I can assure you, *I* did not touch this Irish woman. If you were there, you must be aware of that fact." Take a woman, a terrified, screaming woman, when Grenilde had lived? No, Olaf thought angrily. "I have told you that I have no taste for frigid virgins."

Erin returned his stare, trying not to blink against the contempt in his voice and eyes. She prayed that tears would not come to her eyes, for while he might have no taste for her, his casual hold and intimate press against her were creating a wild rushing sound within her ears, a sound that seemed to sap her of strength, to bring the world sweeping in out of black shadows while she attempted to still the rampant trembling within her. She tossed her head back and forth against the bed, willing herself to speak before paralysis could come to her tongue.

"Perhaps, Wolf of the North, you were not one of the attacking dogs. But Clonntairth was razed on your order; it was your men who so abused poor Moira—"

"The king of Clonntairth could have surrendered," Olaf interrupted impatiently. "All would have been spared. When men fight battles, people will be hurt and killed. It is unfortunate that the innocent are often involved, but that is the way of the world."

"Surrender!" Erin raged. "Clonntairth belonged to my uncle—"

"The conquests of men are also the way of the world," Olaf snapped irritably. "And it is the strong who conquer."

Her fury growing along with the rampant trembling that assailed her, Erin twisted against him to struggle. She stopped in horror as she watched a slow smile seep into his features. He was amply proving himself the stronger and she was succeeding only in making their position even more intimate, making both of them more aware of naked flesh against flesh and the definitive differences in their sexes.

Erin locked her jaw as she stared at him with her emerald eyes burning with a fire more fierce than that of the sun. "Then tell me, Lord of Wolves," she bit out coolly, "what happens when men are of equal strength?"

"Then," Olaf replied lightly, "men compromise. Much as I have compromised with your father."

"Remember your own words, Viking," she hissed, "Your 'compromise' was with my father, not me—" Erin broke off, startled, as there was a tap at the door.

Frowning and distracted, Olaf issued an absent, "Come in."

Erin's eyes flew open with horror. Again she automatically entreated him, the humiliation in her eyes reminding him of his Irish wife's nudity.

He released her and quickly snapped out the command, "Wait!"

Bloodred, Erin furrowed beneath the furs. Olaf ripped a linen sheet from the bed, wound it around himself, then went to the door and opened it. A little man, very small for a Norwegian, bobbed to Olaf and peered beyond him to smile at Erin with a gamine grin she found she couldn't resist.

"Your bath, Lord Olaf," the gnome of a man said with another bob.

"Bring it in," Olaf commanded.

The gnome stepped aside. Two servers walked in with a heavy metal tub, followed by several blushing girls who filled it with steaming water, looking at neither Olaf nor Erin, but giggling as they filed out of the room. The little man stayed behind, arranging an assortment of glass vials upon a large wooden trunk by the door. "Shall I assist you, my lord?"

"No," Olaf said, turning back to Erin. "Erin, this is Rig. Rig my wife, Erin. Rig will serve you any way that you please."

The little man bobbed to her with his contagious grin and Erin found herself shyly smiling back. "Yes, my lady, if you need anything, I will be there."

"Thank you," Erin murmured, her fingers clutching the furs to her chest. He bobbed again and left, winking at her as he closed the door behind him.

As if he had forgotten her, Olaf dropped the sheet

and sank into the steaming water with a sigh, his eyes closed. Erin watched him nervously for a moment, then began to edge out of the bed to bolt to the trunk that held her undergarments and delve through it. She was sure she had been dismissed as she slipped into a light shift, yet she suddenly felt that sensation again at her nape that warned her he watched her. She turned quickly to see that his eyes were half open and lazily upon her. "Come here," he ordered. "I wish you to scrub my back."

"I will not!" she replied instantly, outraged.

She regretted her words as soon as she had voiced them because he rose sopping wet from the tub to stalk her. She started to back away, but there was nowhere to go and his hands were on her shoulders in a flash.

"Lady, you sorely tempt your luck. When I was gravely injured you saw fit to torture me, and yet you call me barbarian. I think I have been very lenient with you, under the circumstances, princess of Tara, so I think we had best start getting a few things settled before I lose my resolve to be temperate with all Irish. I took a wife only because it was the political thing to do. Stay fairly invisible and docile and you will find yourself left alone. We spoke of compromise. Princess, you are nothing but a tool of compromise, however that may personally dismay you. But continue being a spiteful bitch and you will spend your days as well as your nights a bound prisoner. Do you understand? I have been informed that my Irish is quite clear."

She was shaking, her gown soaked by the dampness of his body pressed to hers, but she stared at him a long while. How she hated to give in to him, loathed the steel of his strength that she was powerless against. And she was powerless. Even taking into consideration the fact that she was a strong woman, her strength was like a gentle breeze against an arctic wind.

"I understand your words perfectly," she told him between gritted teeth.

Their eyes seemed to lock in a terrible contest of wills, northern ice against the heat of emerald fields. Then his fingers tightened their steel grip around her shoulders and she muttered heatedly, "I'll scrub your damned back."

He smiled slowly, heavy honey lashes half falling over his sharp eyes. "I think I shall require a massage first."

"A massage," she murmured blankly, frowning as chills crept up her spine while she wondered what new humiliation he was planning.

"A massage," he repeated slowly, still smiling as he grabbed a towel to dry himself. He released her, fully aware that, for the moment at least, she was powerless to do anything but follow his orders. "The first container on the chest . . . bring it."

Erin straightened her shoulders as she moved across the room and forced herself to sigh deeply, as if she were dealing with a child. She feigned vast annoyance as she returned to him, hoping she could hide her trembling from him. She stretched her arm out to him to offer the vial, staying as far away from him as she could.'

He shook his head, refusing to take the vial. "You will need it," he said pleasantly, his eyes, beneath the lowered lashes, continuing to sear her with frost fire. She knew that he watched her for reaction as he spoke and she forced her expression to remain bland and immobile. "It contains a very special oil procured by some of my brother 'barbarians' when they ventured into the southern regions of the continent. It has a pleasant and aromatic scent and, when heated, is quite soothing when kneaded into the muscles by gentle fingers. I am feeling quite tense. It is difficult to sleep when one attempts to do so beside a woman intent upon his early demise."

"You slept quite well!" Erin snapped.

"Did I? Still, my muscles are quite sore."

He turned his back on her and stretched his frame upon the bed. Erin stared at him blankly.

"Well?" he demanded.

Erin approached him and sat gingerly at his side. She opened the stopper and poured an amount of the oil upon his back, then hesitated before tentatively putting her fingers on his shoulders. She began to smooth the oil over his broad back, grudgingly admiring the expanse of bronzed flesh and hard knotted muscle that she stroked. Erin started to feel dizzy. The scent of the oil was subtle and yet enticing on his flesh, but she willed herself to display no reaction.

She rubbed his shoulders, the cleft between his blades, cringing a bit as his muscles rippled beneath her touch, then brought her fingers down his tapering midsection until she reached the trim line of his waist. Then she drew her hands away, about to rise.

"Your back has been massaged."

He twisted, his eyes opening fully as he caught her wrist before she could retreat. He smiled, that mocking smile that didn't quite touch his eyes.

"You do well," he murmured politely in a drawl that was almost a dangerous purr. "You please me so much that I would like you to continue."

She couldn't control the hot flush that crept over her features. "Be glad," he warned her softly, "that all I ask of you is a massage."

Erin's teeth were so tightly locked that the strain was painful, but she poured oil in little streaks along his legs, trying to keep her eyes averted from his buttocks. She worked over his calves, noting that they were strong and hard and well shaped.

Her fingers worked firmly—shaking slightly as she strove to keep them gentle—to a point above the back of his knee. There she halted, determined that she was finished and unaware that he lifted himself on his elbow to watch her.

She suddenly sensed his eyes and looked up at him. He smiled mockingly. "Please . . . continue."

Aware that he would see her slightest flinch, Erin kept her face rigid and impassive. Dear God, how could it be possible that she had come to this? Stroking, touching the very flesh she despised with all her heart and finding that it was fine, firm and disturbing.

"There—" She started to rise again, but he shifted quickly, capturing her wrist again.

"Not quite."

She met his eyes venomously. "No further, Viking."

"As far as I say, Princess."

She stood silently but stubbornly defying him, not caring at that moment if he chose to slap her across the room.

He didn't. He smiled again. "Remember, my wife, things will always go just as far as I say."

Erin took a very deep breath and sat again, suddenly wishing that he hadn't proven to be extraordinarily fastidious and strangely sophisticated for a Viking. She closed her eyes as she touched his buttocks, but she could feel that they too were firm and hard. Suddenly, as she touched him, he rolled in a circle, leaving her unprepared fingers dangling over his manhood. It had a life of its own. It pulsed hot and huge beneath her gingerly fingers. She knew that her face burned red, but she was loath to give him the satisfaction of further response. Barely blinking, she brushed his sex aside as if it were no more of an annoyance than a stray lock of hair might be upon the forehead and rubbed her oil-slick fingers quickly over his hip and up to the lower portion of his steel-flat belly.

He roared with laughter.

A temptation came to her then, an urge to twist and hurt him as she had been hurt by humiliation. Strength suddenly seemed to ripple down her arms, and she lowered her lashes over her eyes as she moved her fingers downward again. But before she could carry out the savage and irrational intent of pure fury, he spoke sharply in warning. "Watch it, Irish. I really wouldn't try anything you're not entirely sure you can handle."

Erin tensed and braced herself, curling her nails into

her own palms, hating him, hating herself. If only she could fight him with a chance of winning. . . .

"Take great care, sweet bitch," he interrupted her tempestuous thoughts softly. "You are in my hands now and I am no longer weak, no longer injured. Nor completely numbed by battle and pain. If you hurt me, you will be hurt in turn."

The strain to keep from striking out at him was great, but she managed to unclench her fingers and proceed to massage his chest, her fingertips extremely sensitive to the golden hair that flourished across that breadth. With lowered eyes she moved her hands to his thighs, and then swallowed nervously as she saw the inner flesh there—and the injury that had healed to a long white line. She couldn't bring herself to touch it, and she fought the memory of his pain and her own cruelty. He had healed marvelously. But that had probably been her doing. She had closed the wound, and she had bathed and packed it with the healing weeds and clay. She had hurt him, yes, but she had also gently helped him.

And even on that long-ago day by the stream, she had been frighteningly aware of him as a man. And when she had escaped him, she had never thought that in a thousand years she would find herself touching him again, frighteningly aware of him again, but much more so with him so casually naked and demanding.

She jerked her hands away once more and folded them in her lap and sat stiffly. She was no longer touching him, but still she could feel him, and what she felt was steel. He was the stronger . . . the conqueror. He was aptly proving it all to her.

"Thank you," he murmured gravely, his amused mockery obvious.

Erin stood quickly and drew away from him and the bed, swiftly retreating to the shuttered window. This time he didn't stop her.

She kept her back to him, hearing his quiet movements about the room as he dressed, fully aware that his eyes were upon her the entire time. The subtle scent of the sandalwood oil was still within the room, a pleasant and masculine scent—a scent she would come to always associate with him.

It was he who spoke again. "I really have no desire to make you miserable," he said quietly. "I simply needed you to understand that I will not have my life made so by a hateful and treacherous woman. I haven't time to deal with your petty dreams of revenge. I am sorry that your aunt died. I have no excuse for what I am—a Viking. But I choose to be a builder now rather than a destroyer. It is a pity that fate brought us together before now, because all I desire is that you be a cordial queen. But fate did bring us together before, and circumstance has brought you here now. Accept that you are my wife—my possession. You may live peacefully and unbothered."

"I was raised an Irish woman. The Brehon laws make me *no man's possession*. How can I accept this?" Her voice was quiet and low, and haunted by misery and despair and pride.

Olaf felt a twinge of pity—and admiration. "Because you must. Brehon laws mean nothing to me. *I* am my own law. Still, I don't seek to hurt you."

"If you wish merely a peaceful coexistence," she asked softly, "why do you wish to humiliate me so?"

"It is strange," he said quietly, "that you can ask such a question. There was a time, Irish, when you did far worse to me. And you are still harboring a dream of ending my life. Keep it a dream, Irish. But today was not for vengeance, but because I believe it will be a kindness for you to realize that you cannot best or defy me. I do not have time to humor you. There are those who do not like this alliance. Dubhlain and Irish cities will be plagued by those who honor neither your father nor myself. There will be wars to fight and cities to rebuild. You must understand that if you cross me, you will be dealt with harshly." He paused for a minute, but she didn't reply. "I will send servants with a bath for you."

"My sister—" Erin began.

"You may see your sister later," he interrupted her. "I plan to send you a lady I believe you will find to your liking."

Erin heard the door close behind him but she continued to stare sightlessly out the window, alternating between the despair that threatened to engulf her and the rage that she was powerless against the enemy who baited her mercilessly to prove his mastery. And wishing that he weren't proving himself to be rational and clean, and, yes, a strikingly powerful and handsome man. It would have been easier to live with her hate undented by his positive assurance that he was not a murderer of women.

A tap sounded on the door again. She absently called, "Enter," beginning to wonder what her life was to be, how she was supposed to fill her days in this Norse stronghold.

"It is me, Rig, my lady. We have brought your tub and fresh water."

Erin blushed as she remembered her gown hid little, but Rig went quickly about his business, supervising the arrival of her tub and the departure of Olaf's. As the room emptied again, he kept smiling and bobbing, his voice very gentle as he said, "Anything you need, my lady, you will call on me. Yes?"

"Yes, Rig," Erin said softly. "Thank you." She smiled at the little man, unaware that she had made her first loyal friend within Dubhlain. He had taken one look at her beautiful, haunted eyes, at the misery in her still-kind smile, and he had fallen into adoration. Olaf was a lucky man. Rig decided. He had married for an alliance; he had unwittingly received a fine and rare gem.

"Your lady comes," Rig murmured, dismayed by his blush of pleasure at her smile. Bowing out awkwardly, he closed the door behind him.

Erin suddenly felt her head begin to pulse with pain. Too much had happened too quickly.

She had been free. A dreamer. Sometimes a warrior. A woman with a vague vision that she would one day defeat the very man who now held her surely beneath his power. A man with apparently very little interest in her except to put her firmly in her place.

Thank God that was his only interest. A blush seemed to spread throughout her body. At least she had not been forced to receive him. That would have left her truly devastated.

If only she wouldn't have played so recklessly with chance! She should have married Fennen. And if she had, surely she would have enjoyed the masculine scent of his body, the touch of firm and strong masculine flesh.

Erin closed her eyes, sickly aware that Fennen had never caused her to tremble like this man, that her Irish suitor's kiss had left her mildly interested, but never quaking inside as she did with the mere glance and proximity of this golden Viking.

It is because I hate him so that I react so weakly and yet so violently when he is around, she thought desperately. He leaves me quaking with fear and fury, that is all.

But there was more she was refusing to admit. Because even as she had abhorred her task, her traitorous fingers had been fascinated by the ripple of muscle beneath them, by the tautening of his fine bronze skin.

She wondered at the obviously very virile man who had chosen to leave her alone. Of course, he certainly held no love for her, but she would have thought that he would feel compelled to relieve the needs that she knew rose easily in a man.

Erin suddenly covered her face with her hands. Of course, it was obvious. He really couldn't care less about her one way or another—and he knew the Irish king would have given him nothing other than a virginal, untalented bride. There must be a woman near, perhaps within this very residence, who was not untalented and not at all adverse to pleasing the great Lord of the Wolves. Good! she told herself. Let him have his whore or whores as long as he leaves me alone.

She did hate him more than ever now. And surely there would be a way to escape eventually.

A choked sob broke from her. Escape . . . To where? She couldn't go home. Her father had done this to her . . . her father, whom she had adored all her life. She was so furious with him, but the hurt outweighed the anger. She wanted to see him. They had parted so badly. She wanted to be held like a child again. She clenched her eyes tightly together, thinking of her mother. Surely Maeve had known nothing about this. If only she could see her mother, feel her aura of gentle strength.

Erin took a deep breath as her thoughts naturally turned to Bede. She wanted to throttle the sister who had betrayed her. How great a sin was it to peel the flesh off a nun, inch by inch?

Erin's headache began to pulse. She was now Olaf's queen, she was surely expected to perform certain functions. Would the Norse respect an Irish queen? Or would they all know that she was but a tool of compromise, a plaything for the king when he was in the mood to taunt?

She eased herself into the water, swept her hair into a knot at her nape, and closed her eyes. Take things as they come, she warned herself. Make your mind go blank when you can, or else you will go mad.

There was a knock. Erin opened her eyes as she heard the creak of the door. She looked at the pretty, smiling face of the woman who ducked her head into the room, and her eyes widened with amazement. The woman who entered smiled a warm welcome. She appeared healthy, rested, and happy. Very happy. Erin gasped out a single incredulous word. *"Moira!"*

CHAPTER

11

❧

Moira stepped quietly into the room and closed the door behind her. "I'm so glad you remember me, Erin."

"Remember you . . ." There had been times when she could not close her eyes without remembering Moira's screams, but it didn't make much sense to tell Moira that. Erin swallowed a little uneasily and blinked. "Of course I remember you, Moira!"

Moira's smile deepened softly. "There were some very bad times at first," she said quietly, "but as you can see, I am fine now."

There were a score of things Erin wanted to say, but she couldn't seem to open her mouth. She hadn't yet assimilated her shock.

"I was badly hurt," Moira continued, moving into the room and delving into a fine cabinet trunk at the foot of the bed, "but I was cared for by Grenilde herself."

"Grenilde?"

Moira hesitated, her lovely gray eyes flashing briefly to Erin's. "My lord Olaf's lady," she said softly. "She is dead now. . . ." Moira shrugged and returned her interest to the trunk. "Since then I have lived with Sigurd, Lord Olaf's chief advisor, and I have found my life pleasant." She selected a gown and laid it upon the bed, then brought a towel to Erin. "You will enjoy Dubhlain, Erin. There is always so much activity! Scholars, chemists, peddlers, priests—they all come to Dubhlain."

Moira held the towel. Erin, still stunned, automatically stood and accepted the embrace of the soft linen.

"It is wonderful that the king of Dubhlain has taken an Irish bride," Moira said. "For those of us who are Irish it will be such a liaison to the Norse . . . not that we suffer," Moira added quickly. "Olaf is a shockingly just man. But sometimes his justice is blind. Wise, but not from the heart. You can be his heart, Erin."

Erin lowered her eyes. His heart! She didn't want to disappoint Moira, but she sincerely doubted she would ever brush the heart of the Wolf.

She still didn't seem to be able to speak. Moira kept up a soft chatter that slowly made Erin more comfortable.

"I have chosen a mauve linen. Will that suit you?"

Erin nodded, and stood still and dazed as Moira helped her dress. "You have such thick, beautiful hair. I will love dressing it."

"Moira." Erin finally found her voice. "You needn't serve me, I can care for myself—"

Moira laughed and the sound was the tinkle of a brook. Erin couldn't believe she could be so happy. "I am happy to serve you, Erin! It is like having a younger sister. Sit, and I will comb your hair."

Dutifully, Erin sat, pensive for several moments before she turned, disrupting Moira's administrations. "Moira! How can you possibly be so well, and so . . . How could you have forgotten . . . forgiven . . ."

That same ethereally beautiful smile came back. "At first, I wanted merely to survive, and so I did. Then I was simply treated well. I have not forgotten, but I have changed. I have lived with these people for three years now. I eat well, I am clothed well. And I-I have come to respect my lord Olaf and love many here. Erin, there are some things that will not change. Olaf has Dubhlain and he is here to stay. As rye in the fields bows to the winds, we too must bow when there is nothing more to be done.''

Erin turned her head around, her eyes shielded from Moira.

Moira began hesitantly again. "Please, Erin, you must accept your fate. If you were to attempt to run to escape your legal marriage, you would make a mockery of your father's alliance. The Vikings would be humiliated, they would demand revenge, the wars could all begin again. . . .'' Moira's voice trailed away.

Erin closed her eyes tightly, fighting tears. Moira was right. She could not run. If not a single guard roamed the city, she still could not run, no matter how she loathed her situation.

It was so painful. Life itself had mocked her. It felt as if the world swam in blackness, so deep was her despair. She opened her eyes again, "Don't worry, Moira," she said quietly, "I will not run."

The strokes of the comb through her hair soothed her scalp. "You will find life here very similar to that at Tara. Most of the Norwegian ladies are kind. Daily tasks are the same. We sew in a lovely chamber with the sun pouring in just like in the Grianan. You will be busy, Erin. There are so many to feed nightly who all must be placed by rank correctly, and now there will be the visiting Irish lords to place as well!''

Erin passed her fingers over her forehead, rubbing it gently. If she couldn't escape the humiliation of finding herself married to Olaf, she must, like Moira, survive the situation, and to do that, she would have to place herself above it. She would use all her power to be not only an efficient queen, but a faultless one. She could take comfort in helping her own people, and she would carefully keep clear of her husband. He claimed he didn't want her to live in misery. He had promised her he would leave her alone as long as she caused no trouble.

Erin pulled her hair out of Moira's hands and tilted her chin. "You must help me, Moira, I do not know what will be expected of me. While men may welcome this alliance, I doubt it shall be accepted by the women."

"It will not be so bad," Moira promised. "Many of the men have already taken Irish wives. Hold still so that I may secure your hair and then we shall find your sister and I will take you to the sun room."

Erin still wanted to throttle Bede or at least shake her until her teeth snapped together. But when she saw her sister's strained features and the agony in her eyes as she entered the chamber, she realized she had to control her anger. Bede would have never hurt her unless she, like Aed, truly believed that the sacrifice was for Ireland and was God's will.

Bede came to her, hugging her with tears in her eyes. "Sister, forgive me."

Forgive, Erin thought. Oh, Bede, you don't know the half of what you did to me! But I do love you, and there is nothing either of us can do. And it would not look well for the new Irish queen to strangle an Irish nun.

She drew away from her sister's arms and grimaced. "Come, Bede, Moira is going to teach us how to live among the wolves."

There were several ladies present in the sun room and only two Irish wives. Erin had never met Norwegian women before, and she was fascinated by their dress. They wore long light gowns of linen with various types of sleeving beneath heavier wool tunics rather than the general, one-piece robe of the Irish. Yet where the Irish took great pride in their mantle brooches, the Norse woman gave great credence to the identical brooches that held their tunics high on their shoulders. They wore many rings and bracelets and armbands and necklaces of gold, glass, and stones. Erin knew that their collection of gold and silver marked them as the wives of the powerful and very rich.

She had never worn much jewelry even as her father's favorite daughter. Moira had fastened golden clips in her hair, but other than that, she was unadorned and simply dressed in the linen. She wondered vaguely if the Norse ladies had silks, or if such fine material was hers only because Irish merchants traded heavily with the Catholics of Spain and Italy.

She froze when she entered the room where busy fingers worked looms and needles and thread. She was an outsider, cast upon them. But Bede, always confident that her God would guide her, swept on through. Moira introduced Bede as a Christian sister and princess of Tara and then she announced Erin as the queen of Dubhlain.

Erin felt like laughing. He was not her husband, she could not think of Olaf in that light, and so she was no queen. She was a game piece for her father and the Wolf.

The ladies did not immediately welcome Erin into their fold, but as Bede watched Erin, she knew her sister had made the best possible impression. Some of the natural resentment faded from the eyes on Erin as she spoke softly and asked their assistance.

Erin spent three hours listening to the suggestions that began to reel in her head. Moira, who hovered in the background, finally interrupted her and said she must come and meet the mistress of the kitchen. Erin looked to Bede to accompany her, but Bede shook her head imperceptibly. Knowing that her sister hoped to either learn more for her benefit or to attempt to make more converts for her God, Erin nodded and left her.

"Moira," Erin asked as her eyes wandered over the elaborately carved staircase that brought them from the second floor to the massive banqueting hall, empty now except for a few old-timers who whittled by the fire and smiled as they passed, "why did you not join in the discussion? It seems to me that you know far more—"

Moira's chuckle with just an edge of bitterness inter-rupted her. "Those ladies are wives of Viking heroes. I am but Sigurd's woman."

"They shouldn't have any more rights than you," Erin said.

"Leave it be, Erin," Moira said. "I am content, but that does not change the fact that I was a prize of war."

Erin could say little more because they passed out of one wing of the U-shaped residence into a small garden and she was startled as she saw men sparring with swords and axes in the distance on a hill.

Moira caught her glance. "They exchange their expertise in the art of warfare," Moira said. "I believe a few of your brothers are out there, and your cousin Gregory."

"My father?" Erin heard herself ask thickly.

"Your father has returned to Tara."

Erin swallowed a lump of pain. He had left her and, in time, Bede would be gone. She would be alone in a nest of hornets except for Moira, who had been turned into a well-kept servant.

Moira brought Erin into the second shaft of the U. The vast workings of the house were there: the kitchen, a smithy, the laundry, food storage, and housing for some of the animals. The kitchen was a large room with a huge central hearth of clay and stone. Cauldrons hung over the fire of the hearth, and spits were set upon heavy chains. Clay bread ovens lined one side of the vast wall; utensils were stacked and stored on wooden shelving. Erin was astonished to see also that water flowed at the turn of a lever from wooden logs into huge vats. Both men and women servants—most apparently Irish—tended meat upon the spit, stirred the cauldrons, and kneaded dough at huge planked tables. A young girl sat in a far corner plucking fowl; another skimmed fresh cow's milk for the cream. The aromas in the kitchen were delicious.

"You will meet Freyda," Moira said. "She is in

charge. When something displeases you, you must tell her.''

Moira glanced anxiously about the busy structure, then suddenly she froze. Erin followed her glance to see a voluptuous woman with long wild hair and a low-cut robe snapping out orders to a harried little man who turned a spit of beef. The monologue—the snatches she caught—was in Irish, which was not surprising because the woman was very dark and certainly didn't appear Norse.

"Moira, what is it?"

"Nothing." Moira shook herself. "Come, I see Freyda."

Freyda was a pleasant woman, plump and beautifully cheery eyed. She had a warm smile for Moira, then openly assessed Erin. "You'll do quite nicely, girl," she told her. "A pretty one for our good King Olaf."

Erin blushed slightly as the woman unabashedly touched her hips, measuring their size. "You're thin, but wide where it counts. I'll see that you eat proper, and our king should father a score of sons!" Erin glanced down at the stone floor uncomfortably, but Freyda merely chuckled. "I will check with you each morning to see if the evening fare pleases you. Today I have already chosen the meats, unless you would care to change it."

"No," Erin answered quickly. "I trust your judgment far more than my own. I will learn the palates of the warriors soon."

Erin realized suddenly that the voluptuous woman who had been scolding the cook was staring at her. She turned her gaze to the woman, wondering how she could feel so instinctively cool toward a fellow countrywoman.

The eyes were leveled mockingly, challengingly, upon her. Then the woman turned and left the kitchen, her hips swaying suggestively.

Her interview with Freyda ended and Erin suddenly

realized that she hadn't eaten all day. "Moira, might we eat something—"

Moira's eyes widened with horror. "I'm sorry, I forgot. Our main meal is at night, and all are usually present. I'll bring you food in the morning from now on. I'm so sorry."

"Moira, please, don't be sorry." It made Erin miserable to have Moira serve her, although she was pleased with her company. "Let's just find something to eat now."

They were given large slabs of succulent beef, which Erin enjoyed until she remembered that Olaf's cattle were also prizes of war. It is Irish food I eat, she thought as she chewed the tasty morsel, and Moira is an Irish servant to the swines in her own land.

Then she was suddenly remembering the other Irishwoman, the one who had watched her so insolently.

"Moira," she demanded, "who was that woman who stared at us?"

Moira made a pretense of licking juice from her fingers. "That—that was Mageen."

"Was she also taken in a raid?"

"Originally, yes. By the Danes, I believe. She lived in Dubhlain when Olaf took the city."

"She looks as if she has free run of the place. Has she not been made a servant too?"

Moira's second hesitation was fractional, but Erin sensed it. "Mageen . . . yes, I suppose she is a servant. Come, we must finish, for there is much more I am supposed to show you."

Erin spent the rest of the afternoon learning more about her new home. She met with the dressmakers, the laundresses and various servants. She learned that she was to have a special room for audiences with those wishing to be hired for court entertainment and that she was also expected to rule over the petty disputes between the women.

But more than that, she learned that the Norwegians were people, which was a curious experience for her.

Beyond warfare, they had the same basic concerns of family and home. She had discovered that she could actually like Norwegians, for she did like little Rig and Freyda.

As dusk turned to darkness, she returned to her chamber to wash for the evening meal. She did so hastily, not wishing to be so engaged if Olaf returned. As she dried her hands and face nervously, she found her mind turning to the strange woman in the kitchen. Mageen, who had stared at her with sardonic insolence. Mageen of the voluptuous body and swaying hips and sultry eyes. Erin realized instantly that only one thing could give a woman such a look. Mageen was Olaf's whore. A shaft of red-hot pain seared through her.

What do I care? she demanded of herself, recovering quickly. Hers was no love match. She had the best she could hope for in a world gone mad. She would not experience humiliation again as she had this morning and last night, because she intended to stay away from Olaf. She was forced to accept the situation, and therefore she would make no more foolish attempts against him.

In spite of her acceptance, she still felt as if she were screaming inside because, obviously, everyone knew about Mageen.

Unable to bear any more thought of Mageen, Erin fled the room. She retraced the steps to the banqueting hall, and then a barrage of nervous flutters attacked her stomach. She had to sit for a meal beside her husband as the queen. To her vast relief, she saw Niall and Bede already standing before the fire that warmed the great hall. She approached them gratefully.

"Niall!"

Her brother's eyes were wary and speculative and pathetically appealing as they fell upon her. "Erin."

"You're staying here?"

"Awhile. Then I must return to Ulster."

She wanted to hug him, to tell him it wasn't his fault. But if she did, she would start crying. Bede finally broke the awkward silence. "Many Irish women will be staying, Erin. You will not be alone. And did you know that Olaf condones and promotes the study of Christianity? This will quickly become home, Erin."

No, Tara was home. This would never be home. I am still surrounded by the enemy, she thought defiantly, but said nothing.

"Brice and Leith will be staying for several months," Niall offered, speaking of his two younger brothers. "And Gregory will be here with you as long as you wish."

Gregory. Thank God for Gregory. I'll not be alone, Erin thought gratefully.

The hall, which had been flooded with idle chatter, suddenly went silent. Erin turned to see that Olaf, resplendent and awesome as always, had entered, his mantle flowing behind his tall golden body making him appear as if he were more than human, a god himself.

His eyes scanned the hall quickly, then locked upon Erin's. He lifted a hand toward her.

Erin approached him with her head held regally high. Remembering her mother's training, she seemed to float across the room.

She felt the heat of his hand as he silently led her to the richly carved chairs at the head of the table. Once she was seated, he released her as if he held dirt.

It was a test, Erin thought, silently raging against the fates that had forced her to live a life of humiliation when she wanted to rip and tear and pummel with anger. It was a test to see if she did or didn't plan to be the docile wife he wanted.

Norwegians and Irish alike filed toward their chairs. The conversation within the hall began to bubble curiously as new allies warily assessed one another. Servants carried in platter after platter.

"So, madam, how did you fare on your first day?"

She could always feel his eyes, just as she could always feel the terrible tension about him. She kept her eyes glued to her plate and the piece of meat she speared delicately with her knife.

"Well," she replied coolly.

As she could sense his eyes, she could sense the cock of his golden brow, the tightening of his fingers around his goblet.

"I assume you have learned the extent of your duties?"

"I was raised at Tara, Lord of Norway. I'm sure I shall find no task too difficult . . . here." She spoke sweetly, making the sound of her sarcasm a double-edged knife. She may have accepted certain things, but she had not accepted the man beside her with his overwhelmingly vibrant power and fundamental masculinity. Every nerve within her seemed to prick when he was near, and she was determined now that since she was here to stay, she would do so with her dignity intact. Conqueror or no, he could not lord it over her if she refused to let him beneath her guard.

He did not reply, but shifted in his carved and inlaid chair to speak to the man beside him. Erin stared down the hall. It was evident that any actual peace between Irish and Norse would take time. Hot-tempered warriors already quarreled garrulously as they filled their mouths. The number of Norse far out-weighed those of the Irish, and there were those of his own men who thought Olaf a shade daft to sup with the enemy.

"Do you expect trouble?"

Erin started to find her husband's eyes upon her again. She shrugged. "I expect nothing, my lord. I am still amazed by what I see, therefore there is little to expect. I should, however, pray against trouble, since your invaders far outweigh the rightful heirs of the land."

He leaned close to her, his breath touching her cheek as he spoke low. "Ah, so if it was the Irish who outnumbered the Norse, you would love to see the spilling of a little blood or perhaps a lot. Mine in particular?"

Erin turned to face him with a smile curving her lips, ice frosting her eyes. "Olaf, I have never pretended otherwise." As before, her words were soft and sweet.

He smiled in return, his arm coming around her shoulders as if they were lovers whispering pleasantries together. "Are you planning to murder me still and escape into the countryside?" It was a softly toned question, as if he had asked her about the color of the sky.

His touch sent little shivers rippling down her spine. She gazed disdainfully upon the powerful broad hand that dangled over her shoulder and then again turned her eyes to meet his. "No, my lord, I would not take the chance of harming my people. I shall wait until the day comes when a Dane shall split your skull."

She was surprised that he found such a comment amusing. He laughed, and the sound was warm and throaty . . . a dangerous sound. The little shivers attacked her again and she turned her attention to the jugglers performing down the hall. Olaf again listened to something being said to his right. Erin surreptitiously took a glance at the Viking who so held her husband's attention and who was seated in a place of authority. He was large, not quite so steeled as Olaf, and probably a hair shorter. His hair was flaming red, his eyes a gray blue. He had stared at her before, but assessed her merely with no comment other than a snort, which Erin had taken to mean that he was not fond of the Irish, but as a woman, she would do. She wondered if he might be Moira's Sigurd. Probably. Poor Moira.

She was not called upon to speak to anyone. The Viking at her right was deeply engrossed in conversation with the Irishman placed next to him.

She began to pray the meal would end. Bede and Niall were far down the hall and, as yet, she hadn't even seen Gregory.

To her dismay she learned that Viking ships had just returned from a journey to Spain. The meal would continue because fresh fruits were being laid out on immense platters.

She ate half an orange, feeling more alone than she had ever felt in her life. How will I bear this day after day? she wondered. She took a long draught of her ale, then sat back in her chair. Perhaps she could feign illness and enjoy her meals in the privacy of her chamber.

The jugglers ended their entertainment. A man began to relate a tale of a Viking King Fairhir who had fought with the god Frey. The tale was amusing, as it was meant to be, and Erin enjoyed the diversion. The man ended his tale and bowed deeply. Cheers rose up about the hall, and Erin believed the man would begin another story. Instead a woman rose from her place at the table far down the hall and motioned him away. Dancers came in his place, but Erin had no eyes for them. The woman had turned mocking eyes to her, a direct challenge. It was Mageen.

She smiled across the distance at Erin. Then with a dismissive blink of her sultry eyes, she sat again, her laughter rising high in response to a jest. Erin felt blood rush to her face with her fury. She glanced at Olaf to see that he merely looked up with temporary interest at the change of entertainment, smiled vaguely at Mageen, and returned to his talk of proper ship-building with the red-haired giant.

But then Erin noticed that many of the ladies about the room, the few Irish and the Norwegian alike, glanced her way. Pity and curiosity filled their eyes until they would catch her return stare, then they would quickly glance away. She kept her head held high until she had simply had enough. She stood, drawing Olaf's eyes to her sharply.

"I wish to retire, my lord. My journey here was wearisome and I have not yet caught up on sleep."

For a moment it seemed as if he might argue with her, then he shrugged as if her presence were unimportant.

Erin escaped the hall to find that Moira awaited her in her chamber.

"Why were you not at dinner?" Erin demanded.

Moira raised her shoulders helplessly. "I prefer to avoid the banqueting hall at night," she said softly.

Erin felt hysterical laughter bubbling within her. "You hide up here because you live with Sigurd while that . . . that witch flaunts herself!"

Moira lifted a brow but said nothing. Erin closed her eyes tiredly. "I'm sorry, Moira. You must do what you wish."

"Come, Erin, I'll help you disrobe."

Erin stood still as Moira assisted her into her night-gown. No words passed between them as Moira combed out Erin's hair. "Erin, would it help to talk?" Moira asked.

Erin shook her head. She couldn't talk when she didn't understand herself. She shouldn't care that all knew Olaf's whore held more power than his wife-by-bargain. She shouldn't care that he had smiled down the table at Mageen. It shouldn't bother her that the man who had lain naked against her only to ridicule and subdue her brought that same naked body next to a woman of her own race who seemed determined to prove that she also ruled.

"I will say good night then," Moira said quietly, crossing the stone floor and attempting a cheery smile as she opened the door. "Lord Olaf shall probably be up soon."

As the door clicked, Moira's words brought new confusion to Erin. She wanted to confront Olaf, to swear and rage and pummel him bodily. She wanted to cry out her frustration. She wanted to go home.

She could do none of those things, not if she wished to establish a relationship of cool propriety and distance between them.

She got in the broad down bed, wondering with surprising bitterness if he would even bother to enter his chamber when it was obvious that he preferred to sleep elsewhere. I should suggest that we maintain separate quarters, she thought. He can have his freedom, I can have mine. We shall not not break into constant war. He does not want me other than to taunt me.

She heard his footsteps, the creak of the door, and closed her eyes. She felt his every movement as he stripped. She could feel him, sense him, smell the pleasant vital maleness of his body as he approached the bed. And she knew that he stood watching her.

"Your wrists, Erin," he said softly. "I have no wish to allow you to become a joyous widow tonight."

She froze, fighting tears that seemed to rush to her eyes. Not again, she thought, please not again, but I *cannot* beg him.

She shifted to stare at his face, studiously keeping her eyes on him. He didn't appear so terrible this evening. There seemed to be a glimmer of sorrow in his eyes.

Her mouth had gone dry. Part of her wanted to lash out at him, demand how he could treat her so miserably when he had assured her father respect, but there was another part of her that simply couldn't bear spending another night in bondage. She wet her lips. "I will make no attempts against you. I-I promise."

"I wish I could believe you." His voice held both determination and regret. "Place your hands out. Despite the fact that you wish me dead by the most odious means, I don't wish to harm you. I will if I must."

He meant what he said, and she was no match for him. She didn't want to scuffle again, didn't want to feel the radiating power of his body against hers. Her lip was begging to tremble. She couldn't allow him to see it. Tightening her jaw, she obediently did so.

He began to tie them together with a silk sash, then paused, staring probingly into her eyes. Suddenly he released her, his voice taking on a harsher quality as he spoke. "If you make another attempt at me, be sure that you do kill. For if you make another attempt to draw blood and I do not die, I will see that you receive twenty harsh lashes as would any petty criminal.''

Erin said nothing. His warning eyes left hers as he moved to extinguish the candles. He silently crawled in beside her, leaving a foot between them—a gulf that could never be crossed.

She slept miserably, free to move, but careful not to. He was like a powerful and hypnotic heat that she did not want to be drawn to. But she wondered miserably how she would endure this night after night after night. She wouldn't, she tried to assure herself. She would speak to him about separate sleeping quarters. And she would somehow manage to alert Mageen to the fact that *she* was the queen, and *not* the traitorous Irish whore who coveted the enemy.

CHAPTER

12

Erin's first week as the new Irish queen of Dubhlain was one spent in almost continual misery. Olaf had elected to stop taunting her, and ignored her, except when he would demand some small task and expected it as his due. Erin did her best to thwart him—leaving his mending to other women, pretending to have forgotten when he wished her to send for food or water or ale. Generally he held his temper, but she was aware of the irritation building within him. She could not help herself. He refused point-blank to allow her a separate chamber. He wanted her where he could keep an eye on her. And so, as the week passed, she lost more and more sleep, knowing he was within inches, sometimes jerking awake in horror to find herself curved against his frame, sometimes finding his arm draped around her. Neither his nakedness nor her accidental touches disturbed him. Erin thought rather indignantly that he assumed he was sleeping with a pet wolfhound. He was supposed to be the animal, the barbarian, yet he left her completely alone whereas she, to her great self-disgust, found it harder and harder to loathe him. One night she lulled herself to sleep with the fantasy dream that she would be rescued by a magnificent Irish warrior. Fennen should have been the man within her dreams. But she awoke time and again, shaking, when she realized that she had bestowed upon her dream prince not only her husband's superbly muscled and powerful form, but his golden clipped hair and hawk-strong features. She had gone so far as to give him eyes of piercing Nordic blue.

After her first week within the walls of Dubhlain, she had escaped Moira and duty to see a bit of the city. The wood-planked sidewalks had amazed her, as had the endless rows of pretty, thatched-roof houses, some of stone, some built with split logs as their foundations. Interspersed with the homes were shops of merchants and craftsmen. The quantity of items available was stunning. Toward the eastern walls of the city were farmlands and fields where cattle and horses grazed. Erin found herself turning toward those unbreachable walls and staring at them longingly. She was so engaged when she heard the thunderous hooves of a war horse approaching. Frightened, she turned to see her husband's sardonic gaze.

"Dreaming of running?" he mocked.

Erin tilted her head to see him above the massive charger, taking care to avoid the prancing hooves of the black stallion.

"A dream only, my lord," she retorted in turn.

He reached a hand toward her. "Come, it grows late. We will ride back together."

"Thank you, I can walk."

"I'm quite sure that you can. However, you will ride."

She had no chance to protest further. He leaned amazingly low from the saddle to slip an arm around her waist and pull her up in fromt of him. She didn't like the feeling that assailed her with his arms around her, and she didn't like his breath against her hair, the heat of his chest against her back, that elemental male scent of him. But he was like the steel of his sword, a physical strength she couldn't match. She sat silently, feeling the muscles of the great horse move beneath her.

"We are lucky you speak our tongue."

Not knowing if he mocked her or not, she again replied in kind. "We are lucky that you speak ours."

She felt his shrug. "If one wishes to invade and conquer a land, it is only wise to know that land and its people."

"And if one's land is being invaded . . ." By her pause Erin stressed "invaded"; she had no need to say "conquered." "It is only wise to know all that one can about the . . . invaders."

He chuckled softly. "Tell me, wife, what else do you do?"

She was glad she did not face him. "The usual, Lord Olaf."

He laughed again, but the sound was a bit hoarse. "Wife, I'll remind you, you do not exactly perform the 'usual' . . ."

A tickle seemed to race down her spine, hot one minute, cold the next. Did he mock her again? She had no reply, but he was speaking again.

"I have the strangest feeling, Erin mac Aed, that you are not at all the usual. Tell me—what other languages do you speak?"

"Latin and that of the Franks."

"Quite accomplished. Latin you will eventually teach me. I wish to understand more about this God I must tolerate for the Irish."

The magnificent entry of the king's residence loomed before them. Erin managed to escape his unguarded arms with a smooth leap from the horse. "If you wish to understand the Christian god, Lord Olaf, speak with my sister Bede. Her commune with Him is far greater than mine."

Erin was fully aware that he watched her as she ran inside. She heard the deep, throaty sound of his laughter echo after her and she pressed her hands to her flushed face, hating him, wondering how it was possible to find so many things so pleasant and stirring about a man she hated, a Viking, a man who mocked her, ridiculed her, ignored her, and held her trapped by bonds to her family and people. A too-proud princess held beneath the twist of his thumb. She was so preoccupied with her thoughts that she literally ran into the man at the foot of the staircase. Pulling away in quick apology, Erin was torn and saddened to find herself staring into the face of Fennen mac Cormac.

"Erin," he murmured softly, breathlessly. "I've been trying to see you alone."

She caught her breath as he placed his hands on her shoulders longingly. "I know how you suffer," he added quickly. "And I have not forgotten you. I don't know how yet, but I will free you from this horror."

"Oh, Fennen," Erin murmured miserably. "There is nothing to be done. I am legally wed to Olaf." Escape, she realized, could never be anything but a dream, unless she wanted to know that she had been the cause of further wars, of fresh bloodshed, of a greater death toll. She smiled sadly as she stared into his earnest brown eyes. She had never really loved Fennen, as much as she had cared about him. He was suffering a far greater pain than she. "You must leave here, Fennen," she entreated him. "You are hurting yourself."

"I cannot, Erin," he swore sincerely. "I cannot leave you to that northern barbarian—"

"He is not a cruel man," Erin heard herself say, and with the words out she had to admit to their truth. "I am fine, Fennen, and we both must accept what is."

"But, Erin," he began miserably, and then his eyes suddenly left hers and he stiffened as he stared over her shoulder. A chill seemed to invade her system as she turned slowly to follow Fennen's line of vision; she already knew what he saw.

Olaf had followed her in. He stood a short distance behind them, his expression as impassive as the stone of his house. Dear God, what has he heard? Erin wondered, a pain tightening around her middle like a band of fear.

But he walked up to them coolly, giving no sign of having heard their words. "My lord of Connaught," he greeted Fennen with brief cordiality. Ice-blue eyes swept Erin's only momentarily as Olaf slipped an arm through hers, drawing her from Fennen's light touch. "Would you excuse us, please. There are things I must discuss with my wife."

Fennen stepped back, tongue-tied, but nodding. My hero, Erin thought with a flash of bitterness. Why was it that even proven warriors such as Fennen seemed to quail before the Wolf?

She felt her husband's arm upon hers as if it were a chain of steel. But as they walked up the staircase, her resentment toward Fennen faded, and she began to nervously wonder again just what Olaf might have heard. I should be grateful, Erin thought. I do not want Fennen hurt, and at least Olaf behaved with civility. But she wasn't grateful. She was terribly nervous. Olaf ignored her so frequently, and now he was leading her toward their room.

"What do you wish to discuss?" she demanded regally, walking ahead of him with a show of annoyance as he pushed the heavy door open.

He didn't reply for a minute and the shivering that had begun at the base of her spine seemed to riddle her body. She found that she couldn't keep her back to him and she turned to face him, forcing herself to maintain an irritated expression.

He leaned against the wood of the door, his arms casully crossed over his chest, his eyes searing into her, his lips a slender line of white, an arched brow rising sardonically.

"I wish to keep the peace, Princess," he said with a surprising quiet. "therefore I do not wish to come across you in the arms of an Irish king again."

"I was not in his arms," Erin protested angrily, but Olaf waved an arm impatiently and interrupted with his voice absurdly sharp for its soft quality.

"If you want your gallant Irishman to live long and healthy, I will not find you alone with him again."

Erin lifted her chin a shade. I should be careful, she warned herself, but she could not be when her anger was rising at a frightening speed. He kept his whore about the hall, and yet she was not supposed to exchange words with an old friend, a man who was a king in his own right. "I was of the belief that I was the queen of Dubhlain," she said sweetly. "I would assume, my lord, that as such I should nurture friendship with the Irish lords as well as the Norwegians."

Olaf paused for a moment, his lashes sweeping over his cheeks, a subtle grin working into his lips. He met her eyes again and moved across the room to sigh and ease his body down on the bed, lacing his fingers behind his head as he kept his eyes on Erin. "Irish," he murmured, "you are slow at comprehension."

Erin remained dead still, her nervousness increasing with his smile and pleasantry.

"Come here," he ordered quietly.

"As you wish," she murmured, approaching the bed with what she fervently hoped was a bored shrug. She paused several feet from him and waited with regal expectancy.

"Come to me, Erin," he persisted quietly.

She paused, pondering the steel beneath the pleasantry of his command, meeting the cool fire in his eyes.

"I don't care to come closer," she murmured uneasily.

He twisted on the bed, leaning on his elbow. She keenly felt his Nordic eyes upon her. "Ahhh . . . that is the problem, Irish. You don't care to work at this . . . and you seem to continually forget that you are granted many concessions." He kept smiling pleasantly. "My back is itching terribly, Princess. If you would just lend a hand for a moment . . ."

She stood silent, wondering if she could run for the door.

Olaf's grin became more wickedly pleasant as he

lifted his palms. "Is it such a great thing that I ask, Princess? Were I to behave in true barbarian fashion, I could jump from this bed and drag you to it."

His voice trailed away as Erin began a furious two-step stalk toward him, sitting beside him uneasily on the bed. He lifted a brow at the scowl storming her features, but slipped his robe over his head and offered her his back. He was ready when she started to rake her nails diggingly over its expanse, twisting to capture her wrists before she could draw blood, meeting the tense anger in her eyes with a caustic grin. "It is a wonder, wife," he said softly, "that you dare to call me barbaric. But I have been pondering this situation, and I have heard that neglect makes the shrew of the maid and the adulteress of the wife. I sought nothing but peace, Erin mac Aed. It seems instead that I do you a disservice. . . ."

Erin's eyes widened with alarm as he pressed her down on the bed. "No!" she protested quickly. "You do me no disservice!"

Her protest came too late. She saw the hard light in his eyes and then felt the bruising determination of his lips on hers. She twisted her head in desperation, but she could not avoid him. He threaded his fingers through her hair and secured her nape, holding her still. She pummeled her fists against his back; he caught her wrists, securing them with one hand, and held her hair once more.

Never had she felt more touched by fire. His mouth was a brand against hers, and even as she struggled against him, the heat seemed to steal over her, robbing her of resistance. He was demanding and consuming, sweeping aside her futile attempt to deny him with subtle persuasion as he parted her lips and teeth to his plundering tongue, seeking the deepest secrets of her mouth. Erin found herself short of breath, unable to move, to protest, and whirling toward an abyss of faintness where she had no control over the trembling, mounting heat that swept through her. His mouth was firm, yet softly caressing, fiery and yet gentle. And she whirled ever closer to that abyss. He no longer entangled his fingers in her hair, but brushed them against her cheek, along her throat, and then insolently over her breast.

Suddenly he drew away. She stared at him, stunned, as he offered her his cold, dry smile and touched her moist lips with the tip of his finger. "I think, dear wife, that you will listen well to my commands and dwell long on the wisdom of dallying with any man, be he Norse or Irish. For I would think once more that you pined with neglect and would strive to see that you were not neglected and left alone."

Erin realized with a rage of humiliation that he spoke coldly, dispassionately. His fiery kiss had been naught but a lesson taught casually by a man well versed in the acts of love. A taunt to remind her that he held the power, and that if she opposed him, there was much left for her to lose if he chose to twist the reins.

He held her no longer, but his fingers hovered mockingly over her breast. A quaking like the earth began in her as her face flushed with the force of her rage. She raised her hand furiously to strike him. He caught it with a flash of his own, and any façade of pleasantry left his voice.

"Irish," he growled, "you are either the most courageous or most foolhardy woman I have ever had the cursed luck to come across. Do you never learn? Let us see. Madam, shall I ever find you deep in conference with the king of Connaught again?"

"No," she bit out acidly. "But you are the fool, my lord. There was never cause to doubt my full obedience to your . . . command. What you do to me is a cross I alone must bear, but I have no desire for others to suffer or men to die on my account."

With her words, Erin scrambled from the bed, lifting her chin with a haughty pride dredged up from the remnants of dignity remaining her. She spun to leave, but he caught her arm and pulled her around to face him. She returned his probing assessment rigidly, barely able to conceal the trembling that still wracked her slender frame.

"It isn't difficult, Irish," he said quietly. "You are free to go now, but I would have you listen, and listen well. I do not wield a tight chain, but when it is constantly pulled upon, it is only natural to jerk it back. Perhaps we have an understanding?"

"A compromise?" Erin demanded bitterly.

"That's right, Irish. A compromise."

She turned to leave the room, daring to speak only when her hand was on the door. "You understand, Viking, it is a compromise—an alliance. By Irish law I can still seek a separation—or divorce." She closed the heavy door quickly behind her, annoyed that she hadn't the strength to slam it even as she hastened desperately to at least once have the last word without his assured and mocking dispute.

Erin plunged into the work of making the massive household run smoothly, finding that she could enjoy the time spent with both Freyda and Rig. She was pleased to discover that she did have a talent for choosing the most tasty beef and arranging meal courses, and also for seating the numerous lords of Ireland and jarls of Norway so that none was slighted. The tension within the women's sun room eased as the Irish ladies joined the Norwegian and Erin found herself not so alone. It grieved her to see that Moira hid in the shadows, serving, but she could not force Moira to take a position that would add to her plight.

Things simmered in the household, then came to a head when Erin discovered that a direct order she had given in the kitchen had been countermanded by Mageen—and Mageen had been obeyed. She learned of the situation when she had been about to enter the sun room to seek out her sister Bede. She stopped when she heard the whisperings.

"It is a pity, because the queen has tried hard . . ."

"If she were Norwegian, it might be understandable . . ."

"He cares not, and so he does nothing . . ."

A titter of laughter. "Poor little thing! A daughter of Aed, a princess of Tara, brought so low . . ."

"Grenilde would never have allowed . . ."

Erin fell back against the paneling of the wall, feeling her heart pounding relentlessly. Dear God, they gossiped about her mercilessly because she had no power in her own house. If Olaf tried, he could not humiliate her more. Perhaps he does try, she thought grimly, remembering how he had mocked her longing survey of the land beyond Dubhlain.

Yet, in her way, she had tried to perform as he had said he wished: She had run his house as requested, and since the evening they had spoken in their bedchamber, she had stayed out of his way, giving him little trouble.

No more, she vowed as she lifted her head and returned to her room. She ignored all further duty for the day, staring out the shuttered window. She could see Olaf, working out in the fields with his men. Her brothers were with him and Gregory. Gregory, whom she had barely seen since her arrival. Her cousin who had survived with her, and then fought beside her, turning to the Wolf because Olaf promised to return Clonntairth when Gregory was strong enough to hold it.

Moira appeared after dusk to nervously remind Erin that it was time for supper in the banqueting hall.

"I am not feeling well. You will please convey my regrets to my hus—to Olaf."

A look of panic crossed Moira's lovely face. "Erin, you mus—"

"Moira." For the first time, Erin spoke to her friend as a mistress. "I have told you what I wish."

She assumed Olaf would barely notice her absence; if anything, he would be slightly annoyed. But when he left the hall for the night, she would be ready to accost him. She was not to speak to Fennen while he not only enjoyed Mageen, but allowed her to usurp Erin's position.

To Erin's surprise, Olaf raged into the room just minutes later. When Erin saw the tic in his taut jaw and the blue fire in his eyes, she regretted her action in a moment of panic, but then she quelled her cowardice and stood tall before his attack. "What do you think you are doing?"

She even managed a sweet and guileless smile. "Compromise, my lord. I do not care to dine with your whore."

"What?"

"I shall not join you in the banqueting hall any more. I am a princess of Tara, Lord Wolf. You wanted your home run smoothly. That, in order to honor my father's agreement, I did for you. But I shall do nothing any more, Lord Wolf. Not when you allow me to be dishonored by your whore."

To her vast surprise, he laughed. "You shall come with me now," he said.

"Only if you drag me. And there are Irish who would defend my rights below in your hall. And I believe that even among your own men you would find those who believe your wife should be respected."

His hands were upon his hips, his head slightly cocked. His blue eyes sparkled dangerously. "I think, wife," he spat, "that you forget who the conqueror is."

"No, Olaf," Erin said coolly, "I never forget."

Olaf stared at her hard. What was the matter with the bitch? he wondered. After all that had taken place, he had done his best to see that she adjusted to her new life. He forced himself to ignore her continual barbs, and he demanded so little of her. Why? he wondered. She was beautiful. The more he saw her, the more he realized just how lovely, how perfect she was: those eyes, like the endless green fields when the sun blazed the dew from the grass; her face, so stunningly aligned; her body, silken ivory, soft and yet firm, built to receive a man. And yet he left her alone when she was far more alluring than any other woman he knew. The answers ran swiftly through his mind.

She despised him. She was his wife and he had always dreamed that Grenilde would be the only woman to hold that title.

Now she still haughtily defied him, eyes blazing, head regally tilted. She still did not know that she was but an inconsequential game piece, and that he was not only the king of the Norse city he had won back with his own hands, but the one man attempting to establish a truce between his men and the Irish.

His jaw twisted with hardness, his lips, full and sensuous, became a grim line in his bronze and golden face. "If you wish to be dragged," he informed her in a deathly quiet tone, "then it appears that I shall be obliged to drag you."

He took a step toward her and she vaulted across their bed to face him over the broad expanse of it.

He was pleased to see her lose the regal cool that had been irritating him beyond reason.

"Drag me, then, dog, but remember this! You may have me flogged, or beat me senseless yourself! But I will not take another step toward running your house until you do something about your whore."

Despite her words, he kept coming, preferring to circle the bed and leave her pinned by the wall. He reached for her.

"No!" Erin screamed, threading her fingers through his golden hair and pulling with incredible strength. She bit into his shoulder so hard that he gasped with surprise and released her, fury evident on his features. "Do for me, a princess of Tara," Erin shrieked, barely aware of the words used in her plea, "at least that which you would have done for your Viking mistress!"

He was dead still. As soon as the words were out of her mouth, she wished she could take them back. She had never seen an expression so dark, so fierce, so forboding. Coupled with his towering size and his lethal power, it was as chilling as a stab of ice.

He struck out at her swiftly with a barely controlled violence that was shattering. One second she had been standing. The next the palm of his hand caught her face and she was thrown across the bed, her head reeling, tears of pain welling within her eyes. She couldn't even seem to find balance to defend herself should he strike again.

He didn't. Instead he left the room and didn't return that night.

In the morning Rig brought her a tray of fresh-baked bread and smoked salmon and cheese. He saw first the pallor of her face, second the little red lines across her face that had been welts.

He lowered his head with a fury for the lord he had served so many years. How could Olaf, merciful to all, mistreat this gentle lady? He would tell the Wolf exactly what he thought one day, even if it meant risking the anger of the sleek warrior.

He noticed that Erin tried to hide her cheek with her hair and smile. He brought the tray to the bed and unobtrusively assessed the damage. It was not that bad. It would fade by afternoon.

"I see that you are still not yourself, my lady," Rig murmured, bobbing as always. "I will make sure that you are not disturbed."

Her liquid emerald eyes touched on him. "Thank you, Rig. I believe I shall stay in my chamber this morning."

Rig poured her a goblet of fresh cow's milk from a horn. He didn't want to leave her. "I thought I would stay with you a spell and tell you a bit of our ways." He didn't give her a chance to protest. "You see, in the beginning, there was nothing but a great chasm called Ginnungagap. Very slowly, two worlds grew up on either side: Niflheim, the dark side, and Muspell, where there was heat and light. At the place where they met, life came about in the form of Ymir the giant. Ymir created himself a cow named Audhimbla from the ice, and from her he gained nourishment. But she licked the salty ice to sculpt the first human form, Buri. Now Ymir fathered the giants who were dark and evil; Buri fathered Bor who fathered Odin, our highest god. Now all of the sons of Bor killed Ymir, and Odin set about to create earth. Ymir's blood became rivers, his flesh, the earth—even the mountains were created from his bones! And light was taken from Muspell to illuminate the earth. And then the sons of Bor created the first man and woman—they gave life and breath to two trees and they became Ask and Embla. Man began to people the earth, in a stronghold made of Ymir's eyebrows called Midgard."

Erin laughed. "People from trees!"

"Yes, of course!" Rig grinned in return, fussing about to straighten the already neat chamber. "But all the giants were not killed, and some day the giants must fight the gods. Surt guards Muspell with a firesword and he will fight the gods on the last day of the world—Ragnarok."

Erin glanced at him, an ebony brow raised high. "The gods and the entire world come to an end?"

"Yes," Rig said mischievously, "and no. I will tell you about Ragnarok another time. Now these three you must remember: Odin, he is the god of wisdom and the god of the dead, and with his Valkyries, he chooses those who must die on the field of battle; Thor, god of warriors and battle; and . . . Frey, god of the earth and things that grow. A charm carving of Frey has been said to make many a marriage fruitful!"

"Oh." Erin straightened and pushed the barely touched tray back towards Rig. "Thank you so much, Rig, but I really can't eat any more, and I would like to sleep awhile longer."

Rig was sorry that he had been dismissed. For a few minutes, he had made her laugh. What had he said? He shook his head with sorrow as he left her, cursing the fool Olaf who had been granted Ireland's greatest gem and then mistreated her.

Erin did sleep. She hadn't done so all night, but with Rig to excuse her presence again, she lay back against her down pillow and found rest in exhaustion. She wanted so desperately to sleep, to stop thinking if only for a little while.

When she awoke she had regained her strength. She touched her cheek and was relieved to discover that the welts were down completely.

She fought against the stupidity of tears and despair. There was so little she could do except threaten him with the Brehon laws, which she refused to admit would be no help in her situation. In Ireland, the lowliest servant or slave, male or female, could eventually buy freedom. A peasant woman could hire a Brehon and take her husband before a magistrate. But the higher one's position, the higher the authority they must go to for judgment. She would be brought to the provincial king—her own husband—and, seeking higher authority—assuming Olaf agreed!—she would be brought to the Ard-Righ. Her own father. The man who had already closed his heart and handed her over to the Wolf on a silver platter.

Olaf could force her to do anything, and it made far more sense to obey than bear the ignominy of being dragged along. But he hadn't dragged her anywhere, he had struck out at her and left her and he had not returned.

She hadn't even meant anything by her words. Despite them, his Grenilde had been the one Viking she had grudgingly admired and respected from afar for all those years. With her gone, he had lost all caring for women. Except for the obliging Mageen who flaunted her authority.

Erin thought again about how dearly she would like to see her mother, to cry out her woes to Maeve. She couldn't talk to Bede, because despite her sister's humor, she believed too staunchly in duty and in the Christian ethics of bearing one's crosses with honor.

Pathetically she whispered aloud, "Father, how could you do this to me?" She closed her eyes again. How she wished she were back at Tara, a child again, crawling upon her father's knee to receive a bauble of colored glass or some such present when he had been away. I am not a child, she reminded herself, and there is no help. Somehow I must learn to deal with all this or I shall go mad.

There was suddenly a tap at her door. Erin considered calling out that she wished to be left alone, then sighed. She had claimed illness, and Bede would certainly insist upon seeing her and she could not hide in the chamber forever. The ladies would find even more time to snicker behind her back.

Erin squared her shoulders. She was a princess of Tara. She would lash out stupidly in anger no longer, but learn to hold her head so high that none would dare underestimate her.

The tapping became more persistent. Erin sat high against her pillow and issued a cool and royal, "Come in."

As she had expected, Bede slipped into the room, but she was accompanied by one of the Norse women, Sirgan who, from the first day, had shown Erin more warmth than the other women. She had also become a great favorite of Bede's, since she was interested in the Christian God, which was rather strange, since she was married to Heidl, one of the fiercest berserkrs known. All the Norsemen were savage fighters, but among them, the berserkrs were a breed apart. The Irish thought them half insane. They screamed and growled like animals in battle, rolled feverish eyes, and were known to break their own teeth by viciously biting their own shields. That Sirgan, a woman of quiet serenity, should be married to such a man seemed strange. Perhaps she had learned to live with the belief that her husband's every battle could easily be his last.

"Sister, I have worried for you," Bede said, sweeping to the bed and taking Erin's hand. "If you ail still, I must ascertain the cause and set about a treatment."

Erin managed a convincing smile for Bede. "I am feeling much better, Bede. I shall be up soon."

Bede smiled in return, then glanced to Sirgan, who hovered behind her near the door. Bede seemed relieved, not just because Erin was well, but because a problem had fallen to her that she didn't know how to handle. If her sister had been ill, she would have been left in a dilemma.

"Sirgan wishes to speak with you, Erin," Bede said.

Erin glanced curiously to Sirgan and smiled. "How may I help you?"

Sirgan approached Erin, a worried frown knitting her brow. She was not a young woman, yet her blond serenity hinted of a past great beauty, and she was still striking and pleasant to the eye.

"I am concerned about Moira," Sirgan said to Erin's surprise. She lifted her hands slightly as if uncomfortable. "She has been with us a long time. She has also patiently endured those of my peers who are not so pleasant to the Irish. Yet today, when Grundred snapped at her about the setting of a loom, she burst into tears and fled the room." Sirgan paused a moment. "Grundred is a spiteful woman. I fear for Moira for I am very fond of her."

Erin listened to Sirgan with a bit of amazement, and then pain. There were those among the Norse who were kind—Rig, Freyda, and now Sirgan. She could not despise them all, and yet she could not allow Moira to be hurt further. She must do something.

"Thank you, Sirgan," she said, "for coming to me like this. I will speak to Moira and see if I might help her."

Bede, looking vastly relieved, left with Sirgan. Erin frowned, then got out of the bed to wash and dress. She realized then that she did not know where to find Moira, so Erin called Rig to bring her to her chamber.

Erin decided she needn't worry about her own looks when she saw Moira's face. Although she was quiet, her cheeks were puffy and her eyes streaked with red.

"I am sorry I did not come this morning," Moira apologized quickly, "but Rig said that you were ill and did not wish to be disturbed. How are you feeling now?"

"Well, thank you," Erin murmured, feeling guilty as Moira was obviously distressed. "I wished to see you, Moira, because I would like to know what is wrong with you.''

Moira's underlip trembled but she lowered her head. ''Nothing, Erin, I believe I am overtired.''

Erin smiled. ''Let's change places today, Moira. You sit and I will comb out your hair.''

Moira protested, but Erin chatted until she had her seated, and then she began to comb her friend's hair, massaging her temples with her fingers. She spoke about the sights she had seen in the streets, and she chattered about the differences between Dubhlain and Tara. Then she spoke seriously again. ''Please, Moira, you must tell me what troubles you. I have heard that Grundred is angry, and I must know what is wrong if I am to keep the peace.'' Erin paused a moment, then decided she needed another twist. ''Please, Moira,'' she said softly, ''if there is trouble among the women, I will have greater trouble with Olaf.''

Moira burst into tears. Erin sank down beside her and held her in her arms, soothing her, perplexed. She felt as if her heart were breaking. When she had been lost and terrified to face the day, Moira had been there, guiding her, making her realize her plight could be far worse. Moira, handling her life with fortitude . . .

Finally Moira began to gasp out words. ''I am with child and I tried not to be. It was sin, of course, but I did not—I did not wish to bear a child out of wedlock, neither Irish or Norse . . . despised by both . . . neither freeman nor servant.''

Her crying became soft, but continued. Erin continued soothing her, then stood with purpose. ''Your child will not be despised, Moira, I promise you. Listen to me. I will demand of Olaf that you be turned over to my father and sent to Tara. He has many men who have lost their families; handsome young men who would love you and accept your child with Christian faith. I will see that Sigurd never touches you again—''

She broke off because Moira was laughing. A little

chill touched her heart. Did she have that kind of power? Just the idea of asking anything of Olaf was an anathema to her. But she had to help Moira, and surely she was due a boon from Olaf and her father for attempting no escape when they had trapped her.

She sat beside Moira again. "Please . . . don't cry and laugh so, you will injure yourself! You must trust me, Moira. I will free you from that Viking monster."

The crazy laughter continued as Moira raised her eyes to Erin. Then she tried to sober herself. "Oh, Erin, bless you, but I do not wish to be taken from Sigurd. I cry only for my child. I am in love with that Viking monster."

Stunned, Erin rose to her feet once more. Her voice seemed to come from very far away. It was as if another person spoke, calmly and confidently. "If you are in love with Sigurd," she said, "and about to bear his child, then he must marry you."

Moira began to weep and laugh again. "Sigurd desires me, but he will not take an Irish wife. He is no king with needs of alliances."

"You will stay here, Moira," Erin said coolly, sobering Moira once more with the regal tilt of her head and composed voice. "And I will return to you shortly. Then we shall make your wedding plans."

Moira watched as Erin sailed purposefully from the chamber, unaware that her mistress was wondering from whence her own absurd confidence had come and praying some miracle might occur so that she might in truth carry out the feat.

CHAPTER

13

Olaf sat on his black war stallion and stared out at the men who practiced their lethal warfaring techniques. He had watched Gregory of Clonntairth and his royal brothers-in-law of Ulster and Tara with great interest. He had been wise never to underestimate the strength of Aed Finnlaith. They had truly been at a stalemate, with either alliance or annihilation the only answer. And although the chosen alliance, solidified by intermarriage, couldn't stop the outlaw raids or the Danes throughout all Eire, Aed and Olaf both sat in relative safety. Combined, their forces were almost indomitable.

It was rumored that Friggid the Bowlegs hid out in the northern regions belonging to Niall of Ulster. One day Olaf meant to flush out the Danish rat, and when he did so, he would have the men of Ulster behind him. That Friggid lived ate at Olaf like a cancer. Like Friggid, Olaf believed that he and the Dane were destined to meet again—to battle to the death. Grenilde must be avenged. Only Friggid's death could ever relieve him of the dark pain that still ate away at his heart.

Musing upon his pain and his situation brought to his mind his Irish wife. A wince ticked at his jaw as he thought of their last meeting, and then he emitted an impatient growl at himself. He tried to be patient with her. He tried to understand her reasoning. But she was trouble. No matter how sweetly she spoke, a blade was behind her words. And no matter how she feigned obedience and "compromise," he knew she did so only as a king might, bending to greater strength as she watched for an opportunity to reassert herself. She would test even the patience of a far more tolerant man with her flashing green eyes that never offered submission and her deceitfully soft and curved form that was constantly rigid with impregnable pride.

She had flagrantly defied him and ignored her position as his wife to humiliate him in his own hall over a petty grievance. And she had taken it upon herself to label Grenilde "mistress." She had deserved his anger.

Then why did it plague him so now that he had struck her? And why had he spent his night miserably before the hearth rather than in the comfort of his own bed? Because she haunted him more daily with her beauty and spirit and he had sworn to stay away from her. His nights were becoming torture even in his own bed, and he had discovered that he had no desire to go elsewhere even to ease the throb within him that she caused.

He snorted suddenly, thinking of women with disgust. He didn't even know what had brought on her temper tantrum. He had not been near Mageen since days before agreeing to the Christian ceremony that had made Erin his wife. A sigh of irritation escaped him. He supposed he would have to do something—at least see if the complaint were warranted. He had promised Aed that his daughter would receive the respect due the princess of Tara, and if his own relationship with her could not be so construed, he owed it to the Irish High King to see that she was honored among his people.

Olaf's scowl became more fierce, and he turned his horse from the scene of the warfare training to ride up the highest dun within the city walls to survey his realm. He didn't like to be bothered with affairs of the household. That, besides the alliance, had been the reason that the idea of taking a wife had been palatable to him even when his heart despised such an action.

His sharp ears long attuned to the sounds of the earth warned him that a horse approached. He shifted in his fine leather saddle, and his amazement caused his scowl to furrow even further into his brow.

His Irish wife rode toward him, she who had begun to plague him waking and sleeping, who haunted him even now with shades of regret over his own, justified behavior. Head high, one with her swiftly galloping mount, she approached him.

She had called Grenilde his mistress. Yet her words had not been cruel, merely desperate. She couldn't understand that Grenilde had been his world. . . . His scowl was suddenly tempered by a grin of respect. Despite the violent result of their last meeting, Erin wished something, and so she came to him. No matter how he twisted the chains of her bondage, she did not accept defeat. Surely by now he would have broken the spirit of a woman less determined than the beautiful princess of Tara fate seemed to have set against him.

He waited, his eyes narrowing as he watched her. Again he thought with some surprise how very well she rode. So fluidly, so controlled. Usually only warriors could handle his massive chargers with such fluid, effortless ease.

The horse halted just feet in front of him. She stared at him with her ebony hair and violet mantle flying proudly in the breeze, her eyes flashing emerald fire.

"Lord Olaf, I would speak with you."

He inclined his head slightly, suppressing the urge to grin. He had noticed that she never addressed him as husband, one of her ways of informing him that she would never consider him such.

"There is a domestic problem that requires your immediate attention. Moira, my woman who belongs to your Sigurd, is with child. She was taken in the raid at Clonntairth several years ago. It is my understanding that she had been with Sigurd since the raid—and also that he was one of her original defilers. You have made peace with my cousin Gregory; you have offered to restore the province of Clonntairth to him. Moira is due as much, my lord, for all she has suffered. As you honor your agreements with my father"—she paused slightly, allowing the dry sarcasm of her words to permeate the air—"I insist that you force Sigurd to marry Moira. She has never offered you trouble of any kind, and despite her position of captive and slave, she has served you and Sigurd well. You cannot allow her to continue to suffer the abuse of the other women, nor allow her child to be born a bastard accepted by neither race." She finished her speech and stared at him defiantly, as if challenging him to oppose her.

He lifted a single golden brow over his mocking ice eyes. "You wish me to force Sigurd into a marriage."

"Certainly. I was so forced."

Olaf suddenly tilted back his granite features and laughed. "An eye for an eye, Princess of Tara?"

Erin momentarily lowered her chin. "No, my lord, there is no recourse for the injustice dealt me."

Her voice was a bare whisper, and yet it touched him, as no other had in a long time. He was possessed by another urge to slap her and also by an even stronger urge to touch her, to feel all that which his eyes had once assessed and found startlingly perfect, to press her against him and see if the passion that flared in her eyes coursed through her blood. The urge was shatteringly strong to teach her that he was her lord and master, and that he had granted her great concessions by leaving her alone. The lessons he had given her were gentle indeed when he was a man with needs—and not an "injustice" of fate.

He jerked his horse around so furiously that the great animal pawed the ground and reared in protest.

He stared at Erin, oblivious of the stallion's flailing of the air, his face suddenly as cold and hard as steel.

But to her amazement, his sharp reply was the one she had scarce dared wish in all her brazen demand.

"So be it!" he rasped.

Then the stallion left her in a wind of dust as Olaf raced down the field to rejoin the training session. Erin stared after him in wonder for only a second, then turned her horse around to bring the astonishing good news to Moira.

She was unaware that he watched her smooth gallop home and that his eyes had once more narrowed with speculation on her expert rapport with the powerful animal. She rode exceptionally well. She rode like a warrior.

Sigurd raged and bellowed when ordered to marry. Olaf allowed him his blustering, then reminded him that they had come to establish a kingdom since none had been offered them at home. Sigurd appeared unhappy, and Olaf did a little raging of his own, at which time the giant with his flame-red hair actually became sheepish.

Olaf realized with little surprise that Sigurd loved his Irish mistress and was proud to finally look forward to fatherhood. It was simply the appearance of things. Olaf offered his general the suggestion that he ask the lady himself, and then none would know that his marriage had been any other than his own idea.

Olaf emitted a long and tired sigh when he finally restored his general to his usual proud manner. He had another task ahead of him that he didn't exactly relish, but Mageen had to be dealt with.

He left his residence behind with anger rumbling in his chest. He hated his life to be cluttered with the petty problems of women. But he owed this perhaps not to the spitfire daughter of the Irish king, but to the Irish king himself.

Erin had returned home ecstatic. Perhaps there was a point to her disastrous marriage; she could wield her power as queen to help her people.

The joy in Moira's face was a ray of brilliance to her heart. Erin discovered it was even possible to be happy as she assured Moira that her wedding would take place that very night.

When Moira left, she was in tears again, but they were tears of joy.

Still riding high on the power that was more dizzying than the feeling of drinking too much ale, Erin wandered to the window and stared down unseeingly upon the courtyard. Her blood was racing, and she felt wonderful and laughed aloud, then quickly sobered as she thought of the night of misery that had preceded her moment of triumph. Olaf had granted her a boon—probably because he regretted his loss of cold control and because of the heated violence he had shown her. But still, she could not, would not, live with another woman ruling her household. She was a princess of Tara.

Erin touched her cheek and remembered the blow that had sent her sprawling. So much for my feeling of power, she thought dryly. But he had not struck her because of Mageen. He had done so because of Grenilde, the blond beauty he loved past death.

She doubted seriously that Olaf bore Mageen any great feeling. She was certain that any emotion resembling love that Olaf had ever experienced belonged only to his lost Grenilde.

Erin knew that Olaf enjoyed taunting her to a point. It was another game of strategy to him, a battle he didn't intend to lose. He had cornered her over Fennen, and in the privacy of their bedchamber he held no qualms about reminding her who ruled his kingdom. But in the great hall, in public, he always granted her a certain deference. He had promised her father she would be respected, and even if he was a Viking, he had his sense of honor.

Would he do something about Mageen? It would be

interesting to see. She chuckled suddenly, thinking that the Lord of the Wolves must be in an uncomfortable position, cast between wife and mistress. Her chuckle died away as she wondered if Olaf particularly cared about her feelings and demands one way or another, but he had made promises to her father.

He had involved himself with Mageen and this miserable façade of a marriage with her. He did, indeed, have a problem. And he was going to have to get out of it himself, just as he had gotten into it.

Erin paled suddenly, as she realized that he might continue to ignore the situation, taunting her, sleeping with the mistress who attempted to rule over his wife.

What do I care? Erin asked herself hollowly. But she did care. Her pride demanded that she care. I will thwart him again and again, she promised herself, and I will not allow his whore to make my life a misery.

Later, as she reached the great hall and set about her duties for the evening, her brooding anger continued to grow despite the coming wedding, which was a victory Olaf had granted her. He had made a concession; in turn, she would feign a certain *outward* obedience. But he would know. She would *make sure* that he knew that within her heart she would never, never, accept him, a Viking, as her liege lord.

"Olaf!" Mageen closed her eyes for a second with the gratitude of seeing him before her. "I have missed you heartily, my lord." She slipped her arms around his neck, having no foreboding of something wrong until he forcefully unwound himself from her grip.

"You have overplayed your position, Mageen. I have come here only to tell you that I will not see you again and that you must leave the city of Dubhlain."

Shocked, her face turned white and she slid to the floor at his feet. "No!"

Olaf sighed with impatience and with a regret that touched him unexpectedly. He picked Mageen up and eyed her narrowly as he sat on a bench by the one planked table in the room, extending his long legs tiredly. He watched her as she stood before him, and he saw a feverish quality to her eyes that was disturbing. She was frightened. He had never imagined this gutsy woman could know fear. She was quite a picture at the moment, her eyes wide, her breast heaving. She reminded Olaf that his marriage had curtailed his activities.

Mageen had offered him her voluptuous comforts on many a night. Damn Erin for creating this problem! But then Mageen had been just as guilty, for if she hadn't set out to taunt his queen she could have remained quietly where she was.

"You cannot mean it," Mageen said huskily. "You cannot mean to send me away. . . ."

"I'm afraid that I do, Mageen. You have heartily offended my wife." He spoke softly, and yet she knew the sound of steel in his voice that meant his decision was irrevocable.

"No!" she said desperately, stamping her foot. "I cannot believe it! The Lord of the Wolves, ruled by a haughty little Irish bitch? What of us, my lord? What of the pleasure I can bring you? She cannot love you as I do."

"She is my queen, Mageen," Olaf stated quietly, rising.

Mageen watched him desperately, realizing that he dismissed her with regret but dismissed her still. He was the king, a man, and yet the king first. Strong, sometimes compassionate, but cold, able to walk away and never look back.

"I will see that you find a home with a suitable household," he told her, still quiet, still firm. "Until then, I'm afraid you are not to appear in the great hall."

Mageen still could not accept what he was saying, not until he turned to leave. Hopelessness welled within her and she lashed out at him, throwing her body against him. "You are a fool! You need not throw me over for that skinny bitch who would slay you in an instant! She will run, Olaf, I warn you, she will make a fool of you with any man and flaunt her infidelities because she despises you so!'' Mageen pressed closer to him, smelling the fine masculine scent of his flesh beneath his tunic, feeling the sinewed arms she couldn't begin to circle with her fingers. She could not let him go; no other could fill her, make her whole. She could not imagine not being able to anticipate his visits even though it had been a long time since they had lain together. ''I tell you, Olaf, she despises you, and she cannot please you! But watch those green eyes of hers, Olaf, for surely they wander. It is said that she would have wed Fennen mac Cormac, who still hovers in Dubhlain. It is probably he whom she wraps her legs around with pleasure—''

Olaf's fingers clenched cruelly into her shoulders and then eased slowly. He was more affected by her words than he cared to admit. ''I will see that you are cared for, Mageen. I warn you now, until I have found a suitable household for you to join, stay away from my wife, for whatever you wish to believe, she is the queen of Dubhlain.''

She fell to the floor again, sobbing brokenly.

Olaf stooped beside her and lifted her into his arms and carried her to her bed to place her on it. He kissed her forehead gently, straightened, and strode from the cottage.

He thought of Mageen with sorrow as he walked toward his own residence. He had come to her for the basic needs that compelled any man, for Mageen was all woman. And their relationship had never been anything more than openly sexual, or so he had thought. He had informed her he wanted no attachments and yet, he knew, emotions could not be controlled. Grenilde was dead; he knew that and still he pained. He could not control that feeling. Nor could he control the fascination that lured him to his Irish wife, the beauty who was proving herself to be pure trouble.

Suddenly he found himself reflecting upon Mageen's

words. Fennen mac Cormac. The Irish king with
whom Erin had whispered in the hall. A young and
handsome king; the man who had stared at her with
such pain and tenderness, who often followed her
about the hall with his eyes.

He had ordered her to talk with mac Cormac no
more, and she had attempted to defy his order before
assuring him she would obey merely because she
wished no harm to befall the Irishman.

An unbidden rage suddenly shook through Olaf's
body. Was there any truth to the accusations? Surely
not. Aed would not have offered him his daughter if
she had known mac Cormac. But fathers did not know
everything. . . .

Was his wife in love with the Irishman? Did she
harbor dreams of escaping with him? Had she lain
with the man, her emerald eyes ablaze with the heat
of passion rather than anger, her supple form en-
wrapped with his, her ebony hair a web of soft clouds
entangling their love?

His anger mounted steadily with the vision, and
with the memory of how she lay beside him night after
night, jerking away with horror each time she unwittingly touched him or curled against him.

He slowly forced himself to relax, wondering at his
fury. He was absurdly jealous over a woman who had
never meant anything to him other than trouble. Then
he shrugged. It was simple. He was a warrior, and a
king. A Viking. A very possessive man. He did not
believe in the Brehon laws. His wife was his property,
and he guarded his property fiercely. If he ever discovered he had been betrayed, he would kill the mac
Cormac first and then wring the beautiful ivory column
of Erin's neck.

Olaf smiled suddenly. Mac Cormac definitely
needed to leave the city. Perhaps his departure could
be hastened.

The king of Dubhlain chuckled aloud softly. You

may make a move, Princess, he thought, but there will always be a countermove.

Olaf sobered and began to wonder about the night ahead. Would his Irish queen appreciate what he had done for her today? He laughed. He would probably never know; he sincerely doubted that she would be waiting to kiss his hand in gratitude.

CHAPTER

14

❧

Olaf entered the great hall to discover that it was already filling for the evening meal. He glanced sharply to see if Erin was present, attending to the duties of the queen. But of course she would be there, creating no problems that night. She had arranged for a wedding.

She spoke before the fire with her brother Leith but she turned to Olaf with her exquisite emerald eyes as if sensing his on her. She approached him, seeming to float across the floor with dignity. "Lord Olaf," she murmured demurely, her eyes downcast for a moment. "Sigurd and Moira will be wed before the food is brought in so that all assembled may witness the ceremony, if that is to your liking."

She looked up at him and he saw in her eyes a glitter that belied her respectful words. She would follow out his every order, never disobeying a command, but always she would defy him within. She would maintain that unshakable cool with patience.

"That is fine. Let the ceremony begin."

Moira and Sigurd were married by a Christian monk, and the night became a festival, with everyone drinking heavily and turning it into a roisterous affair. Olaf noticed that his great red-headed general flushed like a boy and that the Irish woman was radiantly happy to the point of tears.

He was drinking too much himself, he realized, and it irritated him, just like his occasional glances toward his wife, sitting beautifully, regally, and demurely beside him, irritated him. Because when she caught his glance, he saw again that supremacy in her eyes, and despite his intention to keep his vows of peace, he wanted to shake that supremacy out of her eyes, to see her humble before him.

He smiled at her suddenly, his own eyes frosted while the curve of his lips was wicked. He lifted his goblet. "Drink with me, wife, to your victory. A happy union between Norse and Irish."

As he had expected she obeyed, raising her goblet in response, smiling that smile with beautifully shaped red lips that wasn't a smile at all.

Then suddenly he was thinking again of Mageen's spiteful words. "Fennen mac Cormac hovers near . . . it is he whom she probably wraps her legs around with pleasure . . . she wishes to slay you . . . watch those green eyes of hers . . ."

Sigurd distracted him with a great drunken bear hug. He laughed and heaved the man from him, wishing him a fruitful union with a wink. Then he turned to stare at his wife again speculatively but she was gone.

He mused awhile longer at the table, then rose. He could feel the pain pounding at his temple. He had slept so poorly, spent the day not only drilling but handling these petty disputes. He felt the grit of the earth about him and longed for a bath.

Fatigued and irritated with his thoughts of Erin, he left the hall. Finding Rig, he ordered a bath be brought to his chamber.

He entered the room. She was not in bed yet, but securing the drawstring of her gown over her breasts. He smiled as she could not quite cover a tiny jump at his entry as the door slammed. She scampered across the room and far onto her side of the bed, but not before he saw the rapid rise and fall of her breasts beneath the flimsy linen gown or the flush that increased the rose of her cheeks.

He said nothing, but carelessly began shedding his clothes. Rig appeared at the door, ordering his tub be brought in. Water followed. Olaf wondered for a moment what was the matter with Rig, who seemed so very uncomfortable in the room.

Olaf climbed into the tub. Rig stood above him with the last container of water. Half closing his eyes, Olaf stared up at him with a scowl. "The water, Rig. Are you going daft, man?"

Rig dumped the water over him, right on his chest. It was steaming hot and Olaf howled in amazed protest. "What ails you, Rig! Get out of here before I decide a good tan—'

Rig, with a curious glance toward the curled and covered figure of Erin's back, ducked out of the room before Olaf could continue.

For a moment Olaf sat in the steam, thinking of nothing but the tensions the water eased away. But he could not quell either his restlessness or irritation, and he found his eyes turning toward his wife—silent and still, but not sleeping, he was sure—in the bed.

Damn her and her feigned, mocking obedience. Like a fool he had regretted hurting her, and so had ordered his general about and bothered with her petty problems with a whore, and she couldn't manage a grain of honest appreciation.

He smiled suddenly. "Erin," he commanded, his eyes lazily half closed, "I wish you to scrub my back."

She made no reply. Just as she feigned servitude, she feigned sleep.

He spoke again, very quietly. "I know you do not sleep, wife, and I have had a long, tiring day, made more so, I might add, by your demands. I command you to come and scrub my back."

"My lord Olaf," she said coolly, her back still

toward him. "I will obey you in all matters of household, but as to your person, I owe you nothing. You have promised my father respect, and you continually speak of compromise. But last night you saw fit to strike me, proving yourself the barbaric animal that you are. Today, however, you have made things tolerable for me—but what you did was nothing more than your just due to my father and to those you have conquered and with whom you say you desire to live in peace. Therefore we shall keep the peace you desire. I shall bother you no longer since your affairs shall not affect me, but neither shall I expect to be affronted by you. That shall keep the peace. I will keep my distance from you and not anger you. Then you will have no reason to strike me."

He rose dripping and walked to the bed so quietly she didn't hear him until he picked her up bodily in one smooth, fluid motion. He was rewarded for his efforts by a quick look of stunned surprise in her flame-green eyes. Her fingers dug into his chest in her effort to free herself.

"Wife," he said cuttingly, "you call me a barbaric animal, yet you continually feel safe to taunt me. I suppose I must prove to you that I am not an animal, but a civil man wishing nothing other than your most pleasurable existence. You do not care to scrub my back, therefore I will humble myself and scrub yours."

Erin could not dislodge herself from him and one glance into the blue fire of his eyes started her shivering with dismay. She had come to know both his rages and his sword-edged pleasantry, and the latter was the far more dangerous of the two. But there was little time for her to do more than issue the single protest "No!" before finding herself dropped into the tub.

She grabbed desperately at the edges to balance herself but the dripping naked and powerful form of her husband halted her. "How remiss of me," he muttered, catching her wrists with his hand as he hunched down beside the tub, "I can't scrub your back when there is cloth upon it, can I?"

"Damn you, Viking! I don't want my back scrubbed!" Erin cried desperately as he held her with one hand while he slid the other down her body to find the hem of her nightgown and ease the soaking linen up and over her head. He released her wrists only to pull the gown over them, then clutched them once more. "Sit still, wife," he said softly, his eyes bright and sardonically guileless. "I wish to perform a service for you."

She struggled briefly with him, attempting to stand. But that only brought her nude and wet body colliding with his, and she shuddered as if touched by fire as her nipples scraped against the coarse hairs of his chest and her thighs were met by his vital, pulsing masculinity.

She sank back into the tub. He reached between her upthrust knees to burrow for the soap and cloth and she jumped with a gasp.

"Relax, Princess," he murmured, his voice a low whisper with that ever underlying taunt, "Now that I have struck you, as a good barbaric husband, I must make atonement."

She felt him move behind her, sweep her hair into one hand as he soaped her shoulders with the other. But more than his touch on her, she felt his presence, the tension radiating from his body. She could sense each little flicker of movement within him, each nuance of muscle play.

She wound her fingers over the rim of the tub, holding on as if she stood at the brink of a great crevice, and should she let go, she would fall.

What is happening? she wondered desperately. He had taunted her many times before, but this was different. She was finding it impossible to fight, to retaliate, to move. She couldn't think; it was as if her mind were being lulled as well as her senses with the motion and touch and scent of the man she was sworn to despise. Different, but not so different, she struggled to clarify with dismay. She had always been far more terrified of his gentle touch than his anger. The tension had always been between them, lurking, promising an explosion, even as far back as the time at the stream, a tension that held her now in a strange paralysis, causing her to lose more and more coherent thought by the second, making her a prisoner of dangerously erotic sensations.

He did not know if he were goaded by god or demon, if he wished to cherish or punish. It had to do with the drink spinning in his head, but it went further, much further. It went back to the day when she had crippled his manhood with pain and first called him dog, and to his wedding night, when he had discovered he had been granted a rare gem indeed and suffered nightly since in his confusion of grief and need and the fever created within him from the emerald fire of her eyes.

The ebony hair within his hand felt like silk. So did the flesh of the ivory column of her long neck. He cupped his hand in the water to sluice it over her shoulders, then again retrieved the soap to run it along her spine. Her back was long, tucked deeply at the waist, dimpled beneath the water's edge at the top of her buttocks. He silently laved the soap over her, feeling her shivering beneath his caressing fingers. He leaned low to plant his lips against her nape, grazing it lightly with his teeth. She went rigid, but the shivering continued. He saw the knuckles of her long slender fingers grow white over the edge of the tub, and he moved his lips closer to her ear, his breath a caress that brought about a new spasm of shivers. "I'm a barbarian, Princess, a dog of the North. Only following form."

Still behind her, he slipped his hands beneath her arms and raised her, soaping her back again, then dropping the soap as he splayed his fingers over her shoulder and massaged her ivory flesh, moving ever downward to cradle her buttocks and keep the sensuously caressing massage at a fluid flow. He didn't know what force controlled him as desire ravaged his body. Yet his every action was calculated and precise. She shivered so now that her slender form visibly shook.

He touched his lips to her neck again, then moved them slowly down the entire length of her spine, his tongue flicking gently at each vertebra. He shifted his hands to encompass her hips, and knelt, leaning his chest against the tub to nip lightly the shadows of her dimples and the firm ivory cheeks below them.

"No, damn you," she gasped, her voice barely audible. He felt the beautiful play of her hip and bone as she tried to twist from him.

He allowed her to turn within the slick grasp of his hands and saw that her eyes were wildly dilated. He smiled, and the flame that conquered the blue ice in his eyes made her lashes raise high and flutter nervously as she realized she had merely abetted his assault. He released her only momentarily to dig for the soap again, and his hands moved up her calf.

"Please . . ." she whispered, and a roar of triumph surged through his body for he knew that she whispered like a stunned animal, trapped by the spreading sting of the hunter within her own body. She wanted so badly to remain still, to ignore him, to do nothing other than indifferently endure, and she could not. He had evoked the stirrings of the passion and sensuality he had long sensed, and though she could hate him till her dying day, she could never again deny that her body knew a natural response to his touch.

He rubbed the soap higher up her leg, taking his massive sweeps as high as the flesh of her inner thigh, where he left off, rising to bring it over her belly, allowing his fingers to tease the hollows of her hips and the pit of her belly upon the flat sleek midsection. And then with both hands he began to massage her breasts, cupping the weight and fondling slowly in a circular pattern, his thumbs grazing the suds over her nipples.

She remained standing still, her fingers clutched into her palms, a pulse ticking madly at the base of her throat. He gazed into her face as he leisurely held her breasts, feeling the erotic rise of her nipples, dark and rouge beneath the soap. Her eyes were still wide, glazed, her jaw tightened, but her lips parted, as if she would issue a plea again but could not. He leaned closer and touched his lips to hers. She allowed him to do so as if mesmerized, then, at the touch, tried to twist away. He brought his powerful fingers around her neck, holding her still as he bent his head, parting her mouth with his, driving deeply into the moist depths with his tongue. A tiny sound escaped her, but his lips were too sure, too demanding, for her to do anything other than be swept along in the tide. As he held her, he moved his hand over he breast, gliding the soap downward again, his hand massaging the silken flesh between her legs. A sound, a gasp, a moan, a protest, broke into his ravaging mouth, but he continued his massage, his fingers probing surely between her legs to lave her most tender flesh.

Only then did her hands desperately clutch about his shoulders. He was sure they did so in her effort to stand and fight him with a strength rendered useless in the muscles of her thighs.

He broke his kiss, dipping to cup water and sluice it quickly over her body, aware that she braced herself with her hands on his shoulders even as she tried to plead with moist and swollen lips. No sound came from her attempts.

He lifted her, wet, into his arms, and carried her to the furstrewn bed. He laid her down, gazing upon her, her stunned and brilliant emerald eyes, her full ivory mounds with the rouge crests grown hard and dark, her smooth lean belly, her shadowed hip bones, her beguiling ebony triangle that seemed to promise the greatest riches held in modesty beneath, at her long, silken, lithe and shapely legs . . .

Mageen's words came back to haunt him, yet even as a corner of his mind registered that he would kill Fennen mac Cormac with his bare hands if he discovered her touched, he believed in the innocence mirrored by the shock in her eyes. The fires in his own body seemed to leap and flame out and fan beyond control, yet he still endured the agony of his desire. He kept staring at her, drinking in her beauty.

She could no longer think. Something had happened with his touch. She had started to tremble, and then she had seemed to lose control of her limbs completely. A lassitude had stolen over her, and yet it felt as if a great energy were about to be released. Hot liquid seemed to rush through her like the continual tide of the sea. Blackness had seemed to overwhelm her, and then stars, and then light, and then blackness again. Something began, imperceptible at first, but rising undeniably like a firestorm. It began from deep within her, swelling with an ache that was both sweet and debilitating, multiplying with each sure graze of his hand, centralizing like a shattering brand as he sudsed with gentle but unrestrainable fingers between her thighs.

Now she felt weighted down by clouds. She was free as he stared at her, but all she could do was stare back. She had no strength within her, only the strange sweet fire that was both agony and trembling deliciousness.

She felt as if she were drugged. He moved away from her, but she hadn't the wits or energy to attempt an escape. Her eyes followed his body as he moved to the trunk at the door and then returned to her, carrying one of the oil vials. Only when he straddled her, keeping his weight on his own haunches, did she think of flight, and then it was too late. He pinned her to the bed with his eyes as well as his muscular legs, the blue fire that blazed both mocking and strangely tender, reading and countering the trembling emotion within hers.

"I would not think, my wife, of demanding any service of you I wouldn't gladly give in return," he murmured huskily. He poured a small amount of the lotion into his palms and set the vial upon the floor, continuing softly. "Not sandalwood, but an essence of flowers. Perhaps my thorn can be gentled to a rose . . .''

Erin felt she had lost all power of speech. She managed to lift her hands against him, which he captured easily, and then he began to massage her fingers first, bearing the slightest pressure on the muscles, then moving to the palms.

She had to speak, had to stop him. "Olaf . . . leave me be. I-I—'' She tried to rise. She met his eyes, and the firm touch of his hands on her shoulders.

"Lie still,'' he commanded.

His eyes. She couldn't fight him when they were like that. She felt herself pressed firmly back to the bed. "The laws,'' she murmured, only to be interrupted mockingly.

"Damn those Brehon laws! Surely they do not deny a husband the pleasure of serving his wife?''

"You do not serve me,'' she protested, shivering. But he ignored her, and the languor began to steal over her again. She wanted to press against him but she hadn't the strength. She closed her eyes to think, but all she could do was feel. He placed her hands at her sides and his fingers moved soothingly over her collarbone, light and firm, easing her to further lassitude, robbing her of coherency.

She almost cried out as his hands moved over her breasts, caressing them with the light, scented oil, stroking them firmly, gently, circling their weight as his thumbs grazed the nipples over and over again, only to leave them aching and bereft as his massage moved over her rib cage, slowly, deliberately. He touched her hips, and the fire within her centered, low in her belly, as each sweep of his subtle and knowing hands created new laps of flame.

Erin kept her eyes tightly closed, hoping to fight the hypnotism, the spell of fire and need that was encompassing her like the sure waves of the ocean in a storm.

He shifted slightly and rolled her over. She felt his touch upon her shoulders, and down her spine, and with each caress of his fingers, she floundered further in the sea of sensation. He touched the dimples low on her back with fascination, smoothing the slim mist of rose oil over her buttocks, her upper thighs, her calves, and her feet, working the tension lightly from even her toes.

Feeling his own fires burn ever brighter as he touched her was both agony and ecstasy. A strange triumph leaped within him as he watched her stunned and unwittingly, sweetly pliant in his hands. His thorn was becoming as soft and enticing, as ripely primed to be plucked as a full blossoming rose.

His heart was pounding with a drumbeat of desire like nothing he had ever experienced before, and he eased her around again to face him and then stood, watching her again. She opened her eyes, but they were heavy lidded. He smiled slightly. One knee was slightly crooked as she lay there, a last defense of modesty, and yet he knew he would allow her no barriers against him now.

Erin wanted to move, but again, she couldn't. She wanted to close her eyes against him again, but he held them. Warnings were sounding at long last in her mind. She had to move, to protest, but she could only stare at his towering form, the golden breadth of chest, the hard and narrow waist, the manhood that now flamed full and potent. She stared, feeling removed from her body, yet feeling every pore of her body as she had never felt it before. Her lips had gone dry. She tried to wet them with her tongue, and then some form of sanity leaped into a mind more drugged by his touch than any mead could ever do.

A cry escaped her as she realized with a sudden and startling clarity that he was not taunting her. He was at a point where he no longer teased and demanded to bring her to heel. He would have her now.

She desperately struck out at him. "*No!* Don't touch me any more, barbarian!"

"I do not touch you as a barbarian, and we both know it," he assured her in a gentle tone.

He had seen it in her eyes as she first fought sensation, seen the mesmerization switch to fear. Ignoring her frantic blows, he brought his weight quickly over hers, locking her eyes with the demand of his, catching her wrists gently, then pressing her hands down on either side of her shoulders, held palm to palm by his. He curled his fingers with hers, and the tension within them was great. He did not hurt her. He was merely firm, compelling her with his eyes that were a soft but relentless demand. Her fingers curled hard around his as she swallowed, her heart pounding furiously. She attempted wildly to struggle. "Please . . . I beg you, Olaf!"

"Erin, you are mine. My wife. And this too has been our destiny. Be easy, for you know that you tremble at my touch."

He did not fight her, but held her, watching her, commanding with those eyes that she lie still. Her body was still ready for flight, trembling, but she ceased her struggles, as if once more a stunned victim with a hypnotizing potion flaming her blood to a dizzying boil.

He kissed her again, slowly, leisurely, tracing her lips with the tip of his tongue, nibbling upon the full lower section. He darted his tongue into her mouth, then probed deeply. His beard grazed her cheeks, and even that flamed and increased the trembling she could neither control nor cease.

Still holding her hands, he lifted himself slightly and caught her eyes again. Then he shifted to lower himself against her and take her breast into his mouth, fondling the nipple slowly, then more demandingly with his tongue. She tasted delicious, of the exotic rose oil, and the raging desire within himself grew to wilder proportions with the ambrosia that was the taste of her. He glanced at her again, noting her eyes were more than half closed, then repeated the gesture on the other sweetly curved, high and firm mound. Her fingers began to flex, release, and then grip tightly over his.

Too late she realized that he had parted her thighs

with his knee and that the bulk of his weight was between them. He kept lowering himself, soft kisses, gentle bites, the moist hot lave of his tongue taunting her ribs, tasting the drop of clean fresh water and light rose oil caught in her navel, following the slope of her hip.

He wedged his chest deeply between her thighs, forcing them gently to give way fully. He felt their liquid quivering, and a writhing beginning, just beginning in her body, a sensuous rhythm that lay just beyond. He looked up at her face, pale and beautiful in the mantle of fine ebony hair splayed across the pillow and fur. Her eyes had closed, her lips trembled. He heard her whisper "No," but there was barely breath behind the word.

He tightened his fingers firmly around hers, feeling the tension in her hands, then kept his eyes upon her face as he delved into the ebony curls with his tongue. She gasped and shuddered wildly and a mew of protest escaped her. He held her hands more surely and continued, probing gently to find and fondle the tender, vulnerable folds of her womanhood with the most gentle of weapons. Then he released her hands, sliding his own beneath her buttocks, and delved deeply, questing, seeking her feminine warmth. He was rewarded by a surge within her. She arched to his hold, shuddering in tiny spasms.

She moaned out "Please!" and he looked back to her face, seeing that she tossed her head and moistened her dry lips with the delicate pink tip of her tongue. She writhed against him with the natural grace and rhythm of a dancer, undulating sensuously, her tempo increasing wildly as her body's new knowledge of desire and arousal swept away her fear and inhibitions. He felt the drumbeats pound and wrack his fireswept body. The fingers that he no longer held dug into the bedding, then into his shoulders. The world, the bed, the beauty before him, all became cast in a glow of red. Yet still he held himself back, taking her gently first with persuasive lips and tongue until her body replied to his sweet administrations with an ambrosia of moistness.

Still she screamed out when he settled himself between her and entered her slowly, but with a need strong and sure. He held himself still, feeling the pulse of his sex sheathed warmly within her, and he began whispering to her, gentling her, stroking her hair. "Easy, Erin . . . hold me . . . easy."

"Olaf. . . ." She buried her head against his neck, her fingers clinging tensely to his shoulders. He was within her and the pain was like burning steel, yet his broad chest offered a strange security and comfort. He had made her his, and at this moment, she needed his warm strength and assurance.

"Hold me, Erin, the pain will fade. Come with me. . . ." He began to move again, and he was encompassed and embraced fully, accepted by her sweet, giving heat. He drove deeper and deeper, whispering her back into his tumultuous rhythm, feeling again the sensuous undulations beneath him.

Red and black exploded in his mind. Beautiful stars, exploding in rapid fire across the heavens of his mind. The passion he had tortured himself to contain swept through him in wave after wave of hungry need. Control was lost, and deep within her, he demanded and devoured. Tempest-swept, he kissed her lips, and then her breasts, and then her lips again, thirsting and shuddering and straining himself, no longer aware of anything but the female he conquered and surrendered to in turn.

He knew that her slender legs wrapped around him, that her breasts pressed to his chest, arched to his lips, and he knew that she soared with him in the world that was red and black and blazing light. Then she screamed again, a cry echoing with his own groan of ultimate release and triumphant, shuddering, volatile rapture.

He did not release her, but stayed within her as the world slowly took on its proper proportions again.

Then he left her slowly, savoring even the wonderful sensation of withdrawal.

He had intended to hold her, to speak softly, but his words froze as he watched her. Her eyes were closed, her flesh covered in a fine and glistening sheen of perspiration. She didn't move, except to shift her thighs together. Again he started to speak, then scowled, abruptly changing his mind. She shied away from him, and his anger grew as he recognized she was turning from him in shame even after he had carefully, gently, and thoroughly prepared her for their lovemaking. Even after she had enjoyed her first experience after the initial pain, giving as well as receiving, soaring to the peak.

As least, he consoled himself bitterly, she was his. He had felt a base and a very male pleasure in the moment of pain he had caused her and the smear of blood upon them both. He would have killed if he had been betrayed.

He scowled again, looking at the sculpted lines of her back. He was sure she cried silently. Rage rose within him, and then confusion, and then fury with himself. He had not taken her; he had cherished her. He had not merely fulfilled his need.

Grenilde . . .

He had forgotten Grenilde with her, and in forgetting, he had betrayed her memory. He had taken women, but he had not made love since her death. But he had made love to the Irish bitch who despised him above all men, who prayed for his death. He had given as fully of himself as he had ever given, even with Grenilde, and Erin turned from him to cry.

Confusion and rage and heartache swelled within him, and the ice that blanketed his heart returned to his eyes.

He ran a slender finger down his wife's back. "Well, Princess, now you can tell yourself that you have truly been mistreated as expected by your barbarian Viking husband. You have been struck . . . and cruelly raped."

The last was uttered with such soft mockery, she felt as if a sword had pierced her heart. She bit into a knuckle, drawing blood, so that he would not hear her sob. She felt his touch upon her arm, and then heard his voice, suddenly gentle. "Erin . . ."

She jerked away from his touch. "Please! At least now let me be!"

Olaf froze stiffly, then rolled off the bed. He stood and stared at her, his powerful hands gripped into fists at his side. Anger and confusion seized him again, and he inwardly railed at the torment that assailed him.

Then he pulled a pair of trousers from his trunk, threw on a tunic, stumbled into his leather boots, and exited the chamber, slamming the heavy wooden door behind him.

Olaf glanced at the full moon as he wandered beneath it, but he gave it little thought. He had come out to the night to cleanse his mind, not encumber it.

He still didn't know exactly what it was that gnawed at his insides and tore him apart, that left him in fever. He had had her, and that was what he had wanted all along, and yet he wasn't appeased. He wanted her again with a new hunger, and he knew that the hunger could be sweetly quenched, but that it would flame again, a fire burning brighter every time.

Fever, aye, she was like a fever to him. A woman with the provocatively passionate sensuality of a sun-goddess, and she despised him.

Once he had meant to leave her free, to offer peace. Now he could no longer leave her free, but perhaps he could still offer peace.

Grenilde. The name tore across his mind, and he thought of his love with deep and festering pain. But when he closed his eyes, those that he saw were emerald, flashing with brilliance and proud defiance, narrowing, misting.

"Wife," he murmured aloud, "you will learn yet that I am your master. And you will cease your dreams of a different life and lord, of the death of all that is

Viking. For I am a Viking, wife, but I am also the
Ireland that you will know from here on. Aye, emerald
wife, you will break to me. You cannot deny yourself.
By your choice or mine, you will come to me, and I
will take what is mine. But I will reach out my hand in
kindness first, and see if it cannot be taken gently. You
will not cry again when you have been filled with the
full joy of being a woman in my arms.'' He shook
himself, grinding his teeth together.

Then he did notice the moon, and he frowned. It
was a strange moon. Black dancers seemed to play
upon it. Shadows of the gods. . . . A rumbling in
Valhalla.

A sound seemed to stir the breeze, and he thought
of the Valkyries, always seeking out those who were
to die, serving them their drink in the great hall of
Valhalla. He didn't even know if he believed in the
gods, in Odin with his wisdom; Thor, the mighty
warrior; Frey and Freyda, brother and sister, usually
playful and benevolent, deities of fertility. . . .

Olaf scowled fiercely at the moon, at whatever the
shadow dancers meant. Then he returned to the home
which was his pride and slept by the hearth alone in
the kitchen.

Across the vast green and purple fields and hills and
cliffs, Aed Finnlaith woke in the night. He frowned,
wondering just what it was that had awakened him. He
glanced at his wife, but she slept sweetly, her lips half
curled in her dreams.

Nothing in particular, he decided, had awakened
him. But he could not lay his head back and sleep, and
so he rose, clothing himself in a short woolen tunic,
and walked from his chamber out to his silent hall.

The fire had burned low at the hearth; and it offered
warmth but little light. What illumination there was
came from the moon. He passed the dozing sentries
and went out into the night, barely noticing the sharp
chill of the wind.

He glanced up at the moon, and it seemed as if a

shadow passed the gleaming circle, cloaking it in a strange darkness.

A shiver rippled through him, a feeling of something evil born in the night. He tried to shake the spell that seemed to have slipped into his old bones. And then his thoughts turned to his youngest daughter, which seemed to happen so easily to him since his return. Remembrances of her haunted Tara. He could swear at times he heard her soft, rippling laughter like a melody on the breeze and he could close his eyes and see her, her eyes sparkling, her black mane of whisper-soft hair flying behind her as she ran to him.

Perhaps we shall ride back to Dubhlain, her mother and I, he thought. His wife had been horrified that he'd at long last given Erin in marriage to a Viking. But Maeve couldn't possibly imagine Olaf. No one could unless they had seen the towering golden king, felt the power that touched even the air around him.

Yes, he would bring Maeve to see her "baby," and he would pray that the child of his heart would welcome him. He would wait another two weeks, give her a little time to adjust to her new life, and then the High King of Tara would make his first royal visit to the royal Norse household.

He spun around to return to his bed, then felt a prickle at his nape. He turned back to the moon. He didn't like the look of that shadowed moon. It seemed to be a portent of something dark and deadly. Hunching his shoulders against the damp night wind, he walked back to his residence. There seemed to be a keening in the wind, a trembling in the earth. You're an old man, Aed, he thought sadly, with an old man's foolish fancies.

Back in his bed, he slipped his arms around his sleeping wife's body and held her tight against the beating of his heart.

In the deep green darkness of the forest, Mergwin too stared up at the moon. But his eyes were hard and assessing, and he shivered not. He lifted his head, feeling the breeze. He stretched his arms out and called to the earth. He waited, feeling his answers from the heaven. Shadowland. Traitor's moon.

A bolt of lightning jagged across the darkness and disappeared, and the shadow slipped more surely around the moon.

Mergwin spun, his robe and hair and beard all fluttering wildly in the wind. He entered his little cottage and added logs to the fire in the hearth, stoking up a greater heat. He set his cauldron above the fire and into it he began tossing his Druid offerings. His eyes began to burn with the flame, and he chanted, ancient words, the words of the earth. He could not avert disaster. He could only hope to diminish its force.

The Danes were already riding across the land. He could feel them now; the earth trembled. Friggid the Bowlegs sought revenge. Yet that was not the evil he feared. Destiny had long ago decreed that the Wolf must meet the Vulture and, therefore, meet they must. Somewhere in time, one must arise the victor. But had that time come?

Mergwin shook his head. Something else bothered him. Something foolish . . . a mistake that would be a quirk of fate and yet disastrous. And foolish old man! he railed at himself. You haven't the wits to know what, to touch it, to gainsay it.

He sighed and left his hearth. He stepped out into the night again and stared at the moon. Shortly he would ride with his king and with the Wolf. He would have to watch the Wolf carefully, and perhaps discern that danger which he couldn't quite grasp.

CHAPTER

15

The wind was high and rising quickly. On the bluff overlooking the vast expanse of the Irish Sea, Erin stood like a statue, still except for the sweep of her long mantle and raven hair caught in the gusting havoc of the wind.

The sea was gray, churning, boiling. Great waves crashed deafeningly upon the boulder-strewn shore. The water struck, rebounded, and leaped high in the air. Sometimes the wind would catch the droplets of the salt spray and Erin would feel the dampness on her cheeks.

The sky too was gray, ominous and rumbling, warning of a great storm to come. The earth seemed to be cloaked in purple gray with patches of heather bending low to the wind.

But there, at last, Erin finally felt at peace. This tempest, just like fields of rolling green, was part of the land that was hers, inherently Irish.

She had awakened feeling still and sore . . . and as if she had been torn apart. Then, remembering Olaf's parting words, she had begun to cry, feeling hopelessly betrayed and used. But her anger returned, and she had cried again.

Yet beneath her conflicting emotions, she felt a sense of loss. As if she had been given a chance to grasp a glittering gem and been so amazed by its brilliance that she hadn't given herself a chance to examine it properly.

Admit it, she told herself mockingly, perhaps he was right. You have loathed him, yes, but through all your loathing, you have remained fascinated. Perhaps as far back as Clonntairth when he appeared majestically and sternly like a magnificent golden god and then turned to smile at Grenilde. Ever since that day, in a small distant part of your heart, you have wondered about the strength in those arms, the heat in his chest.

And maybe he knew, just as she knew, that the fires created had only begun to burn. She could rail against him for his disdainful indifference, but his taking of her body last night had been the taking of her soul. She would never be quite the same again.

But as the waves lashed and the sky stormed, she was not sure what she felt for him. He was a Viking, yes, and the Vikings were brutal men, in a brutal age, but Olaf raised himself above men and the times and lived by a strange code of honor. He could be cruel, but she had to admit she had given him reason to be. He might have beaten her; any other man with a wife so hostile would have surely done so. And as to rape . . . they both knew how ridiculous such a term was between them.

But what made him what he was? she wondered. He didn't love her, and yet even in her inexperience, she knew no man could have been more tender, more gentle, more determined that she cross the threshold of intimacy with as little pain as possible. But then he had been angry. Yet when he had heard her tears, he had attempted to comfort her. It was when she had stiffly repelled him that he had become again as cold and icily distant as his Nordic homeland.

She smiled a little ruefully. She had heard tales of

captives falling in love with their captors, but she had always ridiculed them. Such women had to be prideless fools. Such tales had been only the most absurd of fantasies to her. But how could she ridicule Moira? She had seen not only the love Moira had borne her Viking lord but the love that red-headed giant had returned.

Erin was no captive, no prize of war. She was the queen of Dubhlain; wife of the Wolf of Norway, legally wed to a man who had little use for her, and she was falling swiftly beneath his powerfully compelling spell despite all that she had promised herself, all that she had vowed. She could never let him know, because he would use her feelings against her as he did everything else, and the contempt he bore her would only grow with his amusement.

But how could she fight him? There was no battle in which they could engage that she could win. Perhaps she did need to speak with Bede and take a few lessons in fortitude, but Bede was leaving that day.

She didn't hear him approach, nor did she know that he had watched her with his sharp hawk's eyes as he neared her, seeing nothing of the dilemma that tore about her heart. He saw only the tall, straight stillness, the whip of her ebony hair in the wind, the royal fall of her mantle. Her head was high as always, her eyes blank upon the surf.

He thought of her with complete softness for the first time, as he thought of her father. Surely Aed had not lied when he had offered him such a prize as this child of his; so beautiful, so vast in spirit, so regal in pride. One with the land, bending, but ever fighting the wind. . . .

A streak of lightning tore across the sky, and a roaring thunder-clap seemed to shake the heavens.

He rode until he stood just behind her.

"They say that on days such as these Odin rides his horse Sleipner across the skies. Sleipnir has eight legs, and when he races, he splits the sky asunder with his speed."

Erin turned to stare at him, surprised at the gentle tone of his voice. She had wondered at first that no one had stopped her from leaving the city walls, and she had assumed he would be annoyed that she had done so. He had little reason to trust her.

His countenance was impossible to read, yet she knew he bore her no anger. His eyes were their ususal stunning blue, and still it seemed that a cloud covered them, making them as mysterious as ever. His mouth, beneath the red-gold beard, was not thin and compressed, nor did it twist in a smile.

He is a stranger, she thought, for all that we have fought, for all that we have shared, he is a stranger. He is a stranger even to his own men because all that he really is is not apparent; he is layers deep, and sometimes we are given insights beneath that overwhelming physical façade, but no matter how long I live with him, I will never know him, because he guards himself and lets no one penetrate his heart.

He dismounted from his horse and approached her, stretching out his hand as he stared into her eyes. Erin felt once more as if an actual power compelled her. She probed for answers within his eyes, unaware that her own were momentarily naked. Slowly she placed her hand in his.

"Come home with me, Princess of Tara," he said softly, gently. "For I seek the solace of my wife."

It was not an apology, nor a declaration of emotion. Yet it was tenderly stated, and she could not deny him.

"I was not running away," she heard herself saying. "I only wished to come to the sea."

He nodded briefly, leading her past the bluff where her horse grazed. "I fear that we will not outrace the storm."

He hoisted her onto her mount and turned to retrieve his own. Erin waited until he had swung upon the stallion and ridden the few feet toward her.

She allowed herself a wistful smile. "Perhaps Odin was also in the need of a ride by the sea."

He smiled in return. "Perhaps," he said softly.

Another streak of lightning lit up the sky; with the thunder that followed it, the rain began.

"Come!" Olaf bellowed above the sound of the tearing wind and the slashing raindrops. "There is a cave—"

He nudged the great stallion into action and Erin followed his gallop down the hill from the bluff.

Despite the whirlwind race of his horse and the tempest of the wind and rain that matched the pounding of his heart, Olaf was feeling a strange and pleasant lightness of heart.

Erin's and Olaf's horses' hooves clattered upon the stone ground as they entered the cave. Olaf dismounted quickly and went to his wife, reaching his arms up to lift her from the saddle. She accepted his touch but didn't meet his eyes.

He walked to the entrance of the cave and stared at the wind-swept deluge beyond and shivered a little with the cold. He looked back at Erin, who stood silently dripping, and shrugged, suddenly feeling a little tongue-tied.

"This will go on awhile," he said, wishing she would talk. He walked deeper in the cave and found the pile of wood he kept there along with a few tattered furs. "I'll build a fire," he said a bit inanely.

She finally spoke, softly, hesitantly. "You come here often?"

He flashed her a surprising smile, the rare one that took his strong angular features and made them appear almost boyish.

"Not often, but sometimes, I like the bluff where you rode today. I like the feel of the sea and the wind. Sometimes I feel that I have been away from the sea too long and that I must go to it again."

Erin stiffened at his words, remembering that he was the invader who had first come out of the black mists in a dragon-prowed longboat. But he was staring at the fire he sparked expertly, nurturing it with kindling, prodding it until he could add dry logs. He glanced up at her again and saw her standing stiffly, her emerald eyes telling him of his mistake.

He lowered his eyes in reflection for a minute and then stood, approaching her, stopping a half foot away from her and placing his hands on her arms.

"Erin, I cannot change what I am. Nor what I have done. But you are my wife now, and I wish to give us a decent chance at our marriage. I said once that I would leave you alone; I have discovered that I cannot do that. But I have also tried to honor your requests. Sigurd and Moira are happily married, and you will no longer be bothered by my past associations."

Erin stared into his eyes, and though she still saw that he was a stranger, she knew too that he was giving her all he could.

She smiled and reached out a hand to touch his cheek, feeling the coarse hair of his beard and rejoicing in the touch. To her vast surprise he caught her hand and kissed her palm. He looked into her eyes and vowed softly, "I will always be gentle, my Irish one."

She threw herself against him, savoring the warmth that filled her through the wet fabric of their robes. He held her, then pulled her away to savor her lips.

She returned his kisses voraciously, loving the darting of his tongue, seeking the depths of the warm cavity of his mouth in return. The scent that was so individually, intoxicatingly him filled her every breath, that scent which was subtle, yet all male, all enveloping. His beard tickled her cheeks as his mouth hungrily sought hers, released it to find her eyes, her brow, her nose.

"We will catch cold if we stand around in these wet clothes," he murmured huskily.

Erin stepped back, swallowing a little, yet determined to appease the hungry fires that had begun to build within her. Today she would take all he had to give her. It might be only desire that brought him to her, but she would have him physically, and she would learn to know each fraction of his steel-framed body, each nuance of muscle, each golden hair.

"Allow me to assist you, lord husband," she said in a low voice.

He felt as if he had suddenly become lost in an emerald sea. He could scarcely believe the truth of his hearing, but it was there. Her voice was soft like a melody. It touched him like a tangible thing, making the nerves of his flesh quiver.

"I would like that, lady wife," he returned just as softly. He watched her as she stepped forward and placed trembling hands upon the brooch of his mantle, and then reached low to remove his tunic. She followed the rise of her fingers with her lips, relishing the tickle of his chest hair against her face as she luxuriated in the taste of the damp flesh. She heard him draw in a sharp breath as the tunic came over his head and she pressed her lips back to his chest, taking a male nipple gently between her teeth. Beneath her she felt the pounding of his heart become one with her, and she understood his tenderness of the night before, because each of her own administrations to him sent a wave of pleasure sweeping through her own body.

Tentatively she pulled away and slipped a hand into his, smiling as she led him closer to the fire. She beckoned him to sit, and removed his leather boots and woolen stockings, planting little kisses upon the hair-tuffed tips of his toes. Again she felt the intake of his breath, and chanced a glance at his face. His eyes were on her, blazing sky blue in the bronze and gold of his face.

She turned her attention to the Norwegian trousers he had worn, and he smiled a little at her perplexity, but forced himself not to help. Her fingers shook like dry leaves as she found the drawstring, but they smoothed without hesitation inside the fabric and over his hips. He caught his breath completely and drew her to him, spanning his fingers through her rain-soaked hair and cradling her to his chest.

"You are the gem of the isle, Irish," he murmured with a husky softness that was a silken caress. He removed her mantle, wanting to strip away the clothes that restricted burning flesh from burning flesh.

But when the mantle was gone, she shook her head with a small, secretive smile and stood, her eyes the radiant green that was the vitality of life and Ireland itself, and she pulled the string on her robe herself, allowing it to fall to her feet. Daintily she removed one shoe and then the other, and then slowly, one at a time, the woolen stockings held up by fine lace garters.

Then she stood, just stood, but it was an offering he might have waited a lifetime to receive. Those eyes that were both tempest and peace, a storm at sea and the greenest fields, held his. Her black mane of lustrous hair curled over her shoulders and breasts, hugging her flesh in its ebony dampness. The crests of her breasts peeked out from those modest ebony tendrils, high and proud, inviting and giving, the color of spring roses. They rose and fell quickly, delineating her sleek rib cage and the hollow of her belly beneath. Then came the hips he knew could move with erotic rhythm, the ebony triangle hiding the core of her enticing womanhood, and the long, lean flanks wickedly inviting.

Swallowing and blinking, he stood to join her, pressing his naked flesh to hers. He rubbed his body against hers, and she emitted a little gasp as he teased her thighs unmercifully, growing against her with a glorious heat.

She placed her hands around his neck, feeling the ends of his hair. Her fingertips had seemed to find new awareness, and she allowed herself free rein, experimenting with the feel of the muscles in his shoulders, his back. He moaned as she ran her nails lightly down his spine, pressed more fervently against her, returning the exquisite torture as she lightly massaged her fingers over his strong hard buttocks, while she kissed his broad warrior's chest, stopping the questing of her lips only long enough to rub her cheek against him, fascinated by the feel of his coarse and yet soft hair against the tenderness of her face.

She ran her hands down his flanks and savored the shapeliness of the bone beneath the flesh of his hips. But in another moment of perplexity, she feared to go further.

It had been a long time since he had been loved, and as the fever flared voraciously within him he knew that he had never been quite so loved. She was his, completely his, and in his arms, there was only the sweetness of her. She was a bit like a fragile and tender flower, brought to bloom by his finesse, and now she reached to him as she might to the sun. Her sensuality was an inherent part of her, and he was the receiver of all her endless passion. She wanted to please him and herself, and she answered his every silent cry, touching that which craved to be touched tentatively, then surely, exploringly, still charting new fields.

He drew her with him as he spread the tattered furs on the ground and lay her down beside him. He kissed her deeply, then buried his face into the perfumed fragrance of that blacker than the blackest night hair. It too touched him, teasing his flesh unbearably as he wound himself within it. He began to kiss her breasts, adoring them, suckling them, yet today she couldn't be still. She kept her hands on him and arched against him, running her fingers over his lean belly as he grazed her nipples with gentle teeth and she moaned against him. Still she hesitated and he whispered words of encouragement.

"Touch me . . . Erin . . . touch me . . ."

She did so and almost jumped at the hot raging pulse, but as he groaned she grew bolder, caressing him with her fingertips, finding the movement that sent him into shuddering oblivion. He found her lips, and his hands moved over her body. Into her mouth he whispered, "Oh, wife . . . my sweet, sweet wife, go on. It doesn't bite, you know."

She started to giggle but then her breath was swept away as he moved his hand between her thighs, teasing and probing until she cried out and sagged against him, whispering for mercy.

The storm that raged outside was nothing to compare with that which swept within her. She felt the ground, she felt his touch with each nerve of her body, and yet she floated on clouds. There were moments of blindness, and then there was brilliant light. She shuddered and quaked and needed, and the tightness within her belly coiled and coiled both painfully and excruciatingly sweetly. She wanted to draw it out forever, yet if she didn't let the deliciousness explode soon, she would surely go mad.

She couldn't stop touching him and tasting the salt of his flesh with her lips and tongue. Something within her snapped and she became wanton, rising above him, tossing her hair like feathers of torture about them both. Sensation became overwhelming, and she moved to appease it. She forgot all hesitation, and she loved him as her desires guided her, learning as she had wished every physical fraction of him.

She glanced at his eyes, blue demanding fire, and sobbed because he swept her beneath him, commanding that the moment had come. They both cried as he entered her, filling her with the vital life she craved. And she, in turn, held him, awed at the beauty of how perfectly she received him, vaguely wondering how she had ever doubted that she could not handle all that he could give. She would never again be able to live without it, could not bear to think that she would not feel him reaching, expanding, grazing her womb, her heart.

He took her to that brilliant sun-streaked plateau where all was the fundamental earthiness and the sweeping thunder of his ever-pulsing, rhythm, and then lifted her to the sky, burning, soaring, flying, straining, craving . . . exploding over the crest of the hill in a moment of ecstasy so intense and volatile that she shuddered in rocking spasm after spasm as she drifted down. She shouted his name, then whispered it, even as he called hers in return, then he drowned out both sounds with the tenderest of kisses.

She smiled lazily, feeling as if the sun itself had left

its warmth within her body. But it wasn't the sun, it was his seed, and she was loath to move, to risk chancing its loss.

He held her against him, waiting as the air cooled the slicked and glistening heat of their bodies. Smoothing back her damp hair, he wondered with a touch of awe how an experience such as this had come between them. But he had been a fool to have ever underestimated her. From the day at the stream when only chance had made him the victor, to the night he had realized he had been given a tempestuous and unique beauty, he had been a fool. She would never be cowed, but neither could she lie to herself. She had become his, but despite his seduction of her, the choice to come to him freely had been hers. . . .

And where he had been indifferent, he was now obsessed. He could not believe in love, but he was amazed at the ferocity of the feelings he bore her. He would protect her with his last breath of life, yet he also felt such a rage of possession that he feared he would slay her if he ever thought she harbored even images of another man.

He closed his eyes, feeling absurdly comfortable on the old raggedy furs and the stone simply because her soft flanks rested beside his, touching them. He moved his arm slightly until it rested beneath her breast, and the sound of the now monotonous rain filled his ears and lulled him to sleep.

While the Wolf slept, a village burned on the outskirts of Ulster. Friggid the Bowlegs did not stare at the flames. He looked southward and smiled. The Wolf held Dubhlain; he had the daughter of Aed Finnlaith, a girl rumored to be the isle's most fair. But the Wolf had formed an alliance; he would come. He would die. Destiny would be met. . . .

Niall of Ulster rousted his men to prepare for battle. The newlywed Sigurd wondered irritably what had happened to the Lord of the Wolves as he set about

preparing the warriors of Dubhlain to follow their liege
into battle.

And in the moss-covered forest near Carlingford
Lough, Mergwin stood in the rain looking like a lunatic
with his wet beard and soaked robes flapping about
him. He lifted his arms to the gray sky and whispered
the ancient words of invocation. He called to the
heavens, and he called to the earth. On a small stone
altar, he slashed the throat of a young doe, watching
her brown eyes glaze over, offering up life, offering up
blood.

Mergwin did not think about the past or present. He
fought the cobwebs of his mind to try to understand
the coming evil. But he couldn't see it, nor did he
know when it would strike. He only knew that it had
been born in the night, nurtured to fruition in the day.

He cried to the land and the sky to help him, to the
trees and the foliage and the earth to bear witness for
him. He offered his sacrifice of blood, and gave his
herbs to the wind and his doe to the earth. He prayed
to the powers that swept the world.

He prayed for Erin.

Olaf leaned on an elbow, and he watched her as he
spoke while his finger swept little lines over her ribs
and lean belly. "The gods have always been fated to
die, you see. From the very beginning."

She had told him that Rig had entertained her with
a tale of the beginning of the gods, had said there was
an end, but had not explained it.

"Surt will lead the forces from Muspell, as has
always been planned. The great battle will take place
on the field Vigrid. The beginning of the end will be
signaled by the coming of three terrible winters. A
great earthquake will shake the mountains, the sun
will be eaten by one wolf, and the moon by another.
Fenrir, the wickedest of fire-breathing wolves, will
swallow up Odin. But then Odin's son, Vidarr, will
slay Fenrir. Thor, who is always fighting the Midgard

serpent, will finally slay him, but step back nine paces himself and die from the venom. Surt will kill Frey." He paused to smile at her a moment. "Frey is really our fertility god."

"I know." She laughed indignantly. "Rig told me."

"Anyway, then Surt shall set the entire world on fire."

"And the earth and everything will end?" Erin asked with a frown. It seemed now, in the back of her mind at least, that Rig had had a reason to cut his tale short, for her to hear it elsewhere.

"Yes, and no," Olaf told her, smiling again, then turning his idle gaze to the spot on her midriff his absent fingers traveled. "The fire will destroy everything, but in time the world will grow green and fresh again. The sun will leave a daughter to bring light and heat back to the world, and sons of Odin and Thor will dwell in a place called Idavoll and they will repopulate the world. And Baldr, most loved of the gods who was killed by his brother Hod, will leave the world of the dead and come to Idavoll—along with the brother who killed him. They will, at long last, live in eternal peace."

Olaf saw that she smiled very secretively and sweetly.

"What is that for?" he murmured, tracing her lips.

"Oh . . . nothing, my lord," she murmured. That was what Rig thought she must learn herself, that fighting would destroy, but in its wake one might find peace. She would never see that perfect peace between Viking and Irish. Mergwin had long ago warned that that would not come in her lifetime, nor that of her children, but she could find her own private peace. She would have moments such as this to sustain her when the world went awry.

A bright ray of afternoon sun found its way into the cave and Erin glanced toward the entrance. "The rain has stopped," she said quietly.

It was he who smiled then. "I know," he said,

mischief shading his grin. "It stopped a long time ago."

Their eyes met, and they laughed together. Then Olaf regretfully placed a last kiss on her belly and stood, reaching down to assist her. "We must go back, before Sigurd sends the guards out."

Erin nodded. Their clothing had dried by the fire and they donned it silently, helping one another adjust mantles and brooches with mute agreement.

At the entrance to the cave, he paused and kissed her briefly on the lips, staring searchingly into her eyes for a minute.

Then he swatted her horse on the flank to move it around, hoisted her up, and mounted his own.

As they began the ride back, Erin watched him surreptitiously. She thought what a beautiful man he was, and she thought with a little pain that he was still a stranger. Riding tall with his mantle flowing in the breeze, he was once more the Wolf of Norway, his mind, his heart, closed to her. She could never quite seem to pierce his armor.

He turned to her as they approached the city, and the ice fire was back in his eyes, raging high and blue. "Come!" he shouted. "Something has happened in our absence!"

Startled, Erin gripped her reins as her horse broke into a gallop behind Olaf's stallion. Her hair whipped across her eyes and she was half blinded, but from the crest of a hill, she saw that behind the wall the courtyard was filling with men holding swords, picks, axes, and shields. Men prepared for war.

Why, Erin wondered later, as she looked from her chamber window to the courtyard below as her husband, cousin, and brothers prepared for war, did her fate in life seem to be to watch those she loved leave?

Tears welled behind her lids, but she held them in check. She was the queen of Dubhlain, and when they rode with the coming of dawn, it would be her duty to hold the stirrup cup to Olaf, and send the men off with cheers and the confidence of victory.

She hadn't spoken to him since they had ridden back. In the courtyard the horses, sensing the excitement in the air, pawed and pranced about. Standard-bearers, servants, smithies, and warriors rushed, and Olaf had been completely absorbed in the preparations. Erin was sure he forgot her existence entirely. She couldn't even get much information from Gregory, Leith, or Brice, and Niall she didn't see at all. He spent his time closeted with Olaf.

Preparations continued late into the night. Finally, exhausted from the previous night and from physical weariness and painful anxiety, Erin climbed the stairs to their chamber. She stripped away her clothing and climbed between the linen sheets, pulling the top sheet and furs close around her shivering body.

It didn't seem fair. She had waited so long for peace, and now, just when tranquility had finally begun to settle in her soul, it was being torn away.

She lay awake a long time, then her lids closed heavily over her eyes and she slept.

She didn't wake when he came beside her, but in her sleep she edged closer to his body as he held her, curving to him instinctively like a small kitten. He didn't find much sleep, but he did discover a certain serenity in being beside her.

When she opened her eyes, he was looking at her, and for a moment, a very brief moment that flickered past so quickly it might not have existed, she thought she saw a tenderness in his eyes, a glimpse of the inner man she had never thought to know. Then the moment passed.

He reached out to touch her hair, fanning the ebony locks across her pillow. "I wonder," he said softly, "if you still cherish hopes of my coming in mortal contact with a Danish battle-axe."

She opened her mouth, and the words that almost slipped out were "I love you." But she caught them.

She stared at him silently because she could not give that of herself, not when she had so little of him.

"Fear not," he told her harshly. "I have no intention of dying to please you."

She wanted to tell him she didn't want his death; surely he knew it, he saw all too clearly the power he wielded over her. But it didn't matter as he swept her angrily into his arms. They clung in an abandon that flamed fiercely with passionate desperation, both forgetting his vow of tenderness.

She chattered at Brice and Leith, saying inane little things that their mother might have said, reminding them to sleep in shelter, to watch prolonged wearing of wet clothing, to eat properly. To Niall she said nothing. She kissed him and accepted his bear hug, silently holding her tears.

"It won't be so bad, Princess," Gregory whispered to her as she stepped back from Niall, "because we will know that you are here safe, and there is no scurvy Dane who can best the powers of Niall of Ulster, Aed Finnlaith, and the Wolf of Norway."

Erin tried to smile. "I wish I were going with you, Gregory. It is always hardest to wait."

Gregory smiled. "Your days of glory are past, cousin, and thank God. If something had ever happened to you, it would have been my fault. And Erin, your brothers know. Leith guessed. He told me the night you were married, and he told Niall and Brice. They've never said anything. I think they are very proud of you, but frightened too. If things would have continued, they would have found a way to stop you. So as it stands, we created a legend."

Erin felt tears spring to her eyes. They had known—Leith, Brice, and Niall—and they had kept her secret. It made it so much harder to watch them ride away.

Gregory kissed her on the cheek. "Please don't cry, Erin. We ride with a formidable force. We cannot lose with Olaf, and we will meet with your father's troops inland. We will be home very soon."

"I'm not going to cry, Gregory," she murmured, kissing his cheek. But her face was damp. She brushed away her tears impatiently with her fingers.

The high, keening wail of a battle horn sounded. Erin saw that Olaf was already astride his horse, waiting. She brought the silver chalice to him. He raised it high and drank while the men shouted of victory and their mounts reared excitedly.

Olaf leaned down in his saddle and returned the cup. He touched her cheek, his ice eyes flaming with brooding blue fire. "Take care, Irish," he said softly.

She caught his hand. Lowering her head, she kissed his palm. She did not look up again, lest he see the liquid swimming in her eyes. She stepped back as the river of men and horses began to clang and thunder out of the city.

CHAPTER

16

Aed Finnlaith saw his son by marriage across the stream. The Norwegian Wolf was unmistakable. Tall upon his midnight charger, he appeared to be more than mortal man; his golden hair seemed to catch the sun and radiate its power about him. Even from such a distance, indomitable force and endless energy charged the air about him.

A shiver touched Aed's bones. I am glad that I ride with this man, he thought, for I am too old to ride against him again.

Horns signaled, banners were waved. The Ard-Righ of Tara rode, crossing the shallowest section of the stream, trying not to show the shock created in his aging flesh by the coldness of the water. He greeted Olaf with a brief embrace while still upon his mount, then both men edged their horses back. In turn he greeted his son Niall, for it was his province they rode to defend.

The troops merged and the tedious march began. They followed the inland road for fifty miles, day following day seemingly endlessly. Then made their turn for the coast.

The Danish attacked out of the night in stealthy marauding parties, but their small hit-and-run attacks were firmly and surely pushed back, step by step. Days turned to weeks, weeks became months. Spring rain and slush became summer rain and slush. Still the main body of Friggid the Bowlegs's army eluded them.

In the brief skirmishes they encountered, Aed found himself fighting nearer and nearer his Viking son-in-law, and more and more he came to believe the man was invincible. Just a mighty, rattling growl from his chest could leave the Danes wavering in indecision that cost them their lives, for never once did the Wolf pause upon the field of battle. He did not fight as the berserkrs. He fought coldly, with unerring precision, and yet he fought like a man possessed.

One night as the dead were buried or burned, Aed approached the strange man he still had yet to truly know, offering him a leather gourd of ale as he leaned against a tree trunk, surveying the fields before him while Viking and Irish went about their tasks of burying or burning the dead.

For a moment the two men stood silently, each feeling the coolness of the night, listening to the occasional forlorn call of a night bird. The cooking fires were being lit. Soon, Aed thought, I'll fill my empty belly and take refuge in my tent, easing my weary body for the night. This was one battle where he rode at the front, yet left most of the strategy to Niall and the Wolf. He had watched with admiring curiosity as Olaf had quietly taken second stance to Niall, advising the king of Ulster craftily and therefore teaching the young king much with honor. It was Ulster they defended; therefore, it was Niall's battle. Niall fought for his land; Aed fought to defend his son and the laws of the greater Eire that had given Niall that land. And Olaf fought because he was committed to Aed and, therefore, to Niall. But Aed sensed that far more drove the young powerful Viking.

Aed watched as Olaf wet a parched throat with the ale, then asked forthrightly, "Do you seek out Friggid

the Bowlegs because of Ulster, or do you seek to
avenge Carlingford Lough?''

The crystal-blue eyes fell on him, then drew away,
staring ahead once more. ''Both, High King.'' He was
silent for a minute, then gazed idly at Aed once again.
''And more,'' he added softly. He returned the leather
gourd to Aed and turned into the trees.

In the moss cool of the forest, Olaf sat on the ground
and leaned his head back against a fallen log. He rode
most of the time with no thought of anything but the
warfare he engaged in, but there were times, nights
like this, when he longed to return to Dubhlain. He
wanted a scalding bath, a pleasant meal, the evocative,
gentle touch of his wife.

He scowled with the thought. There had been
whores along the way; women who entertained the
men and let them laugh and boast of their prowess as
they rode out the weary days. But he had been unable
to allow himself to enjoy the physical soothing of a
woman. He had noted with some amusement that Aed
Finnlaith politely and aloofly steered away from such
entertainment, and he had heard that Aed was eternally loyal to his queen. But the Ard-Righ was an
unusual man.

Thinking of Aed brought Erin to mind. Olaf couldn't
bear the thought of his Irish spitfire in the arms of
another man. Just that image in his mind could make
him roar and snarl for a day. But it was the fact that
she was his, a king's property, that made him feel so
protective. He was, he realized, a very possessive
man, one who would defend all that was his to the
death.

But he didn't really worry about the wife he had
come to know so briefly. He had left Sigurd in charge
of Dubhlain, with strict instructions that his wife was
to be carefully guarded and watched. He didn't believe
that she would attempt to escape, but he didn't know
what went on behind her brilliant green eyes. He had
awakened her passions, yes. In his arms she became a

wild and wanton witch, giving him a pleasure that cleansed his spirit and heart, taking away the dark hauntings that tortured his spirit. But he wondered if she still hated him, if she wouldn't willingly seek out a lover for the purpose of cuckolding the "Viking barbarian" she had been forced to accept in marriage.

His fists clenched together as he thought of her, then he slowly released them. She would find little chance to place horns upon him with Sigurd around, and she was a princess of Tara, something she never forgot. It was unlikely she would stoop to an affair that might be discovered by others.

He closed his eyes, and he could see her before him, her cloak of silky black hair falling over the full curves of her breasts, her long legs moving toward him in a lithe, seductive walk. . . . That picture, he thought with a sigh, is why I cannot seek companionship with a whore.

But it was another picture that drove him on in battle. Grenilde. His golden beauty, his love. He thought of her, then frowned as the picture of her wavered in his mind. He sought to see blue, sparkling eyes and all he could summon were a set of emerald green.

He swore softly. The Irish minx who wanted his head on a blade was a witch. A witch who could be soft, who had laughed with him, loved him, come to him. . . .

"The king of Dubhlain is pensive tonight."

Olaf's eyes flew open and he cocked a brow high and grimly at the insolence of the interruption. He stared with a dark scowl on his face at the robed and bearded old man they called Mergwin who had come upon him without a sound.

"The king of Dubhlain wishes to be alone," Olaf said curtly.

The Druid was undaunted. "There is a haze of light about you, Viking," Mergwin said as he speculatively gazed at Olaf. "If you are to die in battle, it will not be soon."

"That should please my wife," Olaf said dryly.

Mergwin shrugged, stroking his long beard pensively. "You seek to kill Friggid the Bowlegs, my young lord Wolf. I would warn you. It is destiny that you will one day meet. And one of you must die. Perhaps you will slay him. Yes, it is quite possible. But when his death comes, it alone will not give you what you seek."

"Oh? And what is that, Druid?"

"The return of your soul. You must find that in your own life, Wolf of Norway, not in another man's death."

Olaf stood and shook the leaves from his mantle. "So, Druid, you say I will not slay him soon. Do you suggest then that I allow Friggid to continue to haunt these shores, to live to slay me and others upon another occasion?"

Mergwin ignored the sarcasm. "Oh, no, Friggid must die. He is not of the land, Wolf, and the breeze whispers that you are. You must keep seeking him, fighting him."

"Oh?" Amused now, Olaf cocked a brow again.

The Druid smiled. "Look at yourself, my lord. Your mantle is Irish, as is your robe. You speak to me in my tongue. I would hazard a guess that you oftentimes must think to speak in your own. Yes, Viking, you are of the land. You wish to take it, yet it will assimilate you, making you and it one and the same."

Olaf laughed. "Perhaps you are right, Druid. But tell me, my friend, how is it you feel you know these things?"

"I often cast and read the runes for you, Lord of the Wolves."

"The Viking runes?" Olaf inquired with self mockery.

Mergwin merely smiled at the mockery. "I daresay, Olaf the White, that you never set your dragon ship across the sea without the advice of your rune master. Your men would not sail. The Norwegian defeat at Carlingford Lough was foretold by the runes. Even your first meeting with the princess you now call wife.''

Olaf looked at Mergwin curiously.

"Aye, my friend, I know of your meeting with Erin."

"And you did not stop the marriage?"

"No," Mergwin said, smiling slightly. "Your marriage was the destiny of the land."

"Oh," Olaf murmured dryly.

Grinning and feeling curiously lightened by the encounter, Olaf turned to quit the forest. "Lord of the Wolves," the Druid called him back.

Olaf turned with a frown at the tone of his voice.

"The battle will end tomorrow, and the victory will be yours. The rune of the sun, Sowelu, is with you. But watch yourself, my lord, for there is treachery and evil afoot. Tomorrow speaks of danger, yet it goes beyond that. I know not when it will strike again, nor from where, only that it exists and that you must rise above it. Then, and only then, will you find that solace you seek for your soul."

Olaf lifted his brows high again, surprised by the quiet confidence and yet the pleading sound of Mergwin's warning.

"I always take care, Druid," he said softly, not sure if the man was a true prophet or raving lunatic. "I always take care."

One part of Mergwin's prophecy was to come true with astounding accuracy. They had barely broken camp when the troops of Friggid the Bowlegs came upon them in a shocking raid of full force.

Caught between the high ground and the forest, the battle raged in small pockets. Men had to watch carefully to see that they battled foe rather than friend, since the forces quickly became enmeshed.

Olaf saw quickly that Friggid the Bowlegs had reinforced his troops from both Britain and his home shores. The swift attacks along the road had been but a tease compared to the force of men who had been brought to strike from the north.

Morning passed in a rain of clashing steel and spitting blood. Holding a southern ridge with the advantage of a small stream, Olaf noted that Leith and Brice mac Aed fought near him. They were valiant, greeting the Danes with fierce battle cries, and hacking their way ever forward with deliberate determination.

Olaf smiled to himself as he dodged a spearpoint. The throb of victory began to rise in his blood. The Danes were falling back. This was it, the day he would find Friggid the Bowlegs.

With triumph giving renewed vigor to his limbs, he howled ferociously and dove forward into the melee. The Danes, who had been as thick as flies, were thinning to a mere trickle. He heaved his sword and brought down a fire-eyed opponent, then searched quickly for his next victim.

To his horror he saw a Danish battle-axe plummeting toward Leith mac Aed. He roared out a warning; his muscles geared into action. His sword blade pierced through the neck of the accosting berserkr, but all too late. Leith mac Aed, a red stain swamping between his shoulder blades, pitched forward.

Olaf knelt beside him, the battle growing dim in his ears. His troops had pushed forward, and he was alone on the field with the dying youth.

He was accustomed to death, to the screams of the dying, but pain suddenly seemed to lacerate his heart as he thought of the agony this would bring to his Irish ally of Tara—and to his Irish wife.

He hesitated, wondering if he couldn't stop the flow of blood and somehow save the boy.

"You can do nothing, my Lord. Leith of Tara was destined to fall here. You must go on."

Olaf jerked his head up, astounded to see the Druid standing before him again. Mergwin knelt beside Leith. A little chill whispered through Olaf's body. Mergwin had known that Leith would die. . . .

The Druid turned the boy over. Leith opened his

eyes, smiled briefly, grimaced in pain, and rattled his last breath. Mergwin gently closed his glazed eyes. "Go, Wolf of Norway. Your work—your destiny?—for the day is not yet fulfilled."

Olaf rose and took one last look at Leith and then Mergwin. He wondered briefly if the crazed Druid didn't wish him to hurry out and die. He didn't know if he trusted those flaming eyes or not.

But the battle awaited him. He strode over the ridge and down to the sector of trees where the howls and screams of war now vibrated. He moved warily, watching his back, knees bent, sword poised. The battle waged in the trees was dangerous; a neck could be slit from behind and a man could bleed to death before he knew he had been struck.

A fierce roar warned him of attack. He spun lithely and struck, sending his massive sword in an arc, and his opponent crumpled to the ground, a look of shock replacing his snarl.

The battle raged through the afternoon. With the coming of dusk, the Danes had been pushed eastward, almost to the ocean. Olaf again found himself on a ridge, and again the fly-thick Danes began to fall. He shouted the order to his men to push forward. He sent a squad to flank the left, and another in a right curve to see that the enemy would be crushed between them.

It was then that he turned to see he was alone again except for the Dane who charged him in an effort to take him off guard, the Dane who had led the forces that annihilated the Norwegians at Carlingford Lough, the Dane who had caused Grenilde's death, the death of all that had been life to him—Friggid the Bowlegs.

Olaf jumped aside with barely a second to spare as the honed and bloodied edge of the battle-axe whistled by his shoulder to lodge into the ground. He could have slain Friggid then. He could have slipped his sword into his back, but he wanted to kill the Dane face to face. He smiled and stepped back, facing the filthy red-haired, pockfaced Dane.

"Get your weapon, Dane. I want to stare into your eyes when you die."

Friggid returned the glacial smile. "So be it, Wolf. Down to the two of us. The only end." He raised his axe. "You will drink to my life in Valhalla tonight as you sup with the dead!"

He made a mighty rush forward. Olaf warded off the blow with his sword. Steel clashed; two mighty arms shuddered and the men snarled as they broke apart again. Olaf made a swipe at the Dane. He cut his flesh, but the Dane dropped and rolled, playing for time. Olaf followed him again. Friggid threw a handful of mud into Olaf's eyes, temporarily blinding him. He jumped up to deliver his mortal blow, but Olaf sensed the wind of his blade and warded it off with the steel of his sword. The sword shuddered and flew from his hands.

With his vision clearing, Olaf saw the Dane coming for him again. He jumped high to elude a blow to his legs. The heavy axe brought Friggid's weight careening downward, but he was up quickly. Olaf realized he was playing cat and mouse without a weapon. He backed away from the Dane, avoiding the quick succession of blows by agility alone. Then suddenly his sword was thrown before his feet. He knew not from whence it came, nor did he care. He dove to retrieve it.

Friggid shrieked in a berserkr rage and rushed forward, arcing his axe for Olaf's skull. Olaf dodged at the very last second, feeling his hairs split. But the maneuver was successful. Friggid the Bowlegs was carried away with the force and was sent rolling toward the shelf of foliage. Olaf tore after him, but too late. Two Danes rushed into the fray, allowing their leader to escape. Olaf battled both men, raging that Friggid was a coward not to keep the battle man to man, one on one. He slew both the Danes.

Victorious, he had taken the day, but he hadn't taken Bowlegs. He felt empty and drained.

Something rustled in the trees, and he hunched low

and raised his sword again, his eyes alertly darting through the trees. He saw only a patch of white disappearing into the depth of the forest—a patch of a long white robe.

He smiled slowly with wonder and glanced at the sword that had been so opportunely returned to him. He lifted it high in the air and allowed the dying sun to reflect on it. "Thank you, Mergwin," he whispered softly. "Thank you for life."

Some of the emptiness left him and he felt strength return to his drained limbs. He laughed aloud. "Yes," he said softly. "Thank you, my strange friend, for I am very glad to be alive."

Brice mac Aed would allow no one near Leith. He sat against an oak, cradling the body of his brother to his chest, tears streaming down his cheeks. He smoothed the hair from Leith's brow, talking to him, sometimes laughing.

Not even Niall of Ulster, grief drawing his own countenance tight, could separate his living sibling from the dead Leith for proper burial. The Viking forces had long since decided the fierce young Irishman should be left alone to handle his grief; they had gone to tend to their own. But the Irish priests were concerned. They demanded that the body be turned over to them so that Leith's soul might join that of Christ in heaven.

Such was the scene when the Irish High King discovered the death of his son. He did not attempt to confront Brice, he merely stood in the clearing, feeling as if his heart were as brittle as his bones and shattering. Leith. The easygoing one. The one with the crystal laugh. The son who could step in between serious Niall and wild Brice and say a few simple, logical words to cool both rising tempers. Leith. Aed closed his eyes as the pain shuddered through him. He tried to tell himself that he was a lucky man. He was the Ard-Righ of Ireland; he had spent most of his years in battle. He had fathered ten children, and a miracle had allowed each of his offspring to reach adulthood. His sons had been fighting for years, except for Mikel, who trained with the guard at Tara and Shean and Galbraith, who had long ago taken Holy Orders.

He had ten children but that fact did not diminish the pain of losing this son, this special, unique individual.

But he was the Ard-Righ, the leader of men who had fought long and hard for him; men who had given sons of their flesh to the land. He could not show his grief, but neither could he condemn the son who cradled his brother. He approached Brice slowly and placed his hand on his shoulder.

"He was your brother, Brice," Aed said softly, "and he was my son. I would take him from you now."

For a moment Brice held tight to his bloodied burden, then he met the sorrow of his father's eyes.

Aed took his dead son into his arms and carried him from the copse of trees. He carried the son who in life had stood taller, broader than he, and he did not falter.

He brought him to his tent, where he tenderly bathed the dirt from his face, the trail of dried blood that marred his lip. He shrouded his child lovingly in silk, then he gave him up to the priests.

On a distant cliff overlooking the valley copse where the men of the Norse and Irish alliance buried their dead, Friggid the Bowlegs stared on the scene with a snarl of hatred twisting his features. His men were dead or largely scattered. Only two score had made it with him to this point where they regrouped and nursed their wounds.

Friggid began to curse aloud, lifting his fist to the air. "Still he lives . . . still the Wolf lives!"

Olaf the White held Dubhlain, held the daughter of the Ard-Righ of Ireland, and held the provincial kings in the palm of his hand. None of these things would matter to Friggid if only the Wolf lay dead.

He stared at the mourning rites before him as the sun sank behind cliff and valley.

Suddenly he turned to his men, a fever in his eyes. "We ride south tonight! Niall of Ulster will head north, the Irish Ard-Righ will journey south and inland. The Wolf will follow the coast southward. We will join the outlaw bands that fester the inlets and be a step ahead of the Norwegian. We will wait for him and create a trap and we will see him journey on to Valhalla from the very door of the city he took from us. . . ."

The Danes cheered on their leader. Friggid smiled. He cared not if they all died or were slaughtered. The Wolf was a sickness with him. Younger, stronger, charismatically golden and powerful. Olaf had to die, had to suffer pain and loss. He had felt mortal blows, the loss of Grenilde, but now he had another woman. A princess, the Ard-Righ's daughter. A weak point? Friggid wondered. One, at least, he would have to keep carefully in mind.

Ashes to ashes. Dust to dust. The prayers droned on as dirt was spilled on Leith's silken shroud.

Aed Finnlaith had never looked so old as he turned from the stretch of land that had been paid for by the blood of his own flesh.

Olaf walked quietly to the sly Irish fox, his old adversary turned ally and friend. There were no tears in the man's eyes, just a weariness and grief that went beyond physical manifestation.

"My men would honor your son and the king of Connaught," Olaf said quietly, offering the Irish king the only sympathy that could be accepted. "They wish to offer their own tributes to great warriors they believe will surely grace the table at Valhalla. I speak with you because I would not offend you, or the priests who are in your service."

The old king gave him a soft smile. "I am not offended, Wolf. I am pleased to know that those who fought alongside Leith and Fennen would grant them that honor. Valhalla . . . heaven? What difference in those words, friend? Please tell your men that they have my blessing to offer up what prayers they would.''

Olaf nodded, understanding more thoroughly than ever the bond of the soul that had drawn him to this leader. He said nothing else, but saluted the Irish king.

The priests grumbled, but the Norse would have their way to assure Leith mac Aed and Fennen mac Cormac a safe and comfortable journey.

Beside Leith and Fennen they buried their swords, food for their journey to the next world, goblets, brooches, knives, and plates. They dug a great crevice to bury horses with complete bridles and trappings so that they might ride across the sky.

The Vikings preferred cremation, sending the spirit through the air, but there were many who adhered to the policy of supplying the deceased with all their needs within the soil, and the Christian priest would never, never allow the Irish prince and king to flame upon a bier.

Aed and his sons disappeared into his tent for the night. It was a time they must have to grieve alone, as Olaf well knew.

But he found himself restless that night, unable to sleep. He stalked a pattern beneath the stars, somewhat startled to realize he could think of nothing but home.

Once it had only been a house. Palatial, magnificent, the birth of a dream itself. A king's royal residence, but still only a house. And now it was home, because there would be warmth there. His wife . . . So many times he had fought his dreams of her in which she welcomed him, her slender arms outstretched, her bewitching emerald eyes liquid and sparkling with pleasure. Her black hair would be cloaked about her; beneath it he would feel the beating of her heart. He had often wakened from his dreams aching and sweating. Still, there had been no solace from the torment; no other woman would do. I am bewitched, he often thought. She was not his long-lost valiant blond beauty; she was a spitfire of Eire, as hard to tame as the land.

Today he had beaten the Danes again. Friggid might live, but his men were ousted from Dubhlain and Ulster and vengeance for Grenilde had been extracted.

Though that feat had not brought him the inner peace he craved, it was a door, closing upon the past. He could look to the future, but he did not know if his dreams of the future with Erin could come true; his proud and beautiful bride could easily hate him still. She could be celebrating each long day of his absence, praying each night for his death upon a Danish pike.

He was a man well aware that passion, love, hate, and pride all knew thin boundaries. He had awakened her sensuality, he could claim her as a woman. She could not deny the fires he could flame, but possessing her made-for-desire body was not the same as possessing her mind, her soul, or her heart.

He had been away so long. Three full moons. They had hardly had a chance to know one another. When he returned, he vowed, they would start over. Their battles had been fought. He would do his best to please her, to include her in all that was his life. He would include himself in hers. He would make her happy, because he craved her like a thirsty man unable to drink his fill of wine. Because he needed her. . . . Because he . . . He closed his eyes. Maybe he did love her. Maybe all had not been lost with Grenilde.

A noise startled him and he glanced up sharply, sensing danger. He breathed fully again and with an irritated shake of his head.

Mergwin, appearing like a combination of some awesome bird of prey and a madman, moved toward him through the trees.

"By all the gods, Druid," Olaf muttered softly, "you do know how to make man's blood pulse."

Mergwin, adjusting his long sleeves with dignity, peered at Olaf haughtily. "I believe, young lord, that your blood pulses just fine—with or without my presence."

Olaf laughed, then quickly sobered, remembering the events of the day. "I am in your debt, Druid. I believe you saved my life."

Mergwin sniffed. "Save your gratitude, Viking. I did not save your life, but gave fate a hand. You would have beaten Friggid anyway." His voice lowered with pain. "Just as young Leith and Fennen were destined to die."

Olaf shook his head impatiently. "Men create their own destiny, Druid."

Mergwin glanced at him knowingly, but shrugged. "As you wish, Norseman."

Olaf chuckled again. "I like you, Mergwin. And I believe men must follow their own stars. You go about your fate—I will create my destiny."

Once more Mergwin shrugged, but Olaf narrowed his keen blue eyes at the man.

"What is it this time, Druid? The battle is over. Tomorrow we ride for home. My enemy ran in defeat. Can you contest that?"

"No." Mergwin shook his head. "It's just that . . ."

"Just what, Druid?" Olaf demanded.

"Nothing. Nothing. Good night, King of Dubhlain." Muttering beneath his breath, Mergwin left Olaf and hurried for his bed.

Olaf remained in the night air a few minutes longer, inhaling the clean scent of earth and air and summer made all the more sweet by victory and the promise of the morrow. Niall would ride on for Ulster; he and Aed could turn south for home.

He ducked into his tent, found his cot, and slept well.

Mergwin did *not* sleep well. He fumed and tossed, knowing that shadows still rode the moon.

CHAPTER

17

There were days during Olaf's absence when it seemed impossible to believe that she had ever become his wife, days when it seemed she surely must have dreamed the time that passed between them. On those mornings Erin would ride out to the bluff that overlooked the sea and she would try to remember his features twisted into a gentle smile, the tense and exciting set to his countenance when his ice-fire eyes blazed out his need. She tried to recall the day when he had spun ancient Norse tales for her, and she liked to dream that he had come to feel something for her.

But most of the time she was faced with reality. She was his wife, and though the Brehon laws protected women from being mere chattels, Olaf didn't necessarily follow the Irish laws unless they were convenient. In his eyes she was property, and as personal property, he would care for her, protect her, and defend her. He would guard her jealously, and she knew her life could go one way or the other in almost a perfect split. If she obeyed his decrees, he would see that she was respected as he had promised her father. If she stepped out of line . . . She didn't know how far his

anger could take him, only that there was a cold and
relentless side to him. When he chose he could lock
himself away behind the cold blue steel of his eyes and
judge remorselessly.

Bede had returned to her convent the day after the
men rode out, and Erin had sorely missed her sister.
She had wondered at first if she might feel entirely
alien in the Norse city, but Moira somehow managed
to be there exactly when she needed her. And though
the great hall seemed very quiet indeed with all the
warriors, Norse and Irish, gone, the evening meal was
still celebrated with the skeletal guard crew remaining.
Sigurd kept things well in hand, and Erin was never
afraid in her own home.

The troops had been gone just over a month when a
new reality dawned on Erin, one that she first attempted to ignore and then accepted with a strange
combination of excitement and trepidation.

She was with child, and as each day passed, she
became more certain. She felt queasy in the morning,
exhausted at night.

As she lay awake at night, she tried to think of what
it would mean, and wondered at her thoughts. A
Viking . . . she was going to have a Viking child. . . .
No matter how she forced those words through her
mind, it mattered little. The child she carried was his,
the Wolf's. A child to grow to tower above men as his
sire did, strong, and beautiful.

Would he be pleased? she wondered. Didn't all men
crave sons? Or had he lost that desire when he had
lost Grenilde?

The thinking and worrying might have driven her
mad, but Erin could, at times, pretend that she had
never encountered the Vikings at all. Each morning
she rode out of the city walls and raced along the cliffs
by the sea, as if she were a young girl again, a child
with no care but to spend her days in freedom, except
that Sigurd, Erin noted, always rode behind her.

As she rode one morning Erin was startled to see a
woman standing on the cliffs. A strange tremor shook

her, for the woman stood exactly where she had stood the day Olaf had come to her, the day before he had ridden away.

Erin's heart made a little thump and seemed to stand still. She strained her eyes against the wind and the salt spray of the rugged coastline. It was Mageen, and she was standing precariously close to the edge. . . .

With little thought, Erin dug her heels into her mare's flanks and raced across the distance. Mageen did not turn at the pounding hoofbeats, nor did she turn as Erin dismounted and approached her. Erin realized suddenly that her old adversary had not seen or heard her; she appeared in a trance as she stared down the jagged rock to the sea.

"Mageen?" Erin said hesitantly.

There was no response from the pale-faced woman. As Erin watched, Mageen took another step toward the cliff. Instinctively Erin leaped toward her, hurtling them both to the ground, and rolling away from the threat of the ledge.

Mageen's eyes finally registered coherence as they locked with Erin's anxious ones, staring deeply as Erin righted herself to a sitting position beside her— carefully keeping hold of Mageen's wrist. Mageen's eyes offered no gratitude. "Why did you stop me?" she asked softly.

"You were about to kill yourself!" Erin exploded. She noted now that Mageen's beautiful hair lacked its usual luster, that the once superbly voluptuous body was almost emaciated. Her face had changed the most shockingly. Where her eyes had once been rich with bold invitation and laughter, they had become hollow and forlorn, like those of a hunted animal.

"It is best," Mageen said listlessly. She closed her eyes and then stared at Erin again. "You always win, don't you, Erin of Tara? This is but your victory. For you the gold and jewels and crowns, and you but speak a word and I have naught. Even the whores, beggars, and thieves turn from me."

"What?" Erin murmured weakly.

Mageen was spared an immediate answer for a horse was pounding toward them. Sigurd, always the watch dog, was coming after Erin. "Erin! You must come away from the cliff!"

Sigurd was annoyed as he left his horse to come to her side. "I will take care of this. Do you know how close you came to hurtling over the rocks, my lady? Olaf would be furious with us both—"

Erin waved Sigurd's hand aside as he reached to help her to her feet. She couldn't even care that the giant Viking was yelling—actually yelling at her—in front of Mageen. "Leave me be, Sigurd, I am not going over any cliffs. And I will take care of this myself."

Sigurd hesitated, scowling. "A few minutes only, Erin. I will await you by the copse." He remounted his horse and rode the distance, his eyes still on her. Erin watched him with exasperation, then returned her full attention to Mageen. "I never sought your death," she told the other woman. "I never sought to harm you—just to . . ." Erin hesitated, staring into the face that reflected a misery deeper even than any she had ever known. "Mageen, you must know that I did not wish to come here. To lose all respect along with my freedom was more than I could bear."

Mageen closed her eyes again and laughed hollowly. "My lady, were I in your position, I would have torn out my hair and eyes, but not for respect. You see, I loved Olaf." Her eyes opened and focused on Erin's. She spoke again softly. "I wonder if you too, my lady, have not found yourself loving against your will."

Erin flicked her own lashes over her eyes and ignored the statement. "My lord Olaf is not a man worth dying for, Mageen. He loves no one."

Mageen's hand fluttered from the ground and fell back to it. "You do not understand, my lady. I have been barred from the great hall. The merchants will not sell to me. The warriors do not seek out my cottage. There is not a man or woman in the town who will offer me a nod in greeting."

Erin stood up and extended her hand to Mageen. The other woman watched it for a moment, then turned her eyes to Erin's hesitantly.

"Take my hand, please, Mageen," Erin said quietly. "You have taught me how it is possible to use responsibility lightly. I must hold to my stand," Erin said, smiling ruefully. "I was forced into my marriage, but I still cannot allow you a part of my husband. But I knew not of my own cruelty, and it weighs heavily upon me that I might have cost you what is precious and totally yours—your life. If you wish a friend within the town, you have one. Me. And you will come to the great hall this evening and all will know that you are welcome."

Mageen slowly accepted Erin's hand, still staring at the princess incredulously. She stood and finally smiled. "My lady, I thank you."

"Tell me, Mageen—" Erin paused awkwardly for a moment. "Do you do anything other than . . . I mean, do you have any particular talents—"

Mageen chuckled softly, and Erin was glad to see a touch of the woman's saucy humor return to her listless eyes. "Do you ask me if I can be other than a whore, my lady? Aye. I cook and sew and keep a hearth as well as any. Long ago I learned that men were fickle creatures, quick to cast their eyes astray and seek another. It seemed wiser, and more profitable, to be the woman men sought rather than that poor creature they left behind to mend and clean and serve."

Erin shrugged. Mageen's sentiments weren't terribly different from her own, even if their direction took a slightly different course. "Not all men are like that, Mageen," she said quietly. "My father has never swerved from my mother. But that is not what I want to speak to you about. Moira of Clonntairth grows heavier daily with her child. Would you care to serve her? She is a kind and gentle lady who offers no judgment."

Mageen lowered her eyes, trembling. "Aye, my

lady. I would be glad to care for Moira, and the babe that comes."

"Then it is settled," Erin murmured. "We will return, for the wind grows blustery and the air cold."

"You must ride, I will walk back."

"Nay, you may sit ahead of Sigurd. He will take you to Moira."

Erin turned purposefully to gather the reins of her horse and wave toward Sigurd. Mageen halted her momentarily with a hand upon her shoulder. "Erin of Tara, I thank you heartily. You offer me friendship, and I tell you this: I have been but a whore, but I offer in return the full loyalty of my heart and, if ever needed, the life you have saved."

Erin flushed. "I have but repaired the damage I did of my own careless hands."

"Nay, much more." Mageen hesitated a moment, then continued. "You must also care for yourself. A first child is oft uncomfortable to carry."

Erin glanced nervously at her mare and patted the animal's sleek neck. "Is it so obvious then already?" she asked huskily.

"Nay," Mageen replied with a surprising wisdom in her eyes. "I see it, as I see that you too have come under the spell of the Wolf. Guard well his child, Erin, for surely that will bind his love."

Erin said nothing as Sigurd rode up to them once more. She expected further disapproval for her actions, but the man was quiet as he accepted Mageen upon his horse.

Sigurd was thinking only that the queen was certainly her father's cub, truly the child of the wise and indomitable Aed Finnlaith.

Messages had come to the city from the front, so Erin knew that the combined forces rode northward. She was assured that her husband was fine and her father healthy. Those who reported to her also knew that the king of Ulster still rode well, but of her brothers and Gregory, she heard nothing. All she could do was pray and hope that the Danes would soon be encountered and beaten and that the troops would come home.

Though it became harder and harder to believe that her time with Olaf had existed, Erin discovered more thoroughly each day how she missed the man who was both intimate and stranger. Through sleepless nights she thought of him, splaying her fingers over the bed where he should lie. She wondered how he filled his nights, and writhed with the agony of thoughts that he found willing women along the way, women whom he held, women who touched his golden head, crushed themselves to his broad shoulders, availed themselves of his compelling touch.

She would awake exhausted in the mornings to tell herself she was a fool and bemoan the fact that she had been born a woman. She offered him all, while as a man, he expected her loyalty as his due while he . . . She didn't know what he did. She only knew that he would half kill her if he suspected her of disloyalty, and that her own father would approve of his action. It wasn't fair. She knew now too that he distrusted her, that Sigurd was always near because he watched her for Olaf.

Erin spent her days with Moira, sewing tiny things for her friend's child, while keeping her own condition a secret between herself and Mageen.

She kept wondering how Olaf would feel, and how she would tell him. When he did return, would he want her as he had, or would he decide that he had tamed his wild Irish wife and discover he had little use for her?

How would she greet him? Surely he couldn't be displeased with her. Everything had run smoothly in his absence. Sigurd could report that she had cared for his home well and made no attempts whatever to thwart him.

It was midsummer when she was awakened by a roar and cheering from the courtyard below. Dressing hastily, Erin raced down the stairway and outside, anxiously demanding to know what had happened.

Sigurd forgot all protocol and lifted her high off the ground to plant a kiss on her forehead. "It is done!" He explained, "The Danes have been defeated at Lord Olaf's hands and the troops now ride for home."

Erin was dizzy with relief, but still frightened. "My father?"

"Your father lives," Sigurd said. His eyes clashed quickly with those of the young messenger who had brought the message. In the days that had passed, Sigurd had discovered himself growing fond of the wild beauty his king had married and whom his wife loved. He saw no reason to tell her before Olaf's return that she had lost a brother.

"Oh, thank God!" Erin murmured. She glanced up at Sigurd with her emerald eyes alight. "I must plan, we must prepare a great feast—"

"Whoa, Irish!" Sigurd laughed. "They have a long march home. It will be many days before they appear!"

"Still," she murmured, "there are things which I must attend to. . . ."

Her heart began to beat painfully, and tingling ripples began to scurry up and down her spine. He was returning . . . he was coming home. . . .

She was anxious and scared. She closed her eyes, remembering the rough magic that had flared between them that last time they were together. She could remember his harsh words, how he still believed she wished to see him fall beneath a Danish battle-axe. Erin started shaking again. No matter what his feelings, the angers that lurked in his heart, whether he took her in tenderness or tempest, he was conscious of her always, kindling her fires as he did his own.

Had their child been conceived that last time? Or the very first? Or when they had met at the cliffs while the rain raged its deluge? It seemed so long ago.

How he would greet her on his return caused the fear she had so stoically learned to control to rise again. He could be the coldest stranger. His eyes could blaze with the frosts of ice as well as the flame of fire. He was still the Viking conqueror. Always a stranger.

But despite his words of mistrust and her fear, she already ached for him, trembling with the anticipation born of her memories.

One night, unable to sleep, Erin slipped from bed, discarded her nightgown to change into a robe and scamper down the stairway. Perhaps if she could sit before the fire in the great hall awhile, drink another cup of ale, then maybe she could sleep.

But as her footsteps carried her toward the hall, she paused. She could hear Sigurd's voice, and though he attempted to mute it, his voice carried. He was speaking with the captain of the Dubhlain guard, and he sounded worried. Clutching the wall that parted the staircase from the great hall, she curiously tiptoed closer.

"If we could get the Irish of Meath to trust us and ride with us, I would feel no worries. But our troops are skeletal as it is. We cannot pull all of our men away from the city. It would be left vulnerable. I don't know what to do. Olaf is usually always on guard against an attack, but he will not be expecting a scurvy lot of outlaws to spring upon him after he has bested Friggid's troops."

The young captain said something Erin couldn't hear.

"By the blood of Odin!" Sigurd suddenly railed. "I don't know. Perhaps these Irish do not realize our king rode for an Irish king! Or perhaps they don't care about their own kings! But if they refuse to ride with us to rout out these outlaws, then I fear the outlaws might very well attack Olaf and his troops."

Erin felt a chill stealing over her. All this time—all this war—and now the troops, battle-weary and finally victorious, were about to fall into a rat's nest.

She closed her eyes and leaned heavily against the wall. The Irishmen of whom Sigurd spoke had to ride

with the Norsemen! Her father's life was at stake,
Gregory, Brice, with whom she had spent half her
childhood hours quarreling, Leith—so calm and judicial, just like Niall, keeping the peace, mimicking the
fights until she and Brice would laugh and hug and
make up, and Olaf—the husband she awaited, the
Viking whose child she carried, the man she awaited
to share his bed again.

No, it was her father she worried about, and Gregory, and her brothers. . . .

She swallowed sickly, straining to hear the conversation again. Sigurd had been told that the Irish troops
whose aid they needed to enlist were half a day's ride
up the coast. The outlaws were not a hour's ride
farther north. They had received no answer from the
Irish except that they awaited a sign from Saint Patrick. Sigurd would not know until he went into battle
whether he would receive the aid he needed so badly.
If only the outlaws could be drawn out from their lair!

Erin was barely breathing. She knew a sign that the
Irish would accept. A lady in gold appearing before
them. The Golden Warrioress.

I cannot, she thought, I cannot ride again. . . . I am
terrified.

She shook so badly that she held to the wall to
remain standing. The situation had to be desperate for
Sigurd to be worried. The confident, undauntable general was frightened.

I cannot, she thought again. Erin sagged against the
wall, thinking of her father and how she had last seen
him, telling Aed she would never forgive him. If he
were to die, it would be herself she could never, ever
forgive. . . .

Erin heard the chairs creaking suddenly in the great
hall. She turned, fleeing up the stairway and back to
her room. She leaned against the heavy door, breathing heavily. Oh, Gregory! she thought. You were
wrong. The Golden Warrioress must ride again.

Erin began to plan as she moved around the room,
clenching her hands together. She would sneak out

with the next coming of night. Sigurd, her watch dog, would not notice her absence. She would keep him and Moira drinking late at the table, and then surely Sigurd would be safely cloistered with his wife, since he must then rise and prepare his own troops. By the time the Norse arrived, the Golden Warrioress would have led the Irish in an ambush against the outlaws. Then Sigurd would come in time to back her up. But would she and Sigurd be successful in flushing out the enemy?

Mergwin! Erin thought suddenly. If only she could see her old Druid friend. He could advise her, warn her. . . . Suddenly she stopped her pacing. The runes. She could cast the runes and try to foretell if Olaf was in danger. Her husband, she had fathomed, looked caustically on the oracles. But as a Viking commander, he kept a set of runes, for many of his men would make no move without the wisdom of the engraved stones.

She reached for the bag. One stone, Mergwin had told her, would guide a decision. But would she read the message of the stone correctly?

Erin reached into the catskin bag Olaf kept and withdrew a single stone with uneven slashes crossing. She closed her eyes tightly together. It was the stone the Norwegians called Nauthiz, a rune of pain. She tossed the stone away from her, trying to convince herself that she, like Olaf, did not believe in oracles.

"My destiny is my own!" she whispered aloud. But fear riddled through her again. Olaf could be ambushed. She would have to ride.

"I shake and tremble when I can perhaps change things," she murmured. Her decision was made.

Erin slowly calmed herself, and then it all suddenly felt right. It was so terribly hard to be a woman, used for barter, taken but not loved by a husband. Humiliated by his superior strength.

Though she had discovered she loved the bronze giant who was her possessor, she could still rail against the fates that had left her powerless to his mercy, praying he did not discover the love that would give him even greater advantage over her.

She should be glad to ride as the Golden Warrioress again, to have, just for a moment, a time of soothing power once more. And to see death and destruction once more, she reminded herself.

It couldn't be helped, and she forced herself not to think about the terror.

She half smiled a moment. If all went well, she would perhaps admit to Olaf that she was the famed Irish warrioress.

Her smile faded. She could never do that. Like her father, he wouldn't be pleased. He would be furious that she had risked his child—if he wanted his child. . . .

A sob caught in her throat. He had to want his child because she wanted it so much! Her hand moved protectively to her lower abdomen. A boy with golden hair and stunning blue eyes, a Norse giant of a man, yet intrinsically Irish. An Irish cub of the Wolf. And she could love him freely as she was so afraid to do with the father. Her child—oh, dear God, she was risking her child! And she wanted the baby so badly. . . .

No! The risk was minimal—and necessary. She would be careful.

"I am afraid," she whispered aloud.

But she reminded herself her countrymen were out there, men willing to die to keep alive an alliance made by her father and her husband. An alliance that had made her first a prisoner of the Wolf, then of her own heart.

CHAPTER

18

"We attack just as the dawn breaks!" Friggid announced to his scurvy men. They were a ragged lot indeed. Vultures rather than men. The poor remains of his own troops, and the outlaws he had banded together—Danes, Irish, and Norwegians, following no king or loyalty except to themselves. Scavengers of the land. But perfect for his purpose. They fought viciously for whatever they could grab.

"The Wolf is camped on the shoreline by the cliffs. We have but to take him by surprise."

Friggid turned his gaze to the road and stroked the ragged length of his beard, tucking the ends more securely beneath his belt. As he stood there one of the Irishmen came to him, a pleased snarl displaying a row of broken and discolored teeth.

"Have you a wish for an edge, Danish jarl?" the man asked.

"I've always a wish for an edge. Speak up, man."

"Through the trees I have spied a woman riding, wearing golden armor. One against whom I seek vengeance, for she led a raid against a troop of Danes with whom I rode two years hence. She is the one the

Irish call Golden Warrioress. She must seek out the
forces of the king of Meath. We must stop her and
perhaps use her, Dane. If she believes we are the
Irish. . . ."

Friggid grinned fully. "We can allow that famed
Irish warrioress to lead us against the Wolf, and the
alliance will be sadly shaken." Friggid began to laugh.
Justice. At long last justice, against the Norseman,
against the fickle Irish.

He turned to shout to the lot of men once more.
"Hide all your trappings that are Viking! If you speak
not the Irish tongue, speak not at all. We await a lady
in gold!"

Erin was well aware that she was engaged in a risky
business. She kept Sigurd and Moira long at the table,
seeming to drink as much as they while toasting the
prowess of the kings of Dubhlain and Tara. She stumbled up the stairway yawning and did such a magnificent job that Moira, giggling, insisted that Sigurd carry
her the rest of the way.

Then she waited, feeling time creep by.

Among the trunks of haphazardly packed belongings
brought with her an eternity ago when she didn't
believe her father would even deign to sup with a
Norseman, she found the delicate coat of gold-gilded
armor and the helmet and faceplate. She rolled them
carefully into fur bunting and silently crept from her
chamber.

She didn't take the time to saddle a horse for fear
she might be heard. She slipped a bridle into the mouth
of a big bay gelding and covered herself in a huge
woolen cloak so that she might wave her way past the
guards at the gate like any peddler.

Meticulous in her plan to keep all possible chance
of discovery minimal, she rode inland first to a small
farming village crested against a hill. There she offered
the sleepy farmer a bracelet of gold to trade her a
horse for her own, retrade it when she returned, and
to forget she had ever come in the first place.

It was only as she rode through the fields and trails to the coastal road that fear began to plague her. Would she be able to get away with it this time?

Erin gave her head a little shake and mentally squared her shoulders. No one could possibly suspect her of being the Golden Warrioress. She had never been near Dubhlain during any of her exploits. But what if she was forced to reveal her identity when she joined forces with Olaf?

Her teeth began to chatter. It was one thing to dream that she met her husband on equal terms, but quite another to accept the fury that would surely fall her way if she faced him in the light of day. No, whatever happened, she would meet him with her head held high.

Then she began to worry that her ploy to attract the invaders might not work. Perhaps they had already heard of her approach. But that was unlikely. These were outlaws, and the Golden Warrioress had not roamed the land for some time now, and in all that time, she had not wielded her sword. It had lain untouched with her things.

She grew ever more nervous with the coming of the dawn, yet she continued her keenly attentive journey north, hearing every crackle of the trees, every whisper of the wind. As pink streaks trekked across the sky, paling the black of night to dawn's gray, she saw ahead of her the signs of a camp; smoke from a dying fire, broken branches within the foliage, the occasional print of a hoof in the dust.

She had no intention of going too near the men of Meath. She planned only to allow them to see her, and she would ride ahead, finding the outlaw camp, luring the would-be murderers out. But before she did that, she would assure herself that these men were Irish.

Dismounting from her horse, she crept quietly through the foliage, stepping so softly upon the earth that no twig snapped. By the early gold and pink light she felt herself begin to breathe more easily. These men were indeed Irish. Only the Irish would fight with

the aprons of leather and the weapons set before the
smoking fires. Surely the outlaws Sigurd had spoken
of were Norse, Danes probably, with only a few traitorous Irish and Norwegians in their ranks.

Erin hurried back to her horse and, finding a small
alcove within the foliage, rested as she awaited the full
coming of day. Then it was time. She adjusted the
golden helmet and faceplate and mounted her horse
and rode through the camp.

A heavyset warrior raced up to her and quickly
explained the location of the outlaws. Erin nodded her
understanding, waited for the Irish band to mount, and
once more started north with the troop behind her.

They rode as the sun began to creep up in the sky,
casting a golden glow over the summer day, and before
they came upon the second camp, Erin began to
understand her father as she never had before.

It was the land that he loved, and this was the land.
Rich and verdant in her summer cloak of green, the
trees full of life, the air fresh and vibrant. This was the
land, this beauty. This emerald of hill and field, this
vibrant color of sky and nearby sea and growing,
blooming flowers. This was their dream. . . .

She was so lost in her sensitivity to the morning
shrills of the birds and the glistening of drying dew
drops upon the foliage that she almost stumbled on the
signs of the outlaw camp. It was east of the road, set
on the beach of an inland cove that was perfect for her
method of operation. Vast caves and boulders framed
the coves—perfect lairs in which to hide the Irish
troops who would fall upon the outlaws.

She motioned to those following her, pointing out
their destination and signaling them to move out in
small numbers. The horses were left behind as men
began to creep belly down through the remaining
scattered foliage until they reached the refuge of the
cliffs. Erin watched their progress and waited until all
were ready and carefully positioned. Then she began
her own crawl to the highlighted cliffs. She remained
belly down as she carefully climbed the jagged stone,

painfully aware of the sound of her own breathing, of the hot feel of the sand and pebbles beneath her groping fingers.

At the top of the cliff of her choice, she saw that the camp was far larger than she had expected. She wondered sickly about the battle to follow and wished fervently that the sun wasn't striking her eyes so ferociously. It was difficult to see, to truly assess the enemy.

She took a deep breath, fighting back a wave of terror that was nauseating, wishing desperately that she had never struck upon the morning's path. But it was too late for cowardice. Irish men surrounded her; Irish men ready to fight, willing to die.

She stood up, brandishing her sword high and in circles. She saw the men beginning to mill about the camp look up, seeing her, a figure in gold upon the cliff, and the reaction was as always. They were puzzled; they pointed her out to one another. Then they began to shout and grab weapons and run in the direction of the cliffs.

She ducked back to the ground, throwing herself to the hard and dusty stone, her heart racing. Now it was time for her to disappear. But before she could creep down the stone, she realized something was wrong.

The enemy was not rushing for a blind attack. Someone was shouting that it was a trap; the cliff was being carefully surrounded rather than charged. Then the sound of clashing steel came to her too quickly. The battle had already begun.

She had to get down the cliff. It would be suicide to be trapped there. She began a careful shimmy, watching the earth beneath her the best she could. The sounds of howls and steel and thunder were coming from the east, and she could only surmise that the Irish were retreating, seeking out their mounts and attempting to vanish into the summer lush forests.

She saw the sandy earth beneath her feet and jumped the last short distance, gripping her sword tightly. But before she could run, she saw that she was about to be met by an opponent.

It had been a long time since she had practiced with a sword. Too long, she thought with belated remorse, and the steel-clad frame that came after her own was a large one. Weight! she reminded herself desperately. Think of his weight. Seek only to escape him, to run.

Desperately she fought off the sword blows of the tall and heavy warrior. Pure desperation kept her moving, spinning, ducking, leaping, parrying, returning shattering blow with shattering blow. Desperation alone allowed her to entice the warrior to strike out at her and meet the cleft of the stone cliff instead, momentarily lodging his weapon. All she needed was a moment, enough time to run; but looking up, she found that she was faded by another warrior, and shock stabbed through her like a thunderbolt, because the man she faced was her husband.

The steel-cold eyes of the Wolf of Norway bored into her, both searing and freezing her soul. It was only then, in that second in which she stared back in dismay, that she realized she had made a deadly mistake.

The men she had led were the outlaws and Irish. Not Danes. Not Norsemen. Not invaders, but traitors to their own land . . . to her father's alliance. To the Ard-Righ of Ireland, to the Norwegian Wolf. She had joined with the wrong men against her husband.

She thought she had seen him fierce in anger but nothing she knew of him as a man had prepared her for Olaf as a warrior.

The blue steel of his eyes was the same as his towering, knot-sinewed body. It was in the arm that coolly leveled the sword with the emblem of the wolf meticulously carved into the handle. Steel was in the very air that surrounded him, in the golden glow of vibrancy and tension that was his.

He inclined his head slightly. "You have fought a commendable skirmish, lady, but so far you have only played games. Now it is my sword you must meet."

Erin didn't have any more time to reflect upon the tragedy of her foolish actions; she was forced to raise her sword in defense. He was right; so far she had only played games. No matter how she ducked or spun, he was there, and each clash of his steel against hers was more than shattering. He was quick, he was lithe, he was cunning, and staying alive became her only concern.

She noted vaguely that they were watched by a spattering of Vikings, but it meant nothing to her. Someone started to move in but Olaf snapped out that his was a private battle, he was to be left alone. Then she realized that he meant to kill her.

Not even that mattered, because there was nothing to be done. Instinct took over, and even as her strength was sapped with brutal surety, she fought on like a trapped rat, seeking only to survive and prolong her life as long as possible. Even as she fell to her knees beneath the blinding force of his blow against her sword, she sought to ward him off. Not until her sword flew high and away with his next relentless swerve did she accept the fact that all was lost. Sprawled on the dirt with the point of his sword at the pulse in her neck, she closed her eyes and knew that it was too late to plead for mercy, too late for anything but a last glance at the sunshine and a last scent of the salt summer air.

"Dear God, don't!"

It was Gregory's voice. He was screaming; there was a pounding across the ground. "Don't—you can't—"

Olaf spoke, his voice strangely cool and detached, but bitingly in command. "Calm yourself and return to camp. I have no intention of murdering her. Go, all of you."

"But—" It was Gregory, dear Gregory. Gregory who knew Olaf might have slain his wife; Gregory who would feel the urgent, anguished need to defend and protect her.

"Go!" It was the growl of the Wolf in absolute,

furious command. "I have told you she will live. Now leave me."

Erin chanced to open her eyes. The others had obeyed the command. Only Gregory, face contorted with pain, still hedged. Olaf's sword still hovered over her neck. She suddenly became keenly aware of the hard-packed earth beneath her back, of the sand granules that pierced into her flesh, of the sun beating down upon her, of the hard, cold austerity of the golden giant towering over her prone form.

"Olaf—" Gregory pleaded once more.

"I never intended to slay my wife," Olaf spat out with such furious contempt that Erin felt as if she were paralyzed with shock.

"You-you know—" Gregory gasped out.

The sword point moved away from her neck. "Tell me, Gregory, since you insist upon staying," Olaf continued with a deathly cold calm. "What do you Irish do with traitors? I would say that Aed himself, if asked that question, would agree that death was the rightful penalty." He stared down at the ground. "Get up, Erin."

For countless seconds she couldn't move. He reached down suddenly and she stupidly thought that he meant to help her, but he merely ripped the helmet from her head, heedlessly tearing out strands of her hair.

Tears sprang to her eyes, but with her tears came a resurgence to life. She rose with what little dignity she could muster and tried desperately to explain. "I didn't mean to ride against you. I meant to lead an Irish force against the outlaws determined to ambush you—"

His hand snaked out to grasp her hair, his cruel fingers tangled into silken ebony curls.

"Don't!" He ground out harshly. He turned back to Gregory, apparently calm. The only proof of his explosive anger was in his painful grip upon Erin's hair at her nape. "This, my friend, is man's most cunning enemy. A woman. She's beautiful, isn't she, Gregory, this cousin of yours? Her eyes could melt the arctic ice, her hair is the finest spun silk, her face the purest marble, her form as lush as any goddess. And she can smile at you with lips as soft as summer rose petals, but while she's smiling, she's planning your demise. And then, poor lady, she happens to get caught. So what then? Of course, she pleads innocence, and you're supposed to believe because you're so enraptured by the sweet ecstasy of all that feminine beauty—"

"Olaf!" Erin shrieked out. "I didn't . . . I wouldn't go against—"

Her words were cut off by a cry as he roughly jerked her hair, bringing a fresh wave of hot tears to her eyes.

"I promised you once, my lady wife," he grated sarcastically, "that any further trouble from you would result in a heavy toll. I always keep my promises." Staring at her with eyes of ice that were steel against emotion, Olaf tilted his head back and whistled loudly. Seconds later two Norsemen circled the cliffs to stand waiting, fifty feet from them, leading Olaf's magnificent black war charger. Olaf's hand in the air prevented his men from coming close enough to see Erin. The charger moved on to Olaf alone. Comprehension dawned sickeningly in Erin's mind as the massive animal reached his master and Olaf drew from around the saddle a pair of iron shackles hanging from a length of heavy hemp. He intended to lead her behind him as she had done to him that first day they met. Except that she hadn't his stamina or strength nor was her flesh as toughened and calloused against the elements.

"You can't—" Gregory began, but Erin cut him off, echoing his sentiments with a humiliated horror.

"Olaf, please! I beg you, I'm your wife!"

He smiled a smile colder than anything she had ever seen before, and it cut to the quick. It was an anger so sharp she couldn't see that it covered the deepest agony.

"You live because you are my wife," he said quietly.

"If you would only listen—" Erin pleaded.

"Listen!" Olaf bellowed. "I don't need to listen when I can see. You cost lives today, Princess. Men who fought to save Ulster for your brother died here for this treachery." He grasped her hands when he read the panic in her eyes and knew she could instinctively seek to flee, locking the shackles quickly around her wrists.

"No!" Erin gasped out, attempting to bite him.

His hand clenched into her hair once more, tightening unbearably, then he suddenly released her, shoving her toward Gregory, as if fearful of his own anger. "Give her the faceplate back, Gregory."

Gregory made a last valiant and desperate attempt to save Erin as he fumbled to return helmet and faceplate to Erin. "Olaf! Let me stand in for her! Punish me—"

Olaf coldly mounted his charger, his golden brows raised high, his eyes frigidly cold. "I'm sorry. Erin and I have been a similar route before. She still seems to believe there is no law but her own. She must be made to understand that I do not make idle threats, nor do I like my life threatened by my wife each time my back is turned. Go back to camp, Gregory. If you cannot do so by your own will, I will call guards to help you."

Erin somehow saw the anguish torturing Gregory through her own fear. She tried to signal him to go, to make him believe things might go better if only she were alone. "Go, Gregory," she managed to whisper.

"I cannot."

"You must."

Erin watched as her cousin turned, stumbling over the cliffs. Her eyes followed his broken walk, then her vision was directed back to the golden man seized by the icy rage who towered above her on the restless and pawing stallion as he jerked on the hemp, pulling her shackled wrists.

"This, Princess," Olaf bit out, "is justice. Even at that stream, my lady wife, I offered you no malice. And since you have come to my home, I have looked the other way over the daggers you continually throw. No more, Princess. I draw the line here. You will be meted all that you deserve, which should have been your fate from the day we began."

"You won't lis—"

She was unable to finish her statement. His lips compressed tightly and he dug his heels into the stallion's side. The horse leaped to a start, and Erin gasped as she staggered into a run to keep from falling.

Erin spent several minutes trying merely to adjust to the gait of the horse and the rugged terrain beneath her feet. Then she saw where he led her and she almost stumbled as she closed her eyes with horror. They were moving through the camp.

Men paused in various stages of duty, saddling horses, packing gear . . . caring for the dead. The Irish watched her with eyes that spoke of the incredulity and sadness at her betrayal; the looks upon the Norse faces were more venomous.

No man made a move—neither the few Irish who felt pity for the woman who had once ridden with them as goddess, nor the Norse whose tightlipped stares bespoke their feelings that she should be flayed alive rather than punished and humbled before them. She wanted to sink beneath the earth as she was jeered by warriors she had known all her life, and yet that humiliation was not near the pain of seeing what her folly had wrought. Olaf dragged her viciously around and around the men who had fallen. If she lived beyond a century, she would never forget staring upon the glazed faces of the dead men.

Finally that torture upon her ended, Olaf swung the stallion about, whipping her sharply behind him. "We ride on for Dubhlain!" he shouted. "I take my prisoner ahead."

It was a tribute to Olaf as warrior and king that his complete authority was never challenged. His men returned to their tasks, ready to follow behind at the distance dictated by his command.

There was only one man who defied the order. Brice mac Aed, still riding with his brother-in-law, had received a nick in the ribs during the skirmish. He had been having his wound bound when the Golden Warrioress was first dragged into the camp, and when he had finally seen her, he had become numbed and stunned.

But when the Wolf began to ride ahead with her, new life pumped into his veins. No longer aware of his throbbing wound, he tensed his muscles and burst into a hurtling run across the camp. Erin! He had lost Leith, and now he was in panic as the enraged Viking led his sister away.

He had barely reached the central fire before he was once more stunned to receive a flying blow to his legs and find himself crashing heavily to the ground. Ready to fight, he swung around, only to encounter Gregory.

"Get off me, Gregory! Have you gone crazy! That's Erin—"

"Hush!" Gregory pleaded, spitting sand from his lips as he and Brice struggled back to their feet. He grappled his older and larger cousin's shoulders and shook him firmly. "Listen to me, Brice. Listen to me well. He knows it is Erin. And he isn't going to kill her. But she rode against him, Brice. No law in any land would deny him retaliation. Why she did it, I don't know. But he's actually protecting her, Brice. Look at the face of the Viking we have called friend. If he hadn't acted as he had, they would have labeled him a coward and demanded far worse. They would have flayed her within an inch of her life, if they happened to practice benevolence. Erin has to solve this, Brice. If we interfere, we can create disaster. We must wait. We must see how she fares in Dubhlain."

The irrational fire of fear and panic slowly faded from Brice's eyes and his broad shoulders slumped. "She's my sister, Gregory," he said brokenly. "How can I—"

"You must let her go and have faith in the man we have ridden beside in battle so long now. He is a strange man, that Viking we call brother. Powerful but not merciless. Relentless but not ruthless. Erin can far better help herself now."

Why had she ridden against him? Brice wondered sickly. He couldn't condemn Olaf, and yet he couldn't bear that harm might befall his sister. He would wait until they reached Dubhlain. But if Erin didn't appear well before him, he would defy the entire land to take her away.

Olaf did not give the animal free rein. Erin would have instantly fallen and been dragged flat had that been the case. But still he kept up a pace that left her panting before they stood by the cliffs and reached the road. Nor did he glance her way until they were on the road. There he stopped and twisted to stare down upon her.

"Olaf!" Erin gasped out, inhaling desperately. "Have you not done enough to me? Can't you see that my own soul tortures me? Think what you do to me! I will never forgive you—"

"Forgive me!" he thundered. "Wife, never have I met with such a foolish tongue!"

Again the stallion broke into a slow canter. The ride through the camp had been but a prelude, child's play, compared to now. Erin felt the cruel jerk upon her wrists, and instinctively bunched her rapidly tiring muscles to break after the animal. Each time her feet touched the ground it began to feel as if they were pierced by swords. The world began to swim before her. The pounding of her heart was like engulfing thunder and the rasp of her breath was louder than the breeze. Yet she fought against falling, for even at Olaf's speed she would be ripped and torn and bruised.

He pulled up short beneath the shade of a gnarled oak. Erin collided with the flanks of the stallion and slumped to the ground. She took several minutes to breathe, then lifted her eyes filled with both wrath and pleading to his.

"Olaf! I would not ride against my own father!"

"Noble try, Princess," he returned coldly. "Your father no longer rides with me. We parted far north. Surely you are aware of such a fact. If you knew my position and that of the outlaws, you certainly were privy to the knowledge I rode alone."

"Nay—"

"Get up."

"I cannot—" She broke off with a scream as he jerked at the rope. Struggling, she came to her feet, just in time for the great hooves of the charger to start moving again.

The black stallion moved in a slow but fluid canter. Again Erin saw the world spinning and shaking. "I despise you!" she shrieked out. "Better that you do kill me than—"

The stallion stopped abruptly and striking blue eyes were on her again, raking over her as a shaft of cold steel. "Fear not, Princess," he said coolly. "I will not kill you. You are, as you reminded me, my wife. I do not intend to kill you or even leave you battered or bruised. I do not like to gaze upon scars."

A sharp chill crept over the panting heat of her body. "No . . ." she protested feebly, hating the cold and hardness in his eyes. He could not be planning on coming to her, taking her, not like this. Not when this terrible hate raged between them. Better that she fall and break her bones beneath the stallion's hooves. . . .

"Aye or nay, my lady, choices are no longer yours."

She screamed out with pain again as the iron shackles bit around her wrists and threatened to jerk her arms from her sockets as the charger leaped back to motion. A canter again. She wanted to fall, to spite him. Yet she fought against the terrible pain that would come with being dragged against the ragged turf. Not much longer, she thought, stumbling. I cannot run much longer. . . .

The blackness started to descend with greater frequency. She could no longer draw breath into her lungs. Every muscle within her moved in heated agony. Then she fell.

The stallion halted before she had been carried a man's length. Olaf dismounted from the horse, but as blackness swam before her eyes, she received no assistance from him. She felt the point of his blade against her throat. "Up, my lady," he murmured.

Her lips were dry and parched. She could not open them to speak.

"Irish," he said softly, "you will rise. And you will know from this day forth the pain that you cause others. I cannot kill you, as my men lay dead, but I will wield a sword of steel. Perhaps the injustice was mine. Had I blistered your seat the night of our marriage, you might have understood your hate and treachery would truly not be tolerated. But that injustice will not come again."

She could hear him, but only vaguely, and all she could think was that she had never really known him. He would grant her no doubt, give her no chance to explain, and she couldn't stand. She couldn't even open her eyes, or fight the darkness. She could only pray that she didn't heap further indignity upon herself by turning into the dirt to lose the meager contents of her stomach.

"Stand, my lady. I know you well. You have the agility of a cat."

Erin noted dimly that the swordpoint left her flesh. She felt the earth seem to tremble beneath her, but still she couldn't open her eyes. Another horse is coming, she thought vaguely.

"What do you do here, Druid?" Erin heard Olaf demand furiously.

"I have come to stop you, Lord of the Wolves!" Mergwin called out, dismounting from his horse. The evil he had felt was afoot, the evil that had begun with the shadow upon the moon. He had seen but he had not seen enough.

"Druid, I deal with a traitor who cost lives. Irish lives as well as Norse."

"You must stop this, quickly!" Mergwin demanded, coming to the Norwegian king.

Olaf looked at him, shielding the agony in his features with rigid control. "She came against us, Druid. I cannot stop this." She had come against him, wishing his death. All the long nights he had dreamed of her, remembered the soft feel of her skin, the web of blue-ebony hair that covered his shoulders, entrapping him in her sensuality, in her innocence, in her scent. Making all others dim in comparison, haunting his memory, robbing him of sleep as he ached for a glance of emerald eyes embracing his with deepest, misted seduction as he brought himself between the silken prison of her thighs. It had all been lies, even when she came to him, *especially* when she came to him. . . . Trickery. Deceit. She had longed only for his death.

"You are wrong, you have to be wrong—"

"There are twelve dead men out there who can no longer tell you that I am not wrong."

"Keep this up, and you will kill her."

"Nay, Druid, I do not seek her death."

They both broke off as Erin moaned softly. Mergwin vaguely noticed that the Norseman's nails crawled into his own palms with such force that they split the flesh and drew blood.

Mergwin pounded both fists against Olaf's chest and glared like a madman into the cool Nordic eyes of the Lord of Dubhlain. "You must let me tend her. She is with child!"

Olaf raised his arched brows in surprise, then glared at the Druid with naked suspicion and—a very unusual characteristic—uncertainty.

"How can you know that, Druid? And if you can see so damn much, why didn't you foretell this morning? Why didn't you spare us all—"

"I am not a prophet. I see only what I am allowed.

But I tell you, King of Fools, you will kill your own heir—"

Erin had understood little. The world had begun to swirl. She tried to move, but nausea overwhelmed her, and she was wretchedly sick, too sick to care, too sick to feel Mergwin's gentle touch as he ripped the sleeve of his robe to gently clean her face.

Suddenly she felt arms around her. She wanted to fight the touch, but she was powerless. She tried to open her eyes, and her lashes fluttered. She saw blue. Blue with no gentleness, blue that still condemned. Her eyes closed again and she lay limp in the strong arms that carried her as if she weighed no more than a bird.

She was teetering between consciousness and a world of blackness. She wanted the blackness. It took away the pain of her limbs, it took away the terror of reality. But it was not to be hers.

She was set down beneath a shading oak and her eyes finally flew open. He stood towering over her again, touching her this time, his fingers biting into her shoulders. His features were tense and rigid, his bronze flesh drawn tightly over the chiseled bone structure. His lips were pulled into a thin grim line. "Is it true?"

Was what true? She didn't know what he was talking about, and the world was spinning viciously, even the fury of his countenance seemed to swim in and out of focus.

He shook her. "Are you with child?"

Her eyes widened. How could he know?

"Are you?"

She could bring no words to her parched lips. She closed her eyes and nodded. The world still swam, as the pain eased, even the grate of his words was easing. The world was slipping away.

He released her. Someone else was with them. Someone with old and gnarled but gentle fingers. Someone touching her, forcing her to drink a sweet and soothing potion. . . .

She opened her eyes. The curl of a smile played
about her lips. "Mergwin," she breathed in a whisper.

He nodded, but his eyes in the deep sockets of his
wrinkled and weathered face were grave.

It didn't matter. She was in his hands. Her eyes
flickered and closed again. From somewhere, very far
off, she heard Olaf's voice again.

"Thank whatever gods you wish, my lady, that you
carry my son. You will be reprieved until five months
hence. At which point you will find yourself beaten
black and blue for risking that life which is mine in
your vicious quest for revenge."

She wanted to strike him, to curse him, to rake his
eyes from his head with her nails. But she had no will,
no strength to speak against him, in defense of herself.
Mergwin's potion held her tongue and she gave herself
up to the darkness.

There were but ten men still living he could call his
own. Most of the mercenaries who had called him
leader were corpses. And yet for Friggid the Bowlegs,
the encounter had been a macabre victory.

The combined Irish and Norse troops of Olaf the
White quit the cliffs of the beach just minutes before
Friggid left his cave of retreat to stare after the depart-
ing army.

He had inadvertently achieved far more than a rift
in the Norse and Irish alliance, and his laughter echoed
with hoofbeats of the horses that retreated now in the
distance. He had pitted Irish wife against Norse husband. The revered Golden Warrioress had been none
other than the Wolf's mate, the daughter of the High
Irish King.

Friggid's laughter faded as he sank to the ground in
thought. He had dug a sword deeply into the side of
the Wolf. A Viking should have slain male or female,
stranger, wife, or sister, for such an act of treachery.
Olaf had dealt with his offending bride lightly. It was
quite possible the Wolf cared far more for his lovely
mate than the warrior would care to admit. Olaf was

known to be a man of deep passions, capable of thundering rages, ice-cold judgment, searing love and loyalty. The gods had long ago decreed that all men should have a weakness. Friggid now believed he knew what it was.

He could bide his time, return to his homeland to reinforce his strength, to watch . . . and wait . . . and plan carefully. He could never hope to equal the power of the Wolf. But the man could be brought down. The Irish princess could be used again even to a greater advantage.

Friggid would see to it that the agonized howl of the Wolf would echo across the land again.

CHAPTER

19

There was very little she remembered about the trip home. Images slipped in and out of her mind. The color of the sky, the blinding dazzle of the sun when she occasionally opened her eyes, only to close them again and find solace in the blackness. I'm drugged, of course, she thought vaguely. Mergwin, with his potions, could ease the pain of the flesh and the spirit with his secret concoctions of dried herbs.

There was a definite difference when she emerged from the final spell of darkness. She was no longer being jostled roughly along in the hard, coarse litter. She rested on something soft, which smelled of the clean air and a faint fragrance of summer roses. The sheets were cool beneath her fingers, and her head rested on a down pillow. She fluttered her lashes to see the carved arch above the bed, the fine silk draperies tied about the carved posts.

She was home, in her own bed. But it wasn't her bed, and it wasn't her home. That she had come to think so was ludicrous. It was the home of the Wolf, the conqueror, the king of Dubhlain. He had merely been gone so long that she had come to think of it as hers. She had slept in the broad bed alone so many nights, nights when she remembered his touch, the unique, compelling strength of his features, the sweet tempest and serenity of surrender to his passions.

She closed her eyes again. Lying in this bed, it was possible to believe that she had never ridden from Dubhlain. Dear God, why had she ever left? How had she been such a fool? It was incredible to believe that she had simply mistaken the group of men. They had seemed to expect her. But how?

Something had been wrong, because she wasn't a fool. She was the daughter of Aed Finnlaith, a king wise in the ways of warfare and men. Something had been afoot, but Olaf would never believe that, because she had, in fact, ridden at the head of a group of men against him.

I did nothing wrong! her heart cried out. I am guilty of caring, of loving only. Even as I would never have ridden against my own father, she thought bitterly, I would have never ridden against Olaf.

She knew now how completely, how pathetically, she loved him, and that realization cut through her with bitter, bitter pain. Love was a bitter gall to swallow. One could be strong without it, immune to pain, powerful against any abuse of the flesh because the soul could not be touched. But now she was vulnerable. His mere words were more a slashing stab than the keenest blade. He would not even listen to her protestations of innocence. He had already condemned her as a traitor.

Then suddenly she knew he was in the room with her. She hadn't twisted her head, opened her eyes, or heard the slightest rustle of a sound. But he was there, watching her. She could feel the Nordic drifts encompassing her from the icy depths of his eyes.

I will beg that he listen no longer, she promised herself. He mustn't know the power he has to wound me, for I will be lost. I am a princess of Tara, the daughter of the greatest king ever to rule the Irish.

She opened her eyes and twisted her head to meet

his stare. She found him instinctively. He stood by the shuttered window overlooking the courtyard. He was in full dress, resplendent in crimson and black, naturally arrogant in stance, his gold-brooched mantle flowing smoothly over the still breadth of his shoulders.

She was at an immediate disadvantage, aware that her hair was in tangled dishevelment, that her bare toes were protruding from beneath the hem of the sheer white linen gown someone had garbed her in.

She sat up, warily keeping her eyes on him, tucking her toes beneath her gown. She didn't like the cool, still look of him. His moments of greatest calm and smoothest composure were definitely his most deadly. His lowest tones were the most dangerous.

It had been so long since he had ridden away. She faced a stranger again, yet a stranger she had come to know so well.

"So," he said softly, "you have wakened. And you look quite refreshed." He turned fully from the window, crossing his arms over his chest, bracing a leg against a stool. "We can talk."

"Talk? Now, my lord?" She laughed bitterly. "You do not wish to hear me. I have nothing to say to you."

"I suggest you come up with something."

Determined to parry his every thrust with a collected calm to match his own, she ignored the fluttering of her heart. "I attempted to explain everything to you. You chose to ignore me and mete out punishment without any thought of justice or law. You have condemned me, and I will never forget. . . ." How he shackled me, dragged me along with no mercy, she thought to herself, just as I had done to him that long ago day near Carlingford Lough.

"How cruelly I treated you, madam? I'm sure you feel nothing. I took great care to see that you suffered no permanent injury. You did naught but learn a well-needed lesson in justice and humility."

"Lesson! You have no right to—"

"I have every right! I received all rights when I married you!"

Frustration knotted within her to become fury. How dearly she wished that she could shake him, pummel the insolent contempt from his granite features . . . and yet how she wished to touch him, to feel the smooth ripple of his muscles tensing beneath her fingers, bury her face against his neck, inhale the clean, male scent of him.

Her fingers clenched into the palms of her hands and when she spoke it was in a scathing whisper. "You are an idiot, king of fools! Hailed as a wise and merciful man—yet you do not even seek the truth! If you will not listen to me, Viking, seek out your own logic! What if I did wish you dead, lord husband? I would find a better way than risking the lives of my own brothers, father, and cousin!"

His brow lifted slightly. Other than that, he showed no sign of belief or disbelief. "Erin, you are aware that I no longer rode with your father."

"I know now, aye, because you've told me!"

"You are asking me to believe that you just happened to stumble across the outlaws rather than the Irishmen of Meath?"

"Yes."

He kept staring at her and Erin felt that she had to say more. "They were Irish, you see. I believed the outlaws to be Danish or Norse—"

"You have finally hit upon something that I do believe—that you would assume all outlaws to be Viking rather than Irish. And yet I tell you this, Erin. You claim that you met Irish. You did not. The dead men found upon the cliffs and beach were more Viking than Irish."

Erin's breath caught in her throat. "No, they couldn't have been."

"But they were."

She felt as if a stifling band of steel were twisting around her. "But they greeted me in Irish, they wore the leather aprons of the Irish—they spoke of Meath, and the king of Meath is an ally of my father—''

He interrupted her with a snort of disgust. "Erin, you insult my intelligence. You ask me to believe in gross stupidity, when I know, dear wife, that you have the cunning of a fox."

He left his place across the room to stalk her slowly, holding her eyes as he lowered himself beside her. "You have threatened me with torture, death, hell, and damnation since we have met, Princess. On the night of our marriage you intended to kill me. And then again I find myself attacked by you, but I am supposed to believe you meant others to be killed. There were a few Irish men in with the scurvy low bloods who attacked. But I do not believe you are too particular on the nationality of the men you use against me. And how simple to lead! How well your counter-egos mesh! The famed Golden Warrioress—and Princess Erin of Tara, beautiful daughter of Aed, wed to a despised Viking! You must have been in great spirits, my wife, while planning on your widowhood."

"You are wrong!" Erin spat out, feeling a trembling begin within her. He had once been gentle; even in anger, he had seldom been cruel. But now he despised her.

"What would you believe?"

A trembling that she could not control came to her lips. She had to blink to keep the tears that stung her lids from falling. "You could trust me," she lashed out.

"Trust you? Were you bound and gagged, Irish, I would not trust you. My back has been threatened one time too many."

"You have no intention of listening to a word I say," she breathed out harshly, grasping her down pillow with its finely embroidered linen case to her chest as if it could act as a barrier against him. "Think what you like then, and leave me be."

He reached for the pillow and ripped it from her. "Oh no, Irish! We are far from finished with this discussion. I want to hear more about this. I am enjoying this story. How, if you did not have council with these outlaws, did you hear of any of this?''

"Through Sigurd! I went down for ale . . . I was thirsty. I heard him speaking with the captain of the guards.''

"I have spoken with Sigurd. He says he never told you anything. He was afraid you would be anxious. Amusing, isn't it?''

"Sigurd did not see me,'' Erin replied impatiently, wondering if he was listening to her at all. "I waited in the stairwell because I didn't know what I should do.''

She was startled when he rose, turning his back to her as he rubbed his beard and paced several steps away. "When do you expect the child?''

A trembling set up inside of her again as she realized the course of his questioning. "Surely you can count, my lord—''

He spun back to face her. "Yes,'' he said dryly, "I can.''

"You know that you are my child's father.''

"What I know, Erin, is that you would do anything to spite me. But yes, I do believe you carry my child. You were watched meticulously while I was away. You are lucky, Princess, that your dreams of vengeance became more devious. Without the child, you would be in the dungeon, and had you not chosen to barter yourself on that bed to deceive me into trust—''

"Watched meticulously . . . bartered . . . you Viking bastard! You do *not* own me!'' Erin lost all thought of sanity or control. She came at him with a snarl, as if catapulted from the bed, hurling herself at him like a desperate wild creature, her nails raking, her fists pummeling.

He was stunned by the impact and strength of the attack coming from his wife's slim body. He thought fleetingly that it was no wonder even men such as her stalwart brothers had found her difficult to best in swordplay. His own anger and the simple superiority of having spent half his days in battle had given him the easy victory over her on the cliff when he faced the warrioress, but now, taken off guard, he was startled to discover that with fists alone she was pelting him many punishing blows.

"Enough!" he yelled, and using a sinewed thigh to cut between her legs, he sent her off balance so that he could catch her falling form in his arms.

He wanted to toss her on the bed and leave her as refuse, but the feel of her flesh, so warm beneath the sheer linen, the searing flame of her green eyes as they met his, the wild erratic pounding of her heart, that of a caged bird, all combined to sweep the logic from his mind.

She had betrayed him, but the thought meant nothing when the fever of deprivation was leaping from his body, fired by lap after tiny lap of a smoldering flame that encroached upon his limbs, born of a pulsing ache within his groin that grew and thundered like a drumbeat.

He was a fool. She wanted him dead. More than ever she despised him. He had punished her cruelly from the saddle of his mount. He had all but called her whore, and yet she would never know that his actions and words agonized him, twisting into his heart and soul. He wanted so much to believe her, but he couldn't afford to. He was the king of Dubhlain, a man fighting for his tenuous hold on the land.

He wanted to lose himself within her, ease his pain within the warm and giving shelter of her body. Bury his face within the tangled and evocative web of black silk that curled about her in wild dishevelment, feel beneath his shaking fingers the luxurious softness of her flesh, the full, seductive, taunt of her breasts.

His need spiraled in his mind and became a throbbing in his head. He could not speak, because he would stutter out his desire, leave his soul naked before her and bleeding. But he knew she would not accept his caress.

By the thunder of Thor, she would accept him! he raged inwardly, his mouth tightening grimly. He was her husband, her king, her liege—and whatever else happened between them, he would not allow her to turn him away.

He tossed her on the bed, then strode across the floor to check the bolt on the heavy wood door. He turned back to her, making his intentions clear as he faced her with hard challenging eyes that hid the quivering uncertainty within him as he meticulously began removing his clothing, draping his mantle over a chair, his wide leather belt beside it.

Erin inhaled sharply, wedging her toes against the bedding and curling her feet beneath her, edging against the headboard in a rigid stance of defiance like a cornered, spitting and hissing cat.

"You will not!" she cried out. "You will not call me traitor and hint that I would gladly play whore and then think to take me like a possession to be used at your convenience! You will not—"

He continued to watch her. His boots clunked to the floor. His robe was strewn over his mantle.

Tears filled her eyes. He looked so wonderful to her. How often she missed just the mere sight of his nakedness, his warrior's body, muscled like oak, lean and lithe and agile. The broad bronze shoulders. The powerful arms with their clear delineation of muscle and thin lines of blue veins hovering beneath the taut flesh.

I cannot let him touch me, she thought, because I will not be able to deny him . . . deny myself, and he will but think me ever more the harlot.

"If you come near me now, King of Dubhlain," she said with the stilted dignity she could muster, "it will be rape."

"I doubt that," he replied with a shrug of his shoulders. "But if that is your choice, wife, then it shall be rape," he said softly.

He came to the bed slowly but surely, his bare feet silent upon the hard floor. He pulled her into his arms and pressed his lips against hers, undaunted by their stiffness. Her fists flailed against his back, but he ignored the blows. He held her still by her nape and the thick mane of ebony there, tangling his fingers into the silken feel. He prodded her mouth with his tongue, over and over, circling the shape of her lips, thrusting with more and more provocative force until she gasped and gave in to his overwhelming power.

A sob rose in her throat even as she felt the thrust of his tongue in her mouth, the intimate, poignantly missed touch of his hands on her. She must deny him! But despite her anger, he was taking her adrift in a sea of sensation, each tiny nuance of breath and quiver touched her to the soul, robbing her of all else but her need for him. Against her will, she was responding . . . giving in return.

She was stunned when he suddenly pulled away from her, watching her with eyes that had never resembled the roiling tempest of a storm at sea more. She was so startled by her sense of loss, and by those eyes that strangely seemed to combine fire fury and deadly blue pain, that she unwittingly murmured a confused "My lord?"

Color had begun to explode in his mind. Beautiful color, rainbow color. Soft, seductive mauves, pulsing heated reds that met and meshed with the lightning streaking down his middle, coiling in his groin, pulsing inside him like the oncoming tide of the sea. He shuddered inwardly anew with the wanting of her. It was stronger than anything he had ever felt for a woman; it was even stronger than his craving to conquer and rule his land.

But he couldn't take her. She had called him rapist. He could not give her the satisfaction.

He blinked, and the storm was cleared from his eyes. He faced her from the shield of the steel Nordic blue of his eyes, and a mocking curve touched his sensuous lips tauntingly. "I've decided not to rape you, dear wife," he informed her with soft mockery, as he rolled from the bed and stood staring out the window.

A slow freeze of new horror and humiliation settled over Erin. She had responded to his touch when all he had sought to do was prove his power. He had turned so easily from her. Thank God! She wanted him, but not this way! She wanted him loving her, trusting her.

Erin fought momentarily to diffuse that pain, but it was now difficult, as her rage was so intense that she could barely see. "You bastard," she grated with a deathly quiet, drawing the sheets about herself like the tattered remnants of her dignity. "You Viking bastard! You will never touch me again! Ireland has laws, Lord Viking, and I will use those laws against you. I demand that you give me separate quarters while I seek a divorce! Then you will need not worry about my murderous qualities for I will not give a godly damn whether you live or not!"

She was stunned to see that he smiled as he turned from the window. "My lady wife, you are never downed, are you? But you are oft mistaken of your own power. You will not have a separate chamber, and were I to grant you such a concession, it would mean naught, for I would come to you—if I so desired. Nor will I in my own chamber, or my own bed—even if I do manage to control my rapist Viking tendencies— leave you be. You will seek no divorce. You speak of your Brehon laws, but you forget, they mean nothing to me—nor to anyone else, in our circumstance. Our marriage was one of alliance. And as I have told you, Irish, I am a Viking. I hold my own laws. What is mine, I keep. You will not leave this chamber until I say so."

Erin clenched her teeth so tightly she feared they would snap. Each muscle in her body was rigid with her fury. "I will escape you," she uttered desperately.

"Please, Irish," he said quietly, "cease your threats. Your golden mail is being redesigned for you. Shackles and chains. If need be, you will spend your life within your golden armor, reminded of the mistakes of the past." He awaited her reaction, saw none but her tightlipped anger, and stared out the window again.

It was all she could do to keep herself from hurtling

after him again in a heated explosion of her rage. But it would be folly and she knew it. He didn't issue his words as a threat, merely as a painful statement.

"Olaf," Erin said, fighting for control to speak calmly and coolly rather than bursting into tears of tumult and frustration, "I cannot break the images in your mind, but I warn you of this. I did not seek to kill you, nor did I ever before seek escape. But you give me no leave, no room for anything but bitterness. I tell you again I did not intend to come against you. You should look to where the danger lies, for I was tricked."

He turned back to her, but she could read no emotion from his features. He walked across the room to the bed and sat beside her, staring into her eyes.

He reached to touch her chin, but she jerked her head away. "I do not want you touching me," she said stiffly.

He sighed softly. "I believe I have proven that you have no choice in the matter, Erin."

"Then know that what you take is all that you receive, for while you label me a traitor, I will give you nothing."

"You cannot give me what I could take—if I desired."

"There is much, my lord, that I have given you. Love is not owned, it is received."

"I am not a great believer in love, Irish. It is but a weakness that makes fools of men."

He laughed lightly, the strain easing somewhat from his face. "And, Irish, you will not escape me. You can hate me morn, noon, and night, but you will still be my wife—my pregnant wife. But I will make this concession to you. I will accept your warnings that others may wish me harm. And I will seek to see if there is not some way to know if you might ever be believed."

"You are magnanimous," Erin said with cold sarcasm.

He laughed again and she was tempted to scratch at

his eyes. But he caught her hands in advance, knowing the warning sizzle in her eyes. He pulled at her covers despite her rigid and angry protest. "The child is mine, Irish, as it is yours." He touched her stomach very gently, rubbing his knuckles over it lightly. "There are changes in you," he said softly, then his voice went hard again. "Which is another reason you should have been horsewhipped."

Erin lowered her eyes, remaining stiff against his touch.

"Or did you, perhaps, seek to kill the child as it too is Viking?"

She raised her eyes to his, the emerald light in them flaming darkly. "Nay, Olaf, the child is mine. It will be Irish. Mergwin was born of a Viking sire, but, my lord, he is an Irishman."

"It is not an equal world, Irish. The child will be mine."

"Do you keep me here only because of the child, Lord Wolf? Am I a prisoner because you desire an heir? What happens when the child is born? Am I then set aside?"

"I keep you," Olaf said, "because you are mine. And because you have pleased me, and will perhaps do so again. And yes, because I want my child. We shall see where we go from there."

"We will live in misery. So what is left?"

He raised a brow and smiled, the mockery returning. "I did not see you suffer in misery from my proximity or touch today."

Wrath flared within her again at the total injustice of it all. Her hand flashed out across his face so quickly that he had no time to deflect it and could only stare at her in stunned bemusement as she sat, proud even in her nakedness, railing against him. "Never again, Viking, fear not. Bind me, chain me, beat me, threaten me, take me, but I will give to you no more!"

With the ejaculation of her anger, she trembled within. She had to be a fool to strike and defy him when she had no proof of her own innocence and a sure knowledge that he carried out all threats when he believed them just. But she could give him no more. She had made herself vulnerable already and so she sat silently, awaiting his recourse.

He rubbed his cheek with narrowed eyes. "Erin, I do admire your courage." His tone lowered again to warn her his admiration would only stretch so far. "But do not strike me again. I am the barbarian, remember, the one who practices cruelty."

Erin looked away from him, wincing at his sarcasm. "You do practice cruelty, Olaf, far greater than any administered by whips or chains."

"By all the fires of all conceivable hells!" Olaf exploded. "I face my own wife with my sword. And it is cruelty that I do not fall for your pretty excuses!"

He jumped out of the bed and began to dress, his fingers almost ripping the fabric of his clothing as he did so.

Erin didn't reply. She closed her eyes and drew the covers around her again as a shield against her hopelessness.

When he spoke again he was quiet, cold and controlled once more. "You ask what is left between us now, wife. A wall. You despise me; I trust you no further than my own vision. But we are husband and wife, and I want my child that you carry. I will not be denied a part in its growth. Only a trusted few know that it was the queen of Dubhlain who caused the deaths of twelve men—I would not have the families of those dead seeking vengeance. Therefore you may have the run of this house. Do not leave it. You will not be warned again. And one more thing: Do not seek to turn from me, ever. You are my wife, and I will speak to you when and if I choose, and touch you—if and when I choose." He was silent for a moment, his back to her. He sounded bleak when he spoke again. "I am a fool, Erin, for I still like to believe there is hope."

He paused a moment, as if determined that she

digest his words, then added, "If you would rise, Erin, the great hall awaits its king and queen."

There was nothing else to do. She should be grateful. He might have chained her, or sent her to the dungeons, or repudiated her and their child. But nothing had actually changed except his feelings for her, and the terrible anger and bitterness she bore him.

Her fingers trembled as she quickly dressed, then adjusted her mantle. She glanced nervously to where he awaited her by the door.

He was fully dressed already, impatient, his mind on other affairs. Tall and golden and regal, her splendid warrior. The Wolf of Norway, arrogant, powerful, confident . . .

She fought tears as she remembered that he could also be tender only when he had wanted her. His possession. . . .

He stretched out an arm to her and she took it, feeling her lip begin to quiver. How different things could have been. . . .

"Olaf," she addressed him coolly.

"Aye?"

"I obey you now, because you are the stronger."

"I care not why you obey me or heed my warnings, only that you do so."

She would not allow tears to rise to her eyes. As he opened the door, she swept by him coolly. They descended to the great hall in royal splendor—and in rigid misery.

Olaf stood beneath a full moon once more, his soul in torment. Neither he nor Erin had remained within the hall to dine. In his pain and fury, he had forgotten to tell her about the deaths of her brother Leith and Fennen mac Cormac.

Once in the hall, she had quickly ascertained that her brother wasn't present, and she had broken into uncontrollable sobs.

Olaf had not been able to touch her. She would have rejected him, so Brice—a brother—comforted her for the brother lost, while he stood beneath the moon and tortured himself with longing and pain and uncertainty.

She had betrayed him! Or had she? The evidence was against her, and it hurt so very bitterly, because he had just learned to live again. He had just learned that he was to have a child. An heir.

Did she cry for her brother? Or for the mac Cormac? Did she wish that he had died rather than the Irish king? Olaf sighed deeply. He understood pain. He would respect hers. He would seek his night's rest before the hearth.

CHAPTER

20

Longboats filled the coastline and harbor, sleek and magnificent, their dragon hulls and red and white sails billowing in the breeze. The scene was both awesome and beautiful.

As Olaf stood at the harbor within the Liffey to greet the Norsemen who came, the sharp wind whipped his golden hair and mantle about him. There was not, however, a Viking aboard any of the numerous ships who would think to mock the Wolf's Irish dress, for his visage, even from the sea, was an indomitable one. Legs slightly parted, one knee crooked upon a rising ledge, he appeared as something legendary, a golden god. As men had often thought in battle, he seemed to be surrounded by an aura of light. Sigurd stood slightly to his right, and to his left, Gregory and Brice mac Aed.

But when the first visitor set his booted feet splashing into the water to rush ashore, the full and mobile mouth framed by the golden beard slashed into a wide grin. Visitor and king of Dubhlain met with shouts of delight and a shattering embrace. The two men finally parted and assessed one another openly.

It was the visitor who spoke first. He was a man almost of a height with the Wolf, a year or two older, more carefree of manner.

"So, brother Wolf, this is it! The fine city of Dubhlain yours. Taking you from the sea and ending your days of going a-Viking!"

"Aye, Eric, this is it," the Wolf returned. "Welcome to Ireland."

"And a welcome from an Irishman it appears to be." Eric laughed, his blue eyes a shade more gray than Olaf's raking over his brother's appearance.

"Nay, you'll never convince the Irish of that," Olaf said with a shrug. Especially my wife, he added silently.

Eric was already looking beyond Olaf, toward Sigurd. He clapped the red-haired giant soundly on the back. "Sigurd! You old battle-axe. Has this brother of mine taken you too from the seas?"

"We've made a fair trade, Eric. A fair trade. You will see for yourself," Sigurd assured Eric with a broad smile.

"Give your men leave to come ashore, brother," Olaf continued, "and we'll hasten to the great hall. And if you would meet with Irishmen in friendship, I give you Gregory of Clonntairth and Brice mac Aed."

The Irish princes looked at the Norwegian with staunch wariness, but the innate good nature of the Viking was difficult to resist. Once convinced that this was a contingent of Vikings offering no threat further than that of fascinated curiosity, Brice and Gregory stayed at the harbor with Sigurd to direct the landing of the Norse troops as Olaf and Eric climbed the sloping dun to the entrance of the walled city.

With the joyousness of greeting passed, Eric looked at his brother gravely. "I come, brother, with gifts from our father, the jarl. But above that, Olaf, I come to you with warnings."

"Warnings?" Olaf inquired, startled. It had been but three weeks since he had returned from the north country and his battle with the Danes. Was he to spend his life fighting for his tenuous hold on this land?

"Aye, warnings," Eric replied with a troubled shake of his head. "Not for the near future, brother. News travels quickly across the seas. I am aware that the Danes beneath Friggid the Bowlegs met a smashing defeat. Yet already more news comes to us. Friggid had returned to his homeland. Word goes out that he seeks men and that he promises them great riches—aye, he even promises them the city of Dubhlain—if they will follow him against you. It will take him time, Olaf, for brave men fear you. But you must take heed, and defend yourself well, for that Dane is half insane, and he cares not what he risks to kill you."

"Rest assured, Eric," Olaf said quitely, "that I have never discounted that Dane. I know that he will come against me again—and again—until one of us dances with the Valkyries. I will bless the day that I meet him again, for I must. Yet if he issues threats across the seas, you must speak on my behalf. Let the word be carried that Dubhlain cannot be taken. Its walls are stone, and its people, Norse and Irish, will defend it to the death. You taunt me for being Irish, brother, yet by it I have gained much. Half of this fair isle would fight for my defense."

Eric paused, his hands on his hips, his great golden head tossed back as he surveyed first the assured sizzle in his brother's searing eyes, then the walls of Dubhlain, rising high and sturdy behind him. He laughed heartily then, all sense of gravity leaving him. "Brother, I taunt you not. I regale you, for surely you have a foothold on this land, which no man has accomplished before you. I have spoken of business, brother, so now I am free to make my visit one of leisure. You will be pleased to see the gifts we have brought. Silks and jewels and silver plate. Tapestries to deck your walls. And"—Eric paused for a slight moment, giving his brother a licentious wink—"a very special gift to be uniquely yours."

Olaf cocked a sardonic brow. "Spare me, Eric, what is this gift?"

"A woman, brother. A rare and unique beauty. Taken from the Franks, who, it is believed, stole her from distant Persia. Her skin is the color and sweetness of honey, her eyes like almonds of the night—"

"Eric," Olaf interrupted impatiently, "if there is one thing I do not crave, it is another woman. By the gods, I have trouble enough."

"I had heard, of course, brother, that you had married. But I knew it was to form this alliance. That is precisely why I have brought you this jewel of Persia. It is known that you grieve still for Grenilde, but you are a man, brother, and you but keep that grief alive and well by spending your days staring upon your pale and shriveled bartered bride."

Olaf tossed back his head and roared with the first real humor he had enjoyed since his return. "Eric, I thank you for your concern, but believe me when I say I have no use for any woman, no matter how beautiful she might be." Amusement remained in his eyes as he cast a dry glance his brother's way. "Come, you must meet my pale and shriveled bride."

The billowing sails of the dragon ships were visible in the distance from the window of Erin's chamber. She had stared at them first with horror and panic, but then had been informed by Rig that the ships had come in peace, bearing gifts from Olaf's father, a great jarl of Norway.

Her panic first became relief and then anger. Apparently all within Dubhlain had known that a contingent of dragon ships was due, all except her. Olaf had not seen fit to inform her. But then he had barely spoken to her for a fortnight now, so perhaps it wasn't so strange that she knew nothing.

She sank into the hot bath Rig had prepared for her and nibbled nervously upon a nail. Her situation had steadily gone from bad to worse. The pain of loss that had enveloped her upon learning of the deaths of her brother and Fennen had supplied her with a barrier of numbness against Olaf. After that first night in which he had left her alone, he had returned to their room and though he hadn't touched her, the torture had been all the greater. Night after night they had lain awake, together, alone. The tension had left her sleepless, her nerves shattered, until a fortnight ago when he had emitted an oath of disgust and quit their chamber in the middle of the night, and had not returned since. When she was strong she told herself that it was good. But when she was weak, she was in wretched misery, admitting she would rather he fought with her, railed against her, demanded of her anything but what he had done—leave her.

Erin snapped sharply from her thoughts as she heard the sound of boisterous voices traveling up from the great hall. She stepped quickly from her bath, wishing, for once, that she had chosen another to serve her after Moira's marriage. She was curious to meet this new wave of Vikings, men from Olaf's homeland, and despite the loathing she daily attempted to convince herself she bore her husband, her pride and her vanity were at stake. When tales were brought home to Norway on the mouths of these seafarers, she didn't want it said that the Lord of the Wolves had procured himself anything less than a perfect—if Irish—bride.

It was fall and cool, but she chose a light-blue robe of soft silk that needed no belt and therefore concealed well her pregnancy. With a teal-blue mantle of wool over her shoulders, she would be warm.

She brushed her hair strenuously and adorned it with jewels, then set her hand on the carved door. Two deep breaths and a sturdy squaring of her shoulders and she was ready to face any man. She was, she reminded herself, the daughter of Aed Finnlaith.

"It goes on as always," Eric was saying with a laugh as he cast his booted feet on the table. "Swein of Osgood cut off Harilk's ear in a fight, Harilk's brother stabbed Swein, Swein's widow cried out for justice, and Harilk was killed by her uncle. The feud will go

on, brother, no doubt, until both families are reduced
to babes in the—''

Olaf, meditating upon the fire, was startled when his
brother's voice stopped cleanly in midsentence. He
was further stunned to see his brother staring toward
the stairwell with wide eyes and slack jaw, and then
somewhat recoup himself to remove his feet from the
table, scrambling to stand.

He followed his brother's gaze with both amusement
and irritation. Erin was coming down the stairway.

Had there ever been a time, he wondered pensively,
when he had been able to look upon her beauty
dispassionately? With no more absent appreciation
than he gave his magnificent horse? Perhaps not, perhaps he had always been somewhat caught within her
spell, as Eric was now. She was fresh from a bath, her
hair was more luxurious than deepest midnight, curling in tendrils to frame the elegance of her perfect
features and the eternal emerald brilliance of her eyes.
The silk she wore caressed a supple form made even
more beguiling at this stage of her pregnancy when her
breasts swelled against the restraint of the cloth and
the roundness of her belly was a beckoning curve. Her
cheeks were tinged like a rose against purest cream,
her lips were a subtle curve, tinted a slight red.

As he had so often since he had quit their chamber,
no longer able to bear the tension and torture of being
so close and yet unable to touch her by his own
decree, he felt desire pierce through him at the mere
sight of her. Grinding his teeth, he watched her descend the stairs, lifting his brow and forcing a cool
smile of expectancy to his lips.

''Ah, Erin, at long last. We have guests, my love. I
would have you meet my brother, Eric. I am afraid,
being kin of mine, that he is, alas, a Viking, but one I
am sure you will find palatable. Eric, I give you my
. . . Irish wife, Erin mac Aed, Princess of Tara, Queen
of Dubhlain.''

Eric's eyes left Erin momentarily to slide reproachfully to Olaf. Then they once more returned to Erin with unmasked appreciation.

"Erin mac Aed of Tara," Eric breathed, his eyes sparkling as he walked swiftly to the staircase to capture Erin's hand. "I have seen a multitude of women in a multitude of places, yet I come here today to discover that the one I must call 'sister' is the fairest of them all."

Erin smiled, unable to resist the brash charm of this stranger who was her brother-in-law. He was like Olaf, and yet he was not. He spoke to her in Norse, and in dress and manner he was Viking. Yet he possessed a gallantry that Olaf did not. He was, perhaps, as Olaf might have been at one time, carefree and light. He was a raider with few cares, but for all his flippant charm, he lacked certain qualities that the Wolf did possess. He had not his brother's quiet strength, nor towering aura of power and will. "If you come in peace to our shores, Eric, I am glad to meet you. I hadn't known Olaf had a brother, and I am glad to welcome his family."

Eric chuckled pleasantly. "A brother? He possessed, at one time, seven. Three are lost upon distant shores, but I wager, lovely sister-in-law, that you will meet the remaining lot of us as the years pass. The size of our households, my lady, is one of the reasons so many of us go adventuring. We overflow our homes and lands and to gain, we must move outward and seek our fortunes upon faraway lands."

It was Olaf's laughter Erin heard next. "Take care for your comments, brother. My wife does not approve those who seek their fortunes upon the lands of others. She has, upon many occasion, seen fit to subtly remind me that I am but a barbarian invader."

"If my brother has so failed, Erin mac Aed, I will strive to do my best to see that I leave you knowing that we, in Norway, are not so different from the Irish. We humbly farm our lands, and we live the quest of all men, peace and health and harmony within our families."

"Ahh . . . but the peace you seek is only within your own land," Erin contradicted, still smiling.

"Do not attempt to reason with my wife," Olaf warned his brother, striding to the stairway to slip an arm through Erin's and lead her away from his brother toward the hearth where he turned her so that he might possessively slip both arms about her waist and speak over the top of her head. "Erin would have you sending apologies to all you have warned against and replenishing all coffers you have seized."

Erin thought it impossible that Eric did not hear the hostile mockery in Olaf's voice. She felt the taunt with all of her body. It was in his rigid touch, in his voice that whispered against her hair. She wished she had the nerve to slap his hands from her and boldly inform Eric that his brother considered himself shackled by honor and alliance to a traitoress.

But Eric saw nothing amiss. He was smiling broadly. "It seems that Irish carries a bit of the Norse. Am I mistaken, brother? Or may I carry to our father the news that she begins a dynasty within your Irish lair?"

Erin flushed furiously as Olaf spanned his fingers over her belly. "Aye, Eric. The jarl will be pleased to know that the seed of his seed flourishes well in distant isles. Tell him . . . tell him that the Wolf creates fine grandsons for him, to grow to go a-Viking, as his heritage."

Erin stiffened furiously, but the steel of Olaf's hand increased against the protest of her body. She strained her lips into a smile over clenched teeth. "Nay, good Eric. Tell your father, the jarl, that the seed of his seed has entered into a fine and noble race, cultured and learned. He should be proud to grandsire an Irish child."

"Erin," Olaf protested, feigning confusion. "I have spent much time with Irish kings and warriors, and I was led to believe that should a wife be set aside, her child remained with its sire, for that child would be his father's heir, and the Irish guard well the priorities of inheritance."

A chill of fear swept through her spine. Had he then decided that she should remain until his heir was born and weaned, and then return her to her father, their marriage contract put aside honorably as no man was expected to keep a woman as his wife if she had brought a sword against him?

She did not want to tremble as he held her; yet she was aware that he felt the shivering from deep within that she could not control. Dear God, she would never allow him to take her child. Had she slashed her own throat by decrying him so strenuously? He no longer sought her out, no longer cared to sleep beside her. But what else could she have done? Pleaded guilty when she was not? Nay!

"I think," Eric interrupted her thoughts with dry amusement, "that this child, Irish or Norse—whichever you ever decide—will be one to reckon with, judging by his—or her—mother and sire! But what of this great hall, Olaf? You rush me to this splendid place of stone and mortar, but offer not a weary traveler mead or ale to cool his throat?"

"The queen is remiss in her duties," Olaf said coolly, releasing Erin. "Wife, you will see to the comforts of *my* family and friends."

Erin lowered her lashes to hide the seething resentment and sudden rush of pain within her eyes. It was true that Olaf had always welcomed her family with no reservations. He had supported her eldest brother in battle, avenged the brother she had lost, but Eric standing within the hall, offering Olaf the familiarity of kin, struck her anew with pain for that brother she had so recently lost. This was her land; Leith's land. Husband or no, Olaf was a Viking, as was the fur-clad warrior who was his brother. Raiders. Invaders. She was the wife of the Wolf; she could have just as easily been given to a Dane. Perhaps there would have been little difference.

She raised her lashes to see a thoughtful and pensive look in Eric's blue-gray eyes as they fell upon her. "I

would thank you greatly, my new sister, if you would
be so kind to see to my needs.''

Erin looked away quickly at the gentle kindness in
the Viking's voice. Had Eric at long last sensed the
tension that raged within the hall between Irish queen
and Norse king? It was as if he reached out with what
power he had to soothe and smooth the currents from
the air.

"I shall be glad to see that you are served," Erin
said quietly, lifting her chin and sailing on light feet
from her husband. She turned when she would have
exited the hall to seek the kitchen. Her luminous eyes
lit upon Eric once more and she added with a touching
dignity, ''And I am glad to call you brother, Eric.''

Erin did not return to the great hall. It was filling
with the Norse heroes who had come to sample the
hospitality of the Wolf and she did not think she could
stomach the tales of conquest that she would most
likely hear. She spent the morning with Moira, expecting to find a certain solace for her own agitation in her
friend's company. But she grew more miserable.
Moira loved to speak of how their children could grow
as friends, and Erin doubted more each day that Olaf
intended her to see her child grow at all.

As afternoon came, Erin grew more restless. She
had obeyed Olaf's ultimatum and remained within
their residence since their return, but suddenly she
cared little for his warnings. The urge to escape his
Norse walls of stone was overwhelming. With the
commotion taking place as the city and residence were
swarmed with the visitors from the sea, it would be
easy for her to slip outside unnoticed. She could ride
to the cliffs, allow the tempest of the ocean to soothe
her soul, and return.

You are foolish, she thought as she let herself out
through the kitchen, to taunt Olaf further. Yet she was
the wronged party, the victim with no recourse. She
had to go to the sea. It beckoned to her compellingly.

As she rode she could feel the earth fly beneath her,

feel the power and strength of her horse. It was freedom. But from the cliff she could see the harbor and beach at the mouth of the Liffey and the great dragon ships that lay at anchor. Today the ships offered her no threat, and yet they did. They symbolized the gulf that lay between herself and Olaf; a gulf of custom, of society . . . of trust.

I will never forgive him, she reminded herself with poignant pain, and yet she had nothing with which to fight him. He had the power to take everything from her, and give her nothing. If he had tired of her, she was truly lost, and no matter how her dignity and mind cried that she must deny him always until her strength could hold no more, her heart and body cried out for him. She missed him unbearably in the nights, and she tortured herself with visions of him holding another. There had been something beautiful once, if only for a brief time. Something golden and beautiful. A joining that went beyond conquest, fight, anger, or fear. Beyond race, beyond peoples. That day upon this very cliff, long ago now, another world, another time. They had met as a man and a woman, touched . . . loved. . . .

Watching the surf as it pounded and broke against the rock Erin barely heard the hoofbeats until they were upon her. Despite her resolution that she cared not about Olaf's decrees, a shaft of fear bolted through her. She turned from the sea in panic, only to find herself giddy with relief as she saw that it was Brice and Gregory who rode toward her.

"Erin!" Gregory called to her, his tone both scolding and relieved. "Dearest cousin, I never thought you to be a fool!"

Erin stiffened with shock on her mount as Gregory and Brice drew abreast. She glanced from cousin to brother before exploding, "Fool! Gregory, that you of all people should charge me so—"

"Erin, you *are* behaving like a fool," Brice interrupted her firmly. His voice softened. "Did you think, sister, that Gregory and I hadn't demanded of your husband what recourse he had taken? Olaf told us that he ordered only that you remain within his house. That is gentle action, sister, for a Viking—nay, for any man who faced his wife at swordpoint.''

Erin closed her eyes momentarily. "Gentle action! Brice, I did not set out against Olaf! I was misled. If my own brother does not give me the shadow of doubt—''

"None of this matters now!" Gregory exclaimed, stopping the quarrel that was quickly becoming heated. "Erin, we must get back. A messenger has come from Tara, and your husband seeks you out.''

Erin caught her lower lip between her teeth before it could begin to tremble. "Does he know that I am gone?''

"We don't know," Gregory said softly. "I suggest we return quickly. The hall is crowded; perhaps he has not discovered your absence yet, so let's spend no more time talking.'' He turned his mount and nudged the horse to a run. Brice and Erin followed in swift pursuit. They did not slow until they reached the city walls. Once inside, Brice urged her to dismount. "Go back in by the kitchen, Erin, and pretend that you have been busy. Gregory and I will see to your mare.''

Erin nodded with a lump in her throat. "Brice," she said softly, "I tell you, I was not guilty. But I thank you, brother.''

"We are mac Aeds, Erin. And if you tell me you are not guilty, then I will trust you.''

Erin nodded and walked swiftly away from the two. She slipped around to the back and entered the kitchen, grateful to see that all was busy chaos. She chatted with Freyda and several of the cooks, and then moved quickly into the hall, trying to still the tremors of nervousness that could so easily give her away. To her relief, she stumbled upon Eric, who was inspecting the structure of his brother's walls.

"Erin!" he greeted her, grinning. "She who is Irish I seek to feast my eyes upon above any other.''

Some of her nervousness faded away as she smiled

in return. She had never thought she could enjoy a flirtation with a Viking, yet she did. He offered her a friendship that was both respectful of her as his brother's wife and sweetly flattering to her well-bruised ego.

"I doubt, Viking brother," she murmured, "that you have much need to seek to conquer with force, for surely you win surrender with your agile tongue and winning smile."

Eric laughed, his eyes assessing her warmly. "Ah, my Irish lass, I think a man needs not a facile tongue to toast your beauty."

"But surely quick wit and charm are advantageous," Erin started but Olaf's voice cut into her conversation dryly. Her tremors began again as she turned her eyes to his blue stare.

"I have been looking for you, my lady wife." She could not tell from his cross-arm stance, nor from his cool voice, if he suspected her of defying his edict. As he so often did, he seemed to challenge with his words, drawing her into a trap.

"I have been busy about, my lord," she murmured, sweeping past him.

He caught her arm, halting her. For a moment the riveting blue of his Nordic eyes seemed to impale her; then he smiled at Eric. "You will pardon us, brother. A messenger from her father awaits my lady."

"You are pardoned," Eric said cordially. Erin decided there was a bit of the devil to Eric as he caught her free hand and bent low over it to brush it lightly with his lips. "I look forward to the evening, sister. I will enjoy the company of a beautiful woman at my side."

Olaf grunted impatiently and pulled her away. They walked in silence to Olaf's war chamber, but Erin was trembling again, a touch of exaltation mingling with her fear. Was it possible that Olaf might be jealous on her behalf? The longing left her as she began to wonder if he knew that she had disobeyed his edict.

Gregory and Brice already awaited them, along with a small man wearing the colors of her father's troops.

Olaf nodded to the three within the room and moved to the window, leaning against the wall and staring out to the courtyard. The messenger glanced his way nervously, cleared his throat, and began to speak. "Aed Finnlaith, Ard-Righ of the Irish, decrees that his son, Brice, and his nephew, Gregory of Clonntairth, return to Tara upon the morrow. Priests have been assembled to offer masses for the soul of Leith mac Aed, and it is fitting that his family should attend." The messenger again cleared his throat, glancing at Olaf's back. "Aed Finnlaith, Ard-Righ of Ireland, also requests that his daughter, Erin, wife and queen of the king of Dubhlain, should attend these masses. He asks that his ally, his son by marriage, Olaf of Norway and Dubhlain, attend Tara at his leisure, and join with the yearly Fais, the article of government, to be—"

The messenger droned on, but Erin no longer heard him. Home! Her mother—how she longed to see her mother. And Aed! It had seemed an eternity since she had seen her father. Their parting had been so bitter. She wanted to see him so badly, to crawl into his arms, to feel his love, to allow his wisdom to soothe her. Home. A place to regain her strength, to find peace and refuge. . . . She came back to the present as she heard Olaf speaking. "I am afraid that my wife and I cannot leave Dubhlain now. I have been fighting wars too much of my time; there is much urgent within the city that requires my attention. I will, however, endeavor to arrive for the Fais, and I would have you convey my appreciation to the Ard-Righ for his invitation to join with the Irish lords."

Erin felt as if she had received a blow, a knife twisting within her stomach. He wasn't going to allow her to go.

"Olaf," Gregory said in her behalf with a quiet dignity, "Aed asks that his family come together to pray for a brother lost. Brice and I would take it upon ourselves to guard well your wife—"

"Olaf . . ." Erin winced as she realized the voice that pleaded was her own. But she had spoken and she had to continue. "I would dearly love to see my father."

He stared at her coolly. "We will discuss it no more at present." His eyes lit on Gregory and Brice, and new shivers raced along Erin's spine as she saw the reflective gaze. Olaf knew. He knew that her brother and cousin had hurried her back to the city, but he said nothing, except to dismiss the messenger. He stalked past them to the door, then turned. "The evening awaits us. Erin?" He inclined politely, coolly.

She forced herself to swallow the disappointment that had risen sickly within her and nodded. She did not glance at Brice or Gregory, but hurried from the chamber and out to the great hall where she silently took her place at the table. She could not look at Olaf for the tears stinging her eyes as he sat to her left. Vikings and Irish filed to their places with surprising gaiety and curious good humor, but Erin noted little of what took place. Dear God, how she wanted to go home, to her mother, to Tara, to the ancient place of beauty and pride, invincibly, irrefutably Irish.

She was drawn from her thoughts as Eric, who had indeed chosen the seat to her right, bent his head low to hers. "It is interesting, is it not, my lady, to stare about this hall. Men have become friends here. We were born to tear apart one another's throats, heedless that we may be men of like concerns. Yet today I spent hours with your brother discussing the merits of careful horse-breeding; he an Irishman, I a Norwegian. We seem to have much in common, Brice mac Aed and I. Yet were he not your brother, and I Olaf's, it is likely we would have met not across the shoulders of a horse, but within an axe's length of one another."

"It is interesting, Eric, and always good, when men are not seeking to destroy each other," she replied, smiling ruefully at his sharp wisdom.

"It is a pity that those who create the peace cannot find it," Eric said, his eyes touching hers with empathy. He bent even closer. "Yet think of this, Erin of

Tara: the wisest men can oft be the blindest of fools for they rule by integrity, yet not from the heart.''

Erin glanced at him curiously, wondering that he so freely offered her so much.

He smiled slowly, his blue-gray eyes twinkling mischievously. "But then again, perhaps the brother of a Wolf is the only one who would dare to twist his tail and force him to feel his heart.''

He winked at her, raising a brow past her to his brother's chair, then suddenly returned to his food. Erin lowered her head and covertly followed Eric's glance toward Olaf.

His granite features were darkened by a brooding scowl, his brows furrowed in frowning contemplation. She smiled secretively, then pursed her lips. Was Eric indeed managing to twist the Wolf's tail? Could it be jealousy he felt as he watched her talk and smile easily with his own kin?

Her smile faded as Olaf dipped his head to hers and spoke softly. "Tread carefully tonight, Irish, for you have sought to take me for a fool one time too many. I am well aware that you flagrantly disobeyed me, equally aware that your cousin and brother all but tripped over themselves in an attempt to save you from my wrath.''

Erin's throat constricted and she made no further attempt to pick at her food. She sat back in her chair, and she turned toward him and pleaded quietly, "I beg that you do not hold my brother and Gregory responsible for my actions—''

Olaf leaned back and watched her assessively, his blue gaze still brooding and yet alert, again, as if he baited a trap, or watched carefully for reaction. "I hold nothing against the two, for they are brave and stalwart lads, fine, loyal warriors both. They are your kin; it is natural that they blindly seek to protect you.''

Erin attempted to calmly sip from the silver chalice she shared with Olaf. "Perhaps it is not blind loyalty, my lord, but simple trust.''

"Trust, Irish?'' he queried politely. "My back was

turned today, and instantly you defied me. But no matter. You but solved a dilemma for me. I would, perhaps, have allowed you to visit your father in the company of those two. Today you but sealed my reply for me.''

The knife wound of his words struck deeply and seemed to twist. She sipped at the chalice, but her fingers trembled and the mead sloshed dangerously close to the rim. She set the chalice down and knotted her fingers together in her lap, thinking to speak coldly before the tears hovering dangerously became futile sobs.

"That is your final word then," she said coldly.

She did not see the pulse that ticked rapidly against his throat. "It should be," he replied, his voice curt and yet disturbingly husky. "But perhaps, Irish, it will depend upon the strength of your desire to see your family."

Startled by his reply, Erin glanced his way too quickly, her eyes giving away the hope he had raised within her. "What do you mean?" she could not prevent from asking hoarsely.

Maddeningly, he did not reply right away. His eyes were riveted toward the center of the hall where the entertainment was beginning. Erin followed his gaze, clenching her teeth with agony and resentment.

Olaf was watching a uniquely beautiful woman who danced. Her skin was a honey color, her eyes as black as the night and almond shaped. She wore silk trousers that concealed little, and she performed to music unlike any Erin had ever heard before. She danced with a rhythm that offered but one promise: that of seduction.

"He turned her down, Erin of Tara." She turned quickly to catch Eric's gentle eyes upon her. "A man only denies such pleasure when he feels he holds a superior treasure."

Eric smiled and returned to conversation with the Norseman on his right before she could reply. Erin stared at her untouched food, then back to the dancer.

There seemed little reason for her to remain longer within the hall. Olaf would not, most likely, notice her departure.

Yet before she could move, she felt his hand or her arm, and found that once more his eyes burned their ice fire into hers.

"Where do you seek to run to now, Irish?" he demanded softly.

"I do not run," she told him with quiet dignity. "I am but tired, and anxious to find rest within my chamber."

He watched her, slowly releasing her. "Then go to your chamber, my wife, but await me. We have things to discuss."

To Erin's horror, she felt a tremor of heat sweep through her with his mere words. How horrible it was to resent a man with such warranted anger and yet long for him so that it made her melt with weakness.

"It appears to me," she said with applaudable disdain, "that you but enjoy to taunt. There is naught to discuss."

He smiled. "Ah, but, Irish, what has it always been between us? Barter and contract. Mayhap you will discover that you wish to barter again."

"You are mistaken," she murmured a bit breathlessly. "I did not barter, but *was* bartered."

"Perhaps, Irish, we shall see. Go to our chamber—but await me, for I will be along soon."

Erin barely heard Eric's wishes for a pleasant night. She hurried from the table with her heart pulsing a dangerous beat and her breath coming in shortened gasps. She rushed up the stairway and through her door, closing it quickly to lean weakly against. God help her, but what was this new taunt of his? She trembled, she felt afire. How was she to resist him? She *must* resist him and yet she could not bear it were he to seek out the exotic dancer or another. Fool, she chastised herself, for she knew not where he had slept since he had left her bed.

"What do I do?" she whispered aloud, for holding

herself away from him was the only power she had, the only dignity she could retain when he continued to hold her captive as traitor.

A small sob escaped her. If she could only go home, she would not have to know if he sought another. She could find new strength, and ease the pain that cried from within, betraying self, betraying resolve. Seeing him, she ached for him with a searing, shivering agony. How long before the love she couldn't kill with anger and the passions that were constantly a tempest between them broke down the slender barriers of her control and left her truly at the mercy of the Wolf?

CHAPTER

21

The moon was a slender but bright crescent in the sky as Erin stared at it. The stars were a glittering array of splendor against the ink black of the sky. The air that passed through the open window was cold, yet Erin could not bring herself to close it, and so she shivered in her thin linen shift. It made little difference. The tension that riddled through her was far greater than the cold. She didn't think it possible to be more nervous, and still she trembled slightly when she heard the door open and then close, a new wave of jittery sensation sweeping through her.

She did not turn, but waited, aware that he leaned against the door he had so purposely closed, aware that he watched her. She swallowed sharply, wondering afresh what game he played, for if he had decided he wanted her again, he knew he had but to take her. Her thoughts traveled treacherously along that course. She had to maintain her stand against him, and yet she prayed that he would reach out and demand until she succumbed, for then she would have him again and her pride could be retained.

"I must applaud you, wife," he stated finally in a

soft drawl. "It appears you have captured my brother's heart. Eric is most impressed."

Erin shrugged, keeping her back to him. "I find Eric to be courteous and pleasant."

"Strange, since he is kin to me."

Erin ignored his comment. "I would have prepared more graciously for your kin had I been aware that he was coming. Indeed, had I been aware he existed."

"Did you think, madam, that Vikings were truly the spawn of your devil, spewed upon the earth rather than born of mother or father? Surely you must have expected that I did have family."

"You have never spoken of family."

"You have never asked."

Erin shrugged once more, shivering as a ripple in the breeze sent a gust of cold air sweeping inward. They were silent, and Erin felt that the cold but echoed the distance between them. Yet she knew that she had only to turn and meet the steel of his eyes to feel that she was touched by flame.

She didn't want to turn; didn't want to meet those eyes that stole into her soul, threatening to rob her of all pride, lay bare all that sought so desperately to remain hidden in her heart.

"Close those shutters!" he suddenly commanded her gruffly. "Do you wish to endanger your health and that of my child?"

Erin closed the latticed shutters, but continued to stare blankly at them. Silence reigned between them once more, so long that she wondered if she would shortly pound the stone walls and shriek aloud like the wailing death ghosts that haunted the forests.

"Turn around, Erin," he commanded softly at long last.

She did so slowly, lacing her fingers tightly before her and lowering her head slightly to stare at them rather than him.

"I would be curious, Irish, to know why it is that you will not face me."

Erin raised her eyes to his. "And I would be curious, my lord, to know just what game you play."

Olaf hiked a brow high in a handsome show of questioning innocence as he crossed his arms over his chest and smiled dryly. "I am afraid you shall have to explain yourself further if you wish a reply."

"All right," Erin said coolly, lifting her chin. "What is it that you want, my lord? What is it that we have to discuss?"

"It is not what I want, Erin, but what you want."

She turned away from him again, staring at the closed shutters. "You will not bait me, Olaf. I do not expect you to give me leave to travel with Gregory and Brice to Tara."

"Turn around, Erin, and please do not press my patience by making me continually ask you to do so."

She did so, sighing impatiently.

"Tell me, Irish," he demanded softly. "Who is it that you grieve? Leith, or the young king of Connaught? Brother or lover?"

"Fennen was never my lover," Erin replied quietly. "That you well know."

He inclined his head slightly. "Answer my question, I pray you."

"I mourn for them both, Olaf," she replied with quiet dignity. "A brother loved dearly throughout the years, and a friend who was valiant and caring, a noble young ruler of his province."

Olaf was silent for a moment and then spoke to her softly. "Of this I will speak to you no more, and tread no more callously upon your feelings, for the pain that you bear is one that I know, and I would not twist a dagger that pierces within a heart."

He cleared his throat, as if impatient with his own core of emotion. His voice changed abruptly to its more customary deep and politely mocking cynicism. "The question is, Irish, just how dearly do you wish to go?"

She felt a hammering begin in her heart as she realized the strange light in his eyes this evening was one with which she was not familiar. They burned a strange indigo, aloof, but probing with intensity.

"Surely you know," she replied, inwardly bemoaning the fact that she could make her voice no more than a pained whisper, "that I want desperately to see my father . . . to see my home." She silently cleared her throat, but her voice was still husky. "Just as we both know, my lord, that you will deny me."

He did not reply right away. The heat she had expected tinged her body and cheeks a blushing rose as he traveled her form slowly with his eyes. The linen she wore, she knew, was sheer. In the candlelight her form was certainly a silhouette beneath it.

His eyes returned to hers. "Perhaps not, Irish. That is up to you."

"You jest."

"No, I do not. It will depend upon the prize being worth the barter."

"I do not understand why you taunt me with these words of barter," Erin cried with a breathless but caustic bite. "Do you ask me to barter my body, and promise that by so doing I may travel to my father's home? Then I do say, aye, my lord, for it has been my experience to know that you will do as you please whatever my word. You are, as yet, my husband. I have never fought you."

She was surprised to see a subtle grin of amusement seep into the full lips fringed by the neatly clipped beard. "That, Irish, is debatable. But nay, Erin, I do not ask you to barter your body. I am not a fool, lady, nor would you be able to barter what is already mine."

A crimson spread of anger and humiliation covered the lighter hue of soft rose. She had thought to be so cool and disdainful, and still he merely played with her. She had been the fool to assume he wanted her when he had stayed away these weeks. While she grew steadily more rounded and awkward, a beautiful creature, bred to the ways of pleasure in a distant land, awaited to fill his needs if he so chose.

"I beg you then," she snapped, "cease with these

games, for I do grow tired. Say aye or nay that I may
go—''

"A man," he interrupted, "any man, aye, even a
Viking, says aye or nay most oft according to his
mood. If he is in a pleasant mood, relaxed and cajoled,
he is far more likely to say aye. The more that he is
pleased, the more he tends to please."

"Olaf!" Her voice was half sob, half shriek. "What
is it that you want of me? You say that I have naught
to barter—''

"No, that is not what I said."

He stopped her with a voice so quiet it was almost a
whisper, and yet she heard it with her entire being. It
touched her, sent dizzying heat along her spine and
throughout her limbs, just as surely as had his hands
come upon her.

"I said only," he continued, taking a step toward
her, then halting, "that you could not barter your
body, for, aye, wife, that is mine. But I do not seek a
reluctant woman. Nor even a response that is gratify-
ing, but begrudged. You once told me that there is that
which can be taken, that which can only be given. And
you were wise in that, Irish. Please me, Irish. Come
to me, give to me—''

"Again you jest!" Erin snapped coldly, "for I cannot while you label me—''

"Ah, but that is the premise of barter. One must
give to gain. If you wish to go to Tara, then you must
improve my mood, for it is dark at present."

Erin stared at him long and incredulous, the emerald
fire in her eyes seeming to leap out and mesh like
jagged lightning with the blue ice sizzle of his. "I
cannot—'' she began again in a bare gasp, but her
voice faded as he shrugged and turned from her,
yawning as he plucked at the brooch upon his shoulder.

"Then, alas, you shall remain within my walls."

"Olaf!" Erin unlaced her fingers and her fists
pounded into the stone behind her.

He turned to face her once more, one golden brow hiked in polite inquiry.

"You are a bastard!" she raged.

"That has been your general consensus."

Torn and confused, she continued to stare at him. "What difference—"

His brow arched higher, his mocking grin broadened. "Oh, I expect a tremendous difference, Erin. That is the bargain."

Still she hesitated, as if the seconds could give her some divine answer to her dilemma. "You are wrong, Olaf, for whether I walk the steps between us or you, I am still forced."

"Nay, Erin. You will move by choice. Tonight you have but to tell me nay and I will leave the room."

"And deny me leave to travel to my father!"

He shrugged. "I say again, a man in good and gentle humor is far more likely to give. And think on this, Erin. You ask a lot. Guests dwell within our residence, and you seek this after going behind my back to defy my will. It is completely your choice. In fact, I warn you, you must please me greatly for the events of the day have sorely tried my temper."

Erin wound her fingers tightly into her palms, abrading her flesh with her nails. It seemed that he always won his battles with the element of surprise, the twist in method of assault. This one had left her stunned and without defense. If only she could look upon him coolly, and tell him that there was no prize he could offer to get what he asked.

He had truly left her vulnerable, without defense. She was afire with the longing for him to take the steps . . . his steps . . . those that would have left her with pride. Her mind dulled with the needs of her flesh and heart. She could not let him walk out the door. Her pride did not equal the sacrifice of knowing that tonight, with his passions racing strong, he could turn from her, depart the room, and seek out the exotic beauty who had danced well.

His brow lowered as he shrugged and turned once

more for the doorway. She could hesitate no longer. "Olaf!" her voice was a rebellious snap, and yet husky and trembling.

He paused, leaning with an air of expectancy against the solid wood. "I mean what I say, Irish," he said harshly. "No half measures. No rigid kisses from cold lips. You come to me freely, and you offer all."

She trembled and her throat went dry. Olaf, she pleaded silently, if only you would take the steps, you would find all that you seek. Would that I could do that which you ask. I am afraid, afraid that I shall fail. Afraid that my thickening form shall not be as alluring as that which you watched so gracefully dance. . . .

"Erin."

The quiet tone of his voice was compelling, and still she could not move. He spoke again, and she realized that he could truly reach into her heart and soul with the blue steel of his gaze.

"You are, my wife, more exquisitely beautiful to me than ever before. It is my child that rounds your belly, fills your cheeks with the rose of health, and heavily lades your breasts. Indeed, Erin, when the remaining moons have come and waned and you have come full term, your form shall still, for me, be the most uniquely beautiful. You are more than fever to me, Irish, and as yet, I cannot fathom that fever."

Tears hovered beneath her lashes. Do not speak gently to me, she cried out inwardly. Do not flatter and cajole when you speak with the needs of the flesh and not of the heart. . . .

"Irish, I will wait no longer."

Her eyes raised to his with the fire returned to them. She would show him no more of her fears, no more of her heart. He wished to barter. She would live up to her side of the barter. He twisted her soul and she would pay the price he demanded with all of the finesse she possessed.

She took a step from the window and then halted, staring at him as she reached for the hem of her shift and pulled it slowly upward, over her head. Still staring at him, she dropped the garment carelessly, and waited while the Nordic blue of his eyes drew deeper as they swept over her, giving her little clue of their assessment as he continued to await her action.

She began to walk toward him, unaware that the shivering reticence behind the act of boldness made her steps more alluring, the sway of her hips ever more an enticement.

Why was it, he wondered, that each time he saw her, she was a feast he must devour voraciously with his eyes again and again? He did not lie when he told her she held an even greater fascination, for she carried his child beautifully. Her throat and shoulders still so slender, so straight, her breasts enlarged and full, the veins within pale trails of blue that beckoned the gentle touch of his fingers, her nipples darkened to a dusky rose, erect and flowering like petals that bloomed. He could still see the shadows of her ribs below her breasts, and then the subtle swelling of waist, and the roundness of her belly within the angled lines of her hips.

Her legs had not changed. Long and lithe and yet wickedly shapely. She moved with mystery and inborn grace, each step she took a display of fluid seduction. All you need ever do is walk, my wife, he thought, and you would bring pleasure to any man who breathed.

It occurred to him then that he had bartered more than she, for he was letting her go to Tara. But for now it didn't matter. He would have bartered his soul to the Christian devil for this moment. Since he had watched her during the day, her emerald eyes flashing with laughter as she bedazzled his brother, he had known he would give anything, sacrifice the nights to come, just for this moment. Use any means, fair or foul, to have her come to him, reach out to touch, stare into his eyes with her own freely alight with emerald passion and the magic that existed in the sphere of tension between them.

His breath seemed to catch in his throat as she came nearer. The soft and subtle scent of roses assailed his senses, filling him, permeating his bloodstream. He could reach out and feel the midnight web of her silken hair, burrow beneath its fanning tendrils with aching fingers to caress the fullness of her breast. . . .

But he did not. He stood still, outwardly calm, yet trembling within. He was afire, and yet he waited still, for the ecstasy of her touch would surpass that of her sensuous movement toward him.

Erin paused as she reached him, lowering her lashes in ebony crescents over her cheeks. He did not reach for her; he tested her all the way. She shivered with hesitance, afraid again that she could not, rather than would not, give him the pleasure he demanded. But he gave her no quarter, and she had come this far. She could not retreat.

She raised her lashes and met the awaiting, assessive blue of a Nordic sky at dusk in his eyes. Her lips had gone dry, and she touched them lightly with the tip of her tongue and moved her bare feet on the floor to take the last step. She stood before him, not a hair's breadth away, close enough to feel the inferno of heat and power, the strength and muscle play that took place with his every breath, the full and potent extent of desire that was not hidden by his clothing.

"All the way," he whispered, his words a caress on her cheek. She stood on her toes and slipped her arms around his neck, and lightly, lightly brushed his lips with hers, trembling as the soft feel of his beard teased the flesh of her face. Erin edged backward slightly, but still he stared at her with his eyes filled with anticipation. She brought her hands to his face, smoothing a golden lock of hair from his forehead, then splaying her fingers to cup his cheeks and jaw. She grazed her thumb over his mouth, and moved closer once again, pressing her lips to his as she held him, molding her body against his, her breasts crushing to his chest, her hips locking and yet moving against him.

A groan rumbled from his chest as his arms came about her, solidly fusing their contact. The kiss she had begun deepened as he loosened the restraints of passion, stroking her mouth thoroughly with the warm and demanding shaft of his tongue. His hands moved over her back, massaging, commanding, tangling within her hair, exploring her shoulders and spine, lowering to cradle her buttocks and lift her ever more surely against him.

Already she was longing to cry out, to fall weakly against him. But as his lips parted from hers, she allowed the wealth of her tumbled hair to fall about her face, shielding her eyes, as she released her hold on his face to unfasten his brooch, allowing the wolf's crest of silver to fall heedlessly to the floor along with the majestic red fabric of his mantle, which floated down like a blazing cloud.

Her eyes caught his for a moment, and in that breathless span of time, she was aware that she surrendered her will to him, and yet in doing so found the strength of a strange trust. In those brief seconds came hungry admission; their needs were like the bloodred cloud of his fallen mantle, as pure and as honest, as strong and as undeniable, and as valiantly powerful. Erin lowered her eyes, sinking to her knees before him, humble and yet ever proud as she removed his boots.

He set his hands on her head and then threaded his fingers through her hair to draw her back to her feet. But she would not meet his eyes, instead turning her attention to the removal of his belt. He allowed her this action, fondling the midnight silk of her hair between his tense and trembling fingers. He briefly took his hands from her to draw his tunic over his shoulders and allow it too to cascade to the floor, and then she was again in his arms, softest naked flesh teasing his mercilessly, and yet appeasing it with sweet, sensual gratification. He was both amazed and shatteringly pleased as she continued her bold aggression with instinctive expertise, shifting herself against him, stroking his chest with the rhythmic caress of her breasts, his manhood with the subtle undulation of her hips. And still she moved, her lips and teeth grazing his shoulders, her delicate fingers finding strength and command as they caressed his shoulders and arms, explored the whorl of golden hair upon his chest, his nipples and the tautness of muscle beneath.

She lowered herself against him again, touching and caressing with fingers grown bold, with lips that tantalized as they explored with only slight hesitancy and great adventure. All . . . she did indeed give her all, playing the lover's game upon his senses that he had taught her about so well, teasing his thighs, his hips, taking him in a way that shattered and strengthened and flamed fires within him beyond endurance.

He reached for her then with a demanding groan of deepest agony and pleasure, his purpose undeniably intense. He carried her in his arms to the bed, and the eyes that met his were emerald and dazzling, all that he could have desired. She smiled, and again her eyes, with their dusky lashes, held the beauty and mystery that enwebbed him, compelled him with the fascination he could never escape.

He lay beside her, fanning her hair against the pillow. But she had become provocative energy this night, and she rolled against him, sliding her body along the length of his as she raised herself astride him, an arched silhouette of proud and splendid beauty as she took him within her. A shudder of pleasure ripped through him and he clutched her waist, guiding her as she began fluid, sensuous movement. His hands moved to the sleek line of her buttocks, and then suddenly all that was within him erupted into flame, and he caught the thick ebony tendrils of her hair to bring her to him, devouring her mouth with the hunger of his senses. She whimpered slightly at his demand, and yet she strove to match his tempest. His hands roamed her spine again, finding the curve of her hip, keeping her with him. His kiss broke and she rose above him again and again, but even as they met in the storm of their desires, he had to touch her breasts, and lifted himself to caress the tender globes, entangled within wild ebony hair, with his kisses.

He encircled her with his arms, and without departing from her, swept her beneath him, carrying them to the summit with a surge of passion and male demand. He clutched her to him as he felt her release, and caught her lips again with his final, shuddering thrusts, yet when they both lay still, he did not release her, but waited, and in moments began anew, a slow pulsing rhythm that rekindled the flames she had thought herself too complete to feel again.

"No . . ." she whispered weakly, lazy and shivering with the fulfillment of her body. "I cannot. I don't think. . . ."

"Ah, but, Irish, you can. Do not think . . . feel," he whispered in return, smiling knowingly as she moaned and writhed anew. Soon she clutched him ardently again, her nails raking his hair, grazing his back, adding thrill upon thrill to his system. He loved her, he watched her, he luxuriated in her, holding fast to her beauty and splendor. He savored each breathless gasp that came to his ears, he took pleasure in the shudders and cries that again racked her slender body so perfectly fit beneath his. Time. He wished so ardently for it to stand still. And yet the tempest that had swirled between them glided into peacefulness, and sweetly replete and exhausted, she slept. He watched the curve of her lips, parted as she breathed, the fine lines of her face, the sheen on the full elegance of her body. He wound her within his limbs and arms and exhaled a long sigh of the deepest satisfaction and slept.

Erin awoke slowly, content to drift in contentment. When she opened her eyes she would have to face truth, and that was a pain that she wanted to escape.

Her night had been storm and shelter, earth and magic. Yet it had all come about so that she might leave the golden Viking who still slept so soundly beside her.

She had met his price. She could ride to Tara, bring solace to her grieving mother, embrace her father, and sweep away the sorrows of the past. She would be able to mourn for Leith, for Fennen, to offer prayers that their souls would rest with the all-forgiving Christ. She needed that time, needed to feel close to those who loved her now, and those who had done so in their short time on earth.

More desperately than ever she needed to get away, for she could never win a battle when she found herself constantly giving ground. She had sworn never to forgive him; yet she knew, as any man or woman knew who had truly loved, that she would gladly forgive him, were he but to ask for her pardon.

She had oft dreamed of such a day, and in his arms, the dream became painfully real. Olaf, believing, taking her hand, admitting with anguish that he had wronged her, imploring her forgiveness, knowing it was not deserved. Telling her that he loved her above all others.

But that day would never come. She had to admit it, accept it. Tears filled her eyes. When he touched her, when he whispered words of how she pleased him, of how he loved to feel her, move within her, it was so easy to believe, to dream that he would one day love her, trust her, need her.

She had to make herself realize that words spoken in heated passion were easily dismissed. He did not need or love her; he wanted her, and even that was a fragile bond. She would be leaving and that very night he might whisper similar words to another woman. He wanted their child, but he had already warned with thinly veiled threats that he would be within Irish law to set her aside once the child was born.

She choked back a soft sob and became aware of him. His arm was haphazardly cast over her breasts, his muscled thigh and knee curved over her hip and leg. She opened her eyes and twisted slightly to study his features.

His face appeared so much younger in sleep. The

lines of strain were eased, the granite of his rigidly
controlled emotions was relaxed. The structure of his
face was still handsomely rugged, and yet with his rich
honey lashes shielding the piercing Nordic blue of his
eyes, he regained the qualities of reckless youth. His
lips, so full and defined in shape, were slightly parted
beneath the fringe of his clean clipped beard and
moustache. They curved a bit, as if his dreams were
sweet. A lock of sun-gold hair fell across his forehead,
meshed with the thick but clearly arched and defined
crescents of his oft thundering brows. She longed to
touch him, to feel both the softness and coarseness of
his hair, to smooth it from his brow, but she did not.
It was seldom that the Wolf slept so deeply. A sigh, a
shift, a movement, could easily awaken him, and it
was pleasant to gaze at him. A powerful man made
vulnerable to her anguished but thirsting study.

Her gaze moved over his shoulders and she grimaced as she thought it surely a fancy to see him as
vulnerable. Muscle rippled beneath the bronze of his
flesh even as he slept. He was solidly toned. Tight and
sleek and sinewed. The golden king of the wolves. . . .
And I am leaving him. I must, she thought painfully,
then suddenly wondered if he intended to keep his
bargain this morning. It was possible that he had
merely played with her, that he would laugh this
morning and tell her he owed her nothing.

Fuming with the shame of her own eager behavior,
she hastily began to slide from beneath his casually
splayed limbs, trying to caution herself to take care.
But this morning he was deeply asleep. Not a muscle
flickered within his face.

Erin stood and stretched, staggering slightly at the
soreness in her muscles, then looked hurriedly for the
linen gown she had discarded the night before. She
was congratulating herself upon her easy escape when
she froze with horror, hearing a monotonous but firm
tapping begin at the door. She flew to it, hoping to
answer the summons before Olaf awoke.

Rig stood before her, a bit taken aback as the door

was flung open with fury and Erin stared at him in wide-eyed dishevelment. He carried a tin of wash water, which sloshed precariously over his own hands as he took a step backward.

"Your pardon, my lady," he murmured quickly. "I did not know if you wished a bath or no, but I brought this as your brother says he wishes to leave within two hours. He asks that you have your things ready—"

"What?" Erin interrupted, shaking her head with confusion as her brow furrowed. How could Brice know that she had finally received permission to travel with him? Olaf had not been out of the chamber since she had agreed to his bargain.

"My lord Olaf announced last night that you would be accompanying Brice and Gregory home to Tara," Rig said cheerfully, certain he was bearing glad tidings. His smile faded as he saw Erin's face pale and her lips compress. "Is something wrong? Shall I tell your brother that you are not well enough to undertake the journey?"

"Oh, no, Rig. No, no, no. I do certainly intend to undertake this journey." Erin smiled through gritted teeth. "Please tell my brother I will have my things ready shortly and that I will be ready to leave at his convenience." Erin reached for the tin of water and kept smiling as she closed the door. She turned and looked at the figure of the man on the bed, still peacefully sleeping, his lips still curled in a pleasant half smile. She had never seen him appear more comfortable. Even in his sleep it seemed that he was smugly, arrogantly, content.

A bolt of fury whipped through her, and it was all that she could do not to scream her rage aloud. Somehow she controlled herself, and took steps toward the bed with cool purpose. She paused again, her eyes narrowing as she surveyed the relaxed contours of his ruggedly handsome face. Then she raised the tin of water above his head and chest and twisted it with a swift movement, sending a cold deluge on him.

His eyes flew open with instant alarm and he jerked

upward so quickly that she was forced to take a step back. His voice thundered out after his initial sputter with incredulous anger, "What in the name of the gods—"

He cut off as he saw her standing before him, her eyes narrowed and flashing dangerously, her delicate features tense and strained with rigid fury. He clashed his teeth together and his Nordic gaze narrowed in return. His voice, when he spoke again, was crisp and cold, filled with glacial warning and control as he removed himself from the puddle of water within the bedding. "I am hoping, Erin, that you can prove to me you have gone daft to make you behave so foolishly."

He moved toward her, but she did not step back from him. Erin tossed the empty water tin at him in a furious motion that caught him unaware, causing him to grunt and bend with the unexpected pain as the receptacle hit him cleanly in his belly.

"Barter!" Erin raged, planting her hands on her hips with heedless fury. "You scurvy, devious, lying Viking bastard! Heathen dirt! Rat, worm, snake of the earth—"

She was cut off as he gripped her wrist and spun her about so that she fell against the bed, into the sodden coverings. But Erin was wild with her anger. She rose to her knees and began hurtling oaths at him again. "You had already said that I might go. Son of a Norwegian bitch!"

At that he stepped towards the bed, leaning against it with one knee as he caught her chin in a firm clasp from which she could not escape nor fight without punishing pain. "Take heed of your reckless tongue, Erin," he said in a quiet but threatening warning, shaking his golden head of the water that dampened it. "Aye—I had decided last night that I would allow you to go. I never allow my decisions to be influenced by a woman."

Erin jerked herself from his grasp with the strength of her fury. "Damn you!" she hissed, her fists knotting and pummeling against his chest. "Damn you to a thousand hells—"

To her credit, it took several moments of keen concentration for him to secure her wrists and subdue her wild fury. "Watch it, Irish!" he snapped. "You are here still, and I can easily change my mind."

Erin tossed back her head and her hair streamed behind her in ebony disarray, highlighting the emerald fire in her eyes. "Nay, dog of the North, give me no more of your barters, bribes, or warnings! Never again will I heed your words—"

"Never have you given any heed to my words," he retorted, grappling for a wrist once more as she broke free. "Were you ever to do so—"

"You tricked me! You deceived me! You used me—"

Olaf suddenly broke into laughter. "Nay, Irish witch, I but gave you leave to vent your own needs and desires. I believe that I shall miss you greatly."

Erin struggled furiously to elude his hold, panting as she spoke. "That is difficult to fathom, Lord Wolf, as you choose to sleep elsewhere when I am present."

"And does that bother you, Irish?"

Erin dodged to bite the hands that held her. This time he was quicker than she, releasing her so suddenly that she careened backward. Before she could regain her balance, he caught her ankles and jerked her to the edge of the bed, causing her gown to ride high up her waist and her legs to encircle his torso. Suddenly she was no longer seeking to hurt him, but desperately dragging at the linen of her shift.

He leaned low against her, pinioning her hands above her, wicked amusement lacing his eyes.

"I did not know, Irish, that you were feeling neglected. I would have returned to my own chamber sooner."

"Let me go!" Erin hissed stubbornly, trying to ignore the intimate contact with his nudity.

Still he smiled. "Nay, witch, I cannot. I am a captive of all your moods, be they fair or foul. The seductress entices me to weakness, and yet the raving shrew also ignites the fires of my blood. And I cannot behave the gentleman, of course, because I am a Viking. And because I know that my haughty princess is also the most lusty of vixens. . . .''

"Damn you—you cannot do this to me!" Erin wailed, and something within her voice touched a chord within him. "You believe not a word that I say to you—"

"Erin," he interrupted with a strange quality to his voice. "Perhaps you are mistaken. I cannot give you the blind trust that you ask—what happened was too severe. And yet you are a witch, for you do twist my mind with your righteous denials. But you continue to defy me. . . .''

She lay still suddenly, staring into his eyes, trying to fathom if he spoke truth, seeking whatever emotion lay within him. "I defied you only because I so craved the air and my freedom," she murmured uneasily. Her eyes flared with anger once again. "But I am the one misused and abused, my lord. I tell you that it is *my* pardon you should be seeking."

Suddenly he was laughing again, and the sound was husky, from his throat. "I do beg your forgiveness, wife, for neglecting you so long. . . .''

"OHHHH!" Erin grated out exasperated fury. But as she attempted to struggle against him again, she but shimmied herself against the aroused potency of his masculinity.

"Nay, Olaf—" she began, her eyes widening with realization of her position.

"I did not stray, my fiery wench!" He chuckled, his eyes and voice touching her with an unexpected warmth. "I but slept by the heat of my hearth since I could receive none in my chamber. Does that make you happy, wife?"

"Ecstatic," she muttered sarcastically, shielding her eyes swiftly with her lashes.

"Aye, witch, I will miss you sorely," he murmured, and again she was so stunned by the tender warmth in his voice that she noticed not his quick release of her wrists, and could only gasp as he shifted with smooth and expert ease to bring himself within her. His mouth lowered over her parted lips, seizing the advantage. His kiss filled her with his being. He broke it to whisper against her mouth. "Aye, witch, I will miss you as air to breathe, as water to drink. Deny me not this last remembrance of you, for it is not palatable to me that I allow you to go."

Warm waters began a quivering rush through her with the fevered hunger of his words and slow, enticing movement. "Could I deny you if I chose?" she whispered weakly in return, too easily losing herself to the flaming embers of desire.

"Nay, wife," he murmured huskily, thrusting deep and seeming to touch her heart, her soul.

She gasped, parting her lips to capture his, surrendering to the beguiling winds of storm. He gave so little, and yet she grasped at every crumb. But she had no desire to deny him. Indeed, she mourned the fact now that she would leave him, for it seemed that they were destined to part each time they reached out and almost touched.

She responded to him ardently, loving him with a passionate intensity soaring and mingling with his own.

CHAPTER

22

It was snowing. Soft, light flakes whirled delightfully in the air, landing on Erin's woolen mantle and ebony hair in exquisite and delicate patterns.

She had been tired of the weary ride, and cold, but the snow began just as they reached the last hill before the duns and valleys of Tara, and its gentle touch somehow combined with the excitement of nearing home, and her spirits lifted.

She stared across the terrain, and upon the earthworks that fringed Tara, she saw the silhouette of a man. Her eyes narrowed as her horse's hoofbeats continued their monotonous tread. Coming ever closer, she watched the man, a poignant stirring beginning in her blood. He was tall and straight, and yet his hair and beard were very gray. His countenance was a proud one, but weathered and wrinkled with the cares and wisdom of the years. His face is so thin, Erin thought, a pain clutching her stomach.

Suddenly she dug her heels into her mare's flanks, leaving the others behind in a burst of speed. Snow and ground spewed in her wake as she flew across the space that separated them.

Aed watched as she came to him, his old heart seeming to stop and then take flight in nervous reverberations. It amazed him again that she was his, this child of such infinite grace and exquisite beauty. So much a picture of silver dreams as she rode, one with her horse, the delicate snowflakes mingling like diamond drops with the midnight ebony of her hair.

Coming to him . . . coming to him. He watched her face so anxiously as she approached, fear riddling through him. He wanted so badly to embrace her in his arms as the child she was no longer, and the terror of rejection kept him from stretching out his arms. As if he were a drowning man, his past life became an illusion before him. Erin, taking first steps toward him on wobbly legs, Erin flying on her dainty feet to be the first to embrace him when he returned from the field. . . . And always the dazzle of the land within her eyes.

The horse stopped before him and she leaped from the mare's back. Tentatively he met her eyes. He barely saw their brilliance before she was hurtling her slender body into his arms, and where he had stood straight, he suddenly shook.

"Father," she whispered, and the tears that slid from his eyes to his cheeks blended with the delicate flakes of the light drifting snow. He knew he had been forgiven.

Eric surveyed the table and floor with dry amusement. Today Moira had presented Sigurd with a healthy, squalling baby girl, and the Vikings, ready to celebrate at any excuse, had spent the evening in revelry and song—and in a good bit of wenching and drinking. A goodly number of his men had staggered on out to stables or rooms, but a goodly number also lay where they had fallen on the floor. An arm was draped over the table near him. He picked it up and allowed it to drop once more. It fell like dead weight, as the man merely careened with a groan to a more assured resting spot. Eric chuckled softly and drained the last of his ale, thinking of his brother. The Wolf

had drunk with his men, but no amount of ale seemed
to ease his brooding tension. Eric grinned again. The
Wolf had met his match in an Irish vixen and it seemed
he didn't quite understand that fact yet. The longer
she was gone, the worse his temper became. We are
all fools, he mused. We do not see when we are the
conquered. But his brother Olaf had done quite well.
Dubhlain thrived in peace and harmony with her Viking and Irish inhabitants. Olaf's cellars were filled
with meat and grain and mead and ale; his fields were
planted by willing hands, his sheep and cattle well
tended. He was a powerful man, and more. He was
cunning. He knew when to wage war and when to seek
peace. He earned the respect and loyalty of fuidar and
king.

Eric glanced sharply to the heavy doors of the hall
as they swung open. His brother entered, quite sobered, and looking like a host of thunderclouds loosed
by the gods.

Olaf glanced Eric's way sourly as he came to the
hearth and stood before the fire, warming his hands.
"What, brother? You still sit straight? And alone? It is
my observance that few maids may be left in Dubhlain
upon your departure."

Eric chuckled, unruffled. "Brother, there are nights
when I choose to be an observer. There has only been
one with worth to capture my heart within this hall,
and alas, I was condemned to call her sister."

Olaf groaned with impatience, rubbing his temple
with his fingers. "It appears she has taken your heart,
brother."

Eric shrugged. "And your own?"

"I do not give my heart. I did so once, and the pain
of finding it shattered was worse than that of a Danish
axe."

"Grenilde is dead, Olaf. You live, and so does your
Irish beauty."

"Aye," Olaf muttered bitterly. "Irish beauty. Cliffs
are beautiful, my brother, as is the sea, and both are
treacherous."

Eric stood and stretched, nudging a man aside with his foot. "Olaf, you have proven yourself a great prince, the mightiest of warriors, and the most proficient of kings. You are powerful, and you know your strength, and yet you have always been merciful in that strength. You have a far-seeing capacity to pardon those who have wronged you, and the capability to give back where you have taken. You are careful and judicial. And yet it appears, brother, that you have condemned the greatest heart of all that you have conquered, without thought of justice. To build, to dream, you stand outside yourself. You have no fear in battle when you gamble your life, and yet in life itself, brother, I believe you are afraid. Take another gamble, brother. Judge again as the king of wolves might, not the husband. You are missing your wife. Go to her. Bring her back."

Olaf stared at his brother with his temper barely held in check, and yet Eric did not fear his wrath. As he had spoken, Olaf was a man of justice; he would not seek revenge against the truth.

"Brother," Olaf finally said coldly, "does not the sea beckon to you as yet? Hasn't the time for you to go a-Viking come again?"

Eric grimaced ruefully. "That it has, Wolf. But I had thought perhaps you wanted my presence here were you to undertake a journey. Sigurd should have help if Dubhlain is assailed in your absence."

Olaf opened his mouth to speak, shut it, and stared at the flames in the hearth once more. "Aye, brother, I intend to travel and to bring her home. My son will be born in the Viking stronghold of Dubhlain."

Eric said nothing more, but he smiled as he quit the hall to leave his brother to his thoughts and images within the flame.

It was cold, but Erin was warmly garbed against the fresh chill of the air. The chapel had been stifling, and this morning her prayers had wandered continually. On her knees with her back straight as the priest droned on and on, she was vastly discomfited, and endured it only for her mother's sake. If there truly were a heaven, Leith and Fennen would abide there; their sins had been but those of youth. If God existed, he would welcome such men no matter what was said or done by others in their behalf.

She inhaled sharply of the morning air and smiled a little sadly as she stared at the houses in the valley before her. She did love Tara dearly. Under the light blanket of pure white snow, it appeared ever more regal and glittering, this place of kings. There would never be a time in Erin's life when she would forget Tara, or cease to think of it as her beloved childhood home. The stream where she had played, the emerald-green slopes where she had fought and tangled with her brothers, the Grianan where she had sat so many times with Maeve, trying to learn neat little stitches with her toes tapping impatiently as she thought of the vast world outside.

She was glad she had come. She had craved to see her mother, and Maeve had seemed so old and haggard with her grief. Erin knew that her presence was like a healing potion for Maeve. She was able to loosen her grip on her pain and the past as she fretted over her daughter's pregnancy. Erin smiled slightly. It was a wonderful time for them both. Maeve needed so badly to expend her love and energy and maternal instincts, and Erin could not help but enjoy the petting and pampering, so gentle and tender to her bruised soul.

But still, the greatest wonder of coming home had been seeing her father again. The rift between them had been unbearable to them both. Seeing his face lighten with a smile was a boon she would have trudged mountain and vale to achieve; knowing that she had unburdened his heart was pure balm to her own. She had spent uncounted hours with him since her arrival, times of great and touching love she could store within her memory for all the years of her life to come.

Yes, she was glad, so glad, that she had come.

And yet, coming home, she had experienced again a painful loss, a homesickness of new direction. For just as this was the place of her childhood, Dubhlain had become the home of the woman Erin. The great buildings rising of stone, the neat sidewalks of wood, the vast great hall where the meals began with the presence of the king and queen, the chamber at the top of the stairs, with its roaring warmth from the hearth . . . and her husband. How many nights had she lain there alone? And how many with him beside her, a strong comfort in the hours of the night, whether she railed against him or not? And even alone she had known that she lay in his bed, and that in itself had been comfort. Did he, she wondered, ever stretch his arms across the sheet where she should lie, and dream that he might hold her, or imagine with awakening thought that she might be there, beside him, length against length, her hair tangled about her shoulders?

With her thoughts, Erin turned to the northeast, as if she might see past time and space to Dubhlain. She smiled, thinking of the messenger who had brought her word of Moira's daughter. How she wished she might have seen the newborn infant! The messenger had been hesitant at first about divulging any more information about the birth, but at Erin's jubilation he had been drawn into giving her every detail, bringing her to merry laughter as she heard how the giant Sigurd had wept tears of happiness and drunk himself into a stupor that first night.

Erin's smile faded as she recalled that the Norseman bearing the tidings had blushed unhappily when she asked if he carried no word to her from Olaf. No, there had been no word. . . .

Erin spun about suddenly as she heard footsteps behind her. Quickly she brought a smile to her face again, for her father came toward her. She had lied to him with wide clear eyes from the beginning, laughing with delight upon her face and pain within her heart as she assured him that all was well, reminding him,

"I am my father's daughter, Ard-Righ. Always I will make my way and find my own strength."

Aed smiled in return before starting to chastise her. "The day is growing colder, daughter. Let me walk you to our house, that you may warm yourself by the fire. We want no harm coming to you or the babe."

Erin accepted her father's arm with outward obedience and an inward grimace. Olaf could have sent her to no finer keepers than her parents. They watched her with more loyal fervor than a pair of winter hawks.

"Your hands are chilled," Aed scolded.

Erin laughed. "Father, I'm fine. Not at all cold."

Despite her words, he slipped an arm around her and hugged her close. "Aye, Erin, you do look fine. You are like your mother in this. With each child she carried, she looked more lovely, and not a day did she spend feeling ill."

"Then I am heartily glad I am like mother," Erin replied. "I feel most awkward, and oft sleepy, but never ill."

They walked in companionable silence for a spell, but as they neared the house of the Ard-Righ within the valley, Aed paused. He looked at Erin pensively, and she wondered suddenly how many assurances of her state of well-being he believed. "You looked toward Dubhlain, daughter," he told her broodingly. "What were you thinking?"

Erin forced a cheerful shrug. "Nothing much, Father. I was thinking of Moira, I suppose. I am anxious to see her babe."

"Not anxious to see your husband?"

Again Erin shrugged. "He was scarce home when I left, Father. He had much work to do, and kin within the household. If he is able to attend the Fais, he will come within the next few weeks. But perhaps he may not be able to do so. War has kept him from the building that is his dream and goal." She could not tell her father that she believed Olaf would not come because of her. She was heavy with child now; of little use for passions that demanded a lithe and comfortable body. Although his words had stirred her heart with hope, she was convinced that he still believed her to be the worst of traitors.

Aed lowered his eyes. He paused for several moments before speaking. "He will come for you, Erin. He is a man who will want his child born in his household." Again Aed paused, and suddenly his arms, so strong in battle, so tender now, were around her as he hugged her to his chest, his child again. "I am afraid for you, Erin. Mergwin whispers of danger he cannot touch. He cannot see. . . ."

A chill whipped through Erin, but she forced herself to chuckle. "Father, what danger? I can get myself into no trouble, for I can no longer run, but must waddle when I walk! Be I here or there, I will be a new mother soon, busy with a child!"

Her words seemed to relieve Aed somewhat. "Take care, Erin, take great care, my beloved daughter. Mergwin's words so often hold wisdom. . . ." Aed released her suddenly, shrugging a bit sheepishly. "The old Druid was here, you know, waiting to see you."

Erin frowned. "He was? Why did he leave without doing so?"

Aed looked at the ground, and for all his age, Erin thought that he looked a bit like an errant schoolboy. "We were like two old squirrels, bickering constantly. He went on his way, for with both of us worrying, we were crotchety old men indeed."

Erin tilted her head back and laughed, thinking of her father and Mergwin, old friends, battling it out with wit and wisdom.

"I expect," she told her father cheerfully, "that I will see Mergwin soon enough. I know him well, and know he will come to see the child—" She cut herself off suddenly, catching her breath and standing still as the baby gave her a ferocious kick.

"Erin, what is it?" Aed demanded anxiously.

Again she laughed, clutching her father's hand. "Feel, Father! Your grandchild moves! Strong and hearty—and determined. That was very much so an Irish kick, don't you think, Father?''

Aed laughed with her. "Don't forget the strength of his sire," he warned her softly.

Aed led Erin ahead of him into the hall, looking heavenward and praying silently as he did so. "Make the child a son, God, for I am too old to worry over the strengths of another female such as the mother."

Erin dutifully ate the broth her mother had prepared her and escaped to the privacy of her chamber. It was secure and warm, and she changed into a thin shift to sit before the hearth. She hugged her knees, trying to still the nagging fear that Olaf would never come. Wouldn't she be better off? Raising her child as an Irishman within the most royal grounds of the isle? Surrounded by those who loved her, and already loved her child?

That would never happen, she thought, paling slightly despite the warmth of the fire. Olaf wanted his child . . . if the child was all that he did want. No, he would come. Eventually.

She settled her chin on her knees. How had he been entertaining himself? she wondered. No doubt there were times he was glad to be free of her. He could seek livelier, trimmer game, and she had left him alone, free to do so without reproach.

She fought tears as she had done so many times. She loved him so much that the love was a part of her being, her mind, her soul, her heart, her every pore. But she could not give him that love. All she could offer was rigid dignity, for her pride and her self she could not barter with, lest she lose and, in losing, have naught, not even the determination and will that sustained her. Not unless her dream should come ture.

Like a child, she could close her eyes and imagine Olaf, open and vulnerable at long last, his only weakness his love for her. Her image was of a misted green bank, with Olaf so nobly and yet humbly pleading for her heart.

Erin sighed and blinked. Fantasies were for children. She couldn't allow herself to pine for what would never be. All she could do was pray for the strength to live her life with the grace of the Ard-Righ's daughter no matter what came her way.

At least she would have her child. The instincts that grew within her surprised her, for with each tiny kick unleashed against her, she loved the life she carried more. Her child . . . his child. . . .

She trembled suddenly as she remembered how they had parted. Flashes of that passion had come to her oft, leaving her feeling weak and wobbling in the middle of any act, be it sewing beside her mother or, absurdly, kneeling upon the hard floor of the chapel.

But when they had parted, she thought mournfully, she had been so much smaller. She now felt as if she appeared as the tents that warriors set upon battlefields. No matter, she convinced herself with a toss of her head. She would greet him nobly, coolly, with great dignity, in her best robe, with its concealing mantle of wool edged with fox fur, her hair neatly and regally decked with jewels. She could hide her awkward bulk behind the wall of royal finery.

Her eyes closed dreamily with that vision, and she tried to plan the words she would say. "Welcome to Tara, my lord of Dubhlain. Be assured your needs will be well fulfilled, for all within the realm of the Ard-Righ strive for excellence in service and craft. . . ."

Her dreams were rudely interrupted and her eyes flew open as she heard a slight commotion in the hallway outside her door. Erin frowned, about to rise, but to her amazement, her door flew suddenly open.

She blinked once, for surely it was impossible for him to be there. She had imagined him, and his ghost had appeared. But as her eyes widened once more in incredulity, she was forced to realize that Olaf did indeed stand before her.

He filled her small doorway, his hands on his hips, his legs parted, his royal-blue mantle combatting the fierce Nordic blue of his eyes for supremacy. His beard and hair were neatly clipped, his features ever rugged granite as he sought her out quickly. The barest hint of a smile touched the fullness of his lips as his eyes saw her before the hearth.

Erin trembled with the sudden, rejoicing warmth of his presence and with dismay. It was he garbed in royal splendor, he who needed no shield of dignity, and she must appear as a lost waif. . . .

She did. A bit like a wood sprite, Olaf thought. Her feet were bare and tucked beneath her, her black hair like a splendid cape about her shoulders, and her wide, startled eyes were like the fresh beauty of a summer field. The thin white shift she wore revealed more to him than it hid, and a surge of emotion unlike any he had experienced touched him to the core. He wanted to run to her and lock her gently into his embrace, touch her belly with tenderness because of the child that grew within. But suddenly he could not. He froze within the doorway, thinking she would surely repel him with frost-cool anger and endure his touch with rigidity and disdain.

His tongue seemed to be tied within his mouth. He had come this far, and suddenly, in annoying weakness, the Wolf could move no further.

Erin hastily scrambled to her feet, blushing at her dishevelment. Her carefully planned speech departed like the wind and the words that came to her lips were tart. "My lord, you have entered a royal *Irish* household. The custom here is for one to knock on doors rather than barging in."

The tone of her voice gave him power for movement and he stepped within the door, closing it behind him as he raised an ever mocking golden brow. "Surely, even within royal *Irish* households, the door of the wife is that of the husband. But then, if not, you must forgive me, for the Norse habit is usually to enter directly. Most probably because we are so accustomed to invasion, we lack more genteel mannerisms. But then, the *Irish* Ard-Righ himself directed me here and bid me all entrances within his home."

Erin floundered silently for words, unable to speak as he walked slowly toward her, making no secret of his assessment. "I am most surprised to see you," she taunted, her words halting as he circled her and she sought to keep her eyes locked to his. "The Fais does not begin as yet and business in Dubhlain must be most detaining."

He paused directly before her, and she prayed that he would not see how her eyes feasted on him, how her spirit surged at his scent and nearness. He touched her face, and the brush of his calloused hand was gentle, gentle still as he grazed it over her swollen breast and belly. He frowned slightly, and Erin caught her breath with nervousness, too compelled to break away from the touch she had longed to feel. "I fear that we must travel home before the Fais," he said with a regret that she was astonished to recognize as real.

"Why?" she whispered uneasily.

"The babe—"

"Is not due for another two months," she protested too quickly.

"It was a mistake for me to allow you to come," he said quietly, his eyes falling from hers to the hand that rested on her belly. "You should not be traveling now, and therefore we must make haste." His eyes raised back to hers and his voice suddenly rang harsh. "I will accept no argument, Erin. I will speak my piece with your father this night, and on the morrow we head home."

She lowered her eyes to his hand. She had no wish to argue. She was achingly glad he had come, and wherever he chose to be, she was glad to be told she must follow.

The baby seemed to share her heart, for he chose that moment to firmly kick against his sire's hand. Olaf's gaze instantly returned to his hand, and Erin shivered with the pleasure of the startled look in his sharp blue eyes. Again the baby kicked, and the great Wolf of the North could not hide his fascination.

"He is strong, our son," Olaf murmured, his own pleasure showing in his slightly awed tone.

"Perhaps a daughter," Erin corrected.

"Nay, wife, it will be a son," Olaf said assuredly, making Erin purse her lips. He laughed as he saw her face again, and she was startled as he lightly ruffled her hair, momentarily twining his fingers within it and then releasing it. "Irish," he said softly, "I believe you would wish to contradict me were I to say it was day when the sun was shining high above us."

You are wrong! Erin longed to cry out. But she couldn't, no more than she could obey the impulse of her heart to throw herself into his arms with gladness. They stared at one another, the rigid distance between them growing. I've come to know him so well, Erin thought. She could recall the ridge and ripple of his each and every muscle, the tone of his flesh, the angle of bone beneath, and still they met anew each time as strangers, wary contestants.

He stepped away from her. "I have much to discuss with your father," he said crisply. "Prepare your things and then seek your rest, for we leave with the coming of the dawn."

He strode to the door, leaving her as abruptly as he had come to her, then he paused and turned back to her coldly. "Whether you like my form of entry, Irish, do not seek to bar a door against me, be this Tara, your father's home. Wherever we are, you are my wife. And I would not be adverse to proving such a point to you by breaking down an *Irish* door."

Erin met his pointed stare mutely and continued to gaze after him long after he had closed the door. She realized suddenly that the pounding of her heart was rapid against her chest, and that fire seemed to riddle through her in liquid waves.

As usual, he left her wishing she could throttle him, or at the very least douse him, in boiling oil—and shaking with pleasure because he would lie beside her, touch her.

She turned from her dazed scrutiny of the closed door to hurry about her chamber, gathering the things she would take, and setting out her clothing for the journey home—her warmest robe and heaviest fur-lined mantle, thick stockings and high leather shoes.

When all was ready, she gazed at her bed. How many times had she lain there laughing with her sisters, chatting about the lives they would lead, the dreams they would fulfill?

Tonight he would sleep in that bed, and reality would overwhelm dreams with golden strength.

She heard him in the hall this time before he entered, and settled quickly beneath the covers, her heart pounding once more. She had her back to him, but as she listened to the quiet sounds as he shed his clothing, she wished she had not chosen to feign sleep. She longed to turn and look at him, the magnificence of the warrior's body she had so missed.

Erin felt his weight as he lay beside her. She waited, her flesh alive with excitement, for his hands to come upon her. Seconds passed like hours in time, minutes like days, and still she waited. She felt only the adjustment of his body as he turned away from her, his embrace for his pillow.

She thought he slept, and she could not prevent a smothered sob from escaping her. It was only then that she felt him, instantly alert, his hand on her shoulder.

"What is it Irish?" he murmured anxiously in the darkness.

She could not whisper the truth so she softly lied. "The babe, my lord, he sometimes presses hard against me."

His arm came around her, pulling her back close against his naked chest. His massive hand moved with the most gentle tenderness in soothing circles over her belly. "Better, Irish?" he queried, his voice a caress against her hair and ear.

Erin allowed herself to smile in the darkness. "Much better, my lord."

She slept soon and well, content to bask in the strong comfort and security he offered.

CHAPTER

23

Olaf stroked his forefinger and thumb over his clipped beard, assessing the sight before him carefully, the sparkle in his eyes the only hint of his emotion. Rig watched his lord anxiously. The little Viking was proud of his craftsmanship learned during the long winters of his homeland when there had been little to do during the long nights except breed more Vikings and whittle with wood. His confidence fluttered somewhat as Olaf so thoroughly studied the carving he had commissioned. Finally Olaf turned his gaze from the cradle to Rig.

"Rig, I tell you, no prince has ever been offered a finer bed. It is the finest piece of craftsmanship I have yet to see."

A broad grin broke out across Rig's gnomelike features. His eyes watered slightly, and he returned his own gaze to the cradle created with his loyal, loving hands. At the head, carved in painstaking and elegant detail, was the emblem of the wolf, and at the foot, as Olaf had requested, were the crossed swords and maiden of justice—the emblem of the Ard-Righ. When touched the cradle would rock softly on firm supports. The wood had been polished until it shone with natural beauty.

Erin would be so pleased, Olaf thought, his heartbeat quickening. Aye, of course she would be pleased and perhaps understand that he offered her much by ordering that the insignia of her family be included. He had kept his own council, eagerly awaiting her delight when the project was completed. But when Rig had come to him and he had sought her out, she had been nowhere to be found.

It wasn't particularly strange, he thought dryly, that he was unable to find her. He avoided her during the day. At night he slept beside her and held her with a feeling of tenderness that was almost overwhelming, and he was content, even when his flesh cried out that he needed more than comfort. He was willing to bide his time. She was like a fine mead one had sipped and found to be superior; he could settle for no less. And the child within her was his; he could cool his ardor on behalf of his son or daughter, as Erin would be apt to correct him.

But though these days had meant a strange peace and truce between them, it was not without a certain tension, for much lay between them. He still could not allow himself to believe her innocent, for she had been apprehended in the act. A man could not allow himself to be lulled to trust by the pretty tears or even the stalwart pride of a woman. So they didn't try to talk. They passed politely in the halls, they spoke fleetingly of the weather when they joined for the evening meal. And they carefully skirted clear of one another. Except in the night, and in the darkness he could hold her close, savoring the soft little sighs of comfort that told him that she too was glad of the peace and the sweet contentment so fleetingly shared.

"Have you seen the queen?" Olaf demanded of Rig.

Rig shook his head, his heart swimming with the pleasure of Olaf's compliment. "She might be in the kitchen, my lord," Rig said almost absently, imagining the babe that would, within another moon, sleep in his cradle. "Or perhaps in the sun room, conversing with the ladies and sewing."

"Hmmm," Olaf muttered impatiently. He walked to the chamber door and turned briefly to Rig before exiting. "Take the cradle to our chamber, Rig, and leave it before the hearth where she may see it immediately. I am going to find her and bring her up to see it."

"Aye, my lord!" Rig bobbed happily and set about to do as he was told.

Olaf walked swiftly through his great hall and to the kitchens, where he learned from Freyda that Erin had come and gone. He checked the sun room, but Moira, sitting happily with her babe, told him the same, and suggested that he check with Freyda. Annoyed, he stomped his way back down to the great hall, where his ever amused brother watched him from the corner of his eye as he sharpened his sword before the hearth.

"Have you misplaced something, brother?" Eric inquired innocently.

"Aye, my wife," Olaf replied sourly. He turned his attention more fully upon the smugly smirking Eric. "You haven't, by any rare chance, brother, any indication of where she might be?"

"Oh, aye," Eric replied, his eyes nonchalantly upon the great blade he honed. "Those who care for her concerns are conscious of her habits. If I were you, Wolf, I would seek her by the sea."

"By the sea!" Olaf thundered. "The cliffs are too far. I gave her strict instructions not to ride—"

Eric finally looked up from his task. "She does not ride. She walks."

Olaf muttered a number of curses and headed for the main door, heedless of Eric's muffled laughter following him. In moments he had saddled his powerful black and was quickly galloping down the trail that led to the cliffs. He did not slow his gait until he saw her, and then he paused, watching her.

The billow of her mantle hid her advanced stage of pregnancy. She appeared much as she had more than two seasons ago when he had come to find her, to touch her, to bring her home, proud and beautiful against the land, sky and sea; one in spirit with both the tempest of the sea and the endless beauty of the heavens. It had rained that day so long ago, and they had tarried long in the caves, perhaps there creating the seed that now flowered.

He dismounted from the black and walked slowly toward her, aware by the stiffening of her spine that she heard him coming. He placed his hands lightly on her shoulders and dipped his head low to whisper against the tangle of her hair. "You have come too far, my lady. You risk our child."

Erin bit her lip, hesitating before answering. "I would not risk our child, my lord. I am young and in fine health, and the matrons within our hall tell me that the exercise is good."

Olaf frowned behind her, wondering at the marked depression within her voice. He turned her toward him, and his frown deepened to a scowl as he saw the strange defeat in her features.

"Why do you look so?" he demanded sharply. "You have naught for which to appear so distraught with misery."

She smiled with no light to the troubled darkness of her eyes. "Have I not, my lord? I have been thinking of the days, the months, the years to come, and it has weighed on me heavily. We are young yet, Wolf of Norway. The years stretch ahead of us with this emptiness. I tire of it, my lord. Truly I grow weary of treading so lightly about you, of knowing that you still brand me traitor."

Olaf stiffened. "I never desired to brand you traitor, Erin. I was forced to do so when I stared into a pair of emerald eyes beneath a golden visor. I would gladly hear proof that you did not intend to draw a sword against my men or me."

Erin lowered her head and suppressed the sobs that threatened to engulf her voice. "Alas, my lord, there is no proof except that within my heart, and yet my cousin Gregory believes me, as does my brother Brice.''

''Perhaps,'' Olaf said huskily, ''that is because neither ever heard his life threatened so vehemently from your lips.''

''No, my lord, it is perhaps because they offer me their love and trust.''

Olaf hesitated, his forefinger reaching for her chin. ''Do you ask me to give you my love and trust, Erin?''

He didn't receive his answer because she suddenly gasped and stumbled against him, buckling over. A worried frown brought his brows together as he sought to right her, clutching her shoulders once more. ''Erin! What is it?''

''I-I think it is the babe,'' Erin gasped, still stunned by the intensity of the pain that had riddled her. She had been experiencing little cramps all morning, but she had dismissed them as it was still too early for the babe to be born.

''Nay, Irish, it can't be—''

''Ohh!'' she cried out, startled as a flood of warm liquid soaked her skirt and sent her shivering. Her teeth began chattering terribly as the winter wind whipped her.

''Erin?''

''Olaf . . . it—it is the babe!''

Vanity gnawed at her as he stooped to sweep her into his arms. ''Nay, Olaf,'' she protested foolishly. ''I am . . . wet.''

He didn't bother with a reply but strode firmly for the horse.

Still shivering uncontrollably, she again protested. ''You said I was not to go near a horse—''

''Erin!'' he breathed with exasperation. ''You are, in truth, a woman with the full capacity for a ridiculous tongue!'' He set her on the black before leaping up to hold her. ''You can no longer cause the babe to come too soon since he comes now no matter what you do! And I do not wish our child born in frosted grass.''

She made no more attempt to speak as he held her

against him, urging the black to a fluid, unjarring canter. Instead she huddled close, savoring his warmth and yet still unable to stop her teeth from chattering viciously.

It was but minutes, and still it seemed an eternity before they reached the city walls and the courtyard before their residence. Olaf dismounted in a bound and reached for her, taking her in his arms once again.

"I can walk," she objected in a whisper.

His only reply was an exasperated groan. Then he was shouting as he carried her through the great hall.

By the time he kicked open the door to their chamber, Moira was racing behind him, surprised at the timing but calm and efficient. "Set her on the bed, Olaf, and help me get these wet things from her," Moira commanded briskly. The feat was quickly accomplished with Erin still trembling and moving weakly to their will. A fresh warm gown was slipped over her head and Moira issued further orders. "Send Rig for extra bedding, and tell Mageen Erin's time has come. She will know what to do."

"And then?" Olaf queried.

"And then, my lord, go drink yourself a horn of ale, for there will be naught else for you to do but wait."

As commanded, he waited, and as the morning passed to noon, and noon to night, he still waited calmly, helped along by the jovial company of Sigurd and Eric. Then as the meal hour came and went and the moon rode high and midnight approached, he slammed his fist against the stone of the hearth and issued a stream of oaths, clearly alerting Sigurd and Eric to the fact that the Wolf grew worried, as they did.

"It is a first child, Olaf," Eric told his brother, masking his own concern. "Such things oft take long. . . ."

Olaf said nothing but stared into the fire. Aye, the process of bearing new life could take long, but this babe was entering the world early, and Erin had so long ago lost the birthing waters. Her pains had surely been steady and wracking all that time. She was strong, but how much could she endure?

He realized suddenly that he could stand to lose the child. There could be others, but if he were to lose her now . . . He groaned aloud, wishing fervently that he could lend his strength to her. Rather a blade should pierce his ribs than she suffer more.

He turned abruptly as he heard footsteps coming down the stairs. He saw that Moira headed for the kitchen, and that she appeared distressed. She had hoped to avoid him, but he called her name firmly and she looked nervously to Sigurd as if for help before facing Olaf.

"Moira," Olaf demanded quietly. "What is wrong?"

Moira wrung her hands nervously. "She did so well, Olaf, nary a whimper for so long, but now the child must appear, and she is so weakened she has lost the power to aid us and we need her help." The thunder and anguish within his rugged features made her tremble and she hurried to assure him. "My lord Olaf, we do all that we can."

He nodded at her and returned his gaze to the fire. Moira disappeared down the hall to the kitchen, then seconds later started up the stairs again with more steaming water. Olaf stared after her broodingly, his face drawn and haggard.

"There is naught that you can do, brother," Eric told him.

"Aye, but there is," Olaf said suddenly, his voice steely with determination.

Sigurd and Eric could do nothing but stare after him incredulously as his firm gait took him to the staircase, where he bounded up its length in long strides.

He did not knock, but entered the chamber directly, pausing only momentarily to ignore the startled glances of the ladies and to focus his blazing eyes on Erin. She appeared so pale and fragile, her face as pale as the snow, her beautiful black mane of hair a damp tangle about her. Her eyes kept fluttering closed, and although Moira entreated her to catch her breath and push, the air that rustled in spurts from her parted lips was shallow and slow.

Mageen, busy keeping dry linen beneath Erin, said nothing to Olaf, but watched him without protest, efficiently going about her duty. Moira opened her mouth, as if to send him from the chamber, but Olaf lifted a hand, moving across the room and indicating that Moira give him her position by Erin's side.

Moira moved away uncertainly and Olaf took her place. He clasped Erin's hand within his and lowered his head to her face, his Nordic eyes willing her to open her eyes. "You're giving up, Irish. I have never known you to do so in a fight."

Her murky lashes raised, the emerald eyes beneath them dazed with pain. "You . . . mustn't be here," she gasped out. "Please, Olaf, not like this. . . ."

He controlled his hands from quivering to grip hers tightly. The spark of life was gone from her eyes. He had to bring it back, at whatever cost. "You are right, Irish. You are a sight. But I'll stay as I am until my Norse son is born."

"Daughter," she grated irritably. "And Irish."

He smiled at her; her emerald eyes were blazing more clearly. Her features suddenly became pinched and drawn and the hand he held dug into his with painful force. "Again . . ." she breathed. Tears filled her eyes and she cried out weakly. "Olaf, I can take no more. . . ."

It was Moira's voice he heard next, the sound desperate to his ears. "She must bear down, my lord."

"Women are weak!" Olaf exclaimed mockingly, at the same time slipping an arm about her and lifting her shoulders against him. "You will fight, Irish! You will fight now. I will help you. Grit your teeth, my love, and push as Moira asks. Must she do it all for you?"

Supported by Olaf and stimulated to draw upon her last reserves of energy, Erin did as he commanded, feeling somewhat numbed as she strained with her body, then gasped out her breath and sagged against him, almost blacking out.

"We've the head!" Moira called out joyfully. "Just once more . . . once more. Olaf, you must make her try once more."

"Again, Erin!" he commanded harshly. "Again . . . and then you may sleep." He pushed her shoulders forward, forcing her to obey. Barely coherent, Erin caught her breath again and strained. She felt the reward of relief as her body emptied and she heard the cries of joy, and her husband's whisper that came with his tender embrace. "I knew you could do it, Irish. Always the fighter."

The world swam and she lay back exhausted. Olaf gently lowered her head to the pillow. A lusty cry filled the room, and then Olaf was whispering to her once more. "A boy, Erin. Sound and fine." He chuckled softly. "and though his fine locks look a bit mussed right now, it appears that they are going to be a pale shade of gold."

She smiled and opened her eyes once to see the infant, protesting as Mageen cleaned him in tepid water. He was barely swaddled in linens before Olaf took him and knelt beside Erin. "A very fine son, my lady, and I thank you with the fullness of my heart."

She could scarce see her babe, and yet she knew that he was sound and beautiful, even if he did appear somewhat wizened. Olaf's words touched her like a caress, and she allowed her eyes to shut once more. She felt the touch of his lips on her forehead, and then he and the babe were gone.

Moira had a bit of trouble extracting the young heir from his sire, but she was firm. "My lord," she whispered, her gratitude and relief gentle within her voice, "you have done nobly, but now you must leave us. We need to bathe Erin and freshen her linen, and at that we will work best alone. She dearly needs her rest, as the babe now needs his mother."

Olaf nodded slowly, returning his son to Moira. He glanced at Erin once more, but her eyes were closed again. A healthier color was replacing the paleness in her face, and although the strain still marred her features, her lips were parted in the slightest smile of peace.

He strode down the stairway tiredly, his thoughts churning, until he saw the anxious faces of Sigurd and Eric.

A broad grin broke out across the golden nest of his beard. "A son," he informed them. "Mother and child faring well."

Eric emitted a bloodcurdling cry of Viking victory. A horn of ale was pressed into Olaf's hands. He drank long and heartily, and hours after Eric and Sigurd had sought what sleep they could, he stared into the fire.

He had never known love such as he had this night. Love for the wee creature with the tiny hands that had clenched around his tightly, love for the woman with the delicate form but stalwart heart who had carried his seed and given him the child.

Nay, more than that. From the beginning, she had given him life again. She was the soul that he had sought.

It was afternoon again when Erin awoke. Instantly she was reaching for her child, and Moira handed her the babe, smiling radiantly at the experience she had so recently savored herself.

With her son beside her, Erin removed the swaddling linen and checked him eagerly from head to toe. He was perfect. So tiny and yet so perfect. Tiny fingers, tiny toes, tiny, wizened face. His eyes opened as she stared at him, and she was stunned to see that they already resembled the shade of green of her eyes.

"Moira! His eyes!"

"Yes, Erin." Moira chuckled. "His eyes are yours. But that tuft upon his head is definitely his fathers! How Olaf knew last night that it would be so pale I will never understand."

Erin smiled and adjusted her gown to allow the whimpering infant to nestle against her breast and greedily take hold. The thrill at his touch as he first floundered, then instinctively suckled with heedless demand riddled her with loving pleasure and she laughed. "Oh, Moira! He was born a golden-haired boy because Olaf decreed it so!"

Moira grimaced and laughed along with her. "Well, my little mother, the Lord of the Wolves is now demanding that he be allowed entrance once more, so when that little one is filled—"

"A comb, Moira! And a basin! I must wash and fix my hair quickly. He mustn't see me looking so terrible again."

"Shhh. . . ." Moira soothed, secretly smiling. "I will not allow him to enter, until you wish it." She toughened her voice to scold. "And, Erin, you must take great care with yourself as well as the babe. You were sadly weakened last night. It will take time for you to heal. I will comb your hair until it shines, but you will also eat!"

Erin was aware that she had little strength, and yet already the agony of the previous night was dim in her mind, for whatever she had endured, the price had been well met. She stared at the tiny head pressed so hungrily to her breast and her tenderness was overwhelming. He was so warm and so beautifully, sweetly alive. He was hers, and he was the golden son of the Wolf.

She insisted the babe stay beside her as she obediently ate and as she carefully and anxiously primped. When Olaf entered, she was curled around the child, watching his sleeping form with a sweet and dreamy expression that again touched all the chords of love and tenderness within his heart. She turned to him, offering him the most dazzling of smiles, with her emerald eyes shining like the lushest hills in summer. He returned her smile and came to the bed, leaning his length opposite hers so that the sleeping child lay between them.

"He is beautiful, is he not, my lord?" Erin demanded with shy pride.

"Aye, Erin," Olaf said softly.

For several seconds they lay in companionable silence, enjoying the sight of their newborn as any proud parents. Then Olaf reached beneath his mantle and produced a tiny coffer, delicately carved in the Norse fashion. "There was little I could think of to give a princess of Tara," he said a bit gruffly, proffering it to her. "But I have noticed that the Irish are keen on ornaments for the hair, and so I hoped that this might give you pleasure."

Tears stung Erin's eyes as she opened the little casket. It mattered not what the gift was, only that he had thought to bring it, and thought to care.

A little cry escaped her as she saw the contents of the inlaid box. Dazzling jewels in emerald and sapphire hung from delicate strands of gold, a matched pair to secure the sides of her hair. She stared at them fighting to keep her tears in check, but still her lips quivered as she spoke. "I thank you, my lord, for truly it is a wondrous gift."

"They do but match the wonder of your eyes, Irish," he said softly.

Erin couldn't bring herself to meet the blue gaze she knew rested on her. He had wanted this son, and she had given him that which he so craved, and so he offered her tenderness. But was it for this moment, or could it go beyond? She started to tremble, too vulnerable to seek an answer. "Thank you, my lord," she whispered again, then hesitated, the facets of the jewels swimming in brilliance before her eyes. "There is another gift I would ask of you, Olaf."

"Aye?"

"I would dearly love to call him Leith."

"It is an Irish name," Olaf said matter-of-factly.

"Perhaps," Erin murmured, finally meeting his eyes to plead. "It is much like Leif, my lord, which is Norse." Again she paused. "To the Irish, he will be Leith mac Amhlaobh, for that is your name to my countrymen. And to the Norse . . . Leif Olafson. Please, Olaf. I would so like to call him for my brother."

Olaf was silent for several seconds. "Then Leith he shall be."

Tears of happiness finally started down her cheeks. Olaf reached over their sleeping babe to smooth them from the softness of her flesh. She caught the hand that touched her and kissed the palm. But before she could speak their chamber door was rudely opened and Moira walked in with more determination than ever a warrior carried to battle.

"My lord, Erin must take great care. She needs to sleep. And there is a strange-looking lunatic in the great hall demanding that he be allowed to see the child and insisting that Erin must drink some evil-looking concoction—"

Erin and Olaf stared at one another and burst into laughter.

Olaf lifted a brow. "Mergwin?" he demanded knowingly.

"Mergwin," Erin agreed.

"Send the lunatic up, Moira," Olaf said. "Erin will certainly drink his concoction. If there is any potion made by man to heal both health and spirit, that potion will be his."

Olaf regretfully withdrew from the bed as Moira departed. "I will leave you, Irish, for I am certain the Druid will stay no more time than to see the child— and care for you." He appeared momentarily pained. "I will take my things from the chamber tonight and sleep elsewhere so that you may do so undisturbed."

Erin lowered her lashes, her heart pounding. Then she raised them firmly to capture his Nordic blue stare with an inviting emerald one.

"I would sleep less disturbed, my lord, were you beside me," she murmured softly.

A warm trembling swept through Olaf. He was, indeed, captive within her gaze. Finally he broke the bewitching contact. "Irish, I have no wish to quit my bed, so if my bulk brings comfort rather than irritation, I will gladly sleep where I belong."

He smiled and left her.

Erin felt as if the world were hers. She was radiantly dazzling when Mergwin swept into the room, looked at the child, and then accosted her with gruff admonishment. "Daughter of Aed, you will listen to me and rest carefully, regaining your strength as I tell you. For three days hence you will not attempt to rise. . . ."

Erin listened meekly, smiling with contentment and pride as the Druid held the baby long and lovingly and then placed him in the beautiful cradle with the emblems in both Norse and Irish, nodding at all the instructions her old mentor had to give. She obediently drank his potion of herbs. But then she couldn't contain the spurt of merry laughter that gripped her and she threw her arms around his neck, hugging him near.

"Oh, Mergwin! I am so very, very happy!"

Mergwin returned her hug, his heart seeming to tug. All appeared so well. Why couldn't he rejoice with mother and child, exalt in the birth of this special child?

There was darkness still to come. If only he could see the way to the light. . . .

CHAPTER

24

It was easy to slip inside of the city. Incredibly easy. He could barely keep from bursting into victorious laughter.

Instead he sat quietly on the broken-down old mare, his string of fresh fowl slapping against the horse's haunches. He paused in the courtyard of the royal residence, granting his enemy admiration as he appraised the masonry, then feeling the hate rise in him once more as he cast his gaze upward and stared at the shutters with their carved emblems of the wolf.

He had little fear of being recognized within the city. He had sacrificed the magnificent length of his beard to move about undetected, and he wore an Irish monk's robe and dull woolen cowl over his head. He carried a large basket, like a healer who was collecting herbs, and he was adept at the Irish language.

Friggid tarried only long enough at the marketplace to lighten his load, then he led his decrepit mount near the great stone house once more. Again, he found no hindrance when he entered the great hall, for it was known that any man was free to bring a grievance or plea to the king and that none was allowed to starve in

Dubhlain. A man need only ask within the hall and he would be fed. Following that custom, Friggid asked for hospitality, and was duly told to sit before the hearth with a full bowl of mutton stew. As he ate, he watched carefully the comings and goings of the men within the hall. Servants were busy cleaning and occasionally a lady would float up the stairs.

Friggid cast his eyes toward those stairs. It was most likely that the Wolf slept near the upper landing, for he would be first to arms should danger threaten his den.

None paid much heed to the unobtrusive monk, and he bided his time with patience. When the hall was quiet, he crept up the stairs with silent speed, the fever of revenge strong within his blood. From the shade of his cowl he looked about once more, but though he could hear women's laughter coming from a nearby room, no one stood near to challenge him. He sought out the first door. When it was closed behind him he surveyed the chamber, noting instantly the cradle with its fine and detailed carvings. He walked toward it and a grim smile crossed his lips, for he had indeed gambled well. The son of the Wolf slept, the small golden head an undeniable sign of the child's paternity. He was careful as he swept the child from its bed into the basket, for he gambled still that the child would not awaken and cry. He did not want the child injured yet, for the babe was but bait for the man.

Quickly Friggid moved back toward the doorway, for having seen the bewitching queen of his nemesis, the Wolf, Friggid did not think the lady Erin would leave her child for long. Yet before he exited the chamber, he stared about it again, feeling the hated envy roaring inside him. From the furs and draperies on the bed to the highly polished trunks, the chamber spoke of both space and comfort. He could well imagine the Wolf on the bed, enjoying the finest of sport with his proud and beautiful fire-eyed queen.

Friggid's fingers tensed over the basket at his side. Dubhlain had once been his. He should have been the king, the one to demand the unique and dazzling girl as his prize, to build such a hall as a monument to his victory.

"But I have, Olaf, at long last won," he whispered aloud.

Silently he opened the heavy door a crack. The hall was still empty, yet he could hear a light melody as a woman approached. Friggid slid swiftly and quietly from the doorway, and down the stairs. He exited the hall unaccosted, for who would think to challenge a tattered monk?

He left the city on the lame mare, but as soon as he approached the northern forest, he tore off his cowl and roared his laughter to the wind. His men, those he had managed to gather and swear to loyalty, awaited him in the forest with a woman to nurse and care for the child and a worthy mount. His first action on joining them would be to slay the sad excuse for a horse he now rode.

Friggid tossed back his head, and the forest rang with his chilling laughter.

Erin hummed as she trod lightly down the hall. The day had dawned so beautifully, so crystal clear. She had felt marvelous since she had awakened, and with Leith now three weeks old, she had been given leave to resume most of her activities. There was much to be done, for Olaf had decreed that the Catholics within Dubhlain were free to celebrate the Christ Mass with all due ceremony. The most staunch Vikings were awaiting the day with interest, for Erin had told them that there would be great feasting, which always set well with the Viking heart.

To Erin it would be a very special Christ Mass, for upon that day she would be six weeks past childbirth, and she intended to purposely seduce her husband and demand that he believe her loyal. He could no longer deny her, she was certain. For although they had still not spoken of matters of the heart, they had shared much, and in those last trying moments before Leith had entered the world, she was certain he had called her his love. She was not Grenilde, but having lost a brother and dear friend now, she could understand that a man or woman could mourn within the heart and yet find room for a new love. Surely the great Wolf must see this now.

Still humming and smiling with the mere thought of gazing on her sleeping son, Erin entered the chamber and approached the beautiful cradle. Panic seized her instantly when she didn't see the babe, a shiver of freezing cold that sped through her blood and limbs. She forced herself to calm down, for she refused to believe that anything was wrong. Olaf had come and taken him, or Moira. But that couldn't be so, for Olaf hunted with a number of his men in the western forest and she had just left Moira in the sun room where they had discussed the menu for the Christ Mass feast.

Maybe Mergwin, who still enjoyed the hospitality of the city . . . no, for Mergwin, though he loved the child dearly, did not touch the young heir without her or Olaf's permission. Rig? Mageen? Unlikely, she thought quickly.

The building scream that had tightened Erin's throat ripped from her in an anguished wail that seemed to shudder the very walls. She flew from her chamber to the hallway, where already the household gathered in alarm at her call.

"The babe . . . Leith . . . is gone," Erin stuttered quickly, her panicked eyes surveying the warriors from the hall to the ladies of the sun room who gathered before her. Her eyes met Rig's pleadingly. "Rig, where is my child? Did Olaf command that he be brought out? Mageen . . . was he awake and fussing? Oh, please! Someone tell me where he has been taken!"

She was answered only by stares of startled misery. Erin collapsed to the floor, a scream of agony tearing again from her throat. Moira stepped forward, stooping to rock Erin in her arms. "We will find him, Erin. Surely there is an explanation."

One of the burly Vikings in Eric's command spoke. "Calm yourself, my lady. I will ride out and find the Wolf."

He pelted at a furious rate down the stairs. The others began to voice ideas of where they might look, and all rushed about, determined to find the small babe and ease his mother's agony. Erin turned her face into Moira's shoulder and cried brokenly. "He is but three weeks old, Moira. He could not have walked or even crawled away. He is too young to survive without me. Oh, dear God, where is my son!"

The house was searched from top to bottom; no crevice or corner went unexplored. The people anxiously tore the city apart, but there was still no sign of the beloved prince. Erin was barely coherent by the time Olaf appeared in his great hall, shouting out questions to his household as he held Erin's trembling frame against his own.

There were no answers, only further confusion as each man and woman attempted to describe search methods and offer ideas.

Mergwin, who had joined the hunt in the forest with the Viking Wolf he had come to admire more and more with the passage of time, watched the scene with dismay, and the coldness of knowledge gripped his bones like a palsy. The darkness had come. He had thought it was Erin who would face the danger; he had not seen that it would be the child.

He stepped through the milling crowd of warriors, craftsmen, and wives, Norse and Irish alike, and addressed the drawn blond giant who held his sobbing princess against his chest.

"Ask, Lord Wolf," Mergwin stated with pain, "what strangers might have entered the hall today, for in that knowing, we shall discover the whereabouts of the young prince."

The startling blue eyes riddled with pain, lit on Mergwin, and Olaf recognized the wisdom of his words. The Wolf's voice rang through the hall with sharp inquiry. "Who has dwelt here this day? What manner of stranger has sought hospitality within?"

"The monk!"

The answer came from many voices after only a second's silence. Mergwin felt his shoulders sag. The Viking who had ridden to find Olaf and bring him home stepped forward to speak. "He was the only one unknown to us to enter the hall today."

Dread touched Olaf like a hammer to his heart. "Describe this monk to me."

He was cowled in tattered brown, and there was little I noted about his face for it was well shaded." The Viking's brow drew in sharply with his concentration. "It did seem that he walked strangely, as if he still rode a horse."

"Friggid the Bowlegs. . . ."

The soft and incredulous whisper came from Eric, who stood at the edge of the crowd. Erin lifted her head from Olaf's shoulder to stare across the sea of faces and meet her brother-in-law's horrified gaze.

"The Dane?" she queried in a gasp, knowing full well the answer, that it was the same man who had inflicted the torture and slaughter that had filled the fields at Carlingford Lough.

She started screaming and screaming, and there was none who could comfort her. Hysterically and mindless of onlookers, she beat against her husband's chest, hurtling furious oaths and accusations at him, that the Irish never waged war against infants; only *Vikings*, invaders no matter what their country, would do such a thing. How could Olaf have allowed his *dog* fight to come into their home, to endanger *her* infant. She demanded that he find their child, that Viking search out Viking. Her words were screeches, barely coherent.

Olaf endured her hammering blows until she collapsed against him, his lips compressed tightly against her wild accusations. His eyes touched on Mergwin, who came close and gently tore Erin away from Olaf, leading her sob-wracked body up the stairway where he would force her to find relief in a potion to dull the mind.

Olaf sent guards to watch the terrain beyond the walls, and called Eric and Sigurd into his private war chamber.

Eric tapped his brother on the shoulder. "She meant not what she said, Olaf," he offered softly.

It was the cold mist of arctic ice that filled his brother's eyes. "Nay, Eric, she meant exactly what she said. No matter. I will find my son first, and then I will deal with my wife."

They planned the search to spread in a wide arc around the city, and devised signals for the screeching war horns should any party of men come across a trail. Eric didn't believe that Friggid could have recruited a large contingent of men, for he had lost so many troops against the Wolf that even his Danish kin feared to ride with him.

Sigurd, hesitant of Olaf's wrath but ever aware that his leader preferred all thoughts spoken no matter how painful, also had quiet words of warning. "The child might be dead, Olaf. The Bowlegs would think little of snuffing out life, and his hatred for you is intense."

Olaf's rugged features were strained, but he spoke with calm authority. "I do not believe he has harmed my child. Such a death would be fine revenge, but still I would live. It is me he seeks through the child."

He had barely finished speaking when a rapping sounded on the door and a guard announced that a messenger from Friggid the Bowlegs awaited his counsel. Olaf strode from the chamber to the hall like thunder, causing the Dane who awaited him to quail before his barely controlled wrath. Olaf moved heedlessly for the cowering man, lifting him from the floor with a grip on the neckline of his tunic.

"Assure me that the child lives, Dane, or you die here and now."

The face of the battle-scarred messenger turned

purple as he garbled out assurances. "But if I do not return, lord of the wolves, Friggid will slay the child."

Eric placed a hand on Olaf's shoulders and Olaf found the control to set the Danish messenger on his feet. "So speak!" Olaf demanded, and the Dane, like many before him, realized that the quiet ice of the Viking lord chilled one to the very bone.

"If you wish the return of your child, you are to ride to the copse by the southern forest at the coming of the dawn. Bring but one other with you—to carry back the child."

Olaf paused for a moment and arctic winds seemed to touch the messenger with glacial fire. "Nay, I will not do so. If Friggid wishes to face me in battle, that I will gladly do. Carry this message to him: I will meet him alone before the gates of Dubhlain. The child will be carried to safety, and then our men may also retreat. It is our battle. It is not that of Irishman and Viking, or of Dane and Norwegian. It is private, and already too many lives have been lost. Carry this message to your jarl, and bring your reply."

"*No!*" The ardent cry came from the top of the stairs. Olaf looked up to see that Erin stood, her fingers gripped over the bannister, her hair wildly tumbling over her shoulders, contrasting with the emerald flames in her eyes. She seemed to whisk down the stairway, and before he could stop her, she was bargaining with the Danish messenger. "Give him no such message!" Erin cried. "Tell him that I will come wherever he chooses, if he will but release the child. I would make a far better hostage, for I ride well and will cause him no delay. Tell him—"

"Erin!" Olaf roared, at last catching her arm and swinging her hard against him. He turned to the messenger. "Go! Out of my hall now, ere I have you relieved of ears and nose. Carry my words to your jarl, not those of a screeching shrew!"

Erin fought against Olaf's strength and shouted. "Hear my words, for your leader would well want to hear them—"

She did not know if the man heard her cry or not, for he had indeed heard the sincere threat in Olaf's words and cared not to have a bloody pulp between his eyes with which to breathe for the remaining days of his life. She did not have long to ponder, for Olaf was suddenly shaking her ferociously. "Must you forever betray me?" he roared in grating, barely controlled rage. "Fool! You know not this Dane! He seeks to see me so only to slit the throat of *my* son before my eyes, before my execution. Idiot! You think he will trade the child for you? Nay, he will take you both. Are you so eager to know the Dane, to lie beneath him and feel his thrust?"

Erin stared at him long and hard, feeling as if her head still spun and rocked from his shaking. "A Viking is a Viking," she spat, trembling as she spoke, for she knew she must speak harshly when her words were a cry against her own heart. "It has seldom made any difference to the Irish whether they were invaded by Norwegian or Dane."

The piercing dagger his eyes struck within her was staggering, and yet she accepted the pain, for she must. Olaf was right; the Dane sought to kill both him and the child. But she knew she could manage to trick Friggid into releasing her son. Even if the sacrifice was herself, it would mean little, for Leith—and Olaf— would live. She had spent the time when Mergwin thought her safely sleeping planning carefully.

Yet she hadn't planned on the extent of Olaf's rage. He pushed her from him with a furious oath, so cruelly that she staggered against Sigurd and would have fallen to the floor had not the Viking caught her. "See that my lady wife is chained," he ordered, "and chained well lest she bring new treachery to this day!"

Sigurd could have wept with the tempest and misery for those he loved. "I'll take the queen to her chamber—"

"Nay!" Olaf thundered. "The dungeons—for she is a vixen versed well in the ways of an enticing witch, able to beguile men to her will."

Sigurd held Erin by the shoulders, shuffling from foot to foot. "Olaf, I—"

"I know well what I say, Sigurd. Obey me."

"Nay!" Erin screamed, but she was led away despite her protest. "Wolf bastard!" she shrieked, but it was doubtful Olaf heard more than the echo of her oath, for Sigurd was carrying her down the dank steps to the dungeons. Dear God, she wondered feverishly how was she ever to escape the stone and steel prison? She had to! The life of her child was at stake . . . and the life of the Wolf.

Sigurd had not chained her, nor allowed her prison to be a miserable one. He had supplied Erin with warm mead and ample food and water and the finest pelts available for warmth. Yet she knew from the look on the Viking's face that though he cared for her, he would loyally obey the jarl he had followed to Ireland, the Lord of the Wolves.

She was too numb for further tears, too worried to think, and so she paced the cold stone floor with feverish agitation, hoping the release of energy might soothe her soul and allow her to plan. But the plans she had made had gone astray, and now, if she allowed herself to think, she would pine with hopelessness, for she was certain only she could save her son.

Hour passed after hour and still her weary steps trod the stone. I must stop, she warned herself, for she was barely regaining strength from childbirth and she knew she could injure herself. But thinking of that made her think of her tiny, precious infant and her breasts would swell and pain her, instinctively filling. The pain was already noticeable and the babe had missed but two feedings.

Tears finally came to her eyes again as she wondered if he cried, if he suffered, if he was hungry. "I mustn't, I mustn't think these things," she voiced aloud, hearing her own voice echo dismally in the cell of stone.

"Erin!"

It was barely a whisper, and as she went silent, she

wondered if she hadn't imagined the sound of her name. But the whisper came again, and she hurried to the thick wooden door and stared out the small barred square. To her vast relief, she heard the rattle of keys.

"Who is it?" she hissed in anxious question.

The door creaked and she trembled with relief as she saw it was Mageen, a look of terror in her eyes. "Hurry, Erin, for if Olaf catches me, he will surely have me flayed alive."

Erin did not think to dispute Mageen, for she had never seen Olaf in such a fury as today.

"Bless you, Mageen, bless you!"

'Oh, hurry, please, please, hurry!''

Erin followed Mageen through the winding tunnel beneath the royal residence. "We can reach the kitchen through here, and hopefully escape to the rear court unseen," Mageen whispered. "The dawn will break soon; most likely the men seek sleep before they must awaken.'

In a short time they emerged from the dark dank depths to the kitchen, and as Mageen had prayed, the servants who had attempted to remain awake through the night had dozed in their chairs and on clean rushes on the floor. The two women were able to make a silent escape into the not yet unbroken darkness of the night.

"Bless you, Mageen," Erin whispered again fervently. "But I must now have a dagger and a horse!"

Mageen hesitated in the darkness, her voice quivering, but her words courageous. "If you ride to the Dane, I ride with you."

"Nay, I *must* go. You but put yourself in needless peril."

"Who will bring your lad to safety?"

After a long moment Erin sighed. "May God care for you all your days, Mageen, and truly know that you are noble. Now, we must first get past the guards."

Mageen chuckled, and though the sound was still touched by her fear, it was with a certain, cunning pride. "I have become friendly with an Irish smithy who travels from town to town with his craft. He will lead our mounts past the guard, and we will meet him by the west wall where there is a hole left by the absence of a water log they must replace because of the rot."

The dawn was coming fast as they finally cantered for the western forest. Terror beat in Erin's heart, and she silently blessed Mageen again, for she knew the other woman was twice as afraid as she was. Yet she could not allow her fear to govern her actions, for she couldn't afford even a trivial mistake.

As they approached the trees, Erin nervously turned toward Mageen and warned with her eyes that they should stop. If Friggid was within the forest he would know she was there, and she had to have space to assure the success of her venture.

A rustling within the trees told her she had calculated well; Friggid was indeed there, and he watched her, certainly waiting to spring.

She forced herself to call out boldly. "I take no further steps, Friggid the Bowlegs. Show yourself, and do so carefully, for I can turn and ride back as well as forward."

She heard a deep chuckle and then the Dane appeared, flanked on either side by heavy guards. "I have been expecting you, Erin of Tara. I bid you welcome."

He spoke his Irish words well, and it was at that moment that Erin recognized him as the man who had led her astray that day on the cliffs when she had faced Olaf. A sickness churned in her belly, yet she allowed no sign of it to show on her face. "I want my child returned to the city of Dubhlain, and then I will ride with you willingly."

"Willingly?" Friggid raised a lascivious brow and chuckled deeply again so that ripples of fear scathed Erin in the pit of her stomach. "Why should I give up the child?" he demanded more abruptly. "The Wolf will come for his son—and I am aware that he is oft at odds with his wife."

"You do not seek the life of the child, Dane, only that of his sire," Erin said coolly. "And Olaf is a possessive man. He will come for me. I am much lighter a burden than a child. I require no special care."

Again Friggid laughed, and the sound of it made Erin's stomach churn. "Erin of Tara, you are a prize. Aye, perhaps you are the better hostage, for there is pleasure to be found with you that the child cannot give. Dismount from your horse, my lady, and draw near so that I may see all that I am offered."

Mageen uttered a sound of protest, but Erin moved quickly to obey for she had counted heavily upon this very moment. She walked with a cool and calculated sway toward the Dane, hearing his words. "Ahh . . . my lady, now I have both child and wife—"

His words were cut off with a strangled gulp as she moved with an agility he had underestimated, bringing the sharpness of her well-honed dagger against his groin. It was she who spoke with command. "My life means naught if my son dies, Dane, I am willing to die; you will not be so lucky. You will live out the remainder of your days as a woman rather than a man!"

"Halt!" Friggid commanded as his guards started to draw near. He felt the surety of the blade pressed to his groin and quickly grated out a command. "Have the child brought to the queen's woman."

Erin did not release her hold until she saw the blanketed bundle that was her son brought to Mageen. She held her breath until she heard a squall that assured her that her child lived, yet even then she could not allow her death grip upon her dagger to falter.

"She rides to the gates, Dane, before you move. I am very nervous, and I would not want my hand to jerk."

Friggid paused, his gaze tense as he returned hers.

He grinned with slow sarcasn. "The child is hungry. Perhaps you would feed him before we ride away. I would enjoy such a . . . domestic . . . scene."

"I would not," Erin replied. Without glancing from his eyes she called to Mageen. "Go now, I will not turn until I know you have reached the wall."

Erin felt Mageen's hesitation, and then heard her voice ring out with startling clarity and fervor. "Think on this, Dane. The lady Erin is but three weeks from a trying childbed. Touch her now and you will kill her, and you will have naught with which to bait the Wolf."

Friggid's rapacious eyes moved slowly from Erin to Mageen and back to Erin. "She is a prize for which I am willing to wait."

There was another pause, and then Erin heard the sound of hoofbeats against the turf as Mageen finally pounded away. It took all Erin's willpower to continue to stare into the mocking eyes of the Bowlegs, but she did so, waiting . . . and waiting. She was tempted to draw the knife against him anyway, but then she would die, and as ludicrous and hopeless as it all seemed, she was not without hope. Her son lived.

At long last Friggid spoke. "Your woman approaches the wall, my lady. Drop your dagger now for I do not seek to kill you, but I am a master in the art of pain."

Erin allowed the dagger to drop through her fingers. She could have held it no longer. She clenched her teeth as Friggid's hands clutched into her hair and grazed over her swollen breasts. He laughed as her face paled. "I think I have made a fair trade, Erin of Tara, for surely I have never met a female so fine or courageous. Another three weeks, eh? I will grant you that time to heal from the child, but be not dismayed, for then I will take what is Olaf's and use it well."

Erin forced herself to smile in return. "You have made no trade, Dane. You will not lure out the Wolf, for he cares not and sees himself as betrayed—by my hand, so carefully twisted by yours. You have nothing but a woman, Dane."

Friggid merely grinned. "We tarry too long here. Get on your horse and attempt no tricks, or perhaps we can shake Olaf by sending him a delicate finger rather than a lock of hair. Perhaps he will not come, Erin. But I am still pleased with what I hold."

He shoved her toward her horse. Well aware that he would slice her fingers from her with no remorse should she disobey. Erin tossed back her hair and mounted her horse, wondering furiously where he took her.

"Into the forest!" he commanded.

"Perhaps he will follow us now," Erin murmured.

"Nay, my lady. For within your babe's blanket is a warning that you will die if I am not given a day to retreat. If and when the Wolf comes, he will face my defenses. Now ride!"

He meted her horse a sound whack on the rump and she scrambled for balance as the animal jumped and leaped to race with the others that tore through trees and brush. How many men did he have? she wondered, trying to count those she followed. A hundred? More. Easily more. . . .

She swallowed back tears of dismay. She'd had no sleep, and her body seemed to weaken by the moment; the ride was painfully jarring. Yet it was evident that Friggid now planned to put distance between himself and Olaf. It seemed apparent that he had planned this all along, aware that the Wolf would not fall prey to panic and ride out unguarded to be slaughtered.

Olaf was astounded to see Mageen stride into the hall with his son, so stunned that he could only freeze and then reach demandingly for the child, burying his face against his son's blanket despite the babe's squalls of protest. Assured that the babe was well, he then turned to face his ex-mistress with rising fury. "How has this come about?"

Mageen could barely speak. "Erin . . . Erin. . . ."

Olaf called sharply for Moira and handed the child to her. "Care for him as you do your daughter," he requested softly, and then the hard frost returned to his voice and eyes. "Erin betrayed me once more," he stated coldly.

"Nay, my lord," Mageen pleaded, fearfully aware that she could meet his wrath herself. "She did as any mother, seeking only to save her child . . . and husband."

Olaf emitted a furious oath. The pain within him could only be expressed with anger, his terror held at bay with strictest control.

Mageen shivered as she stood before him. "The Dane holds her now, Olaf," she whispered in anguish.

She saw the shudder that ripped through his muscular body. Yet his voice was still harsh. He spoke not of love, but of possession. "He will hold naught that is mine. I shall have her back."

He turned from her, and she did not see the glaze of fevered agony that clouded over the sharp blue of his eyes. His shoulders straightened and he was suddenly shouting orders. "Sigurd—send men both north and south, to Tara and Ulster. This time, the Dane will die. He will scourge this land no more!"

Mergwin, brooding against his terror by the hearth, gazed up with ancient eyes darkened with the most grievous sorrow, and yet he wondered if the Viking Wolf were aware he had truly become an Irishman. He prayed to his old gods that the Wolf would know the value of the treasure he possessed and seek forgiveness of his wife, but at the moment, all he could do was sigh with relief. Motive was not essential; that the Wolf rode to rescue was.

And that he did not ride too late.

For the vision of fire was strong; the scent of smoke that teased the old Druid's senses brought a chilling fear.

CHAPTER

25

Day wore into night, night became day. Days passed
into weeks. And still they rode from the break of dawn
past the setting of the sun.

At first, Erin had been certain that she would die.
The Danes had taken great pleasure in taunting her,
and the pace they set was such that she didn't believe
her health could sustain it.

But in those first days when she had believed that
Olaf would come, her heart had been heavily mixed.
She knew Friggid desired nothing less than Olaf's
death, and he cared not who else was slaughtered in
his course. If Olaf raised forces to come for her, a
multitude would die.

So it was better for her to hope that Olaf thought
himself betrayed one time too many, to hope that he
would feel good riddance to a most annoying problem.
Still she dreamed when she collapsed at night that he
rode behind, yet the dawn would come, and she would
be alone in the winter cold with the Danes riding ever
eastward, fearing the passage of time as Friggid caught
her eyes each morning, counting off the weeks and

days upon his fingers and filling the air with his sardonic laughter.

She missed the babe so badly with her body and soul, but at least his father would guard him, and Moira and Mergwin would love him.

Each day she panicked afresh. She was running out of time. . . .

The Danes were not cruel to her; she was Friggid's prize, and so they let her be. Some were even kind, for it seemed they believed she had courage, and for that they gave her a certain respect. Still it was miserable to travel, and more miserable to think of reaching their destination. But the day came. They had been riding for nineteen days, when at sunset they finally reached a camp in the midst of preparation. Erin felt vast dismay as she stared at the settlement, for Friggid had far more men than she had assumed.

He was building on the site of a decimated Irish village; she knew that this was so, for amid the new buildings being created by the Danish invaders stood several of the distinctly Irish wattle-and-daub huts. Earthworks rose to ring the encampment, and staunch walls built in wood. There was much work still to be done, but a firm defensive post was well on its way to sound existence. A great hall stood in the center of the complex, and to the far rear was a raised dais surrounded by a short fence of crossed logs.

Erin puckered her brow at the sight of the dais, wondering what form of macabre punishment Friggid practiced on that platform and at that center stake.

Friggid came upon her as she stared about. "Your Wolf comes too late, Princess, if he comes at all. Within days my stronghold will be impregnable."

Erin said nothing. Her feeling of desolation was overwhelming.

"Come, Princess," Friggid urged her, and she was lifted from her horse to be led to the hall. It was patterned after Olaf's, Erin noted, if on a much smaller scale. She was taken to a chamber at the head of the stairs and roughly pushed inside. "Relish your time, my lady, for my waiting is at an end. Tonight is the last that you shall enjoy alone.''

Friggid left her with a small salute. The door banged shut behind him, and she heard the heavy thud as a bolt was slid into place.

She wanted to be strong, to be brave, to believe that she was small sacrifice for her son and for Ireland. But she threw herself on the bed and the tears she had held back for the long ride began to fall in great sweeps of despair and hopelessness. Yet the tears were beneficial, for their vehemence combined with her exhaustion gave her the release of a heavy, dreamless sleep.

Servants appeared in the morning to bring her food and bathing water and provide her with clean clothing. Bathed and dressed, Erin knew she must begin to plot some method, however improbable, to escape. She found that with the day she was not bolted into the chamber, and carefully made her way to the hall. The Danes watched her as she skirted them to step outside, but none made any attempt to waylay her and as Friggid appeared nowhere about, she hurried on to survey her surroundings in the light of day.

The planked wall was not so staunch, she decided, and yet she would never escape over its height. Her only hope appeared to be to the west, where high rising cliffs gave the Danes a natural defense against surprise attack. But such defenses, formidable against a mass, were weak against one, and if she was to find a way out, that was it.

She attempted to appear as if she were interested in the building efforts, and she discovered that she was free to walk about. Friggid was overconfident, Erin decided, continually fighting the fear that threatened to lead her to another bout of crying. She could not allow herself to think about her son, or her husband, to wonder what they did in the comfort and warmth of the great hall in Dubhlain. Was she forgotten already? she wondered with a cry in her heart. Nay, do not think so! she warned herself. You must escape! Or you will die rather than feel the hands of Friggid on you.

Resolutely she clenched her fists at her sides. A tremor swept through her, yet it left her with the newborn strength of desperation. Surreptitiously she gazed about, and certain she was unwatched, she turned for the cliffs and found a trail that wound upward to the heights.

She was panting as she reached the crest, and yet she was exuberant, for it seemed she had only to descend again westward and live carefully within the forest until she could find help. The cold would be a deterrent, but she would chance freezing or starvation rather than live with nothing but cherished memories and the touch of the Dane whom she hated.

She rested on a rock, breathing deeply of the fresh air, and then stood, stretching to begin again. But before she could take the first footstep towards freedom, she was startled to a freeze by the voice that accosted her.

"Think not to leave me, Princess, for I have waited long to savor vengeance. And vengeance proves its own reward, Erin of Tara, for the tales and sagas have never exaggerated the beauty you possess, nor the nobility of your courage. You will be a tasty morsel for my pleasure this evening, and fear not that you will dismay me, for I am a man fond of fight."

She stared at Friggid, aware that he had but awaited her at the crest of the cliff. "You will never win, Dane. If not my lord Olaf, you will face my father—"

"Then the Ard-Righ shall die, and Ireland may return to her petty squabbles between king and king. That will give me greater chance for success to bend more and more land to my will."

Erin shivered inwardly, praying that her father would never come, for truly Aed's death would be the greatest disaster to befall the Irish.

Friggid swaggered toward her, reaching for a lock of her hair that played in the breeze.

"And know this, Princess: I want you, but I am prepared for whatever may come. Forget your Wolf

and pray that he does not ride. In time you will learn
to serve me. . . ."

He spoke on, but she could not hear him for his
touch made her shiver. I cannot bear this, she thought
brokenly. Always she would see eyes of the northern
sky before her, and to know another's touch did
indeed seem worse than death.

Erin noted suddenly that Friggid had stopped talking, and then he was whispering again, gazing over her
shoulder to the east. "No . . . not yet. He could not
have caught us so soon. . . ."

Curiously, with her heart beating in a furious cres-
cendo, Erin turned and followed his eastward gaze.
Weakness and joy cascaded over her as she surveyed
the view from the high clifftop. The Wolf was coming
for her!

From the heights she could see the troops, and a
poignant thrill ripped her body. The standards were
waving in the air; the thunder of the horses' hooves
was a drumbeat that made the earth tremble. The
Norse battle horns were sounding, and the war cries
of the men were rising like a beautiful and deadly
music on the air. Horses, thousands of them on the
horizon, pounded across the terrain as far as she could
see. The banners of Aed Finnlaith flew from the south,
those of Niall of Ulster from the north, and from the
east, the great banner of the Wolf, Olaf the White of
Dubhlain.

In the center, even in the distance, she could see
Olaf. His hair was a golden halo that marked him
irrefutably; he was one with the great black stallion,
towering above the others in size and majesty, his
mantle of crimson flaring with the thunder of the
gallop.

He was coming for her. So many times she had told
herself that she must wish he would not come, that the
bloodshed must end. . . .

But now that he was there, she was overjoyed that
her wish had been denied. He had been behind them

all the time, all those nights that she had hoped and prayed.

Erin started to laugh. She turned back to Friggid. "He does come, Dane! The Lord of the Wolves rides this way—against you." She could not contain her laughter. It was hysterical, but it was joyous. It held at bay her tears of sweet pride. She thought that she might be about to die; it was highly probable that Friggid would kill her now. But it didn't matter. He could kill her, but he couldn't take away her love, nor erase what had been—the brief and tempestuous beauty that had passed between a Norwegian prince and an Irish princess. Somewhere in Dubhlain her son lived, indisputable proof of what had been. No, Friggid could not take away her triumph, because Olaf had come for her. A magnificent vision of golden power, he was thundering down on the earthworks and wooden gates of the Danish stronghold. So tall and proud, majestic in his mantle of crimson, more awesome than the sun and moon and stars.

Friggid grabbed her arm, wrenching her to her feet. "So he rides, does he, the wolf at bay. It will do you no good, my princess. He will never have you again. He has had all he will ever have of Ireland. Today he will die."

He twisted her arm viciously, but still Erin laughed. "He will not die, Friggid. If you are fool enough to face him, he will butcher you into little quarters. It is you who will die today."

Friggid's face twisted into an ugly smile. "Be that as it may, Princess, but you will never touch him again. One of you will die."

Their eyes clashed in a war of hate, and then he was twisting her arm behind her back to drag her from the cliff. "Brave words from an Irish lass I hold in my power," he reminded her. She tried to fight him, but the pain was too great. He would, she was quite certain, twist until her arm snapped. Still she merely hampered him the best she could as he pushed and dragged her down the angled trail. She fell, sprawling and bruising herself several times, as they made progress down the winding steps. "Let us move, Princess!" he warned her with a growl when she lay gasping for breath, her shoulder bruised from a collision with the hard ground. "I don't want you passing out on me before this is finished!"

Gritting her teeth, Erin rose. It seemed an interminable walk before they were down the cliff, and amid the preparations in the courtyard that roiled the uncompleted camp into confusion. One of Friggid's anxious men came tearing after his leader.

"They are charging straight for the gates!" one informed him.

"So!" Friggid flared. "You come to me like an old woman!" He spat out his disgust. "Get out there, command your troops! Look to the gates—they cannot trample the gates!"

"It is not the Wolf riding alone. It is the Norwegian, and the troops of Ulster, and of Tara. We are fighting the whole of Eire, half of the provinces . . . Aed Finnlaith . . ."

"I care not who we are fighting! I have always fought the whole of these people! Get to your stations! What is this! Have the Danes become cowards because the Wolf comes back? He is not a god, he is mortal man, and he will bleed before you today."

Faced with the insane fury of his leader the man scurried to do as bidden, shouting orders in turn to his troops. Still having no idea where he was dragging her, Erin ground her teeth hard against each other as he wrenched at her fiercely. "Come, my lady princess," he mocked. "I wouldn't have you miss any of the coming slaughter. I have a prime place for you to watch!" Again she was pulled hurriedly along.

Men floundered for weapons, forming in ranks, shouting, preparing catapults to send deadly hot oil over the walls. The archers assembled along the ramparts.

But still the thunder riddled the earth. A thousand drums could ring no sweeter beat. Erin could no longer see the standards, but she could hear the song of the battle horns and, rising ever to her ears, the war cries of Olaf's men, blending in a wild harmony that was both chilling and melodious.

"Come!" Friggid shouted above the uproar.

Erin cried out as she tripped, but Friggid's hold was merciless. In a matter of minutes, she saw where he was taking her—to the raised wooden dais in the far field.

Erin eyed the structure with horror. They entered through a short logged gate and headed for a sloping platform that led to what appeared to be a whipping stake. Erin panicked as she realized he intended to tie her, and began to struggle in earnest with him on the wooden slope. They fell together and rolled halfway down. She almost escaped him, but he caught the hem of her robe and she flew backward instead. He jerked her to her feet and slapped her hard across the face. The world spun and she could taste blood where her teeth had grazed her inner mouth.

"No more tricks, Princess, or you die now and miss the show. And I went through a great deal of trouble to prepare this for you."

Erin said nothing; she felt tears welling in her eyes, but she wouldn't allow them to fall. Even death would be more welcome than the continued touch of the loathsome Dane.

He slipped his arm around her midriff and carried her up the slope to the platform and the stake. Her mind was still swirling so that she could barely stand. A cry escaped her as he jerked her wrists together high over her head, securing them soundly to the stake with loops of heavy rope. He pulled the loops so tight that she felt stabbing pricks in her hands, the blood barely flowing to them.

His cropped beard came very close to her face, his lips touched her ear as he whispered, "The Wolf is a fool to ride against me today. A fool to ride for a woman. But perhaps you can travel to Valhalla together."

She managed to smile grimly and lift her chin. "Brave words for a man who ties a mere woman to a stake, Friggid the Bowlegs. Brave words for a coward who will not meet the Wolf in arm-to-arm combat, man against man. It is because he is the stronger, Friggid, because you are a coward—" She was cut off as Friggid's palm came across her cheek again. She sagged against the post, remaining upright merely because she was tied.

"Shut up, Princess, unless you are ready to die with a knife through your throat."

Erin swallowed and fought back the pain and nausea overwhelming her. The platform spun beneath her feet, went black, and then began to steady again.

She raised her head. "Whenever I die, Friggid, will not matter. You cannot take the Wolf of Norway. Nor will you ever take this land. He will hold Dubhlain until you are dust in the wind—"

"That would be great solace to take to your grave. Except that you are wrong. You will die, but you will get to see the Wolf die first. You will, I hope, appreciate the stunning view I have provided you."

She lifted her eyes. The dais had been placed on a slight dun; the small log fence that surrounded it was no more than the height of a man's waist, and the slope leading to the platform raised it high over a man's head. She could see over the posting and earthworks. She could see fields beyond the fenced defense post of the Danes; she could see the troops that continued to bear down upon the gates.

Once again, she could see the great black stallion, racing, racing, drawing ever closer . . . And she could see Olaf, flying along with the stallion that sent up great clumps of earth with every hoofbeat.

For a moment she closed her eyes. Was he coming because he loved her? Because he had decided he needed her? Or because of honor, because he was a Viking lord, because she was his property, and he would let no man take what was his? Or because he hated Friggid more than he could ever love her; because he had to avenge Grenilde?

It didn't matter in the glory of the moment. She could close her eyes, but she could not close out the sounds of the coming battle, the war cries of Norse and Irish mingling like a chant that rose with the sound of the horns and the thundering drumbeat.

Take care, my love, she thought, and she opened her eyes again. The fields were alive with the galloping horses. Her husband, her father, her cousin, her brothers . . . Ireland's finest. She had given to her land, but now the men of that land rose valiantly to her defense.

"I go to arms, my lady Erin," Friggid mocked.

She stared without blinking into his dark ruthless eyes. "You will burn in hell, Friggid. When you die, there will be no Valhalla."

"I may discover what it is to burn in hell, Erin, and you will discover what it is to burn on earth." He bowed deeply in mockery, and left her.

She didn't understand his innuendo; she didn't care. She was staring again at the cloud of men and horses. They did not slow as they neared the wooden wall. The first catapults were raised and a scream of horror tore from Erin's throat as ropes were hacked with battle-axes and boiling oil was sent flying over the wall.

She closed her eyes again as she heard the agonized shrieks of horses and men. Archers on the ramparts rained burning arrows into the oncoming rush.

"Oh, dear God!" The scream escaped her in horror as the deep gourds of the catapults were refilled. Furiously she worked at the thongs binding her wrists, her twisting only making the ties tighter. She closed her eyes, praying that in doing so she would not see the burning oil fly.

But her eyes flew open again as a sound of the earth splitting came to her. She stared in amazement as she watched the Danish wall caving in.

Olaf was the first one she saw, and it was as if her heart and the world stopped together in time. The black stallion's hooves tore at the wood, and it crumpled beneath the force. The stallion sailed through the air with his rider. Olaf, at the head of his troops, his mantle and golden hair flowing with awesome majesty, his features unconquerable, relentless, his great sword flashing and gleaming beneath the sun as he wielded it high, and his battle cry—the howl of the wolf—rising, splitting the heavens with fury and vengeance. He was magnificent.

He was still too far away, and yet she believed that he saw her. She believed that she could see the blue ice fire in his eyes that was deeper than the ocean and wider than the sky, searing into her heart.

But then the moment was past. The black stallion had not broken down the wall itself. Hundreds of other horses were pouring into the courtyard. The shattering sound of steel upon steel rose as men engaged in hand-to-hand battle. Axes fell with terrible crunches; arrows flew with burning fire.

Erin trembled, lowering her eyes. Friggid had been a fool. He couldn't possibly withstand this onslaught. He could not, she thought, with a pride increased by love and poignancy, ever best the Wolf. But he had threatened her with such positive assurance. Had he truly thought that his feeble wooden walls would stand against a man who dealt in stone?

She jerked instinctively with terror as something whistled by her cheek. Focusing ahead, she saw Friggid just beyond the logs that surrounded her. He held a bow in his hands, the long string still quivering. Wrenching her head around, she stared about her and then she understood.

The logs that circled her dais had been soaked in oil, and into the logs, Friggid had shot a burning arrow. Already the wood was smoking, catching the flame.

"Dear God!" Erin shrieked. With a frenzy she began working at her binds again, ripping, tearing at her wrists. Tears stung her eyes as she realized the lunatic vengeance that was Friggid's.

Above the din of battle, she heard his laughter.

Perhaps he believed he was going to die. He lived with death; to fall in battle would not be dishonor. But whether he lived or died, he would have his revenge upon the Wolf because Olaf would never get past him in time to save his wife from the flames.

"I salute you, Queen of Dubhlain, Princess of Tara!" Friggid called. "May we all meet in the great court of Valhalla!"

He turned, his face still split with a macabre smile, and left her.

The fire was lapping quickly around the dry logs of the fence. Soon it would rise all around her.

Olaf would seek Friggid out, she thought frantically as the smoke rose around her, and he might very well kill him, butcher him in the fury she had described to Friggid. But it would be too late. Too late for her. . . .

She ceased her struggles for a moment, staring at the rapidly spreading fire. "No," she whispered with disbelief. But Friggid's words haunted her memory: ". . . you will discover what it is to burn on earth. . . ."

"No!" she screamed again, raging at the heavens. But her eyes were already beginning to water. The smoke permeated the air, turning it gray around her.

She twisted her wrists until they were raw and bleeding, and then she sagged against the post again, the tears streaking down her cheeks.

She would not burn to death, she tried to console herself. The smoke would ease her from life long before the flames could touch her.

It wouldn't be so terrible to die. If there truly was a God, she would have her brother Leith and Fennen and Bridget and Brian of Clonntairth at the porthole of the heavens to greet her, to bring her home. No, it wouldn't be so terrible to die. Except that she was young, and her life stretched ahead of her. Her life with the warrior-king, the Lord of the Wolves . . . Olaf. She had never told him that she loved him. If only she could tell him. If only she could be in his arms once more, whisper the words into his lips. . . .

* * *

Olaf had eyes for only one man. Almost thoughtlessly he slashed his way through the men who would engage him in battle. He sat on the black with both hands freed, using only his knees to maneuver the trusted mount. He held his shield high in his left arm; he carried his sword in his right. If Friggid was hiding, he would find him. If he were to lose his own sword and shield, he would meet the Dane with his bare hands.

"Wolf!"

The shout rang out. Olaf stared through the melee of men and saw that Friggid was, at long last, riding to meet him.

Despite the calamity, bloodshed, and intensity of that first, reckless engagement of the battle, the men began to part. Axes and swords were lowered. Half of the scattered makeshift buildings were already burning, but not even that gave destiny pause as the two men approached one another on their mounts. There was suddenly something akin to silence. The petty skirmishes ceased; all watched and waited the outcome of the one-on-one battle that had to be fought between the Viking jarls.

They approached one another, warily but surely, the war stallions, both standing seventeen hands high, prancing skittishly with the scent of smoke and blood in their flaring nostrils.

Five lengths away they halted, taking one another's measure.

It was a clash long in coming. It was for Grenilde, Olaf thought, and it was for Ireland, for the peace he had come to crave, for his son. . . . No. It was for Erin. *She* was the land, and she was his life.

Friggid was clad in a ragged tunic and his armor. Olaf met him in the robe and mantle of the Irish, but he had also sheathed himself in the armor he had long ago learned from his enemy. Friggid has eschewed the use of his axe; he carried a sword and shield as did the Wolf; his head was protected by a helmet of steel, his face by a visor in the shape of a ram.

Olaf still wore no helmet. His bare blond head was golden defiance in the sunlight.

"It is between us, Dane. You and me. Do not lead your troops to suicide," Olaf said quietly. "This is a battle between only two Vikings."

"Yes," Friggid agreed. "The battle is between us. It has always been so. Destined by Odin, by Thor. But it is not between two Vikings. You have turned Irish," he spat contemptuously.

Olaf shrugged. "Perhaps, Dane. But you will remember, Friggid, I am the one to hold Dubhlain. I am the one who rides with the thousands—Irish thousands—now." Olaf's tone of voice changed to a growl. "Where is my wife, Dane?"

A mocking grin slashed its way across Friggid's features. "To the victor, Wolf, go the spoils. Surely you know that law of conquest."

"Then," Olaf spat out, "let us have a victor."

Gregory of Clonntairth suddenly broke from the crowd, racing on foot to Olaf's side. He brought the helmet and visor of the Wolf to his bareheaded liege. Olaf secured them over his head. Only his eyes were visible beneath the sheen of metallic silver; eyes that were the fire daggers of ice crystal. Suddenly the great black stallion reared high, snorting and pawing the air. Olaf cast back his head and screeched out his battle cry.

It was the howl of the wolf, a sound so terrible, so chilling, that even Gregory, stepping back into the ranks of men, felt a tremor shake through his bones. He was tempted to cross himself. He did not, but he noted that the Danes seemed to ease backward.

The ground trembled as the black again hit the ground with all four hoofs, and then there was nothing but a blur of action, a terrible screeching as the two great animals came together.

Olaf and Friggid clashed swords, straining and grunting with the force of their arms. Neither was unhorsed. The war stallions spun on tensed haunches. Again there was a blur of speed. The terrible crunch of massive weight against massive weight, a shattering clash of steel.

Friggid fought like a berserkr, his strength that of a madman who knew all was won or lost with this contest.

But though all had heard of the fury of the Wolf, none had ever seen him fight with such a frenzy. He fought with the furor of a man who had suffered terrible pain and loss. He fought with vengeance, but more than anything, he fought for his mate.

But on the next clash, it was Olaf who was unhorsed. He rolled into the dirt, scrambling for his shield and finding his feet with speed and agility. Friggid bore down upon him on horseback, seeking to both lunge and trample. But his lunge missed his target, and Olaf, ducking and reeling, grabbed at Friggid's arm. Seconds later both men were rolling in the dirt, and they were on their feet, circling one another warily.

The cry of the wolf rent the heavens again.

Swords clashed. Steel penetrated Olaf's armor and tore at the flesh of his arm, but he didn't feel the pain. He wielded his massive sword again, kicking out as he raged at Friggid, sending the shield of the Danish jarl flying through the air. Olaf's arm shuddered with the sickening reverberation as his blade then tore through flesh and muscle and bone.

Friggid stared at him, staggering and stunned. He dropped his sword and clutched at his shoulder and neck where the blood poured out of him, where his life drained away. He fell to his knees, still staring at the Norwegian with astonishment, as if he had never believed he could possibly lose the battle.

Olaf stood over his fallen enemy, shaking. He saw the glazing eyes beneath him and the triumph within them still. Kneeling beside Friggid, Olaf took the bloodied shoulders into his hands and shook the man.

"Where is my wife?" he thundered, filled with a sudden panic. No dying man held triumph in his eyes unless . . .

Friggid didn't speak. His breath was a death rattle beneath his visor. There was a smile upon the barely visible lips.

"Where is she?" Olaf roared.

Friggid's eyes were finding the empty glaze of death, but they blinked once and rolled in their sockets toward the far rear of the walled defense.

Olaf released his enemy's shoulders and stood in anxious confusion. He could see nothing but the wooden buildings of the camp, most of them in a blaze. And there was some type of a fenced area, a platform, probably a punishment dais, but it too was blazing.

A rattle sounded from the ground, the strange echo that was like that of dry leaves rustling in winter.

Friggid the Bowlegs was at long last dead.

One of the Danes stepped forward suddenly, placing his sword at Olaf's feet. "We surrender to you, Lord of the Wolves. We are weak in numbers and had no taste for this battle, but were loyal to our jarl. We expect none, but ask your mercy."

"Leave Ireland, or swear fealty to Aed Finnlaith, and mercy shall be yours," Olaf said distantly, still scouring the camp with his eyes. "I have no more taste for killing; I seek only my wife."

The Dane turned to face as Olaf did, and smoke or emotion filled his eyes with a liquid gleam. "The woman . . . your queen. . . ."

"Speak, man!" Olaf roared in a trembling thunder.

The man lifted his hand towards the dais where the fire was rising high in a rim. "The fire, my jarl. If yet she lives, you could not reach her. Olaf of Dubhlain, believe this: We did not know Friggid's plans for her; we had come to respect her, for she was a courageous woman—"

The howl—the deep, chilling howl of the wolf—rose again. It was the howl of an animal wounded and desperate. "No!" he shrieked again, and then as all watched, he was leaping astride the black stallion and racing toward the far courtyard and the inferno that blazed there.

Troops of the Danes, Ulster, Tara, and Dubhlain alike scrambled on horseback or foot to race after him. He halted before the logs that burned so brightly, smoke rising in billowing black from their heat of red and glowing orange. No man could face it.

Yet between the leaping flames of blazing intensity, the raised platform could still be seen. The fire had not yet touched the princess. Little tongues of it were just now beginning to touch the slope of wood that led to the stake from which the princess hung limply. She sagged against it, her face hidden from them all by a sheer cloud of ebony hair made indigo like fine silk from the reflection of the fire.

The cries of the wolf rang through the smoke-billowed air again. He called out to Thor and to Wodon—and he called out to the Christian God.

He spurred the black stallion furiously. The animal charged, but reared high at the wall of fire, spinning about. The Wolf backed the animal away.

Erin raised her head, and she saw the mountain of men and horses before her, but they meant nothing to her in her dazed state. She saw only one man. The majestic giant on the black stallion. The Wolf, ever a king. His visor was still on his face; the visor with the shape of a wolf's head, and she could still see his eyes, Nordic blue, locked with hers. The ice was gone; they were like a summer sea in a storm, filled with tempest, turmoil, and pain. Was she delirious? Did she imagine it? When she blinked, she saw his eyes again, steel cold with determination, and again they were ice.

He did not love her. He had come because he was the conqueror, because he had to avenge Grenilde, because he was a man who would never relinquish what was his. Yet, as she was his, he had however briefly been hers. He might not love her—but he lived! And he would be forever locked in her immortal spirit as she saw him: a man above men on the black. More powerful, more regal, than mortal man. He was a golden god, and if ever he did fall, he would rule above all men even within the hall of Valhalla, unique in magnificence and splendor.

She smiled because she saw him, because he lived, because she had always known that he was indomitable. . . .

Olaf spun the black around. He raced the animal back a greater distance and spun again.

The black stallion reared high, snorting furiously, pawing the air. A hush fell over the land, as if each man, each assembled warrior, caught and held his breath. Only the lone call of the wounded animal sounded on the deathly still air. Time again halted, waited.

And then the black stallion was galloping, racing, mighty flanks straining and bunching with power and fluidity. Closer and closer came the wall of flame. The man was leaning over the neck of the animal, one with him, whispering, coaxing, encouraging.

They reached the flames. The stallion did not balk but sailed over logs and fire unfalteringly. Olaf did not hesitate. He saw the platform, saw the laps of flame beginning to lick their way upward. He directed the horse toward the sloping wood that led to the platform.

Erin saw him and her eyes widened incredulously. He was going to bring the stallion up the slope and to the platform. He can't do it, she thought, because the sloping wood can't possibly bear the weight of the massive war horse.

But he was coming. The wood splintered and crashed, but always the hooves of the stallion moved ahead of it.

Then he reached her. Olaf was before her. She lifted her head and saw his eyes, arctic blue within the visor that hid his face from her. She watched his sword arm rise, and for a moment she quailed, terrified that he had braved the fire only to slay her himself in his fury. But his blade merely fell across the loop of the rope, and she was falling.

The sword clattered to the platform and she felt herself swept up before she could hit the wood. The

horse pranced nervously and snorted as Olaf drew her
high before him on the saddle with its battle trappings.
Her teeth began to chatter as she so vividly saw the
scene around them. Olaf had to be insane. The hooves
of the charger were going to crash through the platform at any second, and they were surrounded by a
wall of flames.

For ungodly seconds the stallion balked, furiously
working at his bit, and then he constricted his sinewed
haunches and leaped from the platform. For a moment
Erin felt as if they were sailing and then they hit the
ground with a jarring thud. The stallion reared and
screeched in protest. Olaf's mail-clad chest held Erin
firm when she thought she would fall, but the flames
were still burning so high around them. How could
they ever breach the fire? How long before the great
animal and they themselves succumbed to the rising
black smoke?

She had been prepared to die with the glory of him
forever implanted in her soul. But now, though he had
gazed at her with curiously arctic eyes, she was in his
arms and she didn't want to die. She wanted to live, to
know him, to feel him, to lie with him in the passions
of their youth, to touch him with the tenderness of
age. She wanted to at long last tell him how she loved
him, her Viking lord, that she loved him no matter
what his birth, no matter that he could never love her
as his heart was in Valhalla with another golden
beauty.

"Olaf," she whispered, and choked on his name,
barely hearing herself over the snap and crackle of the
flames.

"Do not talk," he commanded harshly. "Take a
breath."

She did as he told her. It was now or never. He
spurred the stallion for the flame.

The onlookers stared on, still silent, scarcely
breathing, Irish, Norwegians, and Danes alike.

Then suddenly it happened. The massive black stallion appeared, forelegs reaching through the air, high,

above a wall of flame. He soared and seemed to fly as if he were the mythical, eight-legged horse of the god Thor. He leaped above the fire as if scaling the heavens, and on his back he carried the Norse king of Dubhlain and his Irish wife out of the fire. And into life.

CHAPTER

26

The cheers and shouts of triumph that greeted Olaf were deafening, but he did not pause to accept the ovations. Fire was still leaping and smoke billowing high. He nudged the stallion and eased him through the surrounding sea of men, sailed him over the remains of the outer defense wall, and across the valley and dune to a copse of sheltering pines.

Erin shivered as she sat before Olaf. She had come from the blaze of the fire to the crispness of the winter's day, and though he held her secure in the saddle, she felt little warmth from the man who had just risked his life to save her.

Within the copse of pines he set her down. Erin swayed, and he held her until she found her balance, carefully assessing her soot-smudged face.

"You appear to have suffered no permanent damage," he said gruffly. Then, to Erin's horror, he released her and turned away, his strides taking him back toward the stallion.

For a brief moment she stared after him, her heart seeming to congeal with the winter air. No, she could not allow him to walk away. If she risked all, if she made herself the greatest of fools, she had to call him back. She was alive, and knowing now how very tenuous and delicate that gift of life was, she could allow herself to waste no more of its beauty. Pain would ravage her if he refused her supplication, but she had to risk that pain.

Her arms reached out to him, quivering like branches in the breeze. She parted her lips and his name escaped her, a cry, a broken sob, a single word of such entreaty that the Viking warrior paused and felt his blood race warm, his body tremble like that of a boy. It was one word she said, his name and nothing more, yet in its utterance he believed he heard what he had so long sought. He was afraid, the Wolf was afraid lest he was wrong. He stood for several seconds, quivering, having to force himself to finally turn.

He saw her arms outstretched, saw the tears that created silent rivulets down her cheeks, cleaning away the smudged soot. Still he paused, seeking now assurance in her liquid emerald eyes that beheld him with all the vibrant wonder of richest spring against the death of winter.

"I . . . love . . . you," she whispered, the words more form upon her lips than substance in the air, and still he heard them. "I know that you will always love Grenilde, and I seek only that which you can give. . . ."

His immobility was at an end. a cry escaped the Wolf, and in two swift strides he was back to her, enveloping her within his arms, cherishing her and caressing her gently, holding her as if she were a flower, fragile and delicate to his touch.

"Erin. . . ."

The breeze seemed to take up the whisper of her name, and she closed her eyes, trembling with gladness in his arms. Time passed them and yet could not conquer them, as they stood there, feeling their love give them new strength, fill them with warmth.

He pulled away from her, and Erin saw that the brilliant Nordic blue of his eyes dazzled, touched by tears that would never fall. His lips fell upon hers briefly, as tenderly and lightly as a caress of butterfly wings. Then he was staring at her searchingly, smoothing back her hair, assuring himself that she was in no way marred or harmed.

Erin's heart seemed to catch within her throat as she tried to speak, and so her words stumbled out. "I never did betray you, my lord . . . never. It was Friggid who led me astray the day we met at arms on the cliff." A tear splashed on her cheek as she added with aching bitterness, "Friggid lies dead now, so he can't bear out my words. I still have no proof . . . but neither did I mean to betray you since . . . I sought only to save our son, for he was a part of you that I could not bear to lose."

"Hush, my love, hush," Olaf murmured, and she was crushed more fully against him. "I know. . . ."

"I never meant what I said, Olaf. I despised the Danes, and I was terrified. But Friggid did mean to kill you, and he would have slain Leith before your eyes and then killed you—"

"Hush," Olaf whispered again, and he held her more tightly, more tenderly, against the cold breeze. As the cleansing winds swept by them, Erin was content to be held, but finally she spoke again. "You believe me, my lord?" she murmured, her voice again catching.

"Aye, Irish."

"But I can prove naught to you—"

"I love you, Irish," he interjected softly, "and so I was afraid to judge impartially. Afraid that I would play a woman's fool."

"Tell me that again, my lord."

"I was afraid to believe, to trust in a woman's beguiling words—"

"Nay, my lord!" Erin protested, pulling away from him yet holding him still. "The other! Tell me the other."

He smiled, and the radiance of the sun was within the gentle curve of his lips. "I love you, Irish. I have for some time. But it was very hard to love a vixen with claws sharpened against a Viking she loathed."

"Oh, Olaf!" Erin murmured, drawing near once more to rest her cheek against his chest. The mail was cold and stiff beneath her soft flesh, but she could feel the deeper warmth and the pounding of his heart. "I was so afraid . . . and it is true, I did not want to love a Viking, but I did, my lord, and to love the Wolf of all men. . . ."

Again Erin lifted her eyes to his, holding them with the ghosts of pain that remained. She parted her lips to speak, but he knew her heart, and his words quieted hers.

"Erin, there will always be a love within my heart for Grenilde, but like that love you gave your brother, it is something locked within memory. It takes nothing from what I offer you, for this tie that binds my body and soul is stronger than any I have ever known. You have made my life as full as my heart, my emerald-eyed beauty. You have bewitched me from the beginning, and long before I knew you held my heart in those deceptively fragile hands, I was beguiled and bonded by your sweet perfection, unable to touch another. But you despised me so much, and you made it so clearly evident."

"So clearly evident!" Erin protested, smiling slightly through the tears that still clouded her eyes. "Hardly, my lord! I was shamefully like molten steel, so easily shaped and willful to your artistry. . . ." She paused for a moment, her lips trembling, and her voice was a quiver, a soft rasp of silk from her throat. "You were walking away, Olaf. . . ."

"Irish—never, never until the moment when you called my name, did I dare believe that you had found you could love a Viking, and of all Vikings, the Norwegian Wolf." He grimaced. "Vikings are proud, my love, as are Irish princesses."

A soft ripple of laughter touched melodiously upon the air, a lilt that was the song of the land in all its emerald beauty. The warmth of that song filled Olaf, and he gazed on his princess with the greatest tenderness, seeing the pain at last fade from the eyes that were deeper and greener than even Ireland herself.

The healing had at long last begun; the past was purged, the bitterness buried. It was winter, and yet the spring was foretold, and all the blossoming springs that would follow in their lives.

Olaf kissed her forehead. "Come, my love. Your father will be frantic to see you. And Gregory and Brice—"

"And Leith!" Erin interrupted. "Oh, Olaf! I have missed him so. I crave to see him, to hold him. . . ."

"Our son fares well in the kindest of hands," Olaf said quietly. "But yes, it is a long ride home, and so we must begin."

He lifted her in his arms and set her high on the great black stallion before leaping with smooth agility behind her. As they rode to rejoin the troops, they were contentedly silent. Erin smiled softly to herself as she nestled against the great strength and warmth of his broad chest and powerful arms, thinking of the dreams she had spun.

He had not fallen to his knees to beg her forgiveness. Yet it mattered not, for he had offered her a declaration of love far more eloquent than any she could have envisioned. He was the Wolf of Norway, and of Dubhlain, she thought proudly. The Wolf did not kneel to the past; he rose to the future.

They paused before the remains of the Danish defenses. Erin twisted to see that Olaf stared pensively before him.

"What is it, my lord?" she queried softly.

She felt his arms embrace her more tightly. "I was just thinking of the words of an old Druid, my love. A very wise man. My soul is mine own again, and not because the Dane is dead, but because I have been given life."

He stood before the hearth, surveying the scene that unfolded within his great hall, a subtle smile enhancing his ruggedly handsome features.

The Christ Mass was being celebrated in Dubhlain this year by the entire family of the Ard-Righ because Aed had decreed that Erin was to travel no more since she had endured so much in the two full moons that had waned since she had borne his grandson.

So the royal residence of stone and mortar knew a warmth and gaiety unlike any seen before. The Irish lords and ladies within the hall were doing their best to explain the holiness of the day to the Norse, who occasionally lifted prayers to Odin to spare them the conversion, but were, for the most part, more than willing to sit back and enjoy.

The Ard-Righ himself argued cantankerously with Sigurd, who laughed heartily with vast amusement, for he had already shrugged and at least outwardly donned the cloak of Christianity for Moira's sake.

Maeve was ignoring all revelry in the hall and clucking over Leith as she held him for Erin, who was busy playing hostess. Brice and Eric were, as usual, talking horses, and Bede, the peaceful nun, was appearing quite harried as she chased after Gwynn's toddler Padraic so that Gwynn might sit with her husband for a moment's respite.

It is a home, Olaf thought, truly a home.

"You are pensive, Lord Olaf."

He twisted with a cocked brow to see the man who addressed him. "Nay, not pensive, Mergwin," he said. "I am but counting the gifts of the gods."

Mergwin smiled secretively but his weathered face betrayed him, crinkling into myriad little folds. "I have read your runes again, Lord Olaf."

"Have you?" Olaf queried, smiling also and yet warily. He had learned not to doubt the prowess of the old Druid.

"Aye, that I have. Your days of conquest are over, Lord of the Wolves."

Olaf's smile became a deep slashed grin across the

strong contour of his jaw. "That, old man, is not a great feat of fortune-telling. I hold that which I crave; I seek to go no further."

Mergwin lowered his eyes, and when he once more raised them to Olaf, they were grave. "You will stem the flow of invasion, Lord of the Wolves. But it is not for you to end the waves of those seeking conquest who will come to these shores."

Olaf swallowed, a feeling of heartsickness sweeping over him. "Do you tell me, Druid, that men will come and I will be able to do naught? That I will have no effect upon the land?"

"Nay, Lord of the Wolves," Mergwin said softly. "I tell you only that you cannot change that which is destined for another century. You will remain strong, and you will live long and healthy, and your children will grow strong behind you. The cycle has come full for you, Lord of the Wolves. It is a time for reaping, for growing, for fertility. You will fight your wars, but you will also find peace. As long as you see truly what you seek."

Olaf's eyes were staring beyond the Druid. They rested with brilliant Nordic blue on his wife as she swept gracefully into the hall from the kitchens. She was in green today. Beautiful, deep green. The color was a highlight to her eyes, a backdrop for the rich, midnight beauty of her hair, a flowing cascade of ebony silk bedecked with emeralds. But the gems were no match for the eyes she turned to him, as if knowing that he watched her.

Mergwin saw the smile she offered Olaf. The tenderness, the love. The blazing tempest of passion that would always arise between the two who were by nature so strong, so proud, so demanding, and yet so giving.

"Your pardon, Druid," Olaf murmured, and Mergwin knew no protest as Olaf swept by him.

Mergwin sank to sit by the hearth, his smile returning as he watched the magnificent king approach his Irish princess. An aura was about them both, Mergwin thought. An aura of gold, of the sun, of energy and power.

He laughed suddenly. But peace? Not exactly peace. They would have their share of arguments in the years to come, for their tempers were as stormy as their passions! But beneath it would always be the love, as sure and strong as the earth and hills.

The weathered lines within his gaunt face increased as he continued to survey the royal pair. The golden Viking in his crimson mantle lowered his head to whisper to the green-eyed beauty who glanced at him with an emerald gaze that was nothing less than dazzlingly, wickedly sultry. She whispered in return, and then the two gazed about the hall where all appeared jovial and content to while away the winter eve. They caught one another's eyes again, bold, brilliant blue and deepest, sensual emerald, and then, like errant lovers, they joined hands and slipped away from their preoccupied guests, heading for the staircase. At the landing the Wolf swept his princess into his arms and carried her up the steps. Mergwin still watched as Olaf's booted foot slammed the heavy wooden door closed in their wake.

"Ah, Norwegian Wolf!" The Druid chuckled to himself. "You have truly become Irish! And you will make your impression deeply felt, in all the time to come."

"What are you muttering about, old fool?"

Mergwin smiled at his old friend, Aed Finnlaith. "Are you in a wagering mood, Ard-Righ? I'll lay you odds that before Christ Mass next, you will hold in your arms a second Norse grandchild."

The Ard-Righ followed Mergwin's eyes to the stairs. "I'll take you on, friend Druid."

Aed paused for a minute, his gaze still on the stairway before he caught the Druid's stare and held it with a twinkle. "Before Christ Mass next, I will hold in my arms another *Irish* grandchild!"

Mergwin chuckled. He lifted a cup of ale to Aed. "As you say, Ard-Righ. As you say."

Author's Note

Fierce invaders, ravaging barbarians, strong, and swift, artists in the field of rapine and slaughter can all be said of the Viking. But it is also true that they were often builders, settlers, and dreamers, giving more to their adopted lands than they took. Their dynasties would follow long behind them.

Olaf the White held Dubhlain throughout his lifetime, and, as predicted, five decades of comparative peace came to the island, although scattered raids did take place over the years. Ireland would not be free from the Viking yoke until over a century and a half past the Norwegian Wolf's marriage to the daughter of Aed Finnlaith, when Brian Boru would rise high to glory and bring about the defeat of Sigtrygg the Silk-beard in April 1014, at the battle of Clontarf.

But not even Brian's victory, which he did not live to enjoy, could rid the land of Viking influence, for after the battle, Sigtrygg ruled on in Dubhlain. Too many invaders, such as Olaf, had become one with the land, leaving their mark upon Eire. Olaf's descendants live today throughout the land. His Irish name, Amhla-obh, became MacAuliffe.

And so he did, perhaps, fulfill all his dreams.

About the Author

New York Times and *USA Today* bestselling author Heather Graham has written over one hundred novels and novellas, including category, romantic suspense, historical romance, and paranormal. Married since high school graduation and the mother of five, her greatest love in life remains her family, but she also believes her career has been an incredible gift. Romance Writers of America presented Heather with a Lifetime Achievement Award in 2003.